The

POET'S
GIRL

A Novel of Emily Hale & T. S. Eliot

by

SARA FITZGERALD

**THOUGHT
CATALOG**
Books

THOUGHTCATALOG.COM
NEW YORK · LOS ANGELES

THOUGHT
CATALOG
Books

Copyright © 2020 Sara Fitzgerald. All rights reserved.

Published by Thought Catalog Books, an imprint of the digital magazine Thought Catalog, which is owned and operated by The Thought & Expression Company LLC, an independent media organization based in Brooklyn, New York and Los Angeles, California.

This book was produced by Chris Lavergne and Noelle Beams. Art direction and design by KJ Parish. Visit us on the web at thoughtcatalog.com and shopcatalog.com.

Made in the United States, printed in Michigan.

ISBN 978-1-949759-18-1

10 9 8 7 6 5 4 3 2 1

For Lucy

Prologue

IT WAS A MISTAKE, I knew now, to come back.

Oh, some things hadn't changed, of course. The honey-colored limestone still gleamed in the afternoon sun and the roofs still sported their thatch. The weekenders from London still strolled up High Street, searching for the best place to stop for a cup of tea.

But the postmistress had retired, and the green grocer had died. The cottage where we shared so many quiet summer evenings together had been invaded by a boisterous family.

Twenty years later, there was no one I remembered—and no one who remembered me.

And Burnt Norton? The old estate was now a school for disadvantaged boys. A place I no longer cared to visit.

Time present and time past...

What did I expect to find here? A happy memory of a warm afternoon in September? A reward for my long years of patient waiting?

Into our first world.

There they were, dignified, invisible...

Oh yes, we were nothing if not dignified. And I was nothing if not invisible.

I was sorry now that I had given away the letters you wrote me. They were the one part of you that no one else in the world possessed. Yes, those boxes were a burden every time I moved. Still, they told me that we had shared something special. I would have liked to have been able to read them all now, one last time.

But the world still had your poetry, and I had that day we visited the abandoned garden. I knew the lines of the poem by heart now. I often recited them when I walked through the Cotswold countryside, matching my steps to the rhythms of the stanzas. It took 11 minutes—almost to the second—for you to read it. Your recording was like a lullaby for me, your sonorous voice turning our memories into metaphors.

But this summer I pondered the phrases anew, hoping for some insight, some clue that would help me understand why it had turned out this way.

Should I have made a different choice? Could I have lowered the curtain after Act One or Act Two? Or was our story plotted by some sort of Master Playwright, and my role already scripted on that long-ago night when I was 21?

It didn't matter now. I would go home and start over. I had done it before, I could do it again. I would find a new part to play, something appropriate for a woman my age.

But it would be different now. The laughter and applause were dying away. And this time, I knew, there would be no bouquet of roses.

The Stunt Show

WHEN A DOOR OPENS OR a curtain rises, anything can happen. What would it be tonight, I wondered as Father rapped his gloved knuckles on the stout front door. The Hinkleys' home was not the Boston Theatre after all. But if there was an audience, there was always the chance that something magical could happen.

We stomped our feet to shake off the slush as the maid ushered us into the parlor. The room felt cozy and already alive with the buzz of partygoers. On the far side, the flames of the blazing fire welcomed us. Eleanor had pushed the couches up against the walls to make more room for her performers. And the lamps had been dimmed, bathing the space in a soft light. It would take a few years off the age of the older matrons in the audience—and help disguise our mistakes if we made any.

"My star," Eleanor called out as she crossed the room to greet us. She hugged me, then turned to Father. "And I'm so glad you were able to join us, Reverend Hale."

"I am, too," he replied. "It's not often I can get free to see Emily perform."

Did he sense the difference, I wondered? The contrast between a home filled with laughing friends and the icy silence of the parsonage? Eleanor had been the exuberant ringleader since our school days in Cambridge. But tonight she was truly in her element, the hyperactive impresaria of her very own show.

"Please help yourself to some punch, Reverend Hale, while I show Emily how I've set things up."

She led me to the fireplace, taking a twirl in front of the hearth. "This is where we'll perform. It will be tight, but we can make it work." She nodded toward the dining room. "I decided to put most of the chairs in there. You'll have to thread through them when you make your entrances from the kitchen. It's the best I could do without an actual curtain or proscenium."

"It will be fine."

"And I did manage to find you a pianist." She ran down a mental checklist, then wrinkled her forehead. "I hope the weather hasn't affected your voice tonight."

I didn't expect to have to sing when Eleanor began putting together her "Stunt Show." There were six skits in all, and three had come out of her own typewriter. But she had pleaded that she needed me to help her fill out the program: "I know you can sing something."

And she was right. Growing up, I had gotten used to performing solos at church and school. Uncle Philip had even sprung for some private lessons. The voice teachers confirmed my sense that I would never be able to tackle the soprano solos of Handel or Puccini. But I was good enough to be able to please a parlor full of friendly Boston Brahmins on a cold night in February.

The climax of the evening, Eleanor had decided, would be a scene from Jane Austen's *Emma*. She would play Emma Woodhouse and I would play Harriet Elton, the character everyone despises. Secretly, I relished the challenge of the role. And I would still be responsible for generating most of the laughs if there were any to be mined from Eleanor's script.

"I've still got a million little things to take care of," she said, waving to another arrival on the other side of the room. "Let me know if you need anything."

"I will."

What was it that I loved about acting? I wondered as I retreated to a quiet corner. *Did it help me escape the constraints of Cambridge and Chestnut Hill? Did it let me try on a different skin? Was it easier to speak someone else's witty lines than to come up with my own?*

I recognized most of the faces around the room. They were friends and neighbors of Eleanor's, members of Mrs. Hinkley's clubs, parents of girls we had gone to school with. Scattered among them were a few men, the younger ones from Harvard, the older ones dragged along by their wives. Usually I had no problem striking up a conversation. But tonight I preferred some quiet. Oddly, I needed to steel my nerves.

I was grateful that Aunt Edith was three thousand miles away in Seattle. I could still hear her words when I said I wanted to become an actress, words that were chiseled into my brain like an epitaph on a gravestone in Mount Auburn Cemetery:

"An actress is no calling for a woman of your station."

A woman of your station. Whatever *that* was supposed to mean.

I had chosen my best green silk dress to wear tonight. I knew that it gave me more confidence. I always loved dressing up in a costume, but there would be no costume changes tonight. I would still be Miss Emily Hale, Eleanor's old friend and the Reverend Hale's daughter.

I glanced around the room, studying my audience. On the far side, Amy was holding court with a group of young men. She looked smashing tonight, but then Amy had always known more than I did about how to apply rouge to suit an audience of two instead of two hundred.

Tracy Putnam was easy to find, with his mustache and broad forehead. For a medical student, he was surprisingly good at comedy. Eleanor had written Tracy and John Remey into our Austen skit; the more Harvard men with acting parts, she reasoned, the bigger the audience and the better the party.

And then I saw him, standing off by himself. Observing the scene with an air of detachment—just like I was. It was Tom Eliot, Eleanor's cousin. He, too, had parts to play tonight.

We had met once before, probably at one of those debutante parties the season Eleanor came out. But now he looked lost and lonely, and just so ever ill at ease.

Shall I rescue him? I summoned up my inner actress and stepped quickly across the room.

"Good evening," I said as I arrived at his side. "You're Tom Eliot, aren't you?"

He smiled. "And you're Emily Hale."

"We met at—" We spoke at the same time, then laughed as our words collided.

He waited for me to go first. "I think it was the party at your cousin's home...the season Eleanor was presented."

"Yes, you're right," he acknowledged. "One of those unforgettable debutante parties."

Was he making fun of me? I tried a different tack. "We missed you at our rehearsal last week."

"Yes, I'm sorry about that." He sounded sincere. "When Eleanor approached me about playing Mr. Woodhouse, I told her I wouldn't be able to commit to rehearsals. I'm afraid I'm feeling overwhelmed by my studies right now...."

"I'm sure you'll be fine." The last thing I needed was a jittery costar. "All you have to do is chime in at the end. And even if you miss your cue, Eleanor's got someone ready to prompt us."

"She told me that all I have to do is play myself."

"The widowed father?"

"No," he chuckled softly. "A hypochondriac. Guilty as charged, I'm afraid. And how about you? Are you the quintessential Mrs. Elton?"

He leaned forward, listening intently, as if he really wanted to hear what I had to say.

"It's true that I *am* a pastor's daughter *and* a pastor's niece."

"Then it sounds as if Eleanor's casting was truly brilliant."

"Well, I certainly hope I'm not as shallow as Mrs. Elton."

"I suspect my cousin knows which of her friends can make an audience laugh."

It was a compliment. An unexpected one. It was not what usually happened at parties like this. Around the room, I could see the Harvard men, moving quickly from guest to guest, prowling for introductions. Young men studying law, business, or medicine, looking for a woman with money or a father who could set them up in the firm. Someone other than me.

"Would you like a glass of punch?" he asked.

"Yes, I would, thank you."

I watched him navigate his way across the parlor. He was taller than he had seemed when he was leaning down to listen to me. But he didn't use that height to take command of the room. He stepped among the guests slowly, carefully, apologizing if he still managed to jostle one of the old ladies.

He was not like the other men I'd seen at parties, who barreled through a crowded room as if they had a pigskin tucked under their arm and were about to score a touchdown. There was a cautious shyness about him. And now I had to find out what it was hiding.

He returned with two punch glasses, his elbows tucked in close to keep the drinks from spilling. He gave one to me, then raised his in a toast: "To our dramatic success."

"To our success," I replied, clinking his glass. I took a sip, swallowing slowly. *Law, business, or medicine?* I wondered. "Tell me more about your studies." I smiled. "The ones that are keeping you from pursuing your acting career."

"I'm working toward a master's in Philosophy."

"That *does* sound challenging." I hoped he wouldn't ask what I was doing with my life, since I didn't know the answer. "I learned about the Greek philosophers back in school. And, of course, I studied The Bible."

"That comes with being a Unitarian."

"Particularly if you're a Hale."

"Or an Eliot, for that matter."

I smiled. So we do have more in common than Eleanor Hinkley.

"Actually," he said, "I've been studying Eastern religions lately. I'm taking Sanskrit with Professor Lanman. That's his wife over there, talking to my older sister." He nodded toward a pair of women on the other side of the room. "It turns out Mrs. Lanman is a Hinkley, though her family spells it with a 'c.' She and Eleanor probably shared a relative back on the decks of the *Mayflower*."

"I forget exactly how you and Eleanor are related."

"Her mother is my mother's sister. They're both Stearnses." He paused, then added, "Stearns is my middle name. When you're an Eliot in Boston, you have to use your middle name or the postman will never get your mail to the right house."

I smiled. "You don't have to explain *that* to a Hale."

His eyes caught mine. "You're funny," he said. "Eleanor knew what she was doing when she cast you in our skit."

"Monsieur Marcel!" Amy swooped across the room to join us. "Comment allez-vous?" she asked Tom.

"Très bien, merci. Et vous?"

"Comme çi, comme ça," she replied.

Amy's long eyelashes were as dark as her jet-black hair, and when she fluttered them, they were one of her most devastating weapons. "Don't mind us, Emily," she said with a giggle. "We're just trying to get into our roles."

"You must have had a chance to practice," I observed.

"I insisted on it, didn't I, Tom?" He frowned slightly. "I must admit I was a bit of a pest."

So he did manage to find time for Amy.

Eleanor rejoined us. "Emily, the pianist has arrived."

It was my escape from a competition I was bound to lose.

"I hope we can talk more later on," Tom said, looking at me intently.

"I hope so, too."

I headed to the piano, checking the clock on the mantel. It was almost eight. Curtain time.

The young pianist was flexing his fingers. "I'm Emily," I announced. "I'm your singer tonight."

"I'm Alex Steinert," he said, extending his hand.

"Do you have a copy of the program?"

He nodded.

"Please remember that I'm not a diva. Don't hold the whole notes too long or I'll be gasping for air."

"Don't worry," he said. "I've done this kind of thing before." He smiled, helping me relax.

"That's reassuring," I replied. Unfortunately, it was too late to practice now. "If you would excuse me. I'd better get myself a drink of water while I still have time...."

I knew my way around the Hinkleys' kitchen. Their maid had moved from managing coats to arranging canapés on a tray. I found a glass in the cupboard and filled it with water. As I sipped it, I tried to conjure up thoughts of springtime, but a young man from Harvard kept pushing them aside.

Eleanor popped her head in. "There you are! It's time. Are you ready?"

I nodded.

"All right, then. I'll say a few words to welcome everyone, and then you can make your grand entrance." She gave me a hug. "I know you'll be wonderful."

She swept back out the door. I straightened the lines of my long dress, smoothing out an imaginary wrinkle. I reached for the back of my coiled-up hair, double-checking to make sure every pin was in place.

"You look lovely," the maid reassured me.

"Thank you."

"Good evening, ladies and gentlemen." On the other side of the wall, Eleanor was taking command of her noisy party. "Please find yourself a seat so we can start our show." I could hear the conversations cease as seats were found and chairs shuffled to better positions.

"First, I want to thank you all for coming out on this cold evening. As most of you know, we're performing for the benefit of the Cambridge Visiting Housekeeper program. It is doing wonderful work to try to help young women find meaningful jobs in our homes. Young women who might otherwise be forced to turn to the streets to support themselves."

I glanced at the maid, wondering if she was listening. Eleanor could turn anything into a melodrama if she tried.

"Our show tonight has two acts," Eleanor continued. "During our intermission, we will conduct an auction of a poster that was generously donated by Mrs. Sohier Welch, otherwise known as my sister Barbara." There was a ripple of laughter. A good sign that the audience was ready to enjoy itself.

"When we pass the basket during intermission, I hope you will all give...and give generously."

"And now, without further ado, I want to introduce my dear friend, Emily Hale, who will start off the evening by singing 'Ecstasy' by Mrs. H. H. Beach."

I took a deep breath, forced my lips into an exaggerated smile, and pushed open the kitchen door. Polite applause spread from one side of the room to the other as I worked my way through the maze of chairs. I took my spot in front of the fireplace, positioning my feet under my shoulders the way my music teachers had taught. And then I signaled Alex to begin.

He launched into his introduction. A love song written by a woman.

Only to dream among the fading flowers,
Only to glide along the tranquil sea;
Ah dearest, dearest,
Have we not together
One long, bright day
Of love, so glad and free?

I relaxed a bit, having hit the high "G" on "dearest" without having to strain. Now I could focus on communicating the words.

I scanned the room, trying to establish eye contact with each member of the audience I knew. Eleanor, Mrs. Hinkley, Amy, Tracy Putnam. And Father, his face still an emotionless mask behind his wire-rimmed glasses and beard.

Ah dearest, dearest, thus in sweetest rapture
With thee to live, with thee at last to die!

I closed my eyes, clasped my hands, and bowed my head. When Alex finally lifted his fingers off the keyboard, the room erupted in applause.

I allowed myself to relax, then smiled and looked up again. I spotted Tom, standing behind Eleanor, clapping enthusiastically.

Think of him while you're singing. Remember you're an actress!

The room quieted, and I nodded for Alex to begin playing the next song.

Julia has a garden fair
On the edge of town....

I could not bring myself to look at Tom; I feared I might stumble or forget the words if I did. But when my eyes searched for the familiar faces, it was his I was thinking of.

He was handsome, but no Adonis. He was pale, but to be fair, it *was* the dead of winter. He probably spent too much time indoors, huddled over his books, studying those Eastern religions.

No flower in all the world so rare
As that sweet one beside me there,
When Julia walked with me.

Another round of applause, another song, more applause. And in an instant, it seemed, my moment was over. I left the fantasy of spring gardens and returned to the reality of a chilly winter night. It was time for the first skit.

I retreated to the back of the room, happy to have a break from the spotlight. From here, I could observe Tom Eliot—without him knowing I held him in my sights.

He was dressed well for the evening, in the style of a dapper Englishman. Silhouetted against the lamplight, his ears jutted out a little. He was probably sensitive about them, but I liked that imperfection. His brown hair was parted down the middle, in the fashion of the day. But a short cowlick stuck out in the back, one his brilliantine must have missed.

A scene out of Dickens's *Bleak House*. Kitty Munro playing a debutante. It all whirled by so fast. And then Eleanor took center stage to begin the auction.

"I thought you might like this."

The voice was like a whisper underneath the rising cacophony of competing bids. Tom was there again, offering another glass of punch.

"Thank you. How did you know I would need it?"

"Three songs," he observed. "A lot of singing." He took a sip from his own glass. "But it was lovely. I was"—he searched for the right word—"mesmerized."

I could feel a flush rise in my cheeks. "Thank you," I murmured, then added quickly, "but they were silly songs. 'Four o'clocks and touch me nots, daisies and forget-me-nots.'"

He sipped his drink in silence.

I jumped in to fill the growing void. "I remember Eleanor telling me that you like to write poetry."

He looked surprised.

A mistake. I heard Amy now, laying out her rules of courtship: "Whatever you do, don't let a man know you've been talking about him with your friends."

"I've been trying to write," Tom said at last. "My father's not happy about it. He tells me you can't make a living that way." He paused. "And perhaps he's right. I know it never would have occurred to me to rhyme "touch-me-nots" with "forget-me-nots.""

Now I had second thoughts about the songs I had chosen. "I suppose the lyrics of Charles Edward Thomas are a bit old-fashioned," I acknowledged. Then I smiled. "Perhaps someday a composer will set *your* poems to music."

He set down his glass. "I sincerely doubt *that* will happen."

Across the room, Eleanor was urging her guests to refill their glasses for the second half of the show. I picked up a program off a chair.

"Now it's your turn to shine." Tom's skit with Amy was next, before our scene closed off the evening.

"Do you like to act?" I asked him.

"Yes, I do."

"Why?"

He seemed to have never considered the question. "I suppose...I suppose it's because I have always been fairly shy....But when I spend time on the stage, everything becomes easier. I'm more confident when I speak up in class, critique one of my friends...argue with my father." He smiled. "And talk to fascinating young women..."

The comment startled me, but Eleanor came to my rescue. "Mother's pleased with how much we've raised so far," she announced. "Are you ready for Act II?"

We both nodded.

"Then on with the show...."

"Good luck, Mr. Woodhouse," I told him.

"Good luck, Mrs. Elton," he mouthed in return.

Eleanor stepped forward to quiet the crowd, then I returned to the front of the room. I set down my glass on the mantel, then signaled to Alex that I was ready.

As he played the opening chords, I felt the heat of the roaring fire behind me. Someone must have put on a fresh log at intermission. The warmth seemed to sweep up under my skirt, climbing the seams of my stockings. It was the perfect inspiration for Margaret Ruthven Lang's arrangement of "Mavourneen."

O the time is long, Mavourneen,
Till I come again, O Mavourneen;

This time I dared to look at Tom. And as I did, I reached down inside of me, remembering that core of longing I had felt since childhood. And I pretended that the words were meant to be sung by a woman instead of a man.

An' the months are slow to pass, Mavourneen,

Till I hold thee in my arms, O Mavourneen!

Tom gazed at me, but I couldn't risk staring back. I was Reverend Hale's daughter, and even if Aunt Edith wasn't there, there were too many other women who might notice and who would inevitably gossip.

I found one face, and then another, trying to make each one of them feel as if I were singing to them alone. But when I came to the last verse, I dared myself to find Tom Eliot's eyes again.

Keep thy heart aye true to me, Mavourneen,
I should die but for thy love, O Mavourneen!

Alex played the final notes, and the applause broke the spell.

I had decided to close with "A May Morning." I remembered dances around the maypole back at school and tried to imagine that I had just been crowned the May Queen.

The song ended in a crescendo of rising chords. The room erupted in applause, and I took a deep bow. I signaled Alex to join me, but he waved me off. I took another bow, then retreated to relieve my throat with another glass of punch.

Now it was Tom's turn. "Monsieur Marcel and His Latest Marvel" was the first of the original skits Eleanor had written for the evening. Her dialogue was brisk, but in the end, this was just a piece of inconsequential fluff. All Amy had to do was play herself. And Tom rose to the challenge of pretending to be a Frenchman.

They delivered their lines well, speaking loudly enough that even the most elderly women could hear them. They demonstrated the advantage of having squeezed in an actual rehearsal.

Tom disappeared during the next skit while his older sister Marian took the floor. Finally it was our turn, with "An Afternoon with Mr. Woodhouse" closing out the show.

Eleanor loved Jane Austen, so it was no surprise she had turned to *Emma* for inspiration. And she *was* the Emma of our own circle. Who else would have cast her bachelor cousin opposite two of her closest friends?

Tom pulled up a chair and took his place, pretending to doze by the fire of the Woodhouse manor. Eleanor sat beside him. I launched into my opening speech.

"Thank you for inviting me over, Miss Woodhouse. Your house is very lovely. Very like Maple Grove, my brother, Mr. Suckling's place. Why, this room is the very shape and size of the morning room at Maple Grove! I can almost imagine myself there."

I prattled on, comparing fictional manor homes and extolling the gardens of England and Surrey. For a moment, I allowed myself to wonder if I would ever have the chance to see them.

I ran through Mrs. Elton's preoccupations, taking particular care to draw out the syllables of "Mr. Sickling's *barouche-landau*" for comic effect. And then, at last, I turned to Tom, pretending to sleep in the chair.

"Your father's state of health must be a great drawback," I observed to Eleanor. "Why doesn't he try Bath? I assure you I have no doubt of its doing Mr. Woodhouse good."

"My father tried it more than once," Eleanor replied, "but without receiving any benefit."

I looked at the clock. "Oh, dear, it's getting so late. Time to be off. I've so enjoyed this gathering." I headed back to the kitchen with a wave of my hand, enjoying the smattering of applause and laughter that I heard in my wake.

"Insufferable woman!" I heard Eleanor say. "Worse than I had supposed!"

I pressed my ear to the kitchen door, knowing that Tom would speak next.

"Well, my dear, considering we never saw her before, she seems a very pretty sort of young lady; and I dare say she was very much pleased with you."

His English accent was quite credible, and he managed to sound 30 years older.

"She speaks a little too quick," Tom went on. "However, she seems a very obliging, pretty-behaved young lady and no doubt will make Mr. Elton a very good wife."

I remembered overhearing Edith the last time she visited, as she tried to reassure Father.

"I'm sure Emily will make someone a very good wife."

But who? And when?

There were a few more lines. I knew Eleanor had struggled with the ending of the skit, but her audience seemed to be forgiving. The applause signaled that I could return to the parlor.

As I arrived at center stage, Tom reached for my hand to form a line. I savored the feel of it. Long, tapering fingers. A firm grip, but not a painful one. A palm that was dry. We all bowed together, then Eleanor pushed me out front to take one more bow on my own. Behind me, I could hear Tom join in the applause.

Then we all nudged Eleanor forward so she could bask in the success of her evening. "Thank you all for coming," she said at last. "I'd also like to thank my friends and relatives who performed tonight. But please feel free to linger on for some more refreshments."

Once again, the emotions washed over me. The giddy expectations beforehand. The high-wire act of the performance. The thrill of the applause. The post-performance letdown. Will I ever grow tired of it? Will anything ever take its place?

Mrs. Hinkley's friends took their turns, murmuring kind words about my singing and acting. A few moved on to talk with Father. "You must be so proud of her!" "What a lovely voice!" "What will she be doing next?"

I was not able to catch his reply.

In a few minutes, he rejoined me. Beneath his mustache, I could see the hint of a smile. "You did very well, my dear." He did not show emotion easily, and, in any case, effusive praise was not in his inventory. Everyone expected me to be good. Everyone expected me to rise to the occasion. I was a Hale, after all.

"I'm sure you would like to stay longer," he said, "but I have an appointment early in the morning. I think we ought to be on our way."

I yearned to linger until all the guests had left, to kick off my shoes and sit on the floor in front of the fire. To gossip and giggle with Eleanor and Amy the way we had back in our school days. But I had no choice. Father was leaving, and I had to leave, too.

And where was Tom Eliot, now that I longed to say goodbye?

Then I saw him, standing by the front door. He was holding a coat that I realized was actually my own. Had he noticed me from the moment I walked in?

I crossed the room.

"Thank you for retrieving my coat for me."

Wordlessly, he spread it open, offering each armhole in turn.

"I enjoyed the evening," he whispered. "You were wonderful."

"And you have a knack for accents," I teased.

A smile played on his lips. Then he arched back his shoulders, and, sobering, turned to Father. "Reverend Hale, I'm Thomas Eliot, Eleanor Hinkley's cousin. I would very much like to call on your daughter. Would you give me permission to do so?"

The question caught Father off guard. He was probably already thinking about next Sunday's sermon. "Why, yes," he replied. "Assuming it's all right with Emily."

They both turned to me. Again, I felt that flush in my cheeks. Then I spoke, in the firmest voice I could muster:

"I think I would like that very much."

The Lord and the Lady

BE PATIENT, ELEANOR COUNSELED. TOM can be shy with women. It was good advice. Two weeks passed before he finally phoned, inviting me to dinner and a Boston Symphony concert.

The buzzer sounded at the foot of the parsonage stairs, and Father answered the door. I checked the mirror one last time. My dress was an old favorite, a lilac sheath that showed off more of my shoulders than Edith might have liked. Eleanor had once told me that the color complemented my eyes. More than the rest of my closet, this dress gave me permission to feel beautiful.

Tom came into view as I descended the stairs slowly. His shoes first, followed by legs, torso, and then his face, now wearing the smile of an impish little boy.

"You look lovely," he said when I reached the bottom of the staircase. "Just like one of those spring songs you were singing the other night."

"I may have overdone that theme."

"No, not at all." He smiled. "In the words of no less an authority than the *Cambridge Chronicle*, quote 'Emily Hale was a favorite,' unquote. I certainly agreed."

"Don't stay out too late," Father cautioned as Tom helped me with my coat and we headed out the door.

He proposed dinner at the Cafe Lafayette, a little French restaurant on Boylston Street not far from Symphony Hall.

"Have you been here before?" he asked as we were led to a small table near the rear.

"My Uncle Philip brought me a few years ago." I took off my gloves and tucked them into my purse.

"This is my first time," he said.

"I think it's a good choice," I reassured him. "We had an excellent dinner. And it's certainly convenient to the symphony." I wondered if the place was a stretch for his budget. Eleanor had warned that his finances were tight.

I broached a new topic. "Your cousin told me you were in Europe last year."

"Yes, I was."

"Where did you go?"

"I lived most of the year in Paris. But I tried to travel as much as I could. You can cover a lot of ground by train. London. Italy. Germany. I liked Munich, but unfortunately, I was rather sick during my time there. Too sick, in fact, to experience much of the local cuisine."

I smiled. "A shame, I suppose, if one likes sausage."

He returned the smile. "The beers were more to my liking."

Our waiter arrived with menus and recited the specials for the day. I wondered what Tom could afford. "Why don't you pick out something you remember from your days in Paris?"

"Is there anything you don't like?"

I shook my head. "When your father is a pastor, you're taught to eat everything on your plate—and be grateful that the Lord provided it."

The waiter returned and Tom chose *coq au vin* and steak and *frites* from the *prix-fixe* menu and a bottle of red table wine. "Bring us two empty plates," he added. "That way we can share."

"Of course, monsieur." The waiter bowed slightly, then retreated to the kitchen. Tom unfolded his napkin, then looked at me intently. "Tell me about yourself."

I had never been asked such a direct question, and certainly not by a man. Oh, I had met my share of Cambridge men through Eleanor and Amy, young men with prominent names, handsome faces, and chests full of *braggadocio*. Men who would talk nonstop about themselves, because what could a woman possibly say that would be interesting?

"What would you like to know?" I asked.

He paused. "Why don't you start at the beginning?"

I wondered how much he knew. Did Mrs. Hinkley's friends gossip after I left? Had Tom asked Eleanor to fill in the blanks of my story?

"I hope I'm not prying," he added quickly. "It's just...it's just that I'd like to know everything about you."

I knew he would hear the story eventually, so I might as well tell him my version.

The waiter arrived with the wine. "I was born in New Jersey. My father served a parish there. I had a younger brother. His name was Billy. And shortly after he was born, our family moved back to Boston."

I paused, wary of dampening the mood. "My father was busy, tending to his new parish in Chestnut Hill and teaching at Harvard Divinity School. It was July, just a week before Billy's second birthday. My mother and I had already decorated the house for the party. And Billy came down with a fever, and he died within a day."

"That's terrible," Tom said. "How old were you?"

"I was five," I replied matter of factly. "My mother had what polite society calls a 'breakdown.' It was an unbearable time. The thing I remember most is that I was the one who had to take down all the decorations before Billy's birthday even arrived."

I steadied myself. "It was a very hard time for Father. Fortunately, my Aunt Edith—she's my mother's sister—she stepped in and said I could come live with them for a while. I was actually quite happy at their home up in Maine. But then my uncle moved to Seattle to start a new church, and my father decided it was too far away. So I came back home. Later I was sent to boarding school in Connecticut, and when I graduated, I came home for good."

"And your mother?"

"She never got over my brother's death." What euphemism to use? "She moved to McLean Hospital."

"I'm sorry," he said.

I took a sip of wine. "As the years have gone by, it's gotten easier. I think that's one reason Eleanor and I became so close. I lost my mother, and she lost her father before she was even born." I hesitated. "I've always looked up to her."

"She was blessed with a strong mother," Tom noted. "And when you have money, it tends to make difficult things easier." He reached for his wine glass.

"That's enough about me," I said, wanting to lighten things up. "Tell me about yourself."

Tom set down his glass. "My parents also lost a toddler, but she was never healthy. Her name was Theodora. She died three years before I was born."

I waited for him to continue.

"There are days when I feel like an orphan," he began, "and days when I wish I was."

"What makes you say that?"

"My parents were 45 when I was born. My brother and my other sisters are quite a bit older than I am. So for most of my life, I've been off in my own little world...and when I came along after Theodora died, all the women in my family became very protective. Sometimes it feels like I am being smothered to death. But other times, it's wonderful to have that kind of support." He paused to light a cigarette and take a puff. "My father, however, is another matter. He's worried that I'm never going to figure out how to make a living."

"Why is that?"

"He's a successful businessman back in St. Louis. Of course, the Eliot family tree has more than its share of academics and clerics on its branches. But he's skeptical that I'll ever be able to earn a living teaching philosophy. Sometimes I think his skepticism is valid."

I thought of Tracy Putnam, already launched on the road to becoming a doctor, the Harvard football players, ready to take the Boston business world by storm. I barely knew Tom Eliot. What kind of man is willing to share his insecurities the way he does? *And why do I find it so compelling?*

The waiter returned with two empty plates and our salads. Tom waited until we were left alone again, then raised his glass. "It seems that we are both outsiders in a world of insiders. So I think we ought to drink to us."

I smiled and lifted my glass to meet his. "To us."

* * *

I could have stayed there for hours, listening to Tom, answering his questions and posing some of my own. I rarely drank spirits, but the first few sips of wine made me feel as if I could breathe again. It was like that wonderful moment at the end of an evening when I finally got to undo my corset. My words seemed to flow more freely, no longer trapped in a brain that was always wondering, "What will he think?" or "What will *they* say?"

But Tom had a plan, and the plan called for us to move on to Symphony Hall for the concert. He checked his watch and asked for the bill. He seemed to know precisely how much time it would take to get there.

Our seats were up in the second balcony, but still with a good view of the stage. On the other side, I could see Uncle Philip and Aunt Irene in their usual seats. I opened my program and began flipping through the ads for music teachers and millinery.

Tom still studied the program's cover. He pointed to Philip's name. "That's your uncle, isn't it?"

I nodded, then pointed across the balcony. "He's over there, where they seat the critics."

"I've learned a lot from reading his program notes."

"He's taught me a lot, too."

"I must admit I don't usually read them until I'm back home, after the concert is over."

"Why is that?"

Tom stretched back into his seat. "I prefer to experience the music without preconceptions. You know, like John Locke's *tabula rasa.* I want to figure out on my own what the composer is trying to say. And then I'm ready to read what Philip Hale thinks."

"I'm different," I spoke up. "I want Philip to tell me what to listen for." I read a bit about the opening selection, a "symphonic burleske" by Joseph Gustav Mraczek. "Will I ruin the first piece by telling you that it depicts a series of pranks by some mischievous boys?"

He smiled. "This should be interesting."

The lights began to dim and the musicians quieted their warm-up routines. I closed my program and buried it under the gloves on my lap. The audience applauded politely as Karl Muck walked out onto the stage and took his place at the podium. The German was lean, intense, and wasted little time playing showman to the audience. He raised his baton and launched into a spirited theme.

In the darkened concert hall, I glanced quickly at Tom. His eyes were closed, his mind intent on the music. His head bobbed slightly as he picked up the rhythms of the prologue, his fingers drumming silently on his thighs. Already he was lost in the melodies, his mental pictures, his imagination.

I closed my eyes to give it a try. In the blackness, my thoughts wandered to a thousand other places. But they always returned to that night in Eleanor's parlor.

I was mesmerized.

I remembered Tom fetching my coat at the end of the evening and helping me to put it on. I remembered the toast he had made tonight. I remembered touching his hand when we both reached for the same *pomme frite.* I remembered how easily my words had spilled out and how carefully Tom had listened.

I opened my eyes and tried to pay attention to the music. I wanted to be able to say something intelligent when the intermission arrived. I longed to live in a world of music and literature and art, and—dare I admit it?—poetry and bigger ideas.

I tried to pick out the different themes and solo instruments, the way Uncle Philip had taught me when he took me to concerts. I remembered how he had placed a stick in my hand and cranked up the Victrola to teach me how to conduct. "Draw a kite in the air," he had explained. "One-two-three-four." I watched as Muck traced the same pattern in the air with his stick, coaxing up the volume with his free hand.

But when the music of the first section concluded, the only rhythm that I heard was the rapid beating of my heart.

* * *

Aunt Edith's rules of courtship specified that a woman could never appear to be too eager. Tom Eliot might turn out to be my soulmate, but he had to be the one to take the lead. For now, he was wrestling with Sanskrit and Pali, while I was studying a script by Hubert Henry Davies.

The directors of the Cambridge Social Dramatic Club had cast me as the female lead in *The Mollusc.* The club operated out of Brattle Hall, an unimposing building a few steps from Harvard Square, and even Edith could not have objected to my castmates: young men from Harvard, young women from Cambridge, Boston, and Brookline. The goal was always to raise money for a charity—with a bit of polite socializing and dancing after the curtain fell.

I was going to play Miss Roberts, whom Davies described as "a pretty, honest-looking English girl of about 24." I was pleased about the "pretty" part. John Goddard Hart had been cast as Tom, the visitor from

Colorado. By the end of the play, he would save me from a life sentence as a governess.

John was a pleasant chap who taught English at Harvard. Still, there was nothing about him that set my heart on fire. It would take every bit of my acting skill to persuade the audience that I loved him.

I wondered whether Tom might surprise me by showing up for a performance, then coming backstage to share his own review. But he was nowhere to be found. And though there were more than enough men who lined up for a dance with "the star," I realized that I still felt acutely alone.

* * *

A week later, Tom finally did call—oblivious, it seemed, to how much time had passed since he took me to the concert. Spring had arrived like a long-lost cousin, and he suggested we take a walk in the Public Garden. It was too early in the season for the Swan Boats to be plying the lake, but the daffodils and tulips had popped up in the manicured flower beds, shaking off their own winter doldrums.

"I'm afraid I've had too many papers due," he offered by way of an excuse as he helped me dodge a boy's out-of-control rolling hoop. "But I missed you."

"I've been busy, too." I was careful to keep up my guard.

"I read the review in the *Tribune*. I'm sorry I missed your performance."

"They're talking about having us do the play again later in the year."

"Tell me about it."

He was interested again. In the swing-swang of my emotions, there was a glimmer of hope. "I played Miss Roberts." Then I laughed. "Three full acts and nobody ever calls me by my first name—even the man who falls in love with me. According to the script, I was simply 'an honest-looking English girl of about 24.'" I decided to leave out the "pretty" part.

"From what I saw of the girls in London, I'd say you fit the bill."

"Did you meet many girls in London?"

"No," he replied. "I was too busy being a tourist."

We arrived at a vacant bench. He took out a white handkerchief and wiped off the dust. Then we sat down, leaving some space between us, but putting ourselves close enough that no one would try to squeeze in.

"Tell me more about the play," he said.

"As we went through rehearsals, I discovered that I identified with Miss Roberts," I said. "She was an orphan. And she was a governess who felt she had reached the limits of what she could teach her charges." I paused. "Sometimes I think I might like to become a teacher."

"What's stopping you?"

I hesitated. "I'm afraid I don't have any credentials."

He spoke up quickly. "In my experience, the best teachers are the ones who teach from the heart, not from the head. Oh, you have to know your subject, of course, but there's something more to it. Take Professor Lanman. Sanskrit is a difficult language, but he's so fascinated with the subject that he makes it come alive. He makes you want to master it because it's so important to him."

I liked the way his eyes lit up when he talked about his professor.

He was quiet for a moment. "Ever since we went to the concert, I've been thinking about that first piece we heard, the one about the rambunctious boys. My childhood was nothing like that."

"How so?"

"I had a hernia when I was young."

I remembered the story Eleanor had shared after her party about the first time their families had vacationed together at the Gloucester shore and how Tom had changed into his bathing suit and his cousins discovered he had to wear a truss to keep a hernia in place. And Tom thought everybody had to wear one.

Tom went on. "I was always watched over, coddled, you might say. That's what happens when you have four older sisters....I didn't do any roughhousing. I spent more time in the world of women....As I listened to the escapades of Max and Moritz the other night, I was struck by how alien their world seemed to me."

I mulled that for a moment. *Perhaps that's what makes him different.* "I never had the chance to run wild," I said at last. "I was always reminded that I was the pastor's daughter or the pastor's niece. Even when Uncle Philip took me to a concert, I always worried that I would embarrass him by coughing at the wrong moment or rustling my program." I paused. "And when I was living with Aunt Edith and Uncle John, I always believed that if I tried very hard to be a good girl, Father would finally want me to come back home." I reached up to straighten my hat. "Now I sometimes feel as if he only wants me there to play hostess."

His gaze caught mine, and I lowered my eyes. *Why did I tell him that?* He was so easy to talk to, it scared me a little. I knew the Rules of Engagement for the males I was likely to meet, but Tom Eliot seemed to play by a completely different rulebook.

I tried to change the subject. "What else do you remember from the concert?"

"I thought a lot about 'The Mephisto Waltz,'" he said. "It struck me that it would have been very hard to actually dance to it. I studied your uncle's notes on it. If I remember his quote from Chrysostom, 'Where there is dancing, you'll find the Devil,' or something close to that. Do you agree?"

"Some of the members of our church would agree with him. But I quite like to dance."

"So do I. We'll have to do it sometime soon."

You missed your chance the other night.

Tom tilted his head back and closed his eyes, stretching out his long legs and letting his arms hug the back of the park bench. "I wish that days like today could last forever," he said.

I tilted back my face, too, feeling the warmth of the sun on my cheeks. "So do I."

We sat quietly, listening to the chirping of birds and the joyful cries of the children running through the park. Then Tom reached into his pocket for his watch. He grimaced when he saw the time. "Unfortunately, I have a late-afternoon class. But if we get started now, I'll have just enough time to see you home."

He rose from the bench and offered his hand to help me get up. We walked silently for a while, each of us lost in our thoughts. We did not touch, even to try to hold hands. Yet I could still sense a difference. I could not name it, the feeling was too new, too unique, too special. All I knew was that when John Hart had kissed me at the end of *The Mollusc*, my body had felt nothing like what it was feeling now.

As we walked through the park, our steps matched each other's in length and in tempo. Uncle Philip might have said we had fallen into the same cadence. For the first time in my life, I felt as if I had a protector. It was a feeling I knew I could learn to love.

* * *

At Harvard, the future doctors studied Linnaeus's system for classifying plants and animals. In recent years, I had learned, the students applied another system of classification to the women they dated: pre-debs, debs, post-debs, and LOPHs. Amy had explained what the last one meant: "Left On Papa's Hands."

I was dangerously close to that category, but if Father was worried about it, he never showed it. It had been so confusing when I returned home from the safe confines of Miss Porter's School. Some of my friends were going off to Radcliffe and Wellesley. Others were headed to Simmons to learn how to type or run a household. The doctors could never diagnose the cause of my headaches, giving Edith ample opportunity to fret about the rigors and stresses of college life—and whether I had the same tendencies as Mother.

By the time I finally returned to whatever passed for my "old self," my friends had moved on with their lives. And I was back in the parsonage in Chestnut Hill, where "a woman's touch" was still missing—and appreciated if I could provide it.

Father and I settled into a comfortable life together. His schedule was full, the needs of his parish always growing, sometimes taxing his health. Beyond Chestnut Hill, he maintained other intellectual circles: the Unitarian church, his old colleagues at Harvard Divinity School, the historical society. He did not seem to care how I filled my days—as long as I came home at night.

Still, I was nervous about inviting Tom to dinner. He was, in fact, my first male caller, and who knew whether there would ever be another? I desperately wanted Father to like him.

But I needn't have worried. Father metamorphosed into the Harvard professor he once had been. Before he had taught homiletics, but now our dining room turned into a philosophy classroom. He and Tom argued over everything from Heraclitus and Plato and Buddha to the sermons and speeches of the more celebrated Eliots and Hales.

For a change, I was happy to sit in the audience, to listen and then serve dessert and clear the dishes as their friendly arguments went on into the night. And as the candles came perilously close to dripping on Grandmother Milliken's tablecloth, I wondered if down deep I had yearned to meet a man who could replace Father in my life. And I wondered if he, too, yearned for a man who could replace our long-dead Billy.

* * *

For its final play of the season, the Social Dramatic Club was mounting *Fanny and the Servant Problem*. Miss Roberts had required someone who was "pretty" and "honest-looking," but Fanny was a music hall performer, a woman so enticingly beautiful that the hero, Lord Bantock, would never spurn her, even after he learned she was the niece of his footman.

It was no surprise that Amy got the part.

But I was surprised at the directors' choice for Lord Bantock. No one, they decided, could play a proper Englishman better than Tom Eliot could, and they were willing to schedule their rehearsals around the demands of his classes.

This time, Tom took his role very seriously. We practiced his lines so many times that I knew I could step into Amy's shoes if I had to. But for now, I did what the club needed me to do, and that meant helping out with the props.

Still, it was different this time. Whenever Amy and Tom shared a scene, I had to quell my growing jealousy. Amy had a veritable toolbox of flirtation skills, and she brought all of them to her role. They were on full display when Lord Bantock walked onstage—and when Tom Eliot walked off.

What keeps me from telling her that he's mine? Well, for starters, I was not truly sure I could make that claim. Tom himself was secretive and private, never suggesting that we go to a party together or join another couple for a double date. But soon the production would be over. One performance tonight and then the Saturday matinee. And then, I hoped, I would have him all to myself again.

The most important exchanges came in Act III, when Fanny tested whether Lord Bantock believed that love was possible among different rungs of the British social ladder. From my perch in the wings, I craned my neck to watch and listen.

Amy ran through the names of the attractive servants in the Bantock household. "The wonder to me is that, brought up among them, admiring them as you do, you never thought of marrying one of them."

"Well," Tom replied, "one hardly marries into one's own kitchen."

During our own rehearsals, I had never stopped to ask Tom what he thought about that. Did he think that we were really social equals? Yes, I was a Hale, but I had never gone to college. And my mother was locked away in an asylum. Within the circle of the Stearns family, I knew Eleanor would always rise to my defense. But what about the rest of Tom's family? His businessman father? His mother, so worried about her precious youngest child? His sisters and brother? All of Tom's friends at Harvard?

From backstage, I watched the scene proceed. I held my breath, knowing the climactic moment was coming. "Oh, you dear boy," Amy said at last. I heard the audience's collective sigh as Amy kissed Tom. "You don't know how a woman loves the man she loves to love her....Isn't that complicated?"

Yes, I agreed, it *is* very complicated.

Onstage, Amy was about to reveal her deception. She reached out in turn to each of the servants, coming at last to Ernest, the second footman.

Estlin Cummings was the youngest member of the cast, and Amy loved to tease him and call him "Eddie," which he disliked. But whenever Amy came on stage, Estlin seemed to stammer and go all wobbly, and the prompter got ready to provide his next line.

Now the cast and crew held their collective breaths, waiting for Amy to kiss Estlin.

"Goodbye, Ernest. We were always pals, weren't we?" Amy's lips brushed his cheek. But Estlin grabbed her shoulders, planting a long, full kiss on her lips. Amy's jaw dropped in shock, and the backstage crew broke into applause.

I touched my lips. *What did it feel like when you weren't playing pretend?*

The play wrapped up quickly to the inevitable happy ending. The cast gathered to take their bows, the applause building as Amy took center stage. Now Tom was presenting his leading lady with a bouquet. Of course, it *was* the club's tradition. But will he ever bring me roses?

The cast retreated backstage. There were props to store, a scene to reset for tomorrow's matinee.

I felt a tap on my shoulder. I turned and it was Tom, holding a small nosegay of violets. "Here," he said. "I wanted you to have these."

I was overwhelmed by the surprise. I pressed the violets to my nose, sampling their sweet scent. "Thank you," I murmured. "You don't know what this means...."

"Come on," he said, setting down the flowers and taking me by the hand. "They've cleared the chairs for the dancing."

Someone had pulled out the Victrola and given it a crank. The record sounded like Jolson, a new song I didn't recognize. Still, it fit my mood.

You made me love you.
I didn't want to do it.
I didn't want to do it.

Tom placed his hand in the middle of my back, pulling me closer. I shut my eyes, cataloging every sensation. A whiff of his after shave, the roughness of Lord Bantock's tweed jacket under my palm, the confidence of Tom's dance steps, Jolson's voice soaring over the room.

"Where there is dancing," he whispered, "you'll find the Devil."

I had danced at debutante parties, formal waltzes in long gowns, always fretting that I might catch a heel on my hem. Dutiful dances with a long list of Boston's finest men, faces I could barely remember now.

I wanted to remember this.

We danced on until midnight, and then it was time to close up the theater. I found the nosegay where Tom had left it, grateful that no one else had claimed it.

He saw me home to Chestnut Hill, a trip that had usually ended with dinner with Father. But tonight I wanted to linger for a moment on the front steps.

"Did I tell you that your performance was wonderful?" I paused. "And I had a wonderful time, too."

"We should go dancing more often."

Then he leaned over and kissed a delicate spot behind my ear. He waited a moment, and then his lips found mine. It was a soft kiss, a tender kiss, the kind of kiss I had always dreamed of receiving.

Perhaps Amy had finally provided Tom with the inspiration he needed to cross this threshold. But in the soft glow of the streetlamps on a warm summer night, I did not care if she had.

Let Us Go Then, You and I

WALKING BECAME OUR FAVORITE PASTIME. As spring edged its way into summer, we spent more time outdoors, strolling and talking about every subject we could think of, the weighty and the mundane. Strolling fit our budgets. But it also let us create a world of our own, if only for the length of a summer afternoon.

It was convenient to meet at the Public Garden. The tulips had given way to the hyacinths, and the hyacinths were about to be upstaged by the roses. This time our feet led us toward Charles Street, near the new statue of Edward Everett Hale that Boston's elite, with the assistance of former President Taft, had dedicated just a few weeks before.

We stopped in front of the tall bronze man standing on top of a granite pediment.

"Do you think you got your money's worth?"

I smiled. Tom knew that like most of the rest of Boston, I had donated some pennies to the fund that had supported the statue. "I do."

"Then you're a much better Unitarian than I am."

I walked around the statue, reading the words inscribed on its base: "Man of Letters. Preacher of the Gospel. Prophet of Peace. Patriot."

"I did expect that he would be depicted as a younger man. You know, delivering a stern sermon or waving a manifesto at us."

Tom arched an eyebrow. "With a few slaves at his feet, throwing off their chains and gazing up at their savior?"

"No, not that," I said, wrinkling my nose at Tom. "But I wonder if he would have preferred to be shown in the prime of his life?"

"That's precisely why the statue appeals to me," Tom pronounced. "With all of Boston ready to give their opinions, the sculptor managed to avoid the usual clichés. The good reverend is looking back at his life. There's fatigue and regret, but still some amusement on his face as the birds land on his shoulders." He paused. "Did you ever meet him?"

I shook my head. "Father worked with him at South Congregational. He always looked up to him. But their lives followed different paths after that."

"When the old man finally retired, the congregation tried to hire my cousin," Tom noted. "When he turned them down, they hired Estlin's father instead."

"Samuel Eliot was your cousin?"

He nodded. "I've lost track of whether we're seconds or thirds or fourths. The Eliots, I've decided, are to Unitarianism like the Borgias are to the Pope."

I laughed. "Well, if the Eliots are the Borgias, then Everett Edward Hale *was* the Pope!"

He chuckled softly in return. I was happy I could make him laugh, this intense, hard-working student of philosophy. *Perhaps he needs more of this. And perhaps I'm the one who can provide it.*

He laced my hand through the crook of his arm, and we moved on, beyond the gaze of the elderly minister. As we headed back around the lagoon, I dared to broach a new topic.

"Speaking of Estlin, I heard that he has started calling on Amy."

"He didn't waste much time."

I hesitated. "He also wrote her a poem. He gave it to her after the Saturday matinee."

Tom stopped and turned to me, looking wounded. "Does that make you feel neglected?"

"I didn't say that."

"But maybe you feel that way."

Maybe I did.

He started walking again. "I don't write those kinds of poems," he said at last. "Oh, I can dash off something quick and sophomoric for my friends, or if the *Advocate* has a hole that needs to be filled on deadline. But I'm not proud of them. I need to let my poems stew for a while....But to be honest, I don't feel I've written anything that's particularly good since I came back from Europe."

He stopped and turned back to me, brushing a lock of hair from my cheek. "I've been so happy with you, Emily. And I wonder why I can't channel those feelings into my verse."

"You've never shown me *any* of your poems," I said at last.

"Maybe I'm afraid you won't like them." He smiled shyly. "But if you insist. As long as you are honest with me about what you think of them."

"I promise," I replied. "Cross my heart and hope to die."

* * *

I didn't raise the topic of poetry again. I thought Tom might bring along a poem the next time we went out, or even recite a short one from memory. A week went by, then two, then three. Then one day, an envelope arrived in the mail, fine cream-colored stationery, addressed to "Miss Emily Hale." I recognized Tom's agitated script from the scribblings in the small notebook he always carried in his jacket pocket.

The envelope contained many pages, several poems, I thought at first. But as I unfolded the pages, I realized there was only one, one that went on and on, longer than I would have expected.

I read the title. "Prufrock," I repeated out loud, testing the sound of it. *What an odd name!*

I put the poem aside for a minute, taking time to fix myself a cup of tea before climbing the stairs to the privacy of my bedroom. I settled into the chair by the front window, and began to read it:

Let us go then, you and I,
When the evening is spread out against the sky...

I read the poem once, twice, three times, swept away by the words and the images. No wonder Tom hadn't just reeled it off as we sat side-by-side on the park bench. There was too much to absorb here, too much to think about.

I grow old...I grow old...
I shall wear the bottoms of my trousers rolled.
Shall I part my hair behind? Do I dare to eat a peach?

I could envision Prufrock, sense his fear and tentativeness. It was a meaty role, calling for a truly great actor. But if this was my Tom, I didn't recognize him. Who *was* this Prufrock? Was he young or middle-aged?

I knew I was no literary critic, no professor of English or even a student at Radcliffe. I had never tried to write anything more than doggerel for my friends. Still, I had studied the great poets at one of the best girls' schools in America. I knew there were some poets who wallowed in banality, and others whose lines continued to echo long after you had read them. Tom was clearly in the second category.

Still, his voice was not conventional. You would not find his verses in the pages of the ladies' magazines or the piano benches of the day.

But if he could write this way in Europe, why couldn't he write this way now?

I remembered what he had told me about his loneliness in Europe, of being sick and miserable in Munich. And then a terrifying thought suddenly made me shudder. I could do everything I could to try to make Tom Eliot happy. I could do everything I could to encourage him to write. But Tom didn't want to write the kind of verses I had sung at Eleanor's. "Prufrock" was not borne out of happiness. And if he were truly happy, would he ever be able to write this kind of poem again?

And then I asked another question, even more disturbing than the first. If Tom fell in love with me, if someday we got married and had children, was there a chance he would ultimately decide that it was the worst thing that could possibly happen to him?

* * *

I paused outside of Emerson Hall to catch my breath. The tall red-brick columns drew my eyes to the inscription over the entrance. I knew it was from the Psalms, probably Number 8: "What is man that thou are mindful of him." At least with the Psalms, I thought as I hurried inside, I'm on more familiar footing than with Sanskrit.

The Philosophical Club was meeting in the small auditorium upstairs and Tom had suggested we go out for coffee afterwards. He had been elected president that fall, one more achievement for his résumé, but one more responsibility that cut into our precious time together.

I passed the statue of Emerson in the lobby, tapping the burnished bronze of the philosopher's outstretched foot. It was supposed to bring good luck on exams. I was willing to accept a bit of luck wherever I could find it.

The lecture was underway, and I found a seat near the back of the room. There were a handful of women present, but I didn't recognize any of them. Probably Radcliffe students, invited to listen to the discussion but not to join the club.

I tried to follow the logic of the speakers' arguments. I could hold my own around the dining table, when Tom and Father debated the nature of faith, belief, and skepticism. But now, as the students held forth on the views of Henri Bergson, I had to admit I was getting lost. *What did it really matter in the end?* I wanted to care, because Tom cared so much. But life was meant to be lived, not endlessly discussed. Did Tom spend too much time in the world of ideas?

Still, he belonged in this world. I could envision him as a professor of philosophy. But would it leave time for his poetry? And what of that leash his father kept jerking?

And where do I fit in all of this? If I can't be on the stage, where *would* I be happy? I knew this world, this world of pastors and professors. It was quiet and comfortable and safe. Perhaps that was precisely the problem.

Around me, people were applauding. The program had concluded; the speakers were rising and shaking hands. The audience filed out, the women regarding me quizzically, the men continuing to argue. I waited patiently, knowing that Tom still had to straighten up the chairs and turn off the lights.

"What did you think?" he asked eagerly when he was finally ready to leave.

"The speakers seemed very knowledgeable," I said. "And very firm in their opinions....But I'm sorry, it was mostly over my head. I wanted to understand their arguments, but it was hard because—"

"—because it's rather like arguing over how many angels can dance on the head of a pin?" he suggested.

"Your choice of words, not mine."

"But you're right," he said. "The sun will come up tomorrow and the earth will spin on its axis, no matter whether philosophers agree on what it all means. But I still love pondering the questions we do. And," he said as he pulled on his coat, "I'm grateful that Harvard pays me to teach freshmen all about it."

He took my arm. "Let's find a quiet place where we can talk."

He led me to a café a short walk from Harvard Square. We found a table near the window and ordered coffee and tea.

I had thought carefully about what I wanted to say about his poem. But I had waited so long, I could barely restrain myself now.

"Your poem was wonderful, Tom. You have a voice. A very distinctive voice."

"Do you really think so?"

I was pleased he cared so much about my opinion. I nodded, then took a sip of tea. "I don't have enough schooling to articulate exactly how you did it. And I will admit I didn't understand everything you were trying to say. But it didn't matter. Your images were vivid. The rhythm of your lines drew me in and kept me reading. I think it is very good."

"I wish I could find a publisher who agreed with you."

"You have to be patient," I said. "It's very different from the kind of poetry people are used to reading."

"Conrad is managing to get *his* poems published."

He talked a lot about his friend Conrad Aiken. Perhaps he had better connections or was better at promoting himself. I could do nothing about that. But there was one thing I *could* do.

"You have to believe in yourself, Tom. Editors and publishers, your rivals and your peers—even me—we can all tell you what we think you should do. But you're the only one who matters...."

I hesitated. "That night we did the skits for Eleanor. I remember you telling me that you would never be able to write poems about May Days and forget-me-nots. So write what you want to write. And if you decide it's rubbish, you can always throw it away. If it never gets published, so be it. But at least you will have written something from your heart, not just what you think a publisher wants to read."

He held his coffee cup in his hands, mulling what I had said.

"All around us, the world is changing," I went on. "You read about it in the newspapers. You can feel it, taste it...and poetry is bound to change, too."

He looked at me intently, his face registering a mixture of surprise and delight.

"But then again," I said shyly, "what do I know?" Day after day, my own world never changed. "I suppose I'm just another one of those girls who 'come and go, talking of Michelangelo.'"

"Never," he reassured me, reaching across the table to take my hand. "Besides," he said, "I wrote that line years before I met you."

"Still," I said, "I think it describes me." I hesitated. "I must admit that your poem scared me a little."

"Really?"

"I wondered who Prufrock was, since you captured him so well. I wondered whether he was you. And if he was you, it was a Tom I didn't know. If I peeled back all of your layers, what would I find? Would I find a poet? A philosopher? The president of the Philosophical Club? Lord Bantock? The man who is able to hold his own with his professors?"

I paused, suddenly feeling bolder. "Or would I find the man who thrills me when he leads me onto the dance floor? Or is Prufrock really scared and indecisive and old before his time? Is he really Mr. Wood-house, taking a nap in front of the fire?"

I took a sip of the tea, remembering a few more lines that had stayed with me.

Time for you and time for me,
And time yet for a hundred indecisions,
And for a hundred visions and revisions,
Before the taking of a toast and tea.

"I started thinking about this poem three years ago," Tom said slowly. "I was in Munich, and I had been sick and feeling very down. Despite everything the city had to offer, it still seemed very alien to me. So yes, I suppose there is some of me in Prufrock...but that's not the way I feel now."

I wondered about that. No, he was no longer Prufrock. But he still had that insecurity, that vulnerability about him. That was part of what had first attracted me that night at Eleanor's. I didn't think I would have fallen in love with a take-charge man. Still, Tom had changed, even in the short time we had been together. He was working harder, doing better, making plans. And even if he was still insecure about his poetry, he was certainly more secure about himself.

He pulled out a cigarette and lit it, a flicker of light before the lamps turned up in the restaurant. We sat in silence, quietly sipping our drinks.

I finished my tea and he put down his coffee cup. He reached across the table and took my hand again. Then he recited his lines:

Let us go then, you and I,
When the evening is spread out against the sky....

He stopped there, and we rose and walked out into the dying light. I knew why he had stopped where he did. The next lines were not quite so romantic.

Estlin Cummings had also written about a sunset, I recalled from the poem Amy had shared, beating its wings in the west like a bird. The poem was not exactly an ode to Amy. But Estlin had still envisioned a special twilight where the poet and his woman could feel protected in their own private world.

I wondered whether I would ever inspire Tom's poetry. Would Prufrock ever master the language of love? Would he ever know the delight of a walk through the burnished leaves of autumn?

And would he ever learn how to cultivate profound words out of a core of happiness?

One Fine Day

CHRISTMAS, I WAS ALWAYS TOLD, was the happiest time of the year. But as snowstorms signaled the start of December, I was fighting to control my rising sense of dread.

The swirl of holiday parties, the gatherings for gift-giving and cocoa-drinking in front of the fireplace—every year the warm celebrations only underscored the emptiness of my own family life. And this year, there was a new cloud: What would Tom decide to do at the end of the next semester?

I knew his heart was set on going to Oxford. He talked about the well-known scholars who were there, how his Harvard professors had encouraged him to apply for a fellowship. But he said nothing about whether he had actually done it. I wondered if he feared he would be rejected—and how he would tell me if he was.

But for now he was still in Boston and I had a part to play. The society ladies had booked the Plymouth Theatre for a revival of *The Mollusc*, this time to help the Milk and Baby Hygiene Association address the city's shocking infant mortality rate.

Miss Roberts's lines hadn't changed since I had first performed them, but my own perspective had. "If you knew how I sometimes long to be free to do whatever I like just for one day. When I see other girls...enjoying themselves—it comes over me so dreadfully what I am missing...."

I was determined to get through December. I would brace myself for the Christmas visit to Mother. I would look forward to exchanging presents with Tom. And then in the New Year, I would resolve to do something, anything, to take command of my life.

* * *

We set aside an evening two nights before Christmas. I had taken pains to wrap my package, trying my best to make it look special. I hoped the gift would not seem too impersonal; I still believed it was a good choice for Tom.

He smiled like a little boy when he opened the pen-and-pencil set.

"It's beautiful," he said, giving me a quick kiss behind the ear. "I'll always treasure it."

I smiled. "I hope it inspires you to greatness…and reminds you that no matter what anyone else thinks, I believe in you."

He looked at me intently, then laughed. "I almost forgot my gifts!" He pulled out a small box. It was expertly wrapped, probably, I thought, by a shop clerk. Inside was a bottle of toilet water from Yardley's of London.

"It's hyacinth," he noted. "I sampled several fragrances, but this one made me think of you."

I unscrewed the cap, then put a drop on the inside of my wrist. "I like it," I announced after I smelled it. "It will remind me that spring is coming. And it will remind me of you."

"And something else," he said, handing over a small envelope.

I opened it to find two tickets. *Madame Butterfly* at the Opera House, the first week of January. "This is wonderful," I said. "I really wanted to see it."

I knew that Tom did, too. My friends often complained when their beaux purchased presents that the men really wanted. There was some of that here, I had to admit. Still, Tom gave me so much more—affection, attention, the possibility of a future soulmate. In the end, those were the gifts that truly mattered.

I had located the bottle of brandy Father kept in the back of a cupboard, out of sight of visiting parishioners. It was bold to offer Tom a glass. But sitting in front of the fireplace, warmed by the flames and Tom's presence, it was what I most wanted to do.

I filled one glass for him, then another for myself. I held the tumbler for a moment, contemplating the deep amber color, thinking of the future. This would be a nice life. It was enough just to be together, sharing quiet moments like this.

"1913 turned out to be a very good year for me," I said at last.

"For me, too," Tom replied.

I tapped the rim of my glass to his. "Then let's hope," I said, "that 1914 turns out to be even better."

* * *

As I grew older, I had learned to forgive Father for sending Mother away. Perhaps if Billy had died while we were still in South Orange, it would have been easier for us to cope. Perhaps our old congregation would have rallied around, offering comforting arms, lowered expectations for their pastor, and a never-ending procession of meals to keep us all fed. But he had just moved back to the big leagues of Boston, and the old Chestnut Hill Chapel was now poised for significant growth.

So there was no time, no place for visible mourning and grief. No matter how hard Father tried, he was incapable of consoling Mother. After sobbing uncontrollably throughout Billy's funeral, she had retreated to her darkened bedroom, refusing food, turning away family and friends. He could not deal with this. He was in a new position; it required all of his energy and focus. He needed to find a quiet place for his wife, where she could get the care and attention she needed.

Edith stepped in to help him make decisions. She knew the demands of a clergyman's life. The old asylum had just moved to a beautiful new site in the countryside. Her sister might be able to recover there. She would find the rest and the quiet she needed, the best doctors Boston had to offer, an escape from the stresses and memories of Chestnut Hill.

Edith could also help raise me. She could take charge of all those things Father knew nothing about: the schools, the clothes, the changes of life a woman would have to explain.

And as I grew older, I came to understand how I had provided Edith with the one thing she needed to make her own life complete: a polite little girl she could try to mold into the spitting image of herself.

So Father had agreed to the plan. He filled his own lonely hours with work: pastoring, speaking, writing, and teaching part-time at Harvard. And if that wasn't enough, he pushed his congregation to replace the country chapel they had outgrown. He pored over the blueprints with the architects, tapping back into his knowledge from the career he had once pursued. He had a vision: not only for the aesthetics of a building, but now for the practicalities of operating a church.

The result was like Father: a building that was solid but not dramatic. There was no grand spire directing the eye heavenward. The church was built to last, and it probably would, long after its pastor had passed on. It would remain a monument to Edward Hale—and to the success his congregation had enjoyed under his leadership.

But even the most intellectually gifted preachers were also expected to be family men. And so on most Sunday mornings, I took my usual seat near the front of the sanctuary. I could always hear the whispers of the older women behind me, discussing my hat or wondering why I never brought along a beau. Perhaps the old timers pointed me out to the newcomers, recalling my family's tragedy and thanking God that it had not been visited on them.

I was not entirely convinced that there was a God. What kind of God sent an iceberg to sink the Titanic or a fever to kill a little boy? And I was often exasperated by the politics of the Unitarians and how those battles seemed to weigh Father down. But in the quiet of the Chestnut Hill sanctuary, I did find a small measure of peace. And this year, more than some in the past, I did find a sense of hope.

On Christmas Eve, we would light candles in the front windows of the parsonage and wait for the carolers to come around. If they asked Father for his favorite carol, he would always choose "It Came Upon the Midnight Clear." It was written by a Unitarian clergyman after *he* had suffered a nervous breakdown.

The third verse always made me think of my parents:

And ye, beneath life's crushing load,
Whose forms are bending low,
Who toil along the climbing way
With painful steps and slow...

We stood in the open doorway and listened. The air was crisp and clean, and the winter sky was filled with stars. It would be nice, I thought, to heat some cocoa on the stove and invite the carolers into the parlor to warm up. Or we could have bundled ourselves up and joined them on their rounds. But Father always valued his quiet, especially on bittersweet nights like this.

We did not share many moments like this one, and I knew I was as much to blame as he was.

"What was Christmas like before Billy died?"

I was not sure what made me pose the question. Father never talked about those days, and it would probably pain him to do so now. But he paused, his eyes brightening. "It was nice," he said. "We were very happy."

He reached to close the door, then added, "And your mother was a very good wife."

*　*　*

Emily Jose Milliken Hale was one of the first new patients when the old asylum in Somerville was moved to the Belmont countryside. Now McLean Hospital was set in a beautiful park, with winding paths and carefully sculpted groves of trees. It was a spot picked out by none other than Frederick Law Olmsted after he had finished his work on Central Park. In his senile last years, his relatives had decided it was a restful place for him to live out his days. If there were dangerous patients surrounding Mr. Olmsted and Mrs. Hale, the administrators did everything they could to disguise them.

Mother had actually shown some improvement over the years. The doctors got her eating again, then taking her baths and joining other patients in the activities room. She painted a little and enjoyed her supervised walks. But the handful of times Father had tried bringing her home, it had turned into a disaster—and so he no longer tried. The doctors speculated that the parsonage brought back too many terrible memories, not only of Billy's death but probably the stern judgments of her husband's congregation. But that was his life, and now this was hers.

The hospital was always busy on Christmas Day. The buildings, big and small, were filled with visiting family members. Mother lived in one of the women's houses, a less expensive residence than a private cottage but still very much like our home. A spruce had been set up in the lounge and decorated with Christmas ornaments. The fireplace mantel and bannisters were strung with garlands of evergreens.

Spouses and parents and children came because that's what they were expected to do on Christmas Day. It was the best way to show the staff that there were still people who cared, people who were watching if clothes weren't changed or baths were forgotten. But I knew that most of the residents probably didn't distinguish one day from another. Certainly Mother never seemed to know the difference.

An aide brought her down to the parlor, and Father and I took turns kissing the deadened cheek. It was still possible to imagine that she had once been quite beautiful. Her brown hair was neatly brushed, a touch of rouge and lipstick applied. I helped Father pick out nice dresses for presents, and the orderlies took care to make sure they were worn. Today she was wearing a forest green silk dress—the gift, I remembered, we had brought the year before.

We helped her undo the wrappings on this year's presents and contributed our own exclamations of delight. We took turns telling stories, watching for a spark of interest. We shared the news from Edith's last letter. Aunt Sarah was staying indoors in Cambridge today, nursing a bit of a cold. I yearned to tell her about Tom, to share female secrets the way my friends did with their mothers. But the doctors said it was best to talk about the people Mother knew from her past, not the strangers of the present. To try to conjure up old memories—as long as they were happy ones.

Still, nothing seemed to register. Father always timed our visits for the hour before the noontime meal. An aide would appear to lead Mother away, making it easier for us to say goodbye. As always, that moment eventually arrived. Mother rose from the sofa, then turned to us and smiled.

I held my breath. Did she finally recognize us?

"Today's a special day," she announced. "They're serving us roast beef and mince pie. I have to get to my seat before someone else gets there first." Then she turned and left without a further word.

Father's shoulders sagged, and he brushed away a tear with a quick flick of his finger. He could put on his pastor's face when he needed to. He could lead every funeral, no matter how tragic, with stoical aplomb. But this was different. On a single day in December, he needed all the reserves of emotional strength that I could muster.

"Let's go," I whispered softly, guiding him toward the door. "I've got a nice Christmas dinner waiting for us back at the house."

* * *

Uncle Philip had introduced me to opera, and of all of the composers, I liked Puccini the best. I had wanted to see *Butterfly* ever since it had premiered in the States. Over the holidays, I made time to read the libretto. To fully appreciate the songs, I knew you had to read the script. It underscored the depth of Pinkerton's callousness and how the geisha's love had blinded her to all the warnings from her friends.

Louisa Edvina had joined the Boston Opera during the previous season, but this was her first time in the role. When the soprano made her entrance, I was briefly disappointed with the casting: Except for her kimono, Edvina looked nothing like a geisha. And Vincenzo Tanlongo was portlier than I had imagined Pinkerton to be. His crisp white naval uniform would likely stir many women's romantic fantasies, but I didn't share that particular one. No, neither Benjamin Franklin Pinkerton nor Vincenzo Tanlongo was the man of my dreams. That man was sitting right next to me.

Could Tom ever be as selfish as Pinkerton? What would happen if he won that fellowship to Oxford? What could happen to a man when he gets on a ship and disappears for a year?

"You're awfully quiet tonight," Tom observed near the end of intermission.

I tried to hide my fears behind a smile. "I'm practicing the fine art of being a geisha."

"Don't practice too long," he whispered as the lights dimmed for the second act. "I might miss the Emily I know."

The curtain rose. Daybreak on a hill in Nagasaki. Edvina began the well-known aria:

One fine day we'll notice a thread of smoke arising on the sea....There is coming a man, a little speck in the distance....He will call, he will call: "Dear baby wife of mine, Dear little orange blossom."...This will all come to pass as I tell you. Banish your idle fears. For he will return I know it.

And Pinkerton does return, but with an American wife. He is too cowardly to face Butterfly, so the consul and Kate Pinkerton are forced to tell her the terrible truth. But he wants his son. The little boy will be happier in America.

And then it all spirals downward after that. The family dagger: "Death with honor is better than life with dishonor." The blindfolded child, waving an American flag. The dagger clattering to the ground and—too late—Pinkerton's cries of anguish:

"Butterfly...Butterfly...Butterfly."

The curtain came down, the applause erupted. It grew louder as Edvina rose from the dead, accepting her roses and sharing a collegial bow with those who had deserted her.

The lights eventually came up again. "Are you all right?" Tom asked, his face full of concern.

I touched my fingers to my cheek and realized they were wet with tears. Tom pulled a clean handkerchief from his breast pocket. "Here, this should help."

"I don't know what came over me," I said, dabbing at my eyes. "I suppose I just got caught up in the story."

"Personally," Tom said, "I thought the production was a bit rough around the edges. The conductor seemed to be struggling to hold it all together."

I said nothing for a moment. Could Tom not feel Butterfly's loss? Was he even capable of crying? He had always understood me so much better than the others did; why couldn't he understand this?

You could always count on Tom to have an opinion, and I usually welcomed them. He knew more, had read more, and had studied more than I ever could. But this time, I didn't want his opinion.

"The opera had its flaws," I conceded at last. "But it still managed to touch my heart."

* * *

The word came three weeks later. Tom had been accepted at Merton College at Oxford starting in the fall. I was happy for him and happy that he was so excited. But I thought of us as a couple now, a man and woman who should plan their futures together. I did not think that Tom Eliot was inherently selfish. But he seemed to forget that there were others who might have a stake in his choices.

For now, I decided to keep my peace. What else could I do? Had I expected a ring at Christmastime? I was still not sure we were ready to take that step. But if not now, then when? Perhaps Tom looked ahead to his year in England as one last gasp of freedom. Perhaps I ought to do the same.

So I pretended to be happy. I prodded Tom to make arrangements. I helped him draw up lists of the things that needed to be done, the books he would take, the clothes he would pack. I put on a smile and encouraged him at every turn. But it was different—and harder—than the role I had to play on Christmas Day. In the parlor of McLean Hospital, I was just a supporting actress. But this was becoming the leading role of my life.

* * *

Sarah Emery Hooper surprised all of us by dying suddenly on a drizzly day in February. My great-aunt had lived into her nineties but had remained sharp and feisty up until the end. By all standards of measurement, hers was a good life, well-lived.

Still, her death cast a pall over my world. First there were the obituaries. Sarah had borne no children, but she left behind a slew of nieces and a nephew. Edith received no special mention for providing Sarah with a home in her later years. As for Mother, she was listed simply as "Mrs. Hale," if she garnered a mention at all.

Reverend Cummings would lead the funeral at South Congregational, but Father and Uncle John would also take part. Tom offered to accompany me, but I gave him a pass. He was cynical about the church, and I knew he dreaded funerals—and the thought of dying even more. "It's best if I can give all my attention to Edith," I explained. "Come by the house later on, and you'll finally be able to meet my aunt and uncle."

The church was full, the service ran long. And as I patted Edith's hand gently, I was overwhelmed with regret. I thought of the hours I had spent with Sarah, at Edith's home or family gatherings. She was a sweet little old lady who sometimes dozed off in her chair. Only now, as the eulogies continued, did I discover the woman I had never known. Traveling to Australia in advance of the Gold Rush. Founding the Boston Cooking School. Serving on the Sanitary Commission. Moving up the ranks of the church until the Unitarians could no longer deny her the first vice presidency. Doing most of it after she was on her own.

I had never asked Sarah to share her experiences or provide any kind of advice. And now I had lost my chance.

The skies had darkened by the time we got home. The dining-room table teemed with platters of food, with more plates staged in the kitchen. I tried to take the lead at playing hostess, but Edith was not about to relinquish that role.

"I'm going to visit your mother tomorrow," she said when we were finally alone in the kitchen. "I thought I should do it before we went back to Seattle."

"I'm glad you'll have the time."

"Has there been any change?"

I shook my head. "We visited her at Christmas. She seems comfortable. But she did not really engage with us. I think Father has given up hope."

"And what about you, Emily?"

I hesitated. "The visits don't make me as sad as they once did. I guess I'm getting better at controlling my emotions." I carried some dishes to the sink. "The service today was different, though. I wished I had known Sarah the way you did. She certainly made something of her life. I still don't know what I am going to do with mine."

"What about your young man?"

"I don't know," I replied honestly. "He's going to Oxford next fall. It's a wonderful opportunity for Tom, but...."

Edith smiled gently. "But you don't know what it will mean for the two of you."

I nodded, turning away from her.

Edith put her arms around me, whispering softly in my ear. "Your father went to Rome, your uncle went to Marburg. It's what all the Harvard men think they have to do. But don't worry, my dear. I saw Tom when he arrived tonight. He looked lost without you. And then his eyes lit up when he finally spotted you across the room.

"The young men all come back to Boston eventually," she added. "And I'm sure Tom Eliot will, too."

* * *

Aunt Sarah, I decided, would become my role model. There was no point in moping about Tom; it would only drive him away. Instead I told my acting friends I was ready to take on any part, big or small.

The strategy worked. The Lend-A-Hand Dramatic Club asked me to play Olivia in *Twelfth Night*. It was a juicy role, with the camaraderie of an all-female cast. There would be two performances: the first in Northampton, to benefit needy students at Smith. Ten days later, we would take the show to the New England Conservatory and the wonderful acoustics of Jordan Hall.

The trip to Smith meant I could see Margaret Farrand again. We had known each other since our childhood days in New Jersey. It would have been easy for us to drift apart when I moved to Boston. But Margaret declared we would simply become pen pals instead.

I knew Margaret's letters had helped to save me in those first terrible years after Billy died. While none of the adults would mention his name, Margaret would recall all of her own memories of Billy. It was what I most needed to hear.

As the years went by, I came to appreciate how brilliant Margaret really was. Her father held an important post at Princeton, her uncle was president of Cornell. But she was no intellectual snob. Rather, she was the sister I never had.

And as we grew older, the long, thoughtful letters kept coming, no matter the paths we followed. Margaret's had eventually led to Smith, where she was about to finish her degree in English.

We made a date to get together for tea before the performance. When we arrived at the restaurant, we fell into each other's arms with a long, warm embrace.

"I'm so excited that I'm finally going to see you perform," she said as we picked out a table. "And Shakespeare, no less!"

"We've got a good cast," I said. "Our set designer teaches at Smith, and he came up with an interesting way to manage the scene changes."

"It sounds as if you've been performing a lot."

"It keeps me busy. But there's no future in it. I'm still envious that you're getting your degree."

"Well," Margaret said, "it doesn't mean I've figured out my future. I will probably end up teaching. But I'm not sure where or how." She set down her cup, her dark eyes flashing. "So tell me more about this Tom Eliot you're always writing about."

I laughed. "Speaking of things that need figuring out....He's going to Oxford next year. He's just won a fellowship that will let him travel to Marburg, too. I'm thrilled for him, but..." I hesitated. "I don't know what it means for the two of us."

Margaret said nothing for a moment. "From what you've told me, he sounds like a serious student. I've spent my life around people like that in the English Department. They may be talented writers, but when it comes to expressing themselves to the people they care about, they're at a loss for words."

"However, if you can be patient," she counseled, "I think you'll find that he's worth waiting for." She smiled, her eyes brightening. "And if I can wait for my special someone, I know you can, too."

* * *

I had hoped Tom would come see me perform at Jordan Hall. I could have gotten him a ticket, but I decided not to press it. He was distracted and impatient, overwhelmed by all the details he needed to take care of. Olivia was a demanding role, and I needed to stay focused on it. There was nothing I could do about the dwindling number of days that were left for us to be together.

He phoned the day after the show closed.

"I just got a letter from my father," he said, "and I had to call you right away to share it." He cleared his throat dramatically and then began to read. "I am much pleased that you have received the scholarship, on account of the honor, as you couldn't get it unless you deserved it. You have never been a 'burden' to me, my dear fellow. A parent is always in debt to a son who has been as dutiful and affectionate as you have been."

Tom stopped, waiting for my reaction. But he plunged on anyway. "He's never told me anything like that before."

"It's very nice," I replied.

We both hungered so much for praise. My latest morsel was on page seven of that morning's *Globe:* "Shakespeare's 'Twelfth Night' was presented yesterday afternoon in Jordan Hall....Miss Emily Hale as Olivia and Miss Marion L. Clapp as Viola were exceptionally good."

I wondered if Tom had seen the review. But if he had, he had already moved on. It was his moment of glory now. And I could not bring myself to dim it, even to share a rare moment of my own.

* * *

The early summer days were counting down now—too rapidly, it seemed—until that day in June when Tom would board a ship in Boston

Harbor and steam across the Atlantic. Today we were going to a garden party at a farm out in Sherborn. The host, Benjamin Apthorp Gould Fuller, was a philosophy professor, just a few years older than Tom. Normally, I would have enjoyed this kind of outing. But passing an afternoon with the Harvard Philosophy Department was not how I would choose to spend what little time we had left together.

Yet, I knew it was important for Tom to socialize with his colleagues. A good contact, a positive reference, all of it could make a difference when he finally arrived at Oxford—and when he returned to Harvard to defend his dissertation.

Tom talked so much about his colleagues that I felt I already knew all of them. Fuller had written his dissertation on Plotinus. Bakeman was the expert on Kant, and Lanman spent hours rowing on the Charles when he wasn't teaching Sanskrit to Tom.

And then there was Bertrand Russell. Tom had audited his classes in logic and scheduled more time with him during office hours. It seemed as if he could never get enough of the visiting Englishman. And I was curious to find out why.

The party at "'Tween Waters" was already in full swing when we arrived. Tom led me through the crowd in the backyard to try to find our host. He finally spotted him, juggling two tall drinks.

"Hello, Ben," he said when we joined him. "I'd like you to meet my friend, Emily Hale."

My friend, Emily Hale. "It's good to meet you, professor," I replied.

"I'm sorry I can't shake hands," he said. "And please, call me Ben. After all, Tom is more of a colleague now than a student."

I felt Tom's arm relax as his lips widened into a smile.

"Let me get rid of these drinks," Ben said, "and then I can take care of your orders." The young professor craned his neck, searching for a guest amid the sea of summer whites and pale floral-patterned dresses. "There he is!" We followed him dutifully as he headed across the lawn.

"Here you go, Bertrand....Bertrand, I'd like you to meet Tom's friend, Miss Emily Hale. Emily, Bertrand Russell."

The older man nodded, taking a sip of his drink.

"It's a pleasure to meet you, Mr. Russell," I said. "Tom has talked so much about you."

"I've enjoyed talking with Tom, too."

He was not what I had expected. I had imagined a towering presence, but Russell was of average height, with a lean face and bony hands. He seemed the epitome of the proper Englishman. Perhaps that was what appealed to Tom.

Ben Fuller was studying me intently. Finally, he spoke up. "I've been trying to figure out why you looked so familiar. Did we see you in *Cousin Kate* two weeks ago?"

I smiled. "Yes, you did."

"You were very good."

"Thank you," I said, feeling my cheeks redden in the summer heat. It was something, I thought, to have made a mark with this crowd.

"I'm impressed with anyone who can act," Ben said. Then he grabbed Tom's arm. "Let's get something for you and Emily to drink."

I turned back to Russell. His pipe was back in his mouth, clenched between his jaws. It made his eyes seem all the more piercing as they roved from my head to my feet, settling back at my neckline. I wished that I had brought a wrap. It was far too warm to wear one, but it would have provided some armor from Russell's increasingly uncomfortable gaze.

"So," he said at last, "you're an actress!"

"Just an amateur, I'm afraid."

He shrugged. "That may be, but it's more interesting than the avocations pursued by most of the American women I've met."

I remembered the stories Tom had shared. "You *are* married to an American, aren't you?"

He smiled at my comeback. "Technically," he said. "But only technically."

Tom had told me Russell had a reputation. But even so, I didn't think the state of his marriage was an appropriate topic of conversation with a female stranger at a garden party.

"I've enjoyed discussing philosophy with your young man," he said. "He seems very intelligent."

"He *is* very intelligent."

Russell took another puff on his pipe. "I think he's looking forward to studying in England."

"I think he is, too," I acknowledged. I tried to change the subject. "Have you enjoyed your time here in Cambridge?"

"Not particularly," he replied. "Everyone seems to be trying to be someone they aren't. But I'll be leaving soon. Doing some lectures out West. We'll see if the Chicagoans are any better."

"Sorry it took so long," Tom said, returning with two tall glasses of lemonade, each topped with a sprig of mint.

He handed me a glass that was wet with condensation. The afternoon was turning hot and sticky.

"Well, Tom," Russell said, raising his pipe in salute, "I hope our paths will cross again. Perhaps I'll see you when we're both back in England."

"I'd like that very much, sir."

Russell nodded as he wandered off into the crowd.

Tom looked perturbed over Russell's departure. "Did I miss something?"

"Not particularly," I replied. "He doesn't seem to like Cambridge....or American women, for that matter."

Tom let out a snort.

"I must confess that I found him to be rather boorish."

"He's a brilliant man," Tom asserted.

I took a long sip of my drink. "He may be brilliant," I said, "but that doesn't mean he can't be boorish, too."

* * *

The time had finally come. Tom was sailing in the morning.

What was there left to say? He was too eager to go now, too ready to write his next chapter. And I had second thoughts of my own. I was getting good reviews. Ben Fuller remembered my performance. But his party had left me on edge. I continued to be disturbed by the way Tom had fawned over Bertrand Russell. Did Tom want the same things out of life that I did? Perhaps we both needed some time and space to figure that out.

He had told me not to come down to the docks, that it would be too noisy and chaotic for me to see him off. He would rather say goodbye where the two of us could be alone, in the quiet of the parsonage in Chestnut Hill.

Father joined us for dinner, and this time he did most of the talking. He regaled Tom with his own stories of traveling to Europe, dwelling on his time in Italy, when he had studied architecture. Did Father regret his own life choices, I wondered now? Would Tom return as a philosopher, a poet—or something completely different?

Then, mercifully, the telephone rang. Father muffled his voice as he spoke into the receiver; it must be a parishioner calling with a concern. Fortunately, he no longer felt he had to be our chaperone. He put on his clerical collar and his hat. Then he shook Tom's hand, gave him one last pat on the back, and went out into the summer evening.

"Let's take our tea in the parlor," I suggested.

I no longer had to ask Tom what he wanted to drink after dinner. The shift from coffee to tea had been gradual since Christmas, but now it was complete. He was transforming himself into an Englishman—perhaps some combination of Mr. Woodhouse, Lord Bantock, and Bertrand Russell—right before my eyes.

We sat side-by-side on the faded velvet sofa, our knees only inches apart. My heart was heavy; there was much I wanted to say. But the ending to our script still hadn't been written, and I was not sure which of the possible parts I was expected to play.

At last, Tom put down his cup, then took mine and set it down, too. He took my hands and held them in his. I remembered the time I had first observed his long, graceful fingers that night in the Hinkleys' home. I always loved the feel of my hand in his.

"I love you, Emily." The words came out of nowhere, like a bolt of lightning from the threatening clouds of a late-summer storm. "I don't know what to do about it, except to tell you that I love you."

He stopped there. The words seemed to suck the oxygen out of my lungs. *How I had longed to hear him say that!*

And yet....and yet.

Was that all? What did those words mean in the end? What was Prufrock really trying to tell me?

They were easy words to say, now that it was the eleventh hour. There were things he could have done, words he could have spoken before. He could have asked me whether he should apply to Oxford. He could have asked me what I wanted to do next year. He could have asked whether I would wait for him. He could have asked whether I wanted to come.

He could have asked me to marry him.

"What do you want me to say?" I replied.

He looked puzzled. "I don't know," he mumbled quietly.

Six months I had waited. And now, the night before he would leave, he had finally found his voice.

I sat silently, mulling how to respond, searching for the right words.

"I'm touched when you say you care for me, Tom. And I care for you, too." I took a deep breath, summoning up the courage to say what was on my heart. "But there's too much at stake. We can't rush through this now, only a few hours before you are set to leave.

"I don't think you've figured out who you are or who you want to be," I babbled on. "A few months ago, I wouldn't have felt this way. But I think you need to go off to England and figure that out. While you're gone, I'll ask myself the same questions. And when you come back...we can see how we feel about each other then."

I had wanted to say, "We'll be able to plan our future together." But the words froze on my lips. That was going too far. Women weren't supposed to take charge of these things. It was up to the men to do that.

He looked stricken, and it frightened me. This was not the denouement I had planned just a few hours before.

"Well, then," he said quickly, "I suppose I ought to be on my way. I've still got some packing left to do."

He rose to retrieve his hat and his cane. I busied myself by clearing away the teacups. When I returned, he was waiting at the front door.

"Goodbye then, Emily."

"Goodbye, Tom."

He took me into his arms as best he could with a cane in his hand. His kiss was long and deep, conveying more than his words or careless actions had ever done before. What was it he had said? I tried to remember now.

I opened my eyes and saw the door close behind him. What was I thinking? Why had I pushed him away like that? I reached for the doorknob. It was not too late. I could catch him before he got to the sidewalk. I could call out to him before he turned the corner. I could still stop him and tell him what I really wanted to say.

Yes, Tom, I love you, too. I will wait for you until you return. I will wait for you as long as it takes.

But my wrist did not turn. The door remained close. The words stayed on my lips.

I heard the voice of Edith reciting the rules that had been drummed into me since I was a child:

A proper woman would never chase after a man. And certainly not out in front of the neighbors.

Killarney Roses

THE WEALTHY FAMILIES DECAMPED TO Newport, and the Hinkleys joined Tom's parents at the Gloucester shore. Harvard and Radcliffe students left for the summer, and the Cambridge Social Dramatic Club lowered its curtain until fall. Even our church shifted to a summer schedule. Tom was gone and so were all of my diversions.

But the lazy weeks of June were quickly shattered by gunshots in Sarajevo. On the far side of Europe, Archduke Ferdinand and his wife were assassinated. The headlines on *The Globe*'s front page shifted to Europe. "60,000 Americans Are Now Abroad; Cancellation of German Steamer Sailings Cause Anxiety for Stranded Tourists." As we read the morning papers, even Father could not quell my rising sense of panic.

I had received nothing from Tom—not even a postcard. Was he preoccupied or distracted? Or was his silence more calculated, a way of punishing me for my cowardice?

But I couldn't dwell on that, for the stories were becoming even more alarming: "Kaiser and England Now Grapple in War; All Europe Is in Arms for Gigantic Conflict or to Guard Homeland."

Was Tom still in Marburg? Would he get caught behind the German lines? Or would he be sent home to the States before the term even began?

I had always let Father monopolize the morning paper, but now I rose early to get to it first. The maps of the continent were a mystery to me, just outlines of places I had heard of but knew little about. Weren't all of the royal families related? What were they fighting over, anyway?

When Eleanor returned home after Labor Day, I had to find out what she knew. We met at the café near Harvard Square, and I wasted no time getting to the point.

"Have you heard anything from Tom?"

"He's all right," she reassured me. "He's in London now."

I sagged with relief.

Eleanor pouted. "You mean you haven't heard from him?"

I shook my head. "I'm afraid our parting was rather awkward...." I did not want to recount our final scene. "But ever since the war broke out, I've been frantic to find out whether he was safe."

"I'm sorry," she replied. "I should have sent you word when we heard."

"It's all right," I said. "You had no way of knowing that he hadn't written." The waiter arrived. I glanced quickly at the menu but decided that a cup of tea was all that my stomach could manage. "So tell me what happened."

"I don't know a lot," she acknowledged. "The first time he wrote me, he was crossing the Atlantic. It was typical Tom. He was enjoying the fact that he could fool some of the Americans into thinking he was English. When he got to Marburg, he stayed with a Lutheran pastor and his family. He was enjoying the food and the countryside, and then the war broke out.

"I don't think he took it very seriously at first. He still thought he would be able to study in Germany. But then all the classes were canceled and England declared war, and suddenly he realized he might get caught behind the lines. He found his way to Rotterdam and from there he finally managed to get passage on a ship to England."

"He said he's been treated very well....It seems that both the Germans and the English believe that we'll eventually join their side."

She paused for a sip of tea. "But you know Tom," she said with a sigh. "He was very blasé about the whole thing. He's never been that interested in politics or world events. I think his mother is just relieved that he didn't rush out and enlist."

"I can't imagine Tom racing for the front lines."

Eleanor stifled a smirk. "Neither can I."

We sat in silence for a moment. I knew I should feel relieved, but I mostly felt weary.

"I have an address in London if you would like to write him," she volunteered. "I don't know how long he'll be there, but I'm sure they'll forward his mail."

"I'm not sure it would be proper for me to write him first."

"So are you prepared to wait forever?" Eleanor's dark eyes flashed. "Look, I don't know what happened between the two of you. But I do believe Tom cares for you more than any other woman he's known."

She hesitated. "The world is changing. They're throwing out the old rules before the new ones are written. And you can either wait for Tom to figure it all out...or you can do something about it."

She took another sip from her cup, then looked at me directly. "Take charge of your life, Emily."

"You're full of unsolicited advice today."

Eleanor shrugged. "I know my cousin....and I think I know you. Besides, I've decided to do the same thing myself."

"What do you mean?"

"I've decided to apply to the 47 Workshop."

"Professor Baker's playwriting class?"

Eleanor nodded.

"That's wonderful!" I said. Then I smiled. "Write a good part for me. It might save me from going mad."

* * *

In the end, I took Eleanor's advice. I sat down and wrote Tom a letter, keeping it simple and straightforward.

Dear Tom,

I was happy to learn from Eleanor that you had finally made it to Oxford. I hope that you are enjoying your studies as much as you expected to. I'm sure this is a very difficult time to be living in England.

I will be performing in "Mrs. Bumpstead-Leigh" the second week of December. It's a good cast, and I'm looking forward to it. Our rehearsals will start soon, and then I will be very busy up until the holidays.

Otherwise Boston and Cambridge are much the same as when you left....

Your friend,
Emily Hale

I didn't know how long it would take for a letter to travel to England, considering all the German gunboats circling the island. Nor did I know how long it would take Tom to respond—or if he would at all.

But a letter did arrive about three weeks later.

Merton College, Oxford

Dear Emily,

Thank you for your letter. I was happy to hear that you are still performing. But please be careful not to push yourself too hard.

I am slowly adjusting to life at Oxford. I try to get up early and write letters to old friends, but I am often pressed for time. I hope that Eleanor has been able to share my observations about my life here. I will try and write more next time.

Yours,
Tom

The tone echoed mine. It was not much of a letter, but it *was* a letter. What had happened to our easy camaraderie, our friendship, or—dare I think it?—our love? Eleanor had shared the letters she had received. They were filled with stories and drawings, madcap film scripts, thoughtful observations about Tom's life and the world around him. His lively letters helped keep the cousins connected. My letter, on the other hand, was dutiful and circumspect.

But perhaps Tom wasn't as lonely as I was. I remembered what he had written Eleanor shortly after he arrived: "I like it quite well enough to wish I had come here earlier and spent two or three years."

What will I do if you stay away that long?

* * *

A role in *Mrs. Bumpstead-Leigh* was just what I needed, especially as Christmas approached. The Amateurs would do two performances in Brookline, then pack up the sets and move to Andover for our final Saturday night performance at the Town Hall.

Ada Briggs inhabited the title role. There was much I could learn from the older actress. She had performed on Broadway as Ada Langley but became frustrated with the minor roles she was given. Eventually, she chose marriage over an acting career, and now she performed as "Mrs. Frederick H. Briggs."

Adelaide Bumpstead-Leigh was at the center of a scheme to find a wealthy husband for her younger sister, Violet. The role called for Ada to move back and forth between posing as a well-bred British aristocrat, then letting her hair down with the rest of her family of Indiana bumpkins. I faced the same acting challenge playing Violet, but Violet also served as the moral center of the comedy. It was easy to play the good girl, the character who would eventually expose her older grifter sister. And in the end, I would be rewarded with love—not from the brother I was supposed to marry, but from the brother I actually loved.

As we said our lines, another courtship script replayed in my brain— the final months of my time with Tom, what was said and left unsaid. *If Tom had found his voice sooner, would I have found mine as well?*

And I was haunted now by the lines spoken by Peter Swallow, the fast-talking tombstone salesman, recalling how Adelaide had spurned him years before:

> *For a few weeks, young man, your loss will seem a big thing to you, very like; but then you'll begin to look about you again, and remember there's other fish in the sea. It's that thought lightens the tragedy.*

Were there other "fish" in Tom's sea now? What did he make of the British girls he met? If you believed the playwright, the typical American girl has "manners that are anything but manners," "bold forward speech," "smartness," and "slang." In sum, "downright illiteracy." British girls, on the other hand, "seem to lack a certain rugged, brute vigor."

I wondered what Tom was discovering.

* * *

It was a busy time of year, but the Andover Town Hall was still packed for our final performance. The laughs had come easily; there were even outbursts of applause. Ada adjusted the pace so that the punch lines would not get lost in the din; the rest of us quickly followed her lead.

The audience rose to its feet when the curtain came down. Ada received the roses, but I was happy with the crescendo of applause I received when I stepped out to take my solo bow. I hoped there was a critic in the crowd.

It was late, and we still faced a long drive back to Boston. Ada had graciously offered me a ride, saving me from having to take the train. I would have liked to change my clothes and remove my makeup, but I did not want to keep Ada and Fred waiting.

"Emily?" One of the props crew stepped forward, carrying a long white box tied with a red ribbon. "These are for you," he said, placing it in my arms. "A delivery boy arrived just before the final curtain."

A large envelope was tucked under the ribbon, addressed to "Miss Emily Hale." Inside was a letter from Conrad Aiken. I had finally had the chance to meet him, right before Tom had left town.

Emily—

Tom asked me to arrange these for you. I had hoped to be able to deliver them in person, but then I discovered you were playing in Andover rather than Cambridge, as Tom had told me. My wife has been ill, so I could not venture so far out to see you.

Tom specified he wanted to send you Killarney roses, and sent along the enclosed note. I hope that Howard's Florist managed to get the order straight.

The other envelope was addressed to me at "Brattle Hall." I pulled out a small card.

Emily

I will always remember my leading lady.

Tom

I untied the ribbon quickly and opened the box. Roses. Pink Killarney roses. I buried my nose in the petals. They were fresh and crisp from the cold, and their sweet perfume overwhelmed me.

He had surprised me. He had remembered. He still cared.

Killarney roses.

An' the months are slow to pass, Mavourneen, Till I hold thee in my arms, O Mavourneen!

"Emily, are you ready?" Ada Briggs's commanding voice broke through the memory.

I closed up the box. "Just let me get my coat."

"What lovely flowers!" she noted. "From a fan or an admirer?"

I smiled. "Both, I hope."

I gathered up my clothes, my coat, my purse, and the flowers, then helped Fred Briggs pack the trunk of his car. I settled into the dark corner of the back seat, balancing the box carefully on my lap. In the tight confines, I could still smell the roses.

I smiled, remembering Violet's climactic declaration of love at the end of the play, pretending now that I was saying the lines to Tom. "It seems as if I could breathe! It seems—oh, it seems as if I could fly! It does, honestly. I never felt like that before."

"But what's made all this change?" the hero asked.

The playwright's directions told me to pause, then to say, very simply and directly:

"You."

* * *

In the new year, The Amateurs invited me back, this time to play the lead in *Eliza Comes to Stay* at Whitney Hall in Brookline. Ada was directing; once again, they wanted me to play a teenager.

"I'm 23 now," I said to Ada. "How long can I keep playing ingenues?"

She laughed. "Enjoy it as long as you can."

I had written Tom, thanking him for the flowers, telling him how much they had meant to me. Now I wrote again, telling him about the play and where we would perform. Secretly, I hoped he would send more flowers. But I was wary. I had not heard from him for weeks.

My new role was a meaty one. Eliza Vandan arrives onstage as an 18-year-old waif, "a curious type of humanity," in the words of H. V. Esmond, wearing a shabby, shapeless frock, her hair knotted into a bun under a little straw hat. When the play opens, the hero, Sandy Verrell, is awaiting the arrival of a young girl he had pledged to adopt. Instead, he gets Eliza. After three acts full of miscues and mismatches, Sandy falls in love with Eliza, now recreated as the glamorous "Dorothy." It was curious, I thought, that Esmond and George Bernard Shaw had both published plays within months of each other, centered on the transformation of a poor girl named Eliza.

Although Sandy was supposed to be an experienced older man, Ada had cast a younger one, Osgood Perkins, in the role. I worried how that might affect our onstage chemistry, but Oggie quickly won me over with his acting talent. His eyes shone with a slightly wicked gleam and he could turn his mustache into a very effective prop. I was always proud of my own comic timing, but Oggie's was even better. His acting was bringing out the best in mine.

Midway through rehearsals, a cast member fell ill, and Ada drafted our set designer, Clifford Pember, to take his place. Clifford had done a bit of acting in the past and had one qualification the rest of us did not: He was actually born in England.

He was easy to talk to, and I had a long list of questions about the London stage that I wanted to ask him. But what fascinated me most were his thoughts about set design. The drawing rooms in the comedies I did were barely distinguishable from one another. Long Island could just as easily be England: a sofa at the center, book-lined shelves behind it, windows scattered right and left, and a doorway on either side of the stage. But Clifford's set for *Eliza* was a character in its own right. The furniture was very modern, the set all in black and white. Red roses provided the only spot of color in the second act; pink flowers signaled the passage of time for the third. I knew there was a lot I could learn from Clifford if I paid attention.

The play was the usual mindless romp that Boston audiences enjoyed. As our rehearsals progressed, I always looked forward to the climactic scene, when I asked Oggie pointedly: "What do you want to do—you don't seem to know." And Oggie's eyes would light up as he replied, "I do know what I want to do." And he pulled me into his arms for a kiss.

Did he kiss me longer than H. V. Esmond had intended? Or was Oggie calculating how long the audience would continue to applaud? Or were we actually enjoying the moment more than we wanted to admit?

What if the war dragged on, I wondered, and Tom didn't come back for years? Would he fall in love with someone else? Could I? Was the attraction I felt for Oggie something more than just the chemistry between two actors playing romantic leads?

I knew that I yearned to be loved. Earlier in Act III, the stage directions called for Eliza/Dorothy to fight back tears, and I discovered I could produce them more easily than I expected. When Lady Elizabeth reassured me that I was indeed loved, I replied:

"That's the best thing I've heard in a month of Sundays—you love me. Oh, don't say it again—just let me be like this for a minute....You love me—somebody loves me at last."

There was little love to be found in the lonely rooms of the parsonage, and certainly none to be found within the confines of McLean Hospital. Perhaps someday I would discover it in the heart of a man in Oxford. But for now at least, I knew that the one place I could find it was the theater.

* * *

Later in life, I would never forget where I had been when I heard the news. The sinking of the *Titanic* was more shocking, but the sinking of the *Lusitania* was more terrifying.

We were deep into one of our final rehearsals when Frances Sprague rushed in to tell her brother. The massive liner had been sunk by a German submarine off the coast of Ireland. It had set out from New York the week before, headed for Liverpool. Fifteen hundred people were on board, about a dozen of them from Boston.

Somehow we managed to finish the rehearsal that day. And then the names of the local passengers were published. I didn't know any of them personally, but some were friends of friends. The wait for news of their fates was agonizing.

Clifford had known Charles Frohman, the famous producer, and Oliver Bernard, the set designer, back in England. Bernard had worked at the Royal Opera House and had been hired to design sets in Boston.

He was accompanying Leslie Hawthorne Lindsey and Stewart Southam Mason as they headed off to their new married life in Suffolk. Their wedding at Emmanuel Church just three weeks before had been splashed all over *The Globe*'s society pages.

I gasped when I saw the large photo of Mrs. Mason in the paper. With her fashionable hat and carefully draped fur, Leslie could have been the transformed Dorothy in the final act of our play. She had performed occasionally with The Amateurs. Her brother had been in Tom's class at Harvard. Tom and I used to walk by the Lindseys' big Tudor mansion when we strolled down to the riverbank. Tom was amused that Leslie's father had made his fortune by inventing a better ammunition belt.

By opening night, our audience was in desperate need of a farce. That morning, the papers had reported that Leslie's body had finally been recovered 20 miles from where the ship had gone down. There was still no sign of her bridegroom.

English parlor comedies with happily-ever-after endings did not provide the kind of acting challenge that tragedies did. But still I focused on my lines, my marks, my cues, and my role as if my life depended on it. It helped that the audience was on our side. When the curtain rose on Clifford's unusual set, there was an audible gasp of wonder and then a round of applause. The laughs started slowly. It was as if the audience felt it was disrespectful of the dead to find humor in anything. But Oggie Perkins was a pro. He gave me a wink in our opening scene, and that was enough to steady me.

He caught my eyes, listened intently, helped me stay in character. When he took me into his arms in the final scene, I felt a surge of affection and gratitude. We clung to each other after the curtain came down, our bodies weak with relief. And then after we took our bows, after all the ices and frappés had been served to the playgoers, I finally let the full import of the devastating news sink in.

Tom was on the other side of the ocean—an ocean where, *The Globe* had reported that morning, 28 other vessels had been sunk in a week. It did not seem to matter whether you were on a merchant ship, a steamer, or a liner carrying a Vanderbilt. The Germans were determined to sink them all.

Tom's fellowship year would soon be over. Would he be able to travel home? Was it safe for him to even try? How long could the war go on? How long would he have to stay in England?

And how could I have let him go so easily?

* * *

It had been months since I had heard from him, and I was desperate for any news that Eleanor could provide. We met at our favorite café in Cambridge. Although Harvard was swinging back into the rhythms of the fall semester, the restaurant was still comparatively quiet.

"How's your writing going?" I asked after we placed our orders.

"Reasonably well," she replied.

"And Professor Baker accepted you into his workshop?"

She nodded.

Something is wrong, I thought. It had been three months since we had talked. She should be bubbling over with gossip.

"What is it?" I asked.

She averted my eyes. "It's Tom."

I gasped. Had there been an accident? Had he enlisted after all?

Eleanor straightened up as if to summon up her courage. "I heard the news earlier this summer. I didn't know how to tell you, but I knew I couldn't let you hear it from someone else."

"Go on," I said shakily.

"He's gotten married."

"Married!" Of all the disasters I had imagined, that was not on the list.

There were marriages of convenience. There were marriages forged out of miscommunications. I thought of Fanny, Miss Roberts, and Olivia in *Twelfth Night*. Violet and Eliza, destined for the wrong suitor. Surely this was just a plot twist.

"You can't be serious!" I said at last.

"I'm sorry, but it's true."

I sat in numbed silence as she began to explain. I tried to focus on the details, but it was as if I only heard every other word.

"It was all very sudden," Eleanor began. "He didn't tell his parents until after it was official. He had never even mentioned the woman to them before. We got the news when we were all together at Gloucester. They are simply beside themselves."

"Who is she?"

"Her name is Vivienne Haigh-Wood. He met her through Scofield Thayer. Did you know Scofield? He was one of Tom's old friends from Harvard. Anyway, she's some sort of artist. Apparently, her father, is too."

She hesitated. "Tom mentioned her once in a letter he wrote me last spring. But he referred to her in a very offhanded way. He was describing the English girls he had met, comparing them to American girls. They seemed to be doing frivolous things together, going to dances and such." She twisted her napkin in her lap. "I didn't share that letter with you.... Perhaps I should have."

"Where did they get married?" I asked. I had to know, even if it didn't really matter.

Eleanor took a sip of tea. "At the registry office in Hampstead. Can you believe it? They got Scofield's sister and Vivienne's aunt to be their witnesses. The wedding was performed at the crack of dawn. It was like one of those rushed ceremonies that soldiers arrange right before they go off to war."

"But Tom's not going off to war?"

"No, of course not. I can't imagine why they decided they had to hurry."

But I could. I remembered Oggie's final lines, that giddy, impetuous moment when the two characters discovered they were in love and didn't want to wait another minute.

"Put on your best hat and we'll go out and buy a special license."

Eleanor hesitated. "There's more."

"Tell me."

"Tom came home for a visit a few weeks ago."

I gasped. "Back to Boston?"

She nodded.

"And he didn't tell me?"

"He's married, Emily."

The words sunk in deeper, like a knife thrust into my heart.

"Anyway, that didn't go well, either," she reported. "It's like a switch has been flipped in his brain. He's not the Tom I remember. He fought with his parents the whole time he was home. Of course, we were all desperate to meet Vivienne, but she stayed home in England. Tom said she was sick and afraid to cross the Atlantic...after the *Lusitania* and all that.

"He was supposed to return to Harvard and teach this fall, but now that's all up in the air, too." She shook her head. "I just don't understand him."

I said nothing for a moment, but then I found my voice.

"He wants to be a poet. We've all made his life too easy. We're all too ordinary and conventional. In the mind of Tom Eliot, we're all keeping him from becoming the great poet he aspires to be."

Eleanor shifted in her chair. "You may be right," she said at last. "Did he ever show you his Prufrock poem?"

I nodded.

"He's finally found someone who's willing to publish it. He was very excited about that. He's got a new friend who seems to have some connections. This fellow wrote his father a very strange letter, telling him how talented Tom was and how he would never be successful if he stayed in America. How Tom shouldn't have to spend his time worrying about earning a living. He closed by asking Mr. Eliot to send five hundred dollars! The letter arrived right after they found out Tom had gotten married. All it did was make my uncle even angrier."

Suddenly I felt very weary. "Where is Tom now?"

"He's gone back to London. His wife was ill, and he said he had to return. But he may still come back. Harvard still wants him. Wellesley, too."

He may still come back. But what difference would it make if he did? I had been patient. I had wanted what was best for him. And now I had lost him for good.

The lines of my plays came back as prophetic taunts. I wanted to forget them, but I had studied the scripts too long and too hard. It seemed as if Adelaide Bumpstead-Leigh was speaking directly to me now.

"You've simply found out the truth; and it's bound to be hard....He isn't what you thought him. Not one man in a dozen is what a nice woman would like to think him. He's selfish, he's greedy, he's egotistical; and the more he fiddle-diddles about the beauty and sacredness of love, the more you'd better look out for him!"

I remembered the violets. I remembered the roses. I remembered the night before Tom had sailed, when the two of us had fumbled our goodbyes, our words, our emotions. How I had stopped myself from chasing out after him.

Boston girls didn't do that sort of thing. But English girls, or at least one English girl, apparently did.

To Strike the Best Bargain

EVERYWHERE I TURNED, THERE WERE memories of Tom. If I walked along the banks of the Charles, I remembered him describing the joys of rowing, how the relentless rhythm of the oars helped unleash bold new ideas in his brain.

If I walked through the Public Garden, the last of the summer flowers taunted me with their beauty. No more hyacinths, of course, but still manicured beds, the hallmark of an orderly, predictable world.

There was old Reverend Hale, gazing at me with sympathetic eyes, asking the question I could not answer.

"Why did Tom fall in love with someone else?"

I suspected that behind my back, all our friends would be whispering. Not Eleanor, of course. But word would get around Cambridge, through the Philosophy Department and then the Philosophical Club, and inside the student houses on the Gold Coast and Ash Street, and then around the table as the directors of the Social Dramatic Club cast their next plays. I could lobby for a new role, but even taking to the stage brought back painful memories of poor old Mr. Woodhouse and bouquets of Killarney roses.

For the first time in my life, I wanted to get as far away from Boston as I could. When I broached the idea of visiting Aunt Edith in Seattle, Father was willing to let me go. And when Edith wired me the train fare, the plan was settled.

Going to visit Edith, even in a strange new western city, felt like going home again. She would always listen, dry my tears, and open her arms if I needed a hug. To be sure, she still tried to run my life for me. But it was a small price to pay for all the love I received in return.

Seattle was rowdy but bustling, thanks to the Alaska-Yukon-Pacific Exposition the city had just hosted. People were building homes around the new site for the university, and John had been recruited to start a church in that neighborhood. It was good, Edith acknowledged, to be far away from the second-guessing of the Unitarian establishment.

As for me, the city turned out to be the perfect tonic for my spirits. I could not imagine a place that was such a contrast to home. Noisy and exuberant, crisscrossed by dusty roads and framed by snow-topped mountains. Filled with people of no particular social standing, all lured by the chance to strike it rich or make themselves over. There were Chinese and Filipinos and Scandinavians—and people who couldn't tell a Hale from an Eliot and wouldn't care if they could. It was a place, it seemed, where everyone could get a fair shake—and a fresh start, if they needed it.

If there was a disappointment, it was that the city was still a cultural backwater. True, it did have a symphony. And the Moore Theatre was very nicely appointed. But the Grand Opera House had no resident company, and plays were few and far between. Particularly when I still yearned to find a role.

But Edith made clear her old rules hadn't changed: "The professional stage is no place for a woman of your social position."

"Then what am I supposed to do?" I mused one morning, when the grey fog seemed to match my mood. "I know I'll never get married."

"Nonsense," she replied. "There are plenty of young men out there."

I was still skeptical, remembering the dreaded LOPHs. "I'll just go back to taking care of Father."

"There are jobs you could find." She sounded tentative. "You could go to work in the right kind of office....Or you could find a teaching job...."

"But I don't have an education," I moaned. I didn't want to complain, but it was true. I was too old, I thought, to think about starting college.

She pulled me close and gave me a hug. "Think of Aunt Sarah," she whispered. "She was on her own for most of her life. Did she sit around and mope? No. She looked for something that needed to be done, and then she did it."

She did it. But what, I wondered, was my "it" supposed to be?

The answer always came back to the theater. A new arts school had opened in Seattle, and it was offering classes in drama. I was not sure they could teach me anything I didn't already know. But it *would* provide a credential, whatever I ended up doing. And Edith agreed a class or two would help fill my empty days.

I was eager to grab a script and show my classmates what I could do. But our teacher wouldn't let me. "You have to mine the raw material first," Mr. Palmer explained. "You have to focus on the emotions your character feels, make a list if you have to. Then you have to find the touchstone in your own life. That way you can call on those memories when you finally start learning your lines."

"Goodness," "devotion," and "snobbery" were the traits I had mastered in my roles back in Boston. But now I worked on more challenging ones: "hurt" and "anger," "loneliness" and "grief." It was painful to go there, but I knew I could dig up those feelings if I tried: Billy's death, Mother's breakdown, being sent away to Edith's....

Being abandoned by Tom.

When Mr. Palmer finally let us perform, it was different than before. Far away from my old crowd, it was easier for me to let down my guard. There were times when I went too far, when I pushed Ophelia's madness perilously close to farce. But Mr. Palmer was gentle when he reined me in, advising which of my techniques worked and which needed to be discarded.

In the dying light of late afternoon, I often walked home along the edge of the new Montlake Cut. I was rather like the canal, I decided. It was nearly finished, but not yet filled with water. It was waiting for some signal to go to work.

I remembered the advice Adelaide Bumpstead-Leigh had given her younger sister when she wondered how she could go on living.

I decided quite a long time ago—just as you are going to decide—that there's something very well worth living for after all!... To strike the best bargain with the world you can!

I tried hard to put a name on each of my emotions and store them away for future use. By the time I arrived home, my cheeks were often wet with a mix of chilly Pacific mist and the remnants of my tears.

But after many long walks and many futile dialogues with Tom Eliot, I reached down into my core and found another emotion. It was pride, a stubborn sort of Yankee pride. It was the pride of Sarah Emery Hooper, of Edith Milliken Perkins, of Edward and Phillip Hale. I was not going to let Tom Eliot destroy me.

I was ready to go back to Boston now. I was surprised when Father wrote that he missed me—and I realized I missed him as well. I missed Eleanor and Amy, Oggie, Clifford and Ada, the smell of Brattle Hall, the sharp bite of the Boston winter, the deep drifts of snow, the hope implicit in the city's rendition of spring.

And if I still needed a nudge, they wrote that there were plenty of roles they wanted me to do. Ada was directing Rudolph Besler's *Don* in February. Friends were planning a benefit performance of *Alice Sit-by-the-Fire* in March. And Edward Vroom, the British actor, was building a company of society people to perform the classics at downtown theaters. Last year Ada had played Roxane opposite Vroom's Cyrano. Now, to my amazement, he wanted to audition me.

So I returned, with no grand plan in place. I accepted every part that was offered and won the lead in Vroom's new production.

The charities we supported had changed. The concerns had shifted to Europe; the Milk and Baby Hygiene Association had made way for the Polish refugees. But I was back among my old theater friends. There was Ada, of course. Frances Sprague and Tracy Putnam were performing with Vroom. And in Cambridge, John Hart was now playing my father.

The Globe pronounced that *Cyrano* was "a greater success" than the play Vroom had mounted the week before. "He was well supported throughout," the reviewer noted, "especially by Miss Emily Hale as Roxane...."

And the Cambridge paper reported that the local drama clubs were organizing outings to go see *Alice* because the cast was "a notable one," the same actors "who made the performance of *The Mollusc* so great a success" two years before.

I would never be Mrs. Patrick Campbell. I would never be Lillian Gish or Mary Pickford. But I was, in fact, an actress. And I had come farther than I had ever dreamed possible since that Stunt Show in Eleanor Hinkley's parlor two years before.

* * *

As 1916 approached, The Drama League of Boston decided it could not let the Tercentenary of William Shakespeare's death go unnoticed.

After a spirited discussion, we agreed to pursue "educational activities"; I volunteered to reach out to Simmons College.

It was a place where young women could learn how to run a household or work in an office or shop. It was a school, I realized, that I might have attended—and a place where I might have been happy. As I stood outside the college's imposing red brick building, I thought it was odd that I had never actually been inside. Particularly since Great-Aunt Sarah had eventually moved her cooking school there.

The college's Dramatic Association, it turned out, was sponsored by Lucia Briggs, an English professor whose father was president of Radcliffe. It did not take me long to find the classroom on the second floor.

"Miss Hale," Lucia greeted me warmly. "Do come in!"

She was shorter than I was but crossed the room with the confidence of a more imposing woman. She wore her brown hair like I did, parted down the middle and pinned up in back. It emphasized her dark, expressive eyes. And she had a large, prominent nose; I wondered if growing up in Cambridge, she had learned the fine art of turning it skyward to show her disapproval.

"I've seen Miss Hale perform several times in Cambridge," Lucia told the students, "and she is a very funny comic actress." A conspiratorial giggle rose from the back row. I smiled and winked at the students.

"Thank you, Miss Briggs." I pulled out my speech from my satchel and took my place behind the lectern.

"I'm very happy to be here today on behalf of the Drama League of Boston as we celebrate the Tercentenary of Shakespeare's death. I considered talking to you about the Bard, but I decided I would be more comfortable talking about my own acting experiences."

I began telling my story, warming to it as the girls laughed at my anecdotes. I talked about the times when props went missing or lines forgotten and how the casts had managed to cover it up. I told about the night Estlin Cummings shocked us all by kissing Amy. I recalled the thrill of performing at the Plymouth Theatre and seeing my name next to Edward Vroom's in the program.

"My goodness," I said when I checked the clock. "The time has certainly flown by. I suppose I should stop in case you have any questions."

A brunette in the front row shot up her hand. "Did you ever have to kiss someone you didn't like?"

The rest of the girls twittered, and I smiled. "I never had to kiss someone I thought was repulsive. But there were some men who made me work harder as an actress."

Another hand went up. I nodded to the redhead.

"Have you ever wanted to direct a play?"

"That's a very good question," I replied. "When I started out, all I ever wanted to do was act. But last year I worked with a very good set designer, and he got me thinking about all the things that go into making a play successful. How to design a set so the actors can move around it. How to build a set when you don't have much to spend. So yes, I have been thinking about it."

"I think that's a good place for us to stop," Lucia chimed in. She led the girls in a round of polite applause.

A few students lingered longer to talk. Their curiosity was infectious, I thought. There was a time, not that long ago, when I had felt the same way, when each outing with Tom had opened my eyes to something new to learn.

"Your talk was very interesting," Lucia said when the last of the students had left.

"The girls were very easy to talk to."

"Have you ever considered teaching?"

I hesitated. Lucia was Radcliffe personified. "I'm afraid I don't have any credentials."

"I'm wondering...." Lucia pressed a finger to her lips. "The drama club got organized just last year. The girls have a great deal of enthusiasm. But they're going to need more that that if they are ever going to put on a play. Would you consider working with them?"

"Me?"

"I can organize their meetings," Lucia continued. "I was an officer with the Idlers at Radcliffe, but I never performed with them. I really don't know how to put on a show." She paused. "I should warn you in advance that Simmons may not be able to pay you anything. But I think you would enjoy it."

I mulled the idea. A new challenge. Joining the world of take-charge women like Lucia Briggs. My mind began to race, thinking of the scripts I knew. Which would be right for the girls of Simmons College?

"I think I'd like that," I said at last.

"Well, I don't see how the college could object," she said. "Let me talk to the dean and get back to you."

The administration thought it was a fine idea. In fact, they asked, could I get the senior class to perform a play at commencement? Lucia said she would help me, and so I agreed.

Shakespeare was always a safe choice—and also appropriate this year. I decided on *The Tempest,* organized the auditions, and picked the cast. Lucia asked the physical training teacher to manage the dancers, and the Household Economics classes made the costumes. The seniors performed it outdoors—and fortunately it did not rain.

We did three acts and the epilogue, but that was enough for the appreciative parents. It was long enough for me, too. I was exhausted but exhilarated. I had taken words on a page and turned them into a play. I had pulled it off. The senior girls had put aside their preoccupations with final exams and end-of-year dances to learn their lines, find their marks, and follow my instructions. I had taken charge. I could direct.

And when the girls called me up at the end to share the applause and one thrust a bouquet of roses into my arms, I felt tears form in my eyes.

This time they were happy tears.

* * *

Eleanor came back from Gloucester in September, and we agreed to get together and catch up.

"How's your family?" I asked, trying to sound casual.

"Mother's fine. My sister's got her hands full with her little ones running around. Tom's mother still wishes he would come home from England, and his father still wishes he would stop asking for money."

I tried to let the words bounce off me.

"Actually, I've been quite angry with Tom myself," Eleanor said. "Only one letter from him in the past year. 'In despair,' as he puts it, over how little time he has. And how he relies on me to keep up with all the gossip from Cambridge...."

That was Tom. Never enough time.

Her mouth twisted peculiarly. "He also asked after you."

The words pierced my emotional armor.

Eleanor went on. "I'm reading along, page after page and then suddenly, in the middle of a paragraph, he says, 'Tell me how Emily is.'" She hesitated. "What should I tell him?"

"Tell him whatever you like."

"Such as?"

"Tell him that I'm looking well. Tell him that you don't see me very much because we're both busy with our plays. Tell him I'm directing the Dramatic Association at Simmons. Tell him I'll be doing *Rosalind* this fall for the anti-suffragists."

I paused. "But don't tell him I'm pining away for him because I'm not."

"I don't think he's happy," Eleanor said. "His wife seems to be quite ill all the time. One thing after another."

"That's unfortunate."

"They've been spending a lot of time with Bertrand Russell. He seems to have taken them under his wing."

I rolled my eyes. "Well, that's unfortunate, too."

"Have you met him?"

I nodded. "At a party, right before Tom left. Tom thought he was brilliant, and I thought he was a lecher."

"He writes Tom's mother all the time. The whole arrangement seems odd to me." She laughed. "But what do I know? I'm on the other side of the Atlantic."

I remembered the garden party, Tom, the professor, summer dresses, and chatter over lemonade. At last I mused, "Do you think we'll ever get married, you and I? Or are we already spinsters?"

"I don't look at it that way," Eleanor declared. "It's all in your attitude. You still meet lots of men doing your plays. And look at Amy. She hasn't gotten married yet, but no one thinks of her as a spinster.

"As for me," she went on, "I have yet to meet anyone I felt was good enough." She laughed. "Tom has been telling his friends to call on me when they arrive at Harvard. Frankly, I find it annoying to have to entertain all of them!"

She paused. "It's not to say I don't enjoy the company of men. I consider Tom to be one of my best friends. And that's one reason why I've been so angry with him. He's treated us both pretty shabbily these last few years.

"No, for now at least, I'd rather worry about getting my plays produced than getting married." She laughed. "And everything I've heard about Tom's married life has only reinforced my opinion."

* * *

The news of the war was relentlessly grim. By the time all the casualties of the Battle of the Somme were tallied, the number had grown to more than a million. Close to 20,000 Englishmen had died on the first day alone.

By April, the United States could no longer stay on the sidelines. Overnight, plays and teas and garden parties no longer mattered. Young men were enlisting. Young men were getting drafted. Young men were going off to fight.

The call extended to Cambridge. John Remey, the butler in our Stunt Show skit, was training to become an aviator. Tracy Putnam had already returned from France with a Croix de Guerre for driving ambulances. Estlin Cummings was talking about volunteering to do the same thing. Oxford, Tom had told Eleanor, had emptied out. When all the native sons had charged off to fight for God and Country, he wrote, the campus had fizzled like a spent balloon.

Later that fall, a small packet arrived in the mail, tied up neatly with twine. Inside I found a thin, buff-colored book, with a handwritten note attached.

Dear Emily,

These little books are hard to find in the States, but I thought you would like to have one.

Your devoted servant,
Conrad Aiken

I turned the slim volume over in my hands. *Prufrock and Other Observations by T. S. Eliot.* A published volume by an unfamiliar poet and a man I no longer knew.

I opened the cover gingerly and read the dedication.

For Jean Verdenal, 1889-1915
mort aux Dardanelles

I remembered Tom talking about his good friend from his Paris days. I did the calculation. Dead at 26! I felt guilty I could not recall what that battle was all about.

And what of Vivienne? Would she care that Tom had dedicated his book to one of his old friends?

I turned the page. Of course, "Prufrock" came first.

Let us go then, you and I
When the evening is spread out against the sky....

I read the old, familiar lines with new eyes. The world had changed since I had first read them, and we had changed, too.

Shall I part my hair behind? Do I dare to eat a peach?

Prufrock, I knew, had finally found his courage.

I leafed through the rest of the slim book, spending time with each of the 11 poems. None was dated, so I could not tell when Tom had started working on it or when he had finished. In the middle were "The Boston Evening Transcript," "Aunt Helen," and "Cousin Nancy." Short, cynical, almost juvenile in tone. It was as if Tom was making fun of the Boston we had shared.

And then I came to the final poem: "La Figlia che Piange." The daughter who cries.

So I would have had him leave,
So I would have had her stand and grieve...

Was this our story?

I supposed I could hide the book high up on Father's shelves, where I wouldn't stumble across it every day. But it would still be there, a memory of a lost time, a lingering pain in my heart.

It would be tempting to go down to the Charles River and heave the book into the water like ashes from a funeral urn. But books were meant to be treasured, not burned or thrown away.

Finally, I made up my mind.

I fished the twine back out of the trash bin, found some stationery and wrapping paper, and began composing my own note.

Dear Eleanor,

Conrad Aiken sent me this. I'm happy for Tom that he's finally published a volume of poetry. Still, I find I can't bear to keep it. But I also can't bear to throw it away.

Hang onto it, my dear. Someday it may become rather valuable.

The Daughter Who Cries

1917

AMY WAS GETTING MARRIED.

Despite flirtations with nearly every one of her leading men, despite the ardent kisses and heartfelt poems of Estlin Cummings, she had, in the end, chosen a very conventional husband. Dick Hall came with a Harvard Law degree and a membership in the Cambridge Social Dramatic Club. But he specialized more on the "social" than the "dramatic," the kind of guy who was happy to work backstage or manage the club's finances.

Their engagement was announced in September, but Amy's dreams of a lavish wedding were dashed by the realities of war. Dick had signed up for the Naval Reserve, and he'd been called up for a patrol ship in the English Channel. There was no time even to get invitations printed; the de Gozzaldis simply phoned around to a hundred of their closest friends.

Fortunately, there was still an open date on the Christ Church calendar. As the organist played the opening chords of the Wedding March, Amy and her father took their first tentative steps down the aisle. Silvio stood tall and proud, steadying his daughter with the practiced stride of the Austrian Army captain he had been when he had married her mother in the same church more than 30 years ago.

My eyes began to mist as Amy passed our pew, her gaze focused resolutely on Dick Hall, waiting for her at the altar. She wore her mother's satin wedding dress, trimmed with netting and lace from Brussels. Atop her dark hair, a wreath of fresh orange blossoms held her mother's veil in place.

Despite all the rush, Amy still managed to star in a beautiful ceremony. I thought of that other frantic wedding in England. Why had Tom rushed out at dawn to marry in secret? If you got married alone in a registry office, did it feel as if it was just the two of you against the world? Would it make a difference as the years went by?

The music concluded as Amy's father presented her to her groom, now dressed in formal naval whites instead of his Harvard tweeds.

Benjamin Franklin Pinkerton.

They tell you they love you. They go away. And they marry someone else.

Dick Hall was no Pinkerton. He and Amy would have a happy life together—as long as Dick survived the war.

"Dearly beloved. We are gathered here today...."

* * *

Afterwards, the guests strolled back to the de Gozzaldis' home on Brattle Street for the backyard reception. It was warmer than usual for mid-October. But most of the leaves had fallen, forming a thick carpet on the sidewalk that slowed our steps—and the pace of my racing thoughts.

"You've been quiet," Eleanor observed.

"I've been thinking about Tom."

"You're going to have to forget him, Emily."

"It's hard to do."

We said nothing for a moment. But like a hungry squirrel by a Public Garden bench, I knew if I was patient, Eleanor would produce another morsel to satisfy my hunger.

"Tom's taken a job at a bank."

"A bank!"

"Lloyd's of London. Apparently, his language skills have come in handy. It pays more than teaching schoolboys. And that makes his father happy."

I shook my head. "I can't imagine Tom being happy at a bank." I hesitated. "How did it all go wrong, Eleanor? When I watched Amy walking down the aisle, I wondered who would ever choose to get married at a registry office?"

"Do you really want my opinion?" she asked.

I nodded.

"I think Tom was afraid he would change his mind. For some reason, he decided he wanted to escape his past. You, me, his family, Harvard and Boston. Marrying Vivienne was the easiest way he could turn his back on all that. So he rushed out and got married before he lost his nerve. Or before any of us could talk him out of it."

She kicked at a stick that was blocking her path. "There's a value to long courtships. Oh, Amy will be fine—she's known Dick Hall for years. But the more I read Tom's letters, the more I believe he made a colossal mistake. And as each month goes by, I think he's reaching the same conclusion."

* * *

If there was anything left to my carefree youth, it came to a stunning end on a dreary March day in 1918. I went out for a walk after the Sunday service and returned to find Father slumped at his desk over his notes for next week's sermon.

It was his heart, the doctor had said, as I huddled with Uncle Philip and Aunt Irene around his bed upstairs. Too much work and too much stress. All the sabbaticals and vacations can't provide a cure when a heart is broken and there's no place for the grief to go.

Within three days, Father was dead. And now I felt truly abandoned.

I moved numbly through the next hours, days, and weeks, trying to make decisions when people forced me to. Father was also "father" to a church, and that family wanted to honor him with an elaborate funeral. After a flurry of telegrams, Edith and John said they could make it back by next week. I told the church I wanted the funeral to be delayed until then so John could perform it. I conferred with Mother's doctors, and they agreed she should not attend.

Both Eleanor and Aunt Irene offered to stay with me so I wouldn't be on my own. But after the frenzy of phone calls, after receiving a living room full of flowers and a kitchen full of hot dishes from women who worried I would starve, I found I appreciated the quiet of the empty house.

It was a beautiful place, a structure that Father had lovingly designed for the large family he expected to fill it. I walked through the halls, admiring with fresh eyes the choices he had made. The warm wood paneling, the polished bannister, the parlor where Tom and I had exchanged Christmas presents and said our muddled goodbyes.

I knew I wouldn't be able to stay. The congregation was setting up a trust fund to provide something for Mother and me. But the house was too big and I wouldn't be able to cover the mortgage. It held too many sad memories along with the good ones.

I entered Father's study and regarded the shelves of his well-organized books. I remembered my childhood days, when we would ride together across the river to Cambridge. Father would drop me off on Berkeley Street before heading to Divinity Hall. And we would talk—about school and the world and anything that interested me. It was, I rued now, the only time in my life that he had really made a point of talking with me—until Tom Eliot showed up and got him talking again.

What should I do with all the books? I would not need Father's tomes on homiletics. But the foreign-language dictionaries might be useful, and some of his books on Dante. They would let me take Father with me wherever I went. And perhaps someday those classical reference books would help me crack the perplexing puzzle that Thomas Stearns Eliot had become.

* * *

In April, I made an appointment with Henry Lefavour. As I entered the president's office, I remembered to take the deep breath I always did before stepping out on stage. My future livelihood depended on this performance.

But the president greeted me warmly and asked his assistant to bring in some tea. "I was very shocked to learn of your father's death," he said. "I got to know him through the Colonial Society....I'm sure it's been very hard on you."

"Thank you," I murmured. My voice caught a little, despite my resolve to be strong.

"How can I help you?" he asked.

I decided to be direct. "My father's death has changed my circumstances. I now need a job and a place to live. I've learned that the college will have an opening in the fall for an assistant dormitory matron. I would like to apply for the position."

He hesitated. "I've heard good things about your work with the Dramatic Association, Miss Hale. But this post is quite different. Tell me why you're interested."

Because I'm desperate? That was true, of course, but not what I should acknowledge. "I've been directing your students for nearly two years now, and I've found that work to be very satisfying. I know I'm not like the other matrons—I'm just a few years older than the students. But I've been through some difficult times recently, and I've learned a lot from those experiences. I think I could offer your students something, and I think they could offer me something in return."

He fiddled with his mustache, saying nothing for a moment. Finally, he spoke. "It's true you don't have the kind of experience we usually want for our matrons. But I know how you've built up the Dramatic Association." His eyes twinkled. "I'm sure managing a dormitory can't be that much more difficult than corralling the senior class into putting on *The Tempest.*"

I smiled, happy that he could appreciate that.

"I will have to get the approval of the Trustees," he said. "But between you and me, they usually go along with my recommendations."

The formal letter arrived three weeks later. I would have a place to live and a salary of four hundred dollars a year.

I read the rest of the letter closely. At the end, he wrote, "We are all rejoicing at the prospect of having you with us."

I felt a glimmer of hope. I would not be alone anymore.

* * *

I hung the last of my dresses in the closet, happy to be done with clearing out the parsonage and moving the rest of my possessions into North Hall. My room was small, but big enough. The dorm reminded me of our house, dating from the same era, the same dark wood throughout. There were parlors and small nooks for conversation, a grand piano and a fireplace in the main lounge downstairs. A kitchen down the hall if I wanted to heat a pot of tea. A view of the green of the Riverway out my window.

Classes were about to start, and nearly all of the girls had moved in. I looked forward to getting to know the newcomers but still glad I had a space of my own. A place where I could mull my own dreams, even if I was nearly ten years older.

There was still the stage, of course. New roles, new theaters, new plays. I hoped that would always excite me. But there was something else. I missed the world around Cambridge, the world I'd known when I rode with Father to Berkeley Street. First my classmates, and then the boys around them. Smart minds, like Tom and Father and Uncle Philip. Had I dreamed of marrying a man like that? Living close to Harvard Square, or Oxford as I imagined it to be. Philosophy, English, it didn't matter what the man decided to teach. Conversations by the fireplace, sharing his writings and research. Private jokes. Best of friends.

It was not to be, of course. Still, when I moved into North Hall, I realized there was some of that here. All that had been missing from my life since my days at Miss Porter's School: asking questions, learning the answers, sharing the camaraderie of college friends.

There was a knock at my door. "Miss Hale?"

It was Miss Bean, the matron in charge of all the dormitories. "President Lefavour has called a meeting in his office at two. Can you be there?"

"Of course."

A half-hour later, I considered the possible scenarios as I crossed over to the main building. Was it a welcome for new employees? An inspirational speech for the coming year? Or something more dire? Miss Bean's demeanor suggested the latter.

The president was pacing as I joined the other matrons. "Please take a seat," he said, gesturing to his conference table. I sat down next to Miss Bean.

"If you've been paying attention to the news," he said, "you know that there's been a serious outbreak of influenza at the military installations around Boston. The health authorities had hoped they would be able to contain it there. But there have been dozens of new cases reported in the past week, and sadly now some deaths. And as of today, we have our first reported case at Simmons."

There was a gasp from the other end of the table.

"There is no need to panic," he cautioned. "Nevertheless, we need to remain alert. The student has been taken to the infirmary in North Hall, where she is being kept under observation. Tomorrow, I'm scheduling an assembly to make sure everyone understands the precautions we will have to take."

"Unfortunately," he went on, "most of the burden will fall on all of you. Our nursing instructors, even our nursing students, have already been dispatched to the bases and the hospitals. It will be up to rest of us, but especially you matrons, to keep an eye out for students or staff members who are showing the symptoms. If anyone complains of fever, nausea, aches, or diarrhea, they should be sent to the infirmary immediately. According to the authorities, the worst thing is for an infected person to shrug off their symptoms and keep pursuing their daily routines. All that does is spread the disease to others."

"At the same time," he continued, "we need to stress the importance of practicing good personal hygiene: washing hands, covering mouths, getting plenty of fresh air, avoiding crowds."

He paused. "I know that we don't like shirkers here at Simmons. And we also have a campus full of young women who are excited to be back with all their old friends. But we have to be vigilant because this disease can be so deadly."

He shuffled some papers, then looked around the table. "Are there any questions?" I was too stunned to pose one. "Very well, then," he said. "I know I can count on all of you to do what will need to be done."

We walked back to the dormitories, talking quietly, trying to calm our collective nerves. I tried to run down a list of all the names and faces in my wing. Did any of them look tired or pale? Was anyone coughing or blowing her nose?

The epidemic was already raging across Europe. One more thing to worry about, one more thing I couldn't control. The chilly weather of London, Eleanor said, was already wreaking havoc on Tom's fragile constitution.

"Miss Bean?" I called out as we began to split off to our dorms.

"Yes, Miss Hale?"

"I just wanted to say...." I hesitated, not wanting to sound dramatic. "I just wanted to say that if things get worse, and you need somebody.... What I mean is, unlike most of the other matrons, I have don't have any close family members who depend on me. So if a student becomes very sick and you need someone to take care of her....I'm willing to do it."

The older woman paused, as if assessing whether I really meant it. "Thank you, Miss Hale. But I hope it won't come to that."

* * *

We followed all the instructions, some that made sense and some that did not. We put aside our bandages for the Western front and began sewing masks for Boston instead. Cheesecloth, folded into five thicknesses and cut into an oblong nine and a half by seven and a half inches. We took the instructions seriously, as if precision could make the difference between life and death. Enough masks that no one would think twice about changing one every two hours, more often if necessary.

First there was one case, but others soon followed. It didn't take long before the infirmary overflowed. The "fluzies," as the girls called their sick friends, were all moved to Bellevue House.

On September 26, the Boston Health Commissioner prohibited public gatherings and ordered theaters and movie houses to close. After consulting with the trustees still healthy enough to attend a board meeting, President Lefavour announced that the college was closed until further notice. The commuters went home, and some out-of-towners returned to their families. The rest of the students hunkered down in their dorm rooms, hoping to stay well.

I moved to Bellevue House, where they hoped there would be room to manage any new cases. There were 28 girls now, and I worked with two other matrons to try to keep them comfortable. We applied cold compresses to feverish heads, changed linens when they were soaked with sweat or feces, dispensed sips of water, read letters from home. Two doctors and a nurse stopped by when they could, but then they, too, developed symptoms and were forced to stay away.

There was not much to be done except to let the disease run its course. There were horrible tales of patients who turned blue or lungs that gurgled up bloody foam. I was dog-tired at the end of the day; I found myself reciting prayers from childhood or making up some on the spot. This was a time, I knew, when prayers were called for. Four girls developed pneumonia, and one of them actually died.

Her name was Sarah Esther Dailey. She was a 19-year-old freshman from Montpelier, Vermont, who had planned to study Household Economics. There had been little time to get to know the freshmen before classes were suspended. Sarah died a week later, her mother by her side. She was Mrs. Dailey's only child.

Later on, Sarah's classmates said all the right things, that she had been friendly and eager to start classes. She would be remembered in assembly and in *The Simmons Review*. But in the end, Sarah was just another statistic in a city that was full of deaths—soldiers and sailors, mothers and fathers, teenagers and children. And, inevitably, somebody you actually knew.

Elizabeth Eaton was now the only student still in bed. She had joined the Dramatic Association last year, but she was a shy girl who seemed happier helping with props and costumes than taking on a part. As I checked her one more time on the third day of her fever, she opened her eyes wide. "Please don't leave me alone, Miss Hale."

"Of course I won't, Elizabeth."

I pulled up a chair. "I'll tell you what. I've got one of my favorite scripts with me. Why don't I read you a bit...and you can help me decide whether the play would be a good choice for our club to do."

Elizabeth managed a wan smile. "I'd like that."

"It's *Alice Sit-by-the-Fire*. It was written by James Barrie, and he starts off with a long explanation that sounds like a novel."

I opened the script and began to read: "One would like to peep covertly into Amy's diary (octavo, with the word 'Amy' in gold letters wandering across the soft brown leather covers, as if it was a long word and, in Amy's opinion, rather a dear)...."

The dialogue began, and I took on a different voice for each part. I looked up and saw that Elizabeth had drifted off to sleep. Still, I stayed by her side, reading silently now, remembering different stages, different audiences. Triumphs of a very different kind.

* * *

The college remained closed until late October, four long weeks while it waited for the epidemic to run its course. Lucia and the other instructors worried how they would make up their coursework. The girls fretted more about the men who were still dying at Camp Devens and the Charlestown Naval Yard, the closed movie houses and the canceled dances.

But the crisis finally passed. Beds were reshuffled among the dorms, the girls who had gone home came back to Boston. The students seemed more serious; life, they had discovered, could be very short.

And, I realized, I, too, had looked death in the face—and I had, in fact, survived.

The newspapers said an armistice was in the works, and each day we held our collective breaths waiting for the announcement. The Dormitory Government went ahead with its plans for a dance, but I worried that the early celebrations could still jinx the outcome. There was a time, I remembered, when everyone thought the war would be over in a matter of days.

But then early in the morning, from a continent away, came the glorious news. I was awakened by church bells; they were followed by the honking of car horns, the ringing of cowbells, the clanging of trash can lids and anything else that might make noise. Classes were cancelled as people surged into the streets, headed for the hastily arranged military parade or impromptu parades of their own.

"Be careful," I warned my girls as they rushed out the door. I sighed. *Overnight, I've become an old fuddy-duddy.* But the memory of cleaning out bed pans and scrubbing dirty linens was still too fresh.

I looked out my window as the river of people flowed toward the Common, but I decided I would rather stay in my room. I thought of Father and wondered if his old congregation would be gathering for prayers. Out of habit, I closed my eyes and whispered, "Thank you, God, that it's all over at last."

The Atlantic would be safe again. Would Tom decide to come home?

Would my life have been different if the archduke had never been assassinated? It was impossible to say and a waste of time to wonder. Tom chose to get married at the end of his fellowship year. Even without the war, he still might have done it.

I went to my desk and found my copy of *The Clod*, the Drama Association's next production. I, too, was behind on my plans for the semester. It would be quiet in the dorm today. It would be a good day to try to move on.

* * *

The letter arrived in June. The envelope was lightweight onionskin—ironic, I thought, considering how it weighed on my heart. In the corner was a small unfamiliar stamp: King George V in uniform. And my name and address, written in Tom's distinctive cursive.

I remembered the letter he had sent me, the one that introduced me to Prufrock. A few more after he set sail for England. But now, the first he had written in four very long years.

Did I dare open it? What was to be gained by rechecking the old wound, unleashing all of yesterday's emotions?

Remembering.

It would be easier this year than last. I was no longer just the minister's daughter who dabbled in amateur theatrics. I was Miss Hale, assistant matron of the dormitories at Simmons College, coach of the Dramatic Association. What was there to be afraid of?

I slid my envelope opener under the sealed flap.

Dear Emily,

I hope this letter finds you well. I have wanted to write you for some time, and at last I found a window of opportunity amid my work and my writing. Eleanor passed along your new address. Eleanor has been so good about keeping me abreast of the news of old friends in Boston, and that has included you.

I was sorry to learn that your father died last year. I have fond memo-ries of him and the discussions—dare I say arguments?—we used to have about philosophy and theology and European politics. How naive we all were! I'm sure you have felt his loss deeply. But Eleanor advised me that you found a good position at Simmons and that you are happy there. And for that I am happy, too.

I feel I know something of your pain because my own father died suddenly this past January. I am sorry that you never had the chance to meet him. I do want to come back to America and help Henry take care of Mother's affairs, but it may be some time before I can make the trip. I have recently received a promotion at Lloyd's Bank, where I have worked for the past two years. The regular hours and steady income make things easier for me. I recently turned down the editor-ship of a new magazine when I decided it would leave me no time for my own writing, which I still desperately want to do. I find that after a long day of working with numbers, the words seem to come more easily at night.

If you felt inclined to write me a letter, I would enjoy hearing from you. As my accommodations seem to change with some frequency, it would probably be best for any letters to be sent to my office at the address above.

England is still recovering from all the years of war, but I am hopeful that life on both sides of the Atlantic will soon return to what we used to think of as normal.

Sincerely yours,
Tom Eliot

I read it once, and then a second time. *What to make of it?* It was a cordial letter, a proper letter. I knew all of the news already. "At last I found a window of opportunity...." Where was his wife? Was she away? I scanned the letter quickly again. He never used the word "we." It was as if Vivienne did not exist. Send any letters to my office. I supposed that address was safe.

I refolded the letter and put it away in my desk. It disturbed me more than I cared to admit. I was flattered he had written, but I knew I wouldn't reply. Nothing had changed. He was still a married man on the other side of the Atlantic. I was not about to give Tom Eliot a chance to break my heart again.

To Sit by the Fire?

1920

THERE WAS A BIG DIFFERENCE, I knew, between being a snob and being well-mannered. And it was important that my students understood the difference.

Even without the guidance of a mother, I had managed to master the practices: the proper way to speak, the correct way to hold a teacup, the socially acceptable way to close a thank-you note. Aunt Edith had taught me most of the rules, but there had also been dozens of church ladies ready to correct me if I strayed from the path of convention.

I had undergone years of "finishing" at good schools, sat through hours of listening to Father's precise words from the pulpit. In our part of Boston, there was definitely "a right way" and "a wrong way" to speak. And my time at Simmons had convinced me that some girls needed help with that if they were ever going to succeed at their jobs.

In the spring of 1920, I made my pitch to President Lefavour. By the fall I had a new title: instructor.

As I wrote for *The Simmons College Review*, my new course in "voice culture" would have three goals:

"1) To correct incorrect speech or tonal placement. Often these faults lie only in the student's carelessness, as ignorance of self-correction.

2) To encourage the student to realize that a good voice is a practical business asset in her work in an office. 'There is no speech nor language where the voice is not heard' may be pardonably paraphrased.

3) To interest the student further in the better literature of the day, and of the past, by helping her to interpret it understandingly and imaginatively to others by the one sure medium at her command—the speaking voice."

When I saw the words in print, I feared they sounded rather pretentious. It was really little more than what I already did as drama coach. But now I had classes to lead, lessons to plan, and grades to award. I was, at last, a teacher.

There was still the stage, of course. I knew I would always need that outlet. But I was more careful about the parts I took on. Memorizing lines was easy, but every good role took an emotional toll. I was moving beyond the age of ingenues, but there were still plenty of maids and mothers, and around Simmons, even male roles that someone had to play. By now I knew which of the Boston drama clubs were well-organized and which directors were tyrants. I could always say no if I had to, pleading the demands of my job. It felt good to have a schedule, a routine and work that needed to be completed. I did, in fact, have a life.

* * *

Five years had passed since I first spoke to the Dramatic Association, and the members were determined to celebrate the club's milestone in a big way. By now, we had a tradition of doing a full-length play in the spring, and we had a lengthy debate over what this year's production should be. Barrie's plays had plenty of roles and could always be counted on to draw an audience. After my suggestion, the club settled on *Alice Sit-by-the Fire*.

I did not tell them that I had once played Amy. I did not recount how the role had helped lure me back from Seattle, rescuing me from that bleak time after Tom got married. Back then I had played Alice's daughter, but now the girls wanted me to play Alice herself. I was always reluctant to act in a college production because it meant one less role for the students. But the club's officers were insistent. "The part calls for an older woman," they argued. In five short years, I had apparently crossed the line between daughter and matron—and I was still under 30.

It would be hard work, I warned them, but in the end we pulled it off. We recruited a long list of sponsors—Lucia, Dr. and Mrs. Lefavour, and more—and ticket sales hit an all-time high. Now we would have more money in our coffers to invest in sets and costumes.

"Miss Hale took five 'raw unbleached school girls' and turned them into actresses," *The Simmons College Review* gushed when it was all over. "Miss Hale did not play Alice, she *was* Alice, from the first to the last scene."

I still appreciated the glowing review, but I was proudest of the review that the club itself received: "May all its birthdays be as successful as this one, and its progress be as great in the next five years as it has been in the five that have just passed."

* * *

When May Day arrived, there was a buzz of news: Lucia was leaving to become president of a women's college in Wisconsin.

I had never heard of Milwaukee-Downer College, and I could not imagine why Lucia would want to desert Boston for the Midwest. At the celebration on the lawn, I finally found her, amid a small cluster of students and professors, downing plates of strawberry shortcake.

"I'm thrilled for you," I said, giving her a long hug. "But what am I going to do without you?"

"I want to talk to you about that," she replied. "Wait here a minute."

I watched as she made time for each student, embracing some, extending her hand to others. Already, I thought, she looked older—and much older than I knew her to be. Was it the longer hemline of her dress? The sturdier shoes? The new way she had arranged her hair at the nape of her neck?

She dispatched the last of the students and took me by the arm. "Let's go for a walk." We headed away from the crowd to the relative privacy of The Fenway, following the curve in the road that took us by Mrs. Gardner's elegant mansion.

"None of us knew!" I said, when we were clear of all the parents.

"It all happened rather quickly," she conceded. "The college's president is retiring after 25 years. The trustees wrote me back in January and said my name had been suggested by one of their former professors. At first, I was reluctant to apply because I have so little administrative experience." She smiled. "In fact, I found out later that my father was proposing the names of other Radcliffe graduates."

She went on. "But after thinking about it and talking to my parents, I realized I had always dreamed of becoming a college president. And I decided I had nothing to lose by applying.

"They narrowed their list to three candidates. I was told that one of them dropped out and the other sent in her materials too late. So the trustees invited me to come to Milwaukee for an interview. I must admit I was terrified. Ellen Sabin, the outgoing president, is a member of the board and she sat in on my interview. She must be close to 70 and she's been running the college for more than 25 years. So she's got some very strong opinions. And then I also had to face the 30 or so men who were on the board.

"They said they were concerned about my lack of administrative experience. I acknowledged that it was my weakness, but I said I was sure I could master the skills I needed. They must have liked what I said because the next thing I knew, they offered me the job."

"How soon do you leave?"

"They wanted me to come for their commencement, but I told them I couldn't drop everything here that quickly. I also needed a break. I told them I would be there by September."

"You'll be wonderful," I assured her. "But I'm going to miss you so much."

"That's what I wanted to talk to you about." We came to a bench along the sidewalk, and Lucia motioned for us to sit down. "President Sabin has been advising me about the vacancies that will need to be filled. She just wrote that the professor of vocal expression is leaving. I wondered if you would be interested in the job?"

"Me?" I was incredulous. "But I have even fewer credentials than you do!"

She threw back her head and laughed heartily. "You're right about that." Then she grew serious. "Ellen Sabin has told me—in no uncertain words—that I should hire a college graduate. But in this case, I disagree—and it's my decision to make. I've watched how you've grown since you came to Simmons, Emily. I remember when the Dramatic Association was a struggling little group. Then you stepped in and....well, overnight it became the biggest club in the college. Everyone knows you're the reason why. And then you just kept taking on more responsibility...your dormitory, your classes. You wear us all out with your ideas!"

I pondered her words for a moment. "When do I have to decide?"

"I should move quickly," she acknowledged. "If you don't take the job, I'll need to start looking for someone else." She paused. "I've tried to defer to Miss Sabin on many things. But you're the one person I'm prepared to fight for. Milwaukee-Downer is a wonderful college, but I know we could make it better. I know that there's more to successful drama clubs than just reading lines and selling tickets. You have a real gift, Emily, and I want you to bring it to my new college."

I was a jumble of complicated emotions. I was thrilled that Lucia wanted to hire me. But to leave Boston, and everything that was friendly and familiar?

I checked the watch face that dangled from the chain around my neck. "We'd better be heading back. I promised the committee I'd help them clean up." We walked in silence for a while, then I turned and asked, "What's Milwaukee like?"

"It's not Boston," Lucia replied with a laugh. "But the weather is very similar, and so far, I've found the people to be very friendly."

I stopped and took in all the familiar sights around me. The Fenway, the green of the Riverway, Mrs. Gardner's house, the college.

"I don't know if I could leave Boston," I said at last.

"It might be good for you," Lucia replied.

"Why?"

She hesitated. "We've never talked about this, Emily, and perhaps I'm out of line to bring it up now. But Tom Eliot was at Harvard when I was at Radcliffe. My father taught him when he was an undergrad. Cambridge is a small town. Everyone knew you were a couple. Everyone assumed you would get married when Tom came home from Oxford...."

"But that didn't happen, did it?" I replied.

"If you stay in Boston, you may never be able to leave him behind."

"I've wondered about that myself."

"Come with me to Wisconsin," Lucia urged. "It will be a great opportunity for both of us."

I gazed out at the abandoned maypole, its streamers now dangling limply in the wind. "You know," I said at last, "I've always loved all the traditions at Simmons, but I always hated May Day. I could never figure out why.

"But today, as I was watching the girls dance around that pole, I remembered a song that I once performed at Eleanor Hinkley's house. Tom was there that night. I think that was when I began to fall in love with him. I guess I was just as silly as the words I was singing that night."

I thought about what Lucia had said, and then I turned and looked at her directly. "You've sold me on Milwaukee-Downer. Now see if you can sell them on me."

* * *

It took Lucia nearly two months, but she finally hammered out the arrangements. It was years before she showed me the letters she had exchanged with Ellen Sabin, fearing I would change my mind if I knew what Miss Sabin thought about me. The older woman had reasserted that many people who teach vocal expression "are not acceptable in a college." She thought the school needed "a well-trained college woman plus the special training that is expected for any special subject."

But Lucia stuck to her guns. I was her choice. Miss Sabin responded that the college already had instructors in music, art, and French who didn't have degrees, and that was enough.

Lucia brought in reinforcements. She wrote back that I was "an unusual person," and that her father, the dean of Simmons, and the head of the English Department had all agreed with her that I was the best choice for the job. That was why she planned to hire me. But, she added, in case it would help, my late father had been a minister and Uncle Philip was a renowned music critic.

Things moved very quickly after that. It turned out they also needed two new heads of the dormitories, and Lucia pushed me for one of those jobs, too. By early July, I had a signed contract to teach vocal instruction and manage Johnston Hall. It was the smaller of the two dorms, and my predecessor would live there in case I needed help. It meant a thousand dollars a year and another room of my own.

I had already planned to go to Seattle for the summer to visit Edith and John and take some more acting classes. But before leaving Boston, I journeyed out to Gloucester to see Eleanor one last time. Sipping lemonade on the wide veranda of the family home, listening to the roar of the ocean, a hint of salt on the breeze, I could see why Tom had loved this place growing up. I wondered if he had found a spot in England that took its place.

There had been no more letters since the one I hadn't answered, and this time Eleanor had little news to share. Tom's mother and brother had gone to England for the summer. Eleanor supposed Tom had his hands full, working at the bank, entertaining his relatives, and meeting the needs of his sickly wife. He was still trying to write poetry, but it had been a struggle.

When it was time to leave, we hugged each other and promised we would write. As I rode the train back to Boston, I thought of all the other men I had known: Oggie, Clifford, John Hart, Tracy Putnam. Would my life have been different if Tracy had been the one to bring me a drink that night we performed at Eleanor's? A spark that might have turned into a flame when we met up again on a Boston stage?

He would have been a good match. He had finally finished his studies at Harvard and graduated near the top of his Med School class. But even Tracy was now off to Amsterdam. And, Eleanor had shared, one of his female classmates would be joining him there.

I recalled the advice Lucia had given me on May Day. It *was* time to put Tom Eliot behind me. Whenever Eleanor began to share her scraps of gossip from England, I should cover my ears and tell her, "No more."

If only I could.

Schadenfreude

MILWAUKEE-DOWNER COLLEGE WAS ON THE northeast side of the city, a short walk from Lake Park and the grand mansions that lined the shoreline of Lake Michigan. Its heritage stretched back 70 years, but the original schools were now consolidated closer to Milwaukee in a cluster of red-brick buildings that reminded me of Simmons.

My job came with one small room and a bathroom and parlor that I shared with other faculty members. The broad staircase of Johnston Hall with its wood bannisters brought back old memories of the parsonage in Chestnut Hill. The benches on the landings, I imagined, would make a good place for a girl to read or daydream. There was a second, narrower stairwell in the back; I knew it was the route girls would choose if they tried to sneak in after curfew.

The dorm was a mishmash of architectural styles. The roofline was trimmed with gargoyles; the one outside my room made me smile each morning when I pulled back the drapes to catch the sun rising over the lake. It seemed the architect was trying to create a red castle in the middle of a Midwestern prairie. Father would have said the man couldn't make up his mind.

The school had traditions, but they were designed to welcome new-comers, not exclude them. The YWCA Club held its reception the very first Friday of the term. Soon after that, the freshmen marched around the campus's main horseshoe drive to receive the "color" that would distinguish them for the next four years. From this point on, the incoming Class of 1925 would celebrate everything purple.

The streets around the campus were wide, lined with beautiful shade trees and large, comfortable-looking homes. Still, Milwaukee was younger, more rough-and-tumble than the Boston I had known. Prohibition had forced the breweries to change their formulas, but the stores and restaurants still sold an array of exotic sausages. I was surprised to encounter old German shopkeepers who eyed me suspiciously, as if we were still fighting The Great War. But I met others who were eager to leave their German roots behind: the Brauns who had become Browns, the Schmidts who had transformed themselves into Smiths.

Lucia was installed at the end of September. At the banquet that night, I tried not to bristle when Amelia Ford, the history professor who spoke on behalf of the faculty, drew some laughs with her jokes about the chilliness of Bostonians. I already knew that my students thought my accent was a novelty. I started out my classes by stressing the importance of proper grammar, speaking with confidence, and finishing off words with a clear, crisp consonant. But my ear could tell the difference in how we spoke, how the Midwesterners transformed "pen" into "pin," "Kenneth" into "Kinnith." Some of the students sprinkled their sentences with "yahs." In time I learned they came from the western part of the state, where their relatives still spoke the languages of Scandinavia. I was careful how I went about correcting them and tried hard not to offend. Some girls tried to mimic my accent, but I never asserted it was the "correct" one. The important thing, I always stressed, was to say exactly what you meant.

Someday it might make a difference in your life.

At my first faculty meeting, I discovered that all of my colleagues were women. There was one male who taught violin on a part-time basis, but he was Ellen Sabin's exception. As I met the new dean, Miss Pieters, and then Miss Brown, Miss Belcher, and on through the ranks, I realized there was not a "Mrs." among them. They were all spinsters like myself.

As the months went by and I got to know them better, I learned that if there had been a time in their lives when they had loved a man, they had moved beyond it. There was no place for a married woman in the classrooms of Milwaukee-Downer. And like nuns in a convent, the professors seemed to expect to stay here until the day they died.

* * *

Milwaukee-Downer didn't have a Drama Club, but it did have a long tradition of plays. I tried hard not to step on the toes of any of the other directors. Miss Brown had arrived at Downer College before the turn of the century and now dominated the December calendar with her annual Christmas play. Mademoiselle Serafon, meanwhile, was going to celebrate the tercentenary of Molière's birth next spring by transforming the Cercle Franco-Americain's annual show into a musical extravaganza. In late spring, the sophomores would produce an original May Play, which, one of my cynical students explained, was simply an elaborate way of crowning their May Queen. Girls—and occasionally faculty members—seemed to create scripts and lyrics for any occasion and at the drop of a hat.

Simmons had taught me valuable lessons. There were students who were natural-born organizers. There were girls who wanted nothing more challenging than a walk-on part as a maid. And then there were the divas, the girls who had to be the star. A few of them actually turned out to have talent.

It was important to guide the girls to the right jobs and roles. And it was better to start small and grow big: one-act plays in the fall and a full-length play in the spring.

I had arrived at Simmons at the age of 24, a stay-at-home amateur actress, not much older than the seniors in the club. But I was almost 30 now, no longer one of them. I could still put on a white wig and play a marchioness if Mademoiselle Serafon was doing Molière. But I knew that a line had been drawn between teacher and student, director and cast. And I was now, irrevocably, on the other side.

* * *

Eleanor's letters remained my lifeline to Boston. And she was finally enjoying some success of her own. She continued to channel her love of Austen into her scripts, and *Dear Jane* had traveled across the Charles River to the National Theatre in downtown Boston. The *Cambridge Tribune*'s review was tucked inside her latest letter: "a delightful success by all who had the pleasure of witnessing it."

Oggie Perkins was also breaking into the professional ranks. And, Eleanor wrote, he was getting married. Jane Rane was a Wellesley grad who had grown up near Oggie in Newton. The wedding was scheduled for June. It seemed like a waste of time to dwell on the "might-have-beens" if Oggie and I had managed to pair up; I simply hoped that he would be happy.

Inevitably, Eleanor turned to the latest news from Tom. He'd had some sort of breakdown the previous fall. He had told his mother not to worry, that he just needed some time off and that the bank had provided it. But Eleanor had found out more of the details from his brother. Tom had gone to Lausanne for three months to see a specialist. It was depression. It was his nerves. His wife was still suffering from one puzzling ailment after another, but she actually seemed to improve when they weren't living under the same roof. He had written a long poem, but his friend Ezra Pound had ripped it apart. He feared it would never get published, or if it did, that he would never be compensated for all the hours he had spent working on it.

I folded the letter neatly, then tucked it into the wooden box of correspondence I had brought from Boston. I checked the time; I had to hurry or I would be late for my Vocal Expression class.

The girls were in their seats when I arrived at Merrill Hall. I had a lesson plan ready, but a different, devilish idea had taken hold instead.

"I learned a new word the other day, class, and I wanted to share it with you. Whenever I come across a word I don't know, I always make a point of looking it up and writing down the definition in my notebook. That's how I try to build my vocabulary."

I turned to the blackboard and picked up a piece of chalk. Eleanor and I had marveled at the impossibly long German words Fraulein von Seckendorf had strung together when she taught us at the Berkeley Street School. This one would be easier to remember.

I wrote down the word, set down the chalk, then turned back to face my students. "Does anyone know what this means?"

I was not surprised by the roomful of blank faces.

"*Schadenfreude.*" I said the word slowly, enunciating each syllable with care. "It's a German word, but I came across it last week in an article I was reading. Did I pronounce it correctly?" I looked quickly at the girls of German descent, but no one challenged me.

"It comes from two German words, 'damage' and 'joy.' It's not a particularly nice state of mind. Rather un-Christianlike, actually. But, if we're honest with ourselves, I think most of us feel this way sometimes.

It means taking pleasure in the misfortune of others. Can any of you think of a time when you felt that way?"

A hand rose slowly in the back of the room. "Yes, Annie?"

"There was a boy I liked in high school," the girl began slowly. "He invited me to the dance at the end of the year. I got a new dress and my mother helped me arrange my hair. And then when the time came, he never arrived. I never figured out what happened; he never talked to me again. But then I learned he had taken up with another girl. I didn't know her; she lived in another part of town.

"And then the next thing I knew they were married. The word went around town that the girl had gotten pregnant and that her father had forced the boy to marry her. He had planned to go East to college, but now he was stuck. And here I am, getting my degree, and leaving him behind."

And here I am, teaching in a college, and leaving him behind. "Yes, Annie," I said at last. "I think you captured the meaning perfectly."

* * *

I had accepted Lucia's job offer so quickly that I had never considered whether Milwaukee even had a playhouse. But it had a surprisingly lively theater scene. Professional venues, vaudeville, and its crown jewel for amateurs like me, the Wisconsin Players.

Its cofounder was Laura Sherry, a homegrown impresario who had studied drama at the university in Madison and married into wealth. Five years ago, she'd had the audacity to take her company to Broadway. The war derailed her grand plan, but the troupe simply moved on to France and performed for the soldiers.

It was the Cambridge Social Dramatic Club, taken to the next level. Mrs. Sherry had acquired a townhouse in downtown Milwaukee, and I began spending time there, reading new scripts, building sets, or enjoying a cup of tea with another actor. I was thrilled when I quickly won the lead in a one-act play called *Tradition*, playing the part of an actress, a role, Mrs. Sherry explained, that was inspired by the playwright's wife.

But Mrs. Sherry was always cooking up something bigger. Twice a year, the Players took over the Pabst Theater, the beautiful downtown venue that Milwaukee's beer money had built. Mrs. Sherry's longtime friend, Zona Gale, had just become the first woman to win the Pulitzer

Prize for drama for her play *Miss Lulu Bett*, and now the whole state was clamoring for their native daughter to return so they could all celebrate her success.

It took me a while to get my hands on the script, but once I did, I read it in one sitting. Lulu was a spinster, a sort of indentured servant who was expected to find happiness responding to her family's relentless demands. The play was not perfect. Gale had adapted the play from her own novel, but her financial backers had forced her to transform the final scene into a happy ending. Still, the play captured the voice of a modern woman, a woman with strong opinions who eventually learned how to express them.

Ibsen had written of unhappy women, but Ibsen was a man, writing in a foreign language and at a different time. Gale's characters were members of an ordinary Midwestern family, the kind of people you'd find in her hometown of Portage—or, truth be known, even in the salons of Boston.

It was different from any role I had ever performed.

Laura Sherry broke the news at the end-of-season meeting. Our big production for the fall of 1922 would be *Miss Lulu Bett*, and Zona Gale herself was coming back to help shape the show. Auditions would be held first thing in September.

It was a prize worth working for. All I needed was Lucia's blessing.

"As long as you do your job, meet your commitments, and fit the rehearsals around your schedule, how could I complain?" she responded when I asked. Then she smiled, a conspiratorial twinkle to her eye. "And if you end up playing the lead, it would be wonderful publicity for our drama program."

I planned to go back to Seattle for the summer. It was the perfect place to study the role and maybe take another acting class. A key scene required Lulu to pare a bowl of apples. Before I left, I got the dining-room cook to teach me the best way to wield a paring knife, and I practiced until I could peel an apple without looking—or nicking my fingers.

The later scenes were more challenging. On a lark, Lulu decides to marry Ninian, her sister's brother-in-law, then learns on their honeymoon that he was previously married—and that he just learned his wife is still alive. She returns home in disgrace. Will the weight of the scandal be borne by the relatives of the apparent bigamist, or will they let everyone think that Lulu has been abandoned? She insists on controlling the narrative of her life.

Lulu eventually gets her happy ending. But before that, she is abandoned. Abandoned by a man who was married to another woman. A man she had believed was hers. As I marked up my script, I remembered the techniques I had learned on my first trip to Seattle. I knew I could find Lulu's emotions if I was willing to dig deeply enough into my own.

By the time I returned to Milwaukee, I was ready. Auditions were set for a Saturday in the rehearsal rooms of the Players' Tudor Revival townhouse. I brought along my résumé, eager to remind Laura Sherry that I did, in fact, have quite a bit of experience.

"Very impressive," she said, glancing at it quickly then attaching it to her clipboard. "This morning I'd like you to read some of Act 1, Scene 2. The dialogue between Lulu and Ninian." She called out to a man on the other side of the room. "Lorimar, can you come help us out?" She turned back to me. "Lorimar Knoll is going to play Ninian. You can start at the place where Lulu and Ninian meet."

I nodded to the actor, then reached for my bag. "I hope you don't mind if I pare a few apples."

She looked up from her notes and smiled. "Not at all."

I pulled out my bowl, a knife and four apples, then settled onto the stool on the empty set.

"Do you need a script?" Lorimar asked.

"No," I replied. "I've memorized the lines." I closed my eyes, focusing on shyness, the embarrassment of being overheard by the new man in town when I was asking questions about him.

Lorimar retreated a few steps, then walked back out onto our imaginary stage. "Hello, kitten!," he called out to an invisible niece. "Ask him what? What do you want to ask him?"

I picked up an apple and began to turn a spiral with my knife. I flashed back to my first encounter with Tom Eliot, feeling a small flutter in my heart.

"I—I think I was wondering what kind of pies you like best."

* * *

I managed to peel two apples before the scene came to an end. Lorimar was friendly and good-looking. Like the character he was playing, he tried to put me at ease. I guessed he was a few years older than me. I allowed myself to wonder if he was married.

Mrs. Sherry asked if I could sing something for her. I knew I could launch into "Mavourneen" but decided against it. The script called for Lulu to sing the old Stephen Foster tune "Goodnight." That was a smarter choice.

When I finished, she asked, "Can you play the piano?"

Aunt Irene had been a concert pianist before she married Uncle Philip, but she didn't have the temperament for teaching children. Fortunately, Philip did. "I can't do anything fancy," I replied honestly, "but I can play well enough to accompany myself."

She wrote down some more notes, then asked me to jump ahead to the final scene. It would be tougher, but I had expected that scene to be chosen. I closed my eyes, reached back into my memories, and thought about the pain of striking out from home.

"Mother. Now, mother darling, listen and try to understand...."

When I finished, the onlookers started clapping. I smiled with relief.

"Before you leave," Mrs. Sherry said, "I'd like you to read some of Ina's part."

I forced myself to smile. I did not want to play Lulu's sister, but I knew better than to admit it. I had to be willing to do whatever the company needed.

"I'm going to have to get my script."

I gave Ina my best shot. I remembered playing Mrs. Elton, another character no one liked. But this was drama, not comedy. I had to tone down my histrionics.

"Thank you," Mrs. Sherry said when I finished the reading. "I'll post the cast list later on, but I'll call you if you get a part."

By the time I got back to Johnston Hall, it was late afternoon and I was exhausted. I fixed myself a cup of tea, slipped off my shoes, and propped up my feet. I had done all I could. And if I didn't get the part, well, perhaps it was for the best. Between my classes, the drama club, and my duties as dorm matron, I had more than enough to fill my days.

Downstairs, the telephone rang. It rang often on Saturday nights, as the girls who didn't have dates tried to organize last-minute plans for the rest of the weekend.

There was a knock on my door. "Miss Hale, the phone is for you."

I caught the hint of surprise in the girl's voice. It was rare that a call was for the matron.

I rushed down the main stairs to the phone stand in the front hall, then picked up the receiver. "Hello?"

"Miss Hale?"

"Yes." I thought I recognized her voice.

"This is Laura Sherry."

"Yes?"

"I'm calling to say that we would like you to play Lulu."

My hand flew up to my mouth, trying to muffle my shriek of delight.

"Miss Hale?"

"Oh, Mrs. Sherry. Thank you, I'm so thrilled."

"I do have one more question for you."

"Yes?" My heart started to race.

"We call ourselves the Wisconsin Players. Because Zona Gale was born here, we know that there are people all over the state who want to see this play. Would you be free to travel with us?"

"What would that entail?"

"We usually leave Milwaukee on Friday morning and do performances on Friday and Saturday nights. Sometimes in the same town, sometimes two or three different places."

My heart sank. "I don't think I can commit to that," I said slowly. "I have to teach on Fridays, and I often have to chaperone events on the weekend. I knew that I could do the dates at the Pabst Theater, but I don't think I would be free to travel."

Mrs. Sherry was silent for what seemed like an interminable length of time. Then at last she spoke. "We'll work around it somehow. I'm going to ask Helen Camp to be your understudy. Helen's done our road trips before. Rehearsals start next week."

* * *

Around me, I could see the girls were slowly changing, cutting their hair, shortening their skirts, aping the images in the magazines and the heroines of that novelist out of Princeton, F. Scott Fitzgerald. There were many rules at Milwaukee-Downer, and Lucia kept revising them. I was expected to inspect the men who arrived for dates, find out where the couples were headed and when they would return. There were set hours when the young women could entertain males in the downstairs parlor. Milwaukee-Downer was a school for good Christian ladies; on Sundays, movie outings were prohibited.

I worried that the volume of rules could backfire, that a silly infraction would be treated as harshly as a major one. A cigarette, puffed hastily on the back staircase in a furtive moment of freedom, was different, I thought, than accepting swigs of whisky from a frat man with a car and a flask.

I didn't enjoy being the enforcer, but I knew it was part of my job. I preferred to be clear about my expectations, win the confidence of my charges, and ask them not to disappoint me. I preferred warnings over citations. But rules were rules, and it was one thing to stretch them and another to ignore them altogether.

Life was full of rules, some written down and others that were not. It was best to learn early on that there was a price to be paid for breaking them.

* * *

The Pabst Theater was slightly larger than the Plymouth—my biggest venue up to now—and its builders had spared no expense. It was their statement that Milwaukee had, indeed, arrived. The lobbies were lined with dark hardwood, with accents of gold and marble throughout. A wide staircase led to the balconies; an immense crystal chandelier hung from the ceiling inside. The red-velvet seats, arranged in horseshoed tiers, were soft and comfortable.

Now, as we moved into the theater for our final rehearsals, I was eager to discover all the marvels backstage. I was most intrigued by the system of weights and pulleys that were used to control the scrims. Laura Sherry took time to explain how it all worked. We had become close over the course of the rehearsals. She was now "Laura," not "Mrs. Sherry," even if she was still clearly in charge.

"I have one more thing to show you," Laura said as she led me into wings. She opened a door and flipped on a light. "A dressing room for the star."

"It's beautiful," I said, noting the wood-paneled walls and touches of marble. "And how convenient! Right off stage and with its own little bathroom."

"We want you to have it."

"Me?" I was incredulous. I was playing the title role, but my part wasn't that much bigger than the others. George Robinson served on the Players' board of directors; he certainly deserved it more.

"The cast all agreed you should have it," Laura said. "We all know how hard you've worked on the play."

And so when the 10th of November finally arrived, I showed up as early as the theater opened and found my way backstage to the dressing room. For a while, I simply sat in front of the mirror, hypnotized by the glare of its bright makeup lights. The image reflected back was pleasant enough; the skin was clear, the jawline firm, the hair still brown without traces of gray. But already, I acknowledged, I was beyond the fresh blush of my youth. The expressive lines were deepening.

Yet I did not really mind. The face I saw was the face of experience. And, I was grateful now, a face that suited Lulu Bett.

I rose to change into my costume, wondering which famous actors and actresses had shared this space, hung their street clothes in the closet, flushed the same toilet, scrubbed off their makeup in the sink. I closed my eyes, trying to feel their spirits, harness their energy.

There was a knock at the door. It was one of the tech people carrying a vase of yellow roses.

My heart froze for a moment, my memories flashing back to the Andover Town Hall. The box of Killarney roses. *Could they be from Tom?*

"They're beautiful," I said. "Please set them there by the mirror."

I found the note nestled in the buds.

Good luck, Miss Hale. We know you will be wonderful.
The Dramatic Club

My emotions were perilously close to the surface, almost to the point of tears. I was genuinely touched by the girls' gesture. But that joy was still pierced by an aching disappointment.

What were you expecting, you ninny! He's a married man!

There was another knock at the door. "Ten minutes to curtain."

I dabbed at my cheeks, willing myself to remain calm and focused. I began to apply my makeup, the final step of trying to become someone else. It was time for me to become Lulu Bett—and to leave Emily Hale behind.

* * *

"The family bond is the strongest bond in the world," Lulu's brother-in-law reminded her. "The family reputation is the highest nobility." As I gazed up to the Pabst's balconies, I remembered the unspoken rules of the Hales and Perkinses.

Could I have succeeded in an acting career?

Lulu evolved from the opening scene to the final curtain. But I found the second act to be the most challenging.

"You see Ninian was the first person who was ever kind to me," I explained to the audience. "Nobody ever wanted me, nobody ever even thought of me. Then he came."

Is that why I still love Tom?

And then there came Lulu's explosion of anguish.

"I thought I was married and I went off on the train and he bought me things and I saw different towns. And then it was all a mistake. I didn't have any of it. I came back here and went into your kitchen again—I don't know why I came back. I suppose it's because I'm most 34 and new things ain't so easy any more—but what have I got or what'll I ever have?..."

Three acts, three costume changes. Zona Gale's happy ending, I had to acknowledge, was my own secret fantasy. The man returns. His estranged wife, it turns out, is, in fact, dead. The two of them *will* live happily ever after.

The curtain came down. And the applause rose through the theater, back up the aisles to the top of the balconies. I felt weak with relief, but there was no time to relax. Our curtain call was tightly scripted.

The cast took the stage, one by one. There was extra applause for little Helen Shannon, who played Lulu's bratty, scene-stealing niece. And then it was my turn. As I walked out, the applause continued to grow. One by one, audience members rose to their feet. I felt a wave of joy and happiness. I joined hands with the other actors and we took a synchronized bow.

But there was still more I was supposed to do. I raised my hand to quiet the theater. "It has been wonderful for all of us to perform for you tonight. But it has been a special thrill because the playwright is right here with us. Please join us in welcoming Wisconsin's native daughter, Miss Zona Gale."

The cast began to applaud, the noise building as Miss Gale rose from her seat on the aisle and climbed the steps to the stage. She had arrived in town near the end of our rehearsals, but she had kept her distance, watching us perform from the rear of the theater, then conferring quietly with Laura about little changes she would like to make. Now, as she crossed the stage, she waved her friend in from the wings, and they took their places on either side of me. We all bowed again and again. Bouquets magically appeared. And then Laura signaled for the curtain to come down for the final time.

When the massive drape finally hit the floor, Miss Gale pulled me close and whispered in my ear.

"You inhabited Lulu Bett."

* * *

I slept in as late as I could—and as long as I dared. Saturday meant both a matinee and an evening performance, and I had to conserve my energies. Then I spotted the envelope slipped under the door. It was from Katharine, one of my favorite students.

I just want to tell you now how proud I was of you last night!...I think you were so consistent throughout the play, and made Lulu so real. Why, she lived for me—and I had to wink back the tears awfully hard in the scene where you read the letter, and in the scene where you leave your mother.

And, before I forget it—you looked perfectly lovely, your ears must have burned if you knew all the things I heard people say about you.

I smiled, but I didn't let myself wallow too long in her effusive praise. I was determined to find a copy of the *Sentinel*.

The review was inside, sandwiched between stories on the funerals of two prominent Milwaukee citizens:

Miss Emily Hale, with her dry wit and her downtrodden air which aroused sympathy and at the same time left an impression of deep and intense feeling, stood out decidedly in the feature role. Handling a difficult part with unusual ease, it was neither overdone nor treated in a casual manner.

In a new city. In a new play. On a big stage.
I had finally arrived.

* * *

The society ladies of Milwaukee showered Zona Gale with teas, receptions, and attention all weekend long. But on Sunday, after the last performance, it was time for the Wisconsin Players to have their turn.

I had looked forward to the reception, but now I was weary. The letdown always descended with the final curtain. Tomorrow I would be back in my classroom. In a few weeks, the cast would be heading to Appleton, and I would be chaperoning a holiday dance.

"Here's our star," Laura called out, ushering Miss Gale to my side.

She extended her hand. "As I told you on opening night, I couldn't have been happier with your performance."

"Thank you very much." Then I frowned. "I must confess I was very disappointed when I caught up with *The Journal*'s review today. I was glad I didn't see it before the final show."

I could not forget the searing words: "Miss Emily Hale, who played Miss Lulu, the kitchen drudge in her sister's household, seemed to forget, at times, that she was the uneducated Lulu and gave her lines in a voice too cultured to belong to so drab a housekeeper."

"If the criticism was valid," Laura said, "it should have been directed at me. You gave me what I asked you to do. I was more concerned about whether the rest of the cast could carry their voices to the balconies. I knew the audience wouldn't miss any of *your* lines."

"I agree," Miss Gale chimed in. "The reviewer didn't seem to understand that Lulu wasn't really a drudge."

"Thank you both, but I still wish I could play her one more time."

"I'm sorry you won't be coming on our tour," Laura said. She turned to Miss Gale. "Emily teaches at Milwaukee-Downer and can't take the time off."

"It will be my loss," she replied.

Laura excused herself to catch a board member, leaving us alone.

"Have you done many parts like this before?" the playwright asked.

I shook my head. "I've mostly done comedies. The kind set in an English country home. Ten years ago, they were very popular in Boston."

Miss Gale smiled. "They're still very popular in Wisconsin." She paused. "Tell me, are you familiar with the original version of my play?"

"Yes."

"Which ending do *you* prefer?"

I smiled. "I suppose I prefer the revised one. I've always liked a happy ending."

"Life isn't always like that, though."

"No, it isn't." I hesitated. "While I preferred the new ending, there was a line from the original script that has stayed with me. Something like, 'I thought I wanted somebody of my own. Maybe it was just myself.'"

She smiled. "It *was* a good line, wasn't it? Perhaps I should have worked it into the final version." She took a sip of her drink. "There was a time when I thought I had somebody of my own. We were both very young. He was a writer, too—a poet, actually." She laughed lightly. "It didn't work out the way I had expected. It was very hard for me at the time. But as the years went by, I looked at it differently. I know it made me stronger...and I learned how to be happy with myself." She took another sip. "Forgive me for chattering on so."

"I don't mind."

She smiled. "Even at my advanced age, I still believe happy endings are possible. And I hope you do, too." She surveyed the room. "Now I'm afraid I'd better go circulate with more of Laura's supporters."

"Of course."

She looked at me intently. "I hope you will keep on acting."

I smiled. "And I hope you'll keep writing such good parts!"

I watched as Miss Gale crossed the room. I wondered about the poet in *her* past. But this was not the time or place for probing personal secrets. Zona Gale was a prizewinning playwright. Her heart might have been broken, but she had found a way to channel her heartbreak into her characters and plays.

There was something, I thought, that could be learned from that.

* * *

In the beautiful dressing room at the Pabst Theater, far away from Edith and the Boston society matrons, I had allowed myself to dream again.

Bigger theaters, more challenging roles. Perhaps I could follow Oggie Perkins to Broadway or track down Edward Vroom and his company.

But the words of *The Journal*'s theater critic troubled me now. In all my years of acting, I had never received such a negative review. I knew artists had to be prepared for criticism, but it still stung me very deeply.

I had always worked hard to perfect my voice; I took pride in the precision of my tongue. I didn't know any other way to speak. And now an anonymous reviewer on a Midwestern paper had pinpointed my biggest liability.

"I don't know why I came back. I suppose it's because I'm most 34 and new things ain't so easy any more—but what have I got or what'll I ever have?..."

Laura and Miss Gale had tried to buck me up, but those lines still haunted me. I had never said "ain't" before, and part of me had wanted to correct myself on the spot. It wasn't the only line of Lulu's that I felt that way about, only the most obvious one. And I knew the reviewer was right; I *had* stepped out of Lulu's character.

Over the holidays, I tried to shake off my depression. But it always came back to the same thing. I needed approval. I needed to be loved. I would never have the courage a professional actress needed to expose herself to audiences paying top dollar and critics waiting to pounce from their good seats on the aisle.

There was another side to theater besides the bouquets and the applause. And without the support of the admirer who had meant the most to me, I knew I would never be able to venture out on those kinds of stages.

And there was something else. The Dramatic Club's fall play had been sacrificed to my acting ambitions. Lucia hadn't objected, but I knew the girls had paid a price. I couldn't give the trustees a reason to question the commitment of that "woman with no degree."

So I focused on my teaching and directing girls in plays. And when Laura Sherry asked me to audition again, I lied—just a little. I told her I had decided I would never be able to top the thrill of my nights of playing Lulu Bett. And for now at least, I didn't want to try.

Bitterness and Beauty

1923

THE PACKAGE BORE MARGARET FARRAND'S familiar hand-writing but clearly held more than just a letter. Eleanor kept me posted on Tom Eliot's private life, but from the English Department at Smith, Margaret kept me posted on his professional one.

I opened the package carefully. Inside was a thin black volume, fewer than a hundred pages. On the cover, printed in gold, I read:

The Waste Land
By
T. S. Eliot

I held it reverently for a moment, then turned to Margaret's letter.

Dear Emily,

Tom Eliot's new poem was published in book form in December. It took me a while to track it down, but I thought you would want a copy.

The reviews have been mixed. I have enclosed Burton Roscoe's; his was one of the most enthusiastic. It is not an easy poem to work through, and I don't pretend to understand everything Eliot is trying to say. But he's certainly given my colleagues a good deal to ruminate and fulminate about!

I turned next to the clipping from the *New York Tribune:*

Received the November issue of "The Dial" today. It contains T. S. Eliot's new long poem, "The Waste Land," a thing of bitterness and beauty, which is a crystallization or a synthesis of all the poems Mr. Eliot has hitherto written. It is, perhaps the finest poem of this generation; at all events it is the most significant in that it gives to the universal despair or resignation rising from the spiritual and economic consequences of the war, the cross purposes of modern civilization, the cul-de-sac into which both science and philosophy seem to have got themselves and the breakdown of all great directive purposes which give zest and joy to the business of living.

Roscoe went on for a few more paragraphs before concluding:

The final intellectual impression I have of the poem is that it is extremely clever (by which I'd not mean to disparage it, on the contrary); the sardonic grin which suffuses it is a rictus which masks a hurt romantic with sentiments plagued by crass reality; and it is faulty structurally for the reason that, even with copious (mock and serious) notes he supplies in elucidation, it is so idiosyncratic a statement of ideas that I, for one, cannot follow the narrator with complete comprehension. The poem, however, contains enough sheer verbal loveliness, enough ecstasy, enough psychological verisimilitude and enough even of a readily understandable etching of modern life, I justify Mr. Eliot in his idiosyncrasies. He may, and I think he does, even play practical jokes on his readers; but that is in character, with the curious, variable mood of this fine poem.

I set the clipping down. *The finest poem of this generation.* Tom would be thrilled, but he wouldn't be satisfied. Roscoe had critiqued his structure, his sentiments. He was puzzled by what Tom was trying to say.

I made a note to look up the meaning of "rictus" and add it to my list of vocabulary words.

Then I opened the book. As usual, Tom had shown off his knowledge of Latin and Greek with an epigram. I stopped there, pulling two of Father's reference books down from the shelf. I parsed out the translation, then read more about Sibyl of Cumae. A woman who seeks eternal life, but forgets to ask for eternal youth. She is left to wither away in a cage.

Like me, perhaps?

I had to be happy for Tom. He had done what he had set out from Harvard to do.

April is the cruelest month....

I read no farther than the first line.

Perhaps it is for you, Tom. But for me, it will always be June.

* * *

My first instincts had turned out to be right: Johnston Hall's back stairway was the route of choice for girls sneaking into the dorm after curfew. But now it also often reeked of cigarette smoke.

No woman would have dared smoke a cigarette back when I was in Boston. But enough of them were doing it now that Lucia had been forced to add cigarettes to the list of prohibited items. Along with electric irons and alcohol lamps, they could set off a fire in the dorms.

All of the girls were bobbing their hair and wearing more makeup. They studied the illustrations in *The Saturday Evening Post* and mimicked the ads in *Collier's*. The late-night talks turned more frequently to the best stratagems for landing a university man from Madison.

On some level, all of it pained me. I had mastered some new and difficult things. Finding a job, paying my bills, moving to a strange city. It was hard to become independent. But it had nothing to do with cigarettes and gin. And there was a danger, I wanted to warn my students, in doing all of it to try to please a man.

But even I could still fall into those old traps. One day, out of curiosity, I purchased a package of cigarettes. I waited until I was on my own, embarrassed I might gag the first time I tried one. But I discovered that smoking calmed me. I liked the way a cigarette fit between my fingers, making my hands feel more expressive and graceful.

I couldn't smoke in the dorm, but I began tucking a pack of Lucky Strikes into my purse. And when visiting the Players' townhouse or going out to dinner with friends, I would sometimes pull out a cigarette and ask for a light. And I wondered if my old friends in Boston were doing the same thing, too.

* * *

The letter from Aunt Edith arrived right after the Christmas holidays. "Would you like to come to England with us this summer?"

I reread her words to make sure I wasn't dreaming. England. Summertime. And Edith and John offering to pay my way.

Milwaukee-Downer shut down during the summer, and the staff who lived in the dorms had to find somewhere else to go. My choices had ranged from a cottage on Lake Michigan to short trips to Seattle or Boston. But Europe? It had been a dream since my school days, ever since Amy had first regaled us with tales of visits to her relatives in Austria and Italy.

The war, of course, brought all the grand tours to an end. Lucia and Margaret had the money and skills to charge off in support of the Allied cause. But the lean times that followed Father's death had made my own dreams recede even further.

But now the war was over, and Edith was offering to pay.

England. Summertime. The green gardens of Surrey.

Tom Eliot.

The daydream stopped there.

It had been nearly a decade since I had seen Tom. But there was far more to England than him. Theaters. Castles. Cathedrals. I knew Edith would want to visit every formal garden she could find.

I reached for a pen and paper to accept her invitation before I had time to change my mind.

* * *

We set sail from New York, bound for Southampton. The ship was comfortable but not luxurious. I loved the coziness of my cabin and being rocked to sleep every night on the Atlantic's rolling waves.

One morning, I rose early and found my way to the bow of the ship. The sun was rising in the East, beckoning across the great expanse of sea. I loved the feel of the wind and salty mist upon my face.

Tom had made his own crossing in that long-ago summer of 1914. I remembered bits of his report to Eleanor. Views out his porthole. Games with fellow passengers. Boredom. Of course, that was his second trip to Europe, and this was my first. I felt alive, as if I was being transported to a different world. A world where no one knew me.

I was not the minister's daughter nor the minister's niece, even if that minister still sat with me in the ship's dining room. Nor was I the instructor charged with teaching proper speech and etiquette.

I was Emily Hale, world traveler.

The possibilities now seemed endless.

* * *

I had spent hours in the National Gallery and the British Museum. I had caught the changing of the guard at Buckingham Palace and strolled the pathways of Hyde Park. Through her contacts in the Royal Horticultural Society, Edith had wrangled invitations to view private gardens and the society's facilities at Chiswick and Wisley. I tagged along with her, confirming in the process that Surrey was indeed very green.

But now the days were running out. Still, I couldn't forget the address. *Lloyd's Bank of London, 75 Lombard Street, The City.*

All summer long, I had felt that Edith was monitoring me closely. For the most part, I was happy, reveling among the settings of Shakespeare and the haunts of James Barrie and George Bernard Shaw. Seeing more live theater than I ever thought possible.

But I still couldn't let go of him. *One more time. That's all it would take.*

Finally, the opportunity came. Edith came down with a cold and begged off of our planned outing. "I still would like to see St. Paul's before we leave," I told her. "I'll just go without you."

I rose early and peered outside my window. A fog was settling on the street outside our rooms. I had always heard about the pea-green fog of London, but it was a surprise to experience it on a warm summer day. I picked out my dress with care, finally settling on a crisp-looking linen frock, hemmed to the middle of my calves. Lilac, like the hyacinths. It would be comfortable for a day full of sightseeing, but still conservative. I was no longer the young girl in the Boston Public Garden.

I found my gloves and arranged a small white straw hat on my head. By now I had learned that I should always pack a brolly along with my *Baedeker*.

I left before Edith rose, saving myself from more explanations. I had no grand plan. It was folly to think that if I headed to the financial district, I would cross paths with Tom. Part of me was afraid I would do just that. But perhaps there was a place close to the bank, a café or a chemist's shop, where I could station myself just to try to catch a glimpse of him.

There were no guarantees. From Eleanor, I had gleaned that he worked at the bank's headquarters, but over time that might have changed. He could be on vacation—it *was* August, after all. He might be ill or accompanying his wife to the doctor.

Still, I forged on, joining the sea of early-morning commuters threading their way down into the subway. The Central Line train arrived quickly, and it was just a few short stops to the Bank station. I merged with the crowd heading for the exits, picked one of them at random, then reconnoitered once I had emerged onto the street.

It was not the closest exit to Lombard Street. If Tom traveled by subway—another of my many suppositions—he would probably use the exit on the other side of Threadneedle and Cornhill. I headed that way quickly, checking the face under every bowler I passed.

I found the row of old-fashioned signs with the logos of the companies that called Lombard Street home. As I drew closer, I spotted the black stallion against the field of green. The front door of Lloyd's.

But where to station myself? The shops and cafés of my imagination had failed to materialize. There was only a line of nondescript financial businesses. But there were doorways and columns behind which I could wait. And if I acted as if I belonged there, who would stop and question me?

So I remained there for nearly 90 minutes, as bankers, clerks, and an occasional secretary filed by, hurrying faster as the top of the hour drew near. It finally sounded from a nearby church tower, and the pedestrian traffic waned. It was time for their workday to begin.

I headed back up the street, deciding to make the pilgrimage to St. Paul's by foot instead of by subway. *What did I expect?* I felt even more foolish than I had when I set out that morning.

When I reached the cathedral, I paused for a moment to pray. I asked God to help save me from my lunacy.

* * *

I spent a leisurely morning at St. Paul's, reviewing its history with my guidebook and studying each work of art on its walls. Afterward I walked some more, down Cannon Street to the Monument to the Great Fire of

London and out onto London Bridge. The fog obscured the view today, and I watched, fascinated, as the boats disappeared slowly into the mist.

I checked my *Baedeker* again. St. Magnus the Martyr Church was just a few blocks away. I found the church and stopped in to take a look. I said yet another prayer.

Five o'clock was drawing near, and so I began to head back. Edith would worry if I was gone too long. Cathedrals and churches, banks and monuments could not be *that* fascinating. I felt small, almost shamed by this whole excursion. *What had I been thinking?* If I hurried back to the subway, I still might be able to make it back in time for afternoon tea.

And then, as if a ghost, he stepped out of the fog a half-block ahead. Despite the passage of years, I recognized him at once, the familiar gait, the eyes cast downward, lost in thought, under the brim of the dark bowler. He was dressed the way I remembered him, but in the fashion of a new decade: a well-cut suit, handkerchief in the pocket, a vest and a tie with a neat Windsor knot. In the crook of one arm was a book; in the other, an umbrella.

I froze, wondering if there was still time to run and hide. And what if he didn't recognize me? Would that only make things worse?

He looked up then, and his quick steps stopped a few strides away. He said nothing. Was he trying to remember my name?

"Emily!"

"Hello, Tom." The words caught in my throat.

In a second, he was by my side. "I can't believe it's you."

I could lie and pretend it was all just a wild coincidence. But I dodged instead. "I've been in London this summer. I wanted to see this part of the city before I had to go back home."

He continued to stare at me for a moment, his mouth forming the same sheepish grin that had once melted my heart. Then he fumbled for his pocket watch and checked the time. "Are you headed somewhere? Would you have time for a cup of tea?"

I pretended I had other plans. "I'm here with John and Edith, and they're expecting me for dinner. But I think I could spare a few minutes."

"I can't stay long myself," he said. "But I know a place around the corner where we could sit and talk—if you had the time."

He touched my elbow lightly, steering me quickly through the stream of pedestrians now crowding the narrow sidewalk. I felt lost, as if I could not breathe. I had been so wrong. I had thought that if I saw him one more time, it would crystallize my anger, let me pummel him with my fists. He would be older, and pale and sickly, and I would wonder how I could have been attracted to him in the first place. It would drive him out of my memory and drive him out of my heart.

But that wasn't how it was. I glanced sideways and still saw my young Harvard philosopher, not the stodgy London banker of my imagination. And now, as he strode by my side, a specter in the fog, there was a rush of warmer memories. The rightness of walking with him, protected simply by his nearness.

He led me to a small tea house, then to a table by the window. He began to call out an order, then realized too many years had passed.

"Are you still drinking tea?" he asked.

I nodded.

"Bring us a pot for two then," he instructed the waiter. "And some shortbreads."

He pulled out a cigarette.

"I'd like one, too," I said.

He paused, raising an eyebrow. I liked the fact that I could surprise him. He reopened his cigarette case and offered me one. He lit his own first, then extended the match toward mine. I took my first puff, hoping he wouldn't notice how my fingers were trembling.

We said nothing for a long time. I was afraid I would say too much and that it would come out all wrong. In the old days, I had been afraid to speak up. But over the years, I had conducted too many imaginary conversations with him. I had been filled with angry words, and I feared that if he pushed a particular button, he would get a stream of them now.

But Tom seemed content to study my face in silence, at least until the waiter brought our order and finally left us on our own.

"You should have told me you were coming to London," he said.

"You should have told *me* when you came back to Boston. The Tom Eliot I knew never was a coward."

He had pushed one of those buttons.

"Touché," he replied. He paused for a moment, and took a drag on his cigarette. "Shall we start over?"

"Yes. Why don't we?"

He took a sip of tea. "What brought you here now?"

I gripped my teacup more tightly. *Did he mean London or this neigh-borhood?* "Edith and John invited me to come with them for the summer. I'm teaching now, so I have my summers off."

"Where are you teaching?"

"I've moved to Milwaukee. I'm teaching at a woman's college there."

He smiled. "It's ironic, don't you think?"

His thoughts were always two steps ahead of mine. "What do you mean?"

"I'm working at a bank and you're the one teaching college students."

I laughed; the tension broke. "Yes. Things *have* changed, haven't they?"

Sitting across from him, I could assess him more objectively now. He *did* look older, his face grayer, like the grimy fog of London. I remembered a healthier face, slightly sunburned from sailboat outings, or walks along the banks of the Charles. His hair was trimmed neatly, but there was a world-weariness about him. I wished I could do something to cheer him up.

"Do you still like working at Lloyd's?" I remembered the words of his long-ago letter.

"It pays the bills," he replied. "I'm making use of my foreign languages, and the bank's been very good to me. But that's not all I do. I'm editing a magazine now. It's called *The Criterion*. I work on it at home late at night. It's a lot of work, but I find it very satisfying."

So many years had passed, there was so much ground to be covered. And yet he had not mentioned his marriage or his wife. Would he just pretend she didn't exist?

"I'm sorry, Emily."

Had he really said that?

"I'm sorry," he repeated. "I know I hurt you deeply, and I can never forgive myself for that."

I took a long drag on my cigarette, willing myself not to cry.

"I don't know what happened when I left Boston," he said. "I was very confused. I wanted some sign from you, but I didn't know how to ask for it or to let you know what I needed. I don't think I knew myself."

I said nothing, thinking back over the long years since that night before he left.

"It's a shame," I said at last. "You became a poet. I teach young women how to speak. And yet, when it mattered the most, we could not find the words we needed."

He reached across the table, his eyes hooded with pain and regret. He took my hand. It stiffened, but I didn't pull my fingers back.

"I know now, Emily, that I never stopped loving you."

My heart leapt. *How long had I yearned to hear that?* But he was a married man, I reminded myself. We were sitting in a public restaurant, a restaurant that was filling up with evening customers. Outside the window, his coworkers might be passing by, heading home for the day.

But he was the vulnerable one. I knew no one in this foreign city, no one but my aunt and uncle, in their rooms on the other side of town. It was Tom's reputation at stake, not mine. And at least for this moment, he didn't seem to care.

At last, I pulled back my hand to pick up my cup and finish the last of the tepid tea. I took a bite of the shortbread, chewing it carefully as I considered what to say.

"I was foolish, Tom. I thought if I saw you one more time, I could put you behind me, move on with my life. But I know now that it can never be that easy."

"Is there anyone else in your life?"

I shook my head, then smiled. "You forget, Tom. I'm almost 32. I live in a dormitory at a college for women. Perhaps there was a time in my life when there could have been someone else. Perhaps a friend of Eleanor's or one of my leading men. Perhaps if I had tried harder, or been more open to introductions. But I don't think it's going to happen now."

I paused then added, "But that doesn't change the fact that no matter what your marriage is like, you are still married."

"Yes," he repeated soberly. "I am still married to Vivienne."

It jolted me to hear the name. Of course, Tom assumed I knew the story, that there was no need for him to fill in the gaps. Still, the mere mention of his wife's name was like an angry cleaver slicing through my fairy tale, reminding me how everything had changed.

Down the block, the church bells sounded the hour. I checked the clock on the restaurant wall. "I do need to be going. Edith will start to worry if I don't make it home soon."

"May I walk you back to the Underground?"

I nodded, then fiddled with my gloves while he took care of the bill.

We retraced our steps, each of us lost in our thoughts. When we reached the entrance to the subway, he turned to me again.

"I don't know how this happened, Emily, but I'm glad that it did."

Was I? Even now I still wasn't sure.

"Will you tell your wife that you saw me?"

For a moment, he looked at me oddly, as if he was not sure what had happened or how to describe it—if, in fact, he could. "I don't think so," he said at last. "Oh, she knows that I have good female friends. Some of them have been very helpful in promoting my work." He paused. "But no, you're different. I want to keep you in a separate place."

My heart began to race; I felt lightheaded in the late-afternoon heat.

"May I write you?" he asked.

He is here and I am thousands of miles away. Is there any harm in that?

"Yes," I replied.

He patted his pockets mindlessly. "I should write down your address, but I don't seem to have my little notebook when I need it."

"It's simple," I said. "Johnston Hall. Johnston with a 't.' Milwaukee-Downer College. Milwaukee, Wisconsin."

"I should be able to remember that."

"I hope so." Down the stairs came the roar of a passing train, reminding us there were other places where other people were waiting for us. "Goodbye, Tom."

"Goodbye, Emily."

There was no kiss, no quick embrace. I turned and ran down the stairs into the Underground. I longed to steal one more glimpse of him but feared what might happen if I stopped to look back. So I kept moving forward, having no idea what tomorrow might bring or where this path would eventually lead.

A Work in Progress

1923

A COLLECTION OF POETRY WAS waiting for me when I returned home to Milwaukee. The copyright notice revealed that *Ara Vos Prec* had been published a few years before, but the inscription was fresh:

> *For Emily Hale with the author's humble compliments,*
> *T. S. Eliot*
> *5.ix.23*

There was more, but maddeningly, it was in Italian. I thought it was from Dante, and eventually I figured it out:

> *But let my Treasure,*
> *where I still live on,*
> *live on in your memory.*

I smiled. *Indeed it will.*

The next month I received a copy of *The Criterion*, along with a short note from one Richard Cobden-Sanderson:

> *Mr. Eliot asked me to provide you with a complimentary*
> *subscription to his magazine. Enclosed please find a copy of*
> *Volume II, Number 1.*

It would be nice to receive an actual letter rather than a book of old poems or a scribbled note from a subordinate. Still, Tom *was* taking the time to share some of his life. I should be grateful he had written at all.

I leafed through the magazine. I was trying to read more of this sort of thing now, trying to hold my own with my colleagues in the English Department. The girls might stay up late talking about their beaux, but my peers were consumed by arguing over the latest books and plays or who would make the best presidential candidate now that we had a say in it.

The magazine included an essay by Tom, and I decided to read that first. It was a weighty topic—"The Function of Criticism"—and I struggled at times to follow his argument. He had never talked down to me, never wielded his Harvard degree like a badge of superiority. Still, the essay reminded me that he inhabited another world, a world far removed from the classrooms where I taught.

I had reread "The Waste Land" many times by now, reviewed his endnotes in hopes that they would help me understand it. I found phrases I liked, the descriptions of the Thames and the neighborhood around The City, now that I had seen them for myself. But as a whole, Tom's poem remained a puzzle.

My colleagues in the English Department seemed to agree.

I wrote down the words in this new essay that I would need to look up: "autoletic" and "otiose" and "obnubilation." He challenged the views of another critic, but the battle lines of the English literary establishment meant nothing to me. Instead I was drawn to those short sections where the Tom I knew shone through.

I have had some experience of Extension lecturing, and I have found only two ways of leading any pupils to like anything with the right liking: to present them with a selection of the simpler kind of facts about a work—its conditions, its setting, its genesis—or else to spring the work on them in such a way that they were not prepared to be prejudiced against it.

It would be wonderful to talk with Tom about teaching.

I turned to the next article that caught my eye: "A New Shakespearean Text," by one W. J. Lawrence. I turned to a blank page of my notebook and prepared myself to take notes. There was always something new to be learned about the Bard.

* * *

More issues of the magazine followed after that, and finally, so did some letters. There was no predicting when I would hear from him and no predicting which Tom would be the one to write.

In some letters, the witty Tom came to the fore. In some, he vented about the stresses of his life. In others, he used me as a sounding board for a debate he seemed to be having with himself.

I was puzzled by that. The Tom Eliot I had known in Boston had been cynical about organized religion, fascinated by the spirituality of the Orient, willing to argue with Father about the existence of God.

Now he was seriously considering being baptized as an Anglican.

I didn't spend much of my time worrying about denominational distinctions. I was surrounded by professors who were Congregationalists, Presbyterians, and Episcopalians. The Tom I had known had rejected all of them. But something had changed, and he wanted to know what I thought.

I wasn't actually sure. In recent months, my own religious practices had surprised me. My colleagues were all "good Christian women"; our baccalaureate services were dutifully staged at the nearby Congregational church. But away from Boston, I felt liberated from the sense of duty that used to make me get out of bed on Sunday mornings. Nevertheless, I found that I wanted the kind of family a congregation could provide. And even in the ethnic smorgasbord of Milwaukee, I could still find Unitarians.

But Tom's dilemma was starker. He struggled with the nature of sin and redemption. He was rereading Dante and pondering the nature of Hell, Purgatory, and Paradise. He wrote that some of his old friends mocked him. What happened to "the voice of our generation?" they demanded to know. But he didn't care about them; he wanted to know what I thought.

It doesn't matter what the others say, I wrote. *You need to be true to yourself, wherever that leads you.*

I addressed my letters to Tom's office. I always tried to be sympathetic and friendly, but I was always careful about what I wrote. A secretary might be the one to open a letter. I made no mention of Vivienne. I made no mention of the times we had spent together. I was determined to protect Tom from embarrassment. I was an old friend, and nothing more.

The letters continued, over the weeks and months and years. And when the Tom of my youth picked up his pen, there would be a phrase, a word, a memory that would let me ignore all the didactic arguments of the peevish, exhausted banker. Something would touch my heart and keep me sending a letter in return.

I think of you when the hyacinths bloom....

I still remember the warmth of your hand as I held it that foggy summer day when you came out of the mists of London....

You were always there for me, Emily...even when I wasn't there for you.

I was grateful he never mentioned Vivienne.

I put each letter in my box of memories. And as they piled up over the months and years, I realized I would probably have to invest in a chest.

* * *

Every year, the college's yearbook arrived on campus with a painful reminder of my academic inadequacies: Dean Pieters had a doctorate from Columbia, Amelia Ford had one from Wisconsin, Mary Edith Pinney got hers at Bryn Mawr. Even the physical education instructors boasted bachelor's degrees from Oberlin. And next to the name "Emily Hale" was a big, blank space.

But I worked hard to succeed in other ways. The Dramatic Club had rechristened itself the Mountebanks and was growing in size and drawing rave reviews. Laura Sherry spoke with the club and helped me make other connections. Otis Skinner came for tea during his run in *Sancho Panza* at the Pabst. Eva LeGallienne visited while performing in *The Swan*. Glenn Hunter came, too, leaving behind an autographed photo for the adoring girls who had seen his films.

Lucia wanted to bring name speakers to campus, and I volunteered to help. For starters, I landed Edna St. Vincent Millay and Robert Frost.

I remembered the first time I had read "The Road Not Taken," back when I was mulling over what to do with my life. I wrote Tom eagerly about arranging Frost's appearance and was just a little disappointed when he wrote back that he considered Frost "old-fashioned" and "too easy."

At least, I mused, I can figure out what Frost is trying to say.

The reading was set for an evening in late March. The hall was full, humming with the audience's anticipation. It was more nerve-wracking, I discovered, to wait by the door for the featured speaker than to hide out backstage, about to perform.

Frost arrived later than he was supposed to, shrugging out of a wet overcoat and trying his best to clear his throat from the effects of the frigid lakefront air. He was a disheveled contrast to the sartorial tidiness of Tom Eliot. As I ushered him to the front of Merrill Hall, I could not resist dropping names.

"I wonder if you know an old friend of mine from Boston. Thomas Eliot?"

"I assume you mean Thomas *Stearns* Eliot," Frost muttered. "I know him by reputation, but not personally. I left England just as he was arriving. I didn't like it there, but he seems intent on staying permanently."

Frost rambled on. "He's a good friend of an old friend of mine, Ezra Pound. We both owe whatever success we have had to Ezra."

From the front row, Lucia signaled it was time to start. I quieted the audience and made my introduction. Frost shuffled onto the stage, nearly dropping the sheaf of poems he had brought to read. *Perhaps I should have given him more time to get ready.*

He took his place at the lectern, then seemed annoyed. "Excuse me," he said, "but one of my cufflinks has come undone." He lifted his sleeve, displaying the flapping sleeve of his shirt. "Could someone help me?"

From the front row, Evangeline Fisher, one of my best students, rose from her seat and headed to the platform. She refastened the cufflink with an expert twist of her wrist.

"Thank you, my dear," Frost called out as she retreated. "May I ask your name?"

"Van," she replied. "Van Fisher."

"Thank you, Van," Frost repeated, then turned back to the audience. "Let's give Van a round of applause."

I shook my head as I returned to the wings.

Why do poets always seem to need a mother?

* * *

In April 1925, I received a letter that was different from the others.

My dear Emily,

*It has been ten years, ten years since I allowed myself to get caught
up in a vortex of pretty girls, drinking, dancing and punting outings
on the River Cherwell. A few months of madness that led me to a
morning in June when I signed my life away in a registry office in
Hampstead. Dante had his hell and now I have mine.*

*I have struggled all these years to make the best of it, believing that
the struggle would eventually lead to redemption. But every new
doctor, every change of venue, every new treatment only seems to make
matters worse. My successes give me no joy, and I worry now that my
wife's madness will only become my own.*

*I must sort all of this out myself, as best as I can. I know that if you
were near, you would provide me with a sympathetic ear. No judgments, no solutions. Just your warm, calming presence. And your
letters these last months have provided me with all of that. But I fear
that I must take a break, for the infidelities of my heart only cloud the
decisions that I ultimately must make.*

*Perhaps this hiatus will be a relief to you. I sincerely hope it will bring
you no more pain. I have brought you enough of that already, a pain
that I certainly deserved, but that you never did.*

As always,
Tom

April *was* his cruelest month.

I knew I had to respond, to send at least one more letter. But I didn't
rush to write it. The blackness of his mood scared me, but there was little
I could do to help from thousands of miles away. He was right, after all.
These were his choices, and he had to find a way to live with them.

Dear Tom,

I understand.

I regret that I am so powerless to help you, but you know that I will always be there if you need me.

It would be presumptuous of me to offer you advice. But at the ripe old age of 33, I have learned one thing. It has seen me through the madness of my mother, your departure for England, and the death of my father. Each of us must find our own way to our happiness. No one can do it for us.

Your friend,
Emily Hale

* * *

Once again, I took that advice to heart. Keeping busy was the best antidote to despair. I decided that in the coming school year, the Mountebanks would perform two full-length plays instead of just one. Directing *Alice Sit-by-the-Fire* would make it easier.

And I'd had an epiphany about all the celebrity speakers I had arranged. Most had more celebrity than they had speaking talent. And you didn't have to be Eva LeGallienne to be able to talk knowledgeably about the theater.

I decided to test the waters. The League of Women Voters was a good place to start, but quickly I branched out to the South Side Women's Club, the Shriners auxiliary, the Colonial Dames of Wisconsin. (The colonists, I joked to the women, apparently had survived the trip west from Boston.) I provided whatever my audience wanted, Shakespeare or poetry, tales from my trip to England, speeches on theater trends in New York and Europe. I knew I could never expect to command the kind of fee that Frost or Millay or Helen Keller could charge. But someday, if I built up my résumé, I might be able to earn something.

But there was more at stake. Tom had become famous, and if something ever happened to Vivienne, if the two of us were ever to have a future, I needed to become somebody, too. A university instructor, a star of the Wisconsin Players. And now a public speaker, with a calendar packed with appearances. My essays might never grace the pages of *The Criterion,* but there were still people who would turn out to hear what I had to say.

I was still a work in progress. But Tom had managed to give me the time and space I needed to get the job done.

* * *

I always felt a mix of emotions when Commencement arrived. I looked forward to summer vacation, but each June also meant saying good-bye to my seniors. And the Class of 1926 had been the best I had ever taught. Two of the Mountebanks, Marion McBride and Mary Spicuzza, had been elected class officers. I never dreamed how close we would all become.

The girls had arrived on campus at the start of my second year. From the start, Marion was a determined, take-charge leader. Mary, meanwhile, was a bundle of energy topped by a curly mop of red hair that would never be tamed into "the flapper look," even if she had tried. She came from a large Italian family who lived over the warehouse in downtown Milwaukee that was the base of their banana business. A decade before, they had traded in their pushcarts to purchase a truck, christened it with a bottle of Chianti, and extended their market all over town. They were successful enough that they could send their clever eldest daughter to Milwaukee-Downer. She was thought to be the first Italian-American to pass through its doors, and, I knew, one of its rare Catholics.

But Mary never tried to hide her roots. "Call me Spic," she told all her newfound friends. In a faculty meeting, Amelia Ford mused whether the faculty should discourage this. The word, she explained, was an ethnic slur that was creeping across the Mexican border. The Spicuzzas got their bananas from Central America; surely they must know that?

But if Mary had embraced the nickname, who were we to object? She had a fearlessness that immediately caught my eye—and that I envied in a woman so much younger than me.

The Commencement Play was the final ritual of the school year, performed in the Hawthornden, the spreading lawn beyond the back steps of Merrill Hall. This was the college's 75th anniversary, and Lucia had recruited her father's successor, Ada Louise Comstock, to deliver the major address. There would be two performances of the play this year, and Lucia made clear that she wanted something "big."

I decided to do *Sherwood,* Alfred Noyes's retelling of the Robin Hood legend. There were dancers, an eight-member orchestra, and nearly two dozen singers from the Glee Club. Mary begged to play Shadow-of-a-Leaf, the half-fairy, half-mortal who ushers Robin and Marian into Paradise. By the time I finished casting the roles, 125 people had a part. "No one will be left for the audience!" I joked.

The first night we were forced inside by a storm, but the weather cooperated for the final performance. It was a high-wire act from start to finish. At the last minute, I'd had to recruit one of my former students, Leonore Fischer, to play the role of Blondel. She managed to flub one of her cues, leaving a gaping silence. *What to do?* I stepped out from the wings, breaking into a madrigal I had learned back when I was taking voice lessons. The crowd applauded when I finished, and I prayed no one beyond the cast figured out what had actually happened.

When it was all over, when we had swatted away the mosquitoes and the leads had recited the epilogue, and the parents, faculty—and, by the looks of it, most of the Italian population of Milwaukee—broke out into raucous applause, I shared one last hug with the cast behind a branching hawthorn tree.

Three days later, I was grateful to be seated in the back row on the stage so Mary and the rest of the seniors couldn't see me dab my eyes when they crossed in front of the faculty to receive their diplomas. I remembered the dinners in my studio to welcome the new Mountebanks after they were chosen. I remembered the corsage of sweet peas and lilies-of-the-valley that Mary had pinned on me after I helped the city students put on their play. I yearned to find a way to tell her she was special, but we were not supposed to give our students gifts. And then one day as I was paying my bills, I came up with an idea: "To Mary Spicuzza," I wrote on the check, then added on the description line: "One Hundred Percent Ability in What She Does."

I knew Mary and the girls had saved me. They had filled that spot in my heart that might otherwise ache with emptiness. Not every student, of course, but the ones who had a special spark. The ones who had the same kind of passionate ember that burned inside of me.

It was hope. It was optimism. It was a willingness to take a risk. And, for now at least, that flame helped keep me from becoming an embittered spinster, aging away in my red-brick castle in a land filled only with women.

Vita Nuova

1926

IT WAS A DREARY DAY in November when Lucia summoned me to her office. Why did Milwaukee's winters always seem colder than Boston's? Were the days longer, the winds stronger, the snows deeper? Or did winter just seem to arrive earlier, settling in like an unwanted relative who waited until May to finally pack up and leave?

But Lucia's announcement broke through my gloom. "We're promoting you to assistant professor." And not only that—after more than five years, they owed me a sabbatical. I could have six months off with pay starting next spring.

I managed to keep calm as I left her office, but once outside, I danced down the corridor of Merrill Hall. I knew how I wanted to spend the time. Uncle John had been assigned to King's Chapel in Boston, and he and Edith were taking a sabbatical of their own before he started. Once again, Edith had invited me to come along to England.

My mind began racing with all the things I wanted to do. I was teaching Literary Interpretation now, and I could gather up stories about the poets and the playwrights, visit their homes and the theaters where their works had been staged. Turn up more anecdotes for my speeches, as well.

And return to Tom Eliot's side of the Atlantic?

I would save that dilemma for another day.

* * *

We sailed in February. In a rapid exchange of letters, Edith and I had plotted our route. We would travel first to the continent, then meet John in the British Isles for the rest of the summer. Ultimately, Edith was in charge because she was the one who was paying the bill.

Our path was set by the weather. First Madeira, then Algiers and Gibraltar. We planned to stay four months in Italy: Naples, Rome, Milan, Genoa, Venice, and Perugia. But we focused on Florence, where we would linger for three months in a small pension near the Ponte Vecchio.

Each morning, our landlady dropped off a tray outside our door with a pot of strong, dark coffee, crusty rolls, and sweet butter. I always jumped up to retrieve it, and if Edith was still sleeping, I would slip out to our tiny balcony and watch the city shake off its slumbers.

Our previous stops had been a relentless march through museums and gardens and "must-see" sights. But in Florence, we had the luxury of time, time to try to live like the Italians did, time to explore the city through the eyes of Dante, the de Medicis, and Michelangelo.

Firenze. I practiced rolling the syllables off my tongue. How odd that the English had come up with their own name for the city, when the Italians' was so lovely.

I remembered when Tom had pulled out a dog-eared copy of *The Divine Comedy* as we sat together in the Public Garden. He liked reading the verses in Italian, then checking the English translation on the facing page.

He had told me all about the politics of medieval Florence, how Dante had been exiled and eventually welcomed back, figuratively if not literally. His ornate tomb was empty—his remains were actually in Ravenna—but I still decided to make a pilgrimage. It was odd that Tom had never been there. Maybe one day we would make the trip together.

I should write him. I had decided not to seek him out while I was in England. But I decided I should still let him know I where I was.

Dear Tom,

Edith and I are in Florence. As I write this, I am sitting on our balcony, taking in all the sights and the smells: Wistaria vines climb the walls around me, irises and roses are in the garden below. In the distance, I can see orchards of olive trees and cypress, and at night, the fireflies come out and dance around the pergola, and the nightingale offers a concert.

You would be proud of the way I am reading Dante, picking up a bit of Italian and Latin and exploring all the sights. I started with The Divine Comedy *and I've almost finished it.* Vita Nuova *will be next.*

We head to England later this summer. Once my sabbatical is over, I will return to Milwaukee in the fall as an assistant professor. I hope this letter finds you well and happy....

I could have provided him with our address in London, but that would make it too easy. If he wanted to see me, he should tell me, even if it meant missing him on this trip.

When we were in Boston, I had counted our separations in days or weeks. Now they were measured in years, if not decades. What did another year matter if he was still married to Vivienne?

Edith arrived in the doorway behind me.

"Are you still in contact with Thomas Eliot?"

It was too late; she had seen the name on the letter. "We started writing each other a few years ago. I seek his advice for my classes. It's nothing serious."

"Are you sure?"

"He's still married, Aunt Edith. That hasn't changed."

"I don't want you to get hurt again."

"I don't want to get hurt, either," I replied. "But it's different now. He shares his work. We discuss poetry. It's a friendship, nothing more."

"Besides," I said, "I'm nearly 36. I've accepted the fact that I will probably never marry. But I'm surrounded by single women who have built happy lives for themselves. They're brilliant women who are committed to their work. And I'm a different woman now, too."

She gave my shoulders a squeeze. "I'm proud of you," she said. "But never say never."

She leaned over the balcony railing to survey the street below. "Why don't we go try to find a new place to have lunch?" She paused, then added, "Who knows? We may even meet a handsome Italian."

* * *

I held off posting my letter until we left for Venice. I loved that city as much as I loved Florence, the canals, the bobbing gondolas bringing back memories of the Charles River and the waterfront of Boston. Each night, the Piazza San Marco was taken over by a crowd of tourists and a concert, startling the doves but not to the point that they stopped swooping down to snatch bird seed out of my hand.

Mussolini and his fascists were coming up with more and more reasons to stage a festival, and tonight the plaza was filled with hundreds of fresh-faced singing children. The world was changing so quickly but the old wounds still festered around us. *How long would the children know such joy?*

In Milan, Edith had arranged for rooms in a 16th century villa in the hills north of the city. When no one was watching, I allowed myself to escape into dramatic fantasies, climbing the grand stone staircase as if I were a queen, summoning an imaginary maid to my high-ceiling bedroom, threading through the columns of the sun-drenched loggia to meet an imaginary lover. Falling asleep with a smile on my lips at the silliness of it all.

Finally, it was time to escape the heat of Italy for the mountains of Switzerland. It was ironic that I finished *Vita Nuova* just as our train crossed the border.

I flipped back to a sonnet that had touched my heart in a surprising way. *What would it be like to be loved the way Dante had loved Beatrice? Would it be beautiful and wonderful? Or would it be terrifying to be the object of a man's obsession? To feel that you always had to be so perfect?*

I put down the book. Beatrice had solved that particular problem by dying. It was certainly not the fate that I wished for myself.

* * *

At last we reached England. But this time, we moved on beyond London. We joined up with John, then headed for Devonshire, stretching our legs by taking long walks across the purple moors. Each little town had a memorial to its war dead, and as we paused before yet another Honor Roll, I wondered how many names were on the walls at Oxford and Cambridge, and which of the young men Tom might have known.

We returned to London at the end, and I decided to head back to St. Paul's.

This time I avoided the financial district. I found a seat in the cathedral, halfway to the altar. The tourists filed in, listening as a guide recounted its dimensions. Now and then a penitent joined me in the pew, genuflecting and kneeling in prayer. A workman climbed a shaky ladder to study a spot on the stone wall that needed repair.

This is Tom's world now.

I wondered if he had become an Anglican yet. Even as I was opening up myself to new experiences, he had managed to erect all sorts of walls between us. Crossing to the other side of an ocean. Getting married. Abandoning his academic career. Rejecting the religion of our youth.

My eyes were drawn to the frescoes around me. Religious faith was founded on a mystery. And so was my continued love for Tom.

* * *

When I got back home to Milwaukee, there were several letters waiting for me.

Dear Emily,

Your letter from Florence arrived on a beautiful spring day, and I was very happy to receive it. Since I last wrote, I have left the bank and taken a new job at a publishing house called Faber & Gwyer. The bank forwarded your letter to my new office, which is located on Russell Square.

Because it was such a glorious day, I proposed to a friend of mine, William Stead, that we go for a walk. He is an American, who came to England in the diplomatic corps, and has since become an Anglican cleric. We have discovered we have much in common, including, it seems, poetry and challenging wives.

As we walked around the square, he turned and said, "It would be nice to be in love on a day like this."

I agreed and told him about receiving your letter that very morning. It filled my heart with warm memories, and, I must confess, a lightness of spirit that I had not experienced for many, many years....

A challenging wife. A very careful reference to Vivienne. And yet, Tom could still feel the hope of springtime.

I could see Russell Square again, the sidewalks and well-kept gardens, perfect for a stroll. The buds beginning to form on the trees that lined its paths. I remembered our walks in the Public Garden, and I hoped that he could, too.

* * *

The next letter included a copy of a poem. It was entitled "Journey of the Magi," and once again, Tom had inscribed it in a formal way: "for Emily Hale from T. S. Eliot. 16.viii.27." It was discreet enough for me to be able to pass it around the English Department.

I liked this poem more than some of the others. Tom had assumed the identity of another character, this time one of the three Wise Men, looking back on his life.

There were times we regretted
The summer palaces on slopes, the terraces,
And the silken girls bringing sherbet.

I now wished I had seen him in London to meet for a meal and catch up on his news. Tell him about my classes, seek his suggestions on the authors I should teach.

But there was virtue in patience. Perhaps it was true that absence made the heart grow fonder. And that if given enough time, Tom Eliot might actually remember what we had once shared and discover that he still needed—and wanted it.

* * *

Sabbaticals, I knew, were designed to refresh the academic soul. But, as the new school year started, I felt more and more restless.

Would I turn into Amelia Ford, going on 20 years teaching history? Would I become the next Emily Brown, spending 30 years at Milwaukee-Downer? Of course; everyone loved Miss Brown, but I knew the girls also laughed behind her back at all of her elderly eccentricities.

Will I ever want to leave? Will I know when the time has come?

I had been careful not to encourage Tom. He wrote that he had, in fact, finally joined the Anglican Church. William Stead had helped arrange his baptism in a small country church, away from his disapproving literary friends. Tom's wit had always been a delightful contrast to the pieties of Father and Uncle John. I hoped he didn't lose that in the process.

As the school year unfolded, our letters shifted to more scholarly topics. His latest enclosed the speech he had just delivered to the Shakespeare Association. Inside, he had written: "E.H. from T. S.E. 1927." It would have been nice if he had chosen to sign it "Tom." Still, I liked the intimacy of the initials. To the world, he was "T. S. Eliot," but to me, he was "T. S. E."

Much of the essay seemed esoteric, but then I came to these words:

"What every poet starts from is his own emotions...his nostalgia, his bitter regrets for past happiness—or for what seems happiness when it is past."

Was it possible to transform regrets into poetry? Had Tom made use of our memories? I wished I could find more of them in his poetry, amid all the disturbing images and the often-bitter words.

It was not the stuff of which my own memories were made.

* * *

I could always count on Amelia Ford to keep me up to date on the news of the world, at least as it was communicated through the pages of *TIME* magazine.

"In the Foreign News section," Amelia said, handing over the latest issue. "There's an article about your friend, T. S. Eliot."

I leafed through and found a photo of Tom, and underneath a cutline: "The reader must judge for himself." The article was headlined "New Subject."

> *Last week a sleek, brilliant citizen of the U.S. became a subject of His Britannic Majesty King George V. He is Thomas Stearns Eliot, relative of the late Charles William Eliot, President Emeritus of Harvard University....His many adverse critics, in no wise surprised by his change of nationality, hint that a certain superciliousness toward U.S. letters caused him to feel more at home in England, where neo-literary figures abound profuse as the autumnal leaves.*

It was a sarcastic commentary, I noted, that would only reinforce Tom's opinion that he had made the right decision. But would it always be like this? Would Tom never muster the courage to be the one to break his own news to me? I didn't mind learning bits from Eleanor, but didn't I deserve better than the thousands of faceless readers of *TIME?*

Was it not enough for him to go to Oxford, marry an Englishwoman, and become an Anglican? Did he have to disavow America, too? Was he afraid that if he did not draw one more irrevocable line, it would be too easy to slink back home to his family?

Or even too easy to come crawling back home to me?

* * *

The first snowfall was the signal for Emily Brown to swing into action with her annual Christmas play. She began each school year scribbling down names in a thick notebook, secretly casting roles among the new girls and the old. The suspense built until the first snow fell. Then she arrived at chapel and finally announced the name of the girl who would make the perfect Fezzywig or Barnaby Rudge.

I thought it was madness to link a production schedule to the vagaries of the weather, but you didn't argue with Professor Brown. In her younger days, she had gone to England nearly every summer, looking for props or new inspiration for her plays. Back before the war, she had returned with the sheet music for a silly song about five golden rings and a partridge in a pear tree. Now it was a regular staple in her plays and echoed in the dining hall and chapel services as Christmas approached. I helped her as much as I could, but I learned, very early on, that she really didn't need much help.

I envied Professor Brown's focus, her drive, her energy. I would love to be able to spend every summer in England, free to visit Tom for longer than a furtive chat over tea, untethered from the leash of Edith's financial support.

"I wish I could go back to England this summer." My confession spilled out as I helped Miss Brown tidy up after one of our last rehearsals before the December show.

She peered over the rims of her glasses. "What's stopping you?"

"I can't afford it."

"Nonsense," she replied. "If I could afford it, you certainly can." She shut her notebook with a bang. "I did things differently when I was younger, traveled lighter, spent less money. I'll teach you some of my tricks."

She made good on her promise. It was possible, she explained, to find cheap lodgings in the university towns during the summer months. She knew where to inquire, and before long, I had located a place in Cambridge—at half the cost of what I would have paid to stay in the States.

Suddenly I felt liberated. I wrote Margaret Farrand to see if she would like to join me. We could live the life of students, pursue our academic interests, catch up on old times. I was thrilled when Margaret said yes.

And then I mustered the courage to write Tom:

I'm returning to England this summer. I will be traveling for a bit, then staying in Cambridge for a month, starting in late July. It would be good to see you again.

A few weeks passed, long enough for me to fret that he'd had a change of heart. But then his letter came.

Dear Emily,

I'm sorry it took me so long to write. A few weeks ago, The Criterion *lost its financial backer and I have been scrambling to try to keep it afloat. For now, at least, I think I have succeeded.*

I would like very much to see you. Please let me know when you will be in Cambridge and I will try to come visit.

It has been a while since I felt I had any poetry left in me. But I recently completed the enclosed poem, and it has just been accepted for publication. I am sending it along. I hope, as always, that it meets with your approval.

I was never sure what to expect when I began to read one of his poems. This one was called "Salutation."

There were odd, disturbing images and talk of bones and God and the Virgin Mary. The new Anglican Tom, I thought. And then he shifted perspective, addressing his words to a "Lady of Silences." "Calm and distressed." "Rose of memory." He spoke of love, both satisfied and unsatisfied. And then, close to the end, "...we did little good to each other...."

Does he still love me? Would he tell me if he did?

The Conversion

MARGARET'S PARENTS SAW US OFF in New York at the beginning of July. Our cabin was in Tourist Third Class, a comedown from past voyages financed by fathers or uncles. A stack of three bunks, with room for only one of us to get dressed at a time. No bell to ring for service; instead you stood in the cabin doorway and yelled for a steward. But Margaret was smart enough to slip ours a dollar on the first day, and he brought us hot water every morning.

Our third bunk was occupied by a curly-haired young woman named Beatrice Foster. She had been a city girl at Milwaukee-Downer but would not be returning in the fall. Instead her parents were sending her to Europe in the hope it would provide some more "finishing." They had asked Lucia if I would be willing to chaperone her for the ocean crossing, a request that was hard to turn down, particularly after they said they would sweeten it with a gift of some English pounds. Still I hated the prospect of a 19-year-old eavesdropping on my late-night talks with Margaret, when the two of us had so much to catch up on.

Our departure was chaotic. Margaret pronounced that Beatrice's motto should be "Let Close Calls Teach You Safety." Back in Milwaukee, I had told her the boat sailed at noon and to arrive an hour early. Over lunch, we discovered she had neither her tickets nor her passport; fortunately, they had been delivered to the boat, as was her unlabeled trunk. We were lucky when we just happened to spot it, sitting out on an open deck.

But once we got past that, Beatrice turned out to be a pleasant traveling companion. She tried to be neat and didn't stay out too late at night. And Margaret and I enjoyed prompting her to share all the details of her ship-deck flirtations, which seemed only to multiply with each passing day.

"Were we ever that young?" Margaret asked as we monitored Beatrice one morning from our chairs on the starboard deck.

I pulled my lap robe a bit tighter in the freshening breeze. "I think I was once. Half a lifetime ago."

The sun had finally come out, and the waves—and our stomachs—had finally settled after our first stormy days at sea. Now Beatrice provided most of our entertainment as she tried to manage the gaggle of seniors from Williams College who had taken a fancy to her. Between the two of us, Margaret had dubbed them "the four musketeers." They were on their way to a summer of motoring through France and Spain before returning home to go to work. Despite their wealthy pedigree, they seemed rather harmless—almost pre-war, we decided, in their manners, their drinking, and the respect they showed for women.

I nodded toward the young men. "I don't think they know how old we really are."

"I think you're right," Margaret replied. She closed her eyes and tilted her head back, taking in the sun. "I don't know what it is about this trip, but I feel so separated from my past. It's a wonderful feeling."

"You're not with your parents," I observed. "I feel the same way. It's very different from traveling with Edith and John. Oh, the food's terrible on our deck, and I'd give almost anything right now for a nice soak in a hot tub. But we're also free to be whatever we want to be." I smiled. "If we only knew what that was."

Margaret hesitated, her eyes squinting shut to block out the bright sunlight. "There's something I've been wanting to tell you. But I didn't want to share it in front of Beatrice."

"Oh?"

"I think I've met my soul mate."

"Margaret!" I knew I sounded more shocked than I intended. I glanced quickly from Beatrice, giggling within her circle of beaux, then back to my friend. Studious Margaret, who always seemed to have her nose buried in a book. Who still wrote long, long letters to her mother, beginning with "Dearest Lamb." How could Margaret have fallen in love—and without letting me know?

"His name is Willard. Willard Thorp." She began speaking more quickly as she warmed to her topic. "He studied theater at Harvard, and then President Neilsen hired him to teach speech and rhetoric at Smith.

"Why didn't he see you off when we left?"

"That's the hard part. He's at Princeton now, getting his doctorate. Now that he's there, I realize how much I miss him. I think I'm in love with him and I think he's in love with me. But it's so hard to figure out how we can be together and still pursue our studies."

I felt a mix of happiness for Margaret and yet my own feelings of regret. I did not know what to say.

Finally, she spoke up again. "There's something else you should know. He's younger than me. Eight years younger. It doesn't bother me, and it doesn't bother him. But it bothers my parents. They're worried about his motives." She let out a nervous laugh. "It's not as if I'm an heiress and he's after my money." She hesitated. "But I am careful about what I tell my mother."

She smiled. "I hope you can meet him soon because I know the two of you have so much in common."

A younger man. I remembered Oggie Perkins, but eight years younger? I remembered my students' boyfriends or their older brothers. It was hard for me to imagine loving someone that much younger. My mothering instincts always seemed to kick in too quickly.

I thought back to Amy's summer flirtation. Her bashful younger actor had since turned into a literary phenomenon. Estlin Cummings was now celebrated alongside Tom Eliot for his distinctive poetry—and unique punctuation. Did Amy have a glimpse of that future and decide she wanted a more conventional husband?

"I'm happy for you," I said at last, trying to keep my voice even. I hoped Margaret did not read my emotions. A few days before I left Milwaukee, I learned Zona Gale was getting married—at the age of 53, no less. Her husband was an older man, a widower from Portage whom she had known since childhood. What was happening to all my independent women friends?

"You never mentioned Willard in your letters."

"I hope you're not upset..."

"Why would I be?"

"I think I didn't trust my happiness," Margaret said softly. "I think I was afraid that if I talked about Willard, it might tempt the Fates. I'm still worried that it could all disappear."

She paused. "But to be honest, there *was* something else. I didn't want my happiness to come between the two of us. I know you still love Tom, and I know that he isn't free to marry you. I didn't want to cause you any pain."

I appreciated that she felt that way. But I knew Margaret wouldn't be the one to cause me pain. Tom and I were perfectly capable of doing it ourselves.

* * *

I had always loved the ambience of Harvard Yard, but even Massachusetts Hall was a mere pup compared with the venerable colleges and chapels of the other Cambridge. I had visited Oxford with Edith, but we had made the trip on a dreary day when a cold rain made the soot-covered buildings seem even bleaker. My friends had always said that Cambridge was the prettier town, and as the long sunny summer days stretched on, I had to agree.

I was not sure what to expect of our landlords, the Lings, but it turned out they came from northern England, not China, and were very friendly and gracious. They had fallen on hard times and had turned to renting out their top two floors while they lived with their little girl in the English basement. Our rooms were far better than I expected, furnished simply but with everything we needed, and spotlessly clean. On the top floor, Margaret and I each had our own bedroom, and down below, our large bay window looked out on the Cam River itself, a narrow canal in this particular stretch. The Lings took pride in their three garden allotments and treated us to salads with fresh lettuce and honey from Mr. Ling's beehives for our tea and our toast. As she straightened things up, Mrs. Ling also filled our rooms with vases of garden flowers—love-in-a-mist, coreopsis, and huge white African daisies.

The buses *did* rumble down Chesterton Road at daybreak, but we didn't mind the noise because we were eager to get to the library early. We had been nervous the first day, wondering whether we would ever pass muster with the guardians of the collections to get our reading cards. But once we mastered that bureaucracy, we were like children in a candy store. Margaret still wanted to pursue a doctorate; she was fascinated by the Victorians, particularly Charles Kingsley, who had graduated from Magdalene College nearly a century before. But she could just as easily decide, on the spur of the moment, to request a first edition from 1585 and get lost in it for hours. For my part, I was determined to learn all I could about the theater—English, French, German, historic, and contemporary. It was wonderful to look up from my books and see the towering spires of King's Chapel out the open window as the songs of the chapel choir's morning rehearsal drifted inside.

On the weekends we did day trips, but when Tom wrote that he could arrange to come the following Friday, we quickly changed our plans. He proposed taking the late-afternoon train and suggested we meet for dinner at The Eagle, an old pub near Corpus Christi College. I asked Margaret if she would like to join us for a drink. I knew my nerves would be steadier if she came along.

"I don't want to impose," she replied.

"Don't be silly," I said. "Besides, it won't hurt *your* academic career if you get to know T. S. Eliot."

It had been two years since I had seen Tom, 15 years since he had left Boston. Next year he would turn 40. Where had the years gone? It was easy to feel young and alive here in Cambridge, among the eager students, barely scarred by The Great War. But as they passed us by, they probably saw two middle-aged women, our faces showing more of the lines of life's pains and disappointments.

And what would Tom see? I was careful, as always, when I picked out my dress for our dinner. I settled on a lightweight summer dress patterned with bright flowers. My skirts were shorter than I once wore them, but my neckline was still discreetly high. My vacation budget did not include any money for a London shopping spree, but we were surprised to discover that even wearing last year's styles, we were more fashionable than most of the women we saw.

I knew the stage tricks for making a woman look younger than her years, but I still applied less makeup than I would if I were acting. I knew I had an audience of one, and he would be sitting just a few feet away, on the other side of a table in a dimly lit pub.

My stomach knotted as Margaret and I found our seats in the wood-paneled restaurant. *This is just another role, and you've played it before.*

"There he is," I whispered as I caught sight of Tom taking off his bowler as he entered. He looked much as I remembered him, the slicked-down hair accentuating his large ears, reminding me of the Lost Boys of Barrie's *Neverland*. And as always, the well-tailored suit, a vest even in summertime, a handkerchief folded into his breast pocket.

As I waved to help him find us, his face broke into a smile. He waited for a couple to pass by out the door. He was somebody now, but he still didn't barrel his way through crowds.

I rose to greet him; he gave me a quick kiss on the cheek. It was the careless kiss of a longtime friend—one step, I supposed, beyond a handshake.

"Tom, this is my longtime friend, Margaret Farrand. Margaret, Tom Eliot."

Tom extended his hand to shake Margaret's.

"I'm honored to meet you, Mr. Eliot."

"The pleasure is all mine, Miss Farrand. I've heard so much about you from Emily."

"Please," I interjected. "Enough of this 'Mr. Eliot' and 'Miss Farrand,' or I will abandon you both."

Tom's eyes twinkled. "Are you here as our chaperone, Margaret?"

"You'll have to ask Emily," she replied. "She insisted I had to meet you. I told her I would stay long enough to have a drink."

"Margaret's teaching English at Smith," I said. "She's interested in the work of Charles Kingsley. I was confident you would have an opinion of him."

Tom smiled. "Well, I do, but I wouldn't want to bore you with it...."

"Oh, please," Margaret replied. "I would be interested."

They ordered tall glasses of ale, and then Tom launched into a speech about Kingsley and his battles with the Catholic and Anglican hierarchies, the major themes of his *Hypatia*. Margaret listened as if hypnotized; I still marveled at the quickness of Tom's mind, the range of subjects he knew.

At last he came up for air—and a long sip from his glass. "I'm sorry," he said. "I don't usually talk so much. But once I get started on a topic like that, I sometimes find it hard to stop."

"You've given me much to think about," Margaret replied. "And now, as I promised, I'll be on my way." She rose from her chair, and Tom did, too. "It was a pleasure to meet you, Tom." She nodded to me. "I'll see you back home later on."

Tom retook his seat. The noise of the restaurant filled the silent void as more regulars arrived, greeting their friends and ordering "the usual."

So much time had been lost, I thought. So much to catch up on. But I was nervous about exploring that. I just wanted to be with him.

"You're looking well," I murmured at last. "Better, I think, than the last time I saw you."

"Yes," he replied. "I've been able to resolve some things."

"You've made some interesting choices."

"Becoming an Anglican?"

She nodded. "And an Englishman. I've been wanting to find out more about all of that."

He took a long quaff of ale. I was confident this was not the first time Tom had been asked to explain his decisions. But I had known the Boston Tom, the Tom from the long line of Unitarian Eliots. A different man than the one his British friends knew.

"I've made a mess of my life, Emily. I ruined Vivienne's life by marrying her. And after many years, and reading and studying with clergymen, I decided that the only way forward was to atone for my sins. Break with the past. Start over again spiritually. Try harder this time.

"I wrote you of my friend, William Stead. He has been a great help to me. First of all, he was a good listener. Then he guided me to the clergy who could help me do what I wanted to do. And so I was baptized quietly, without a lot of fuss. So, yes, I have become an Anglican. I have been baptized, I have made my confession."

I tried to act blasé. "And has it helped?"

"Yes," he replied, "it has."

I thought of his fevered arguments with Father, how he had avoided Aunt Sarah's funeral, the smugness of the poem he had written about his cousin's Sunday worship service. He had been so cynical back then. But I had ignored it; I was so awestruck by his brilliance, the joy of watching his quick mind wrestle with a question, even if it involved philosophers whose distinctions eluded me.

And even if I had not witnessed his religious struggle firsthand, I knew his conversion could not have been easy. There would be no blithe pieties, no blind adoption of a denominational rulebook. Tom had wrestled with the devils in his own life. Now he would face down the Devil himself if he had to.

I still admired that kind of confident commitment. Yet the lines he had drawn could hurt others, too. "You've renounced your citizenship," I observed. "Are you ever coming home again?"

"I hope so," he said. "My family wants me to visit, and my mother is declining....But the time never seems to be right."

"Too busy, I suppose." Immediately, I regretted the edge to my words.

"Yes," he replied.

The waiter returned, interrupting the awkward moment. I scanned the menu quickly, trying to focus on the choices, then made an easy one: a plate of fish and chips.

"I really liked the poem you sent me last fall." This was a safer topic. "The one about the Magi."

"Faber put it out in a holiday pamphlet. I imagine they'll want me to produce one every Christmas now." He hesitated. "What did you like about it?"

"You created a very real character this time." I smiled. "It reminded me of 'Prufrock.' It appealed to the actress in me."

"Have you been doing more acting?"

I shook my head. "I take on an occasional role in the college plays. But mostly I direct the students." I paused, making sure he was paying attention. "I have been doing some other engagements around Milwaukee. Poetry readings and scenes from plays. Lectures about the theater."

"I started work on a play myself a few years ago," he said. "But I never finished it. I've been thinking about another idea now."

"I'd love to read it when you're ready."

His dark eyes flickered with light, reminding me of the eager young Harvard student instead of the weary husband. "I would like that," he said. "My friends tend to focus on the themes and the verse. But you probably know more about stage direction than anyone I know."

He values my opinion. Not about the choices he had already made. Those were done, sometimes capriciously, sometimes not. But here was a new respect, one borne out of the work I had done, the reading, the studying, the acting, the directing. This was one world in which there was a chance I could be his peer.

The waiter arrived with our dinners, and the mood shifted, too. We settled into easier topics, sharing news of family and our mutual friends. I regaled him with funny stories about the college's annual Hat Hunt and Professor Brown's Christmas plays, happy that I could make him laugh again. I told him about our ocean crossing, how Margaret and I had used a nightgown and our red bed-curtains to transform Beatrice into a Grecian statue for the masquerade. About our final night with the boys from Williams, how one had juggled oranges and I performed Ruth Draper's comic monologue about the Italian lesson.

"Hank, Clint, Curt, and Bill," I remembered out loud. "Their names could not have been more perfect for rhyming. So Margaret and I lay in our bunks the night before our last dinner party, and we made up limericks for the place cards." I paused, testing whether I could still remember one. "There once was a boy named Bill. Of Beatrice, he never got his fill...."

My tongue was loosened by the glass of ale, but I was happy to see Tom laughing. "Perhaps I should stick to free verse!" I said, taking another sip.

But no matter how hard I tried to keep things light, happy, and uncomplicated, a cloud always seemed to cross over our table. Tom had been forced to find new backers for his magazine, to cut back the production cycle. His longtime secretary had contracted tuberculosis and had to resign; she was expected to die any day now.

And Vivienne? Her latest diagnosis? How he had "ruined her life" by marrying her? Thankfully, there was no more talk of that.

We finished off with cups of tea and generous slices of apple pie. At last, Tom signaled the waiter to bring him the bill.

"What brings you to Cambridge?" I asked. Of course, the answer, I hoped, was "you," but that masked my real questions: "What did you tell your colleagues?" and "What did you tell your wife?"

"I didn't lie to anyone," he said quickly. "I simply told them I was going on a retreat. Which is true in a way. But no one knows I'm in Cambridge."

Then he answered my unspoken question. "Vivienne and I don't spend much time together now. Our home is under repair right now. She is often off taking treatments or visiting friends. In the meantime, I have places I go when I need a quiet place to do my work. No one would think it strange for us to be apart."

There was a sad look in his eyes. His gaze drifted away, lost in distant memories. At last he spoke again.

"Do you remember that garden party we went to, out at Ben Fuller's farm?"

I nodded. *Of course I do.*

"You were right about Bertrand Russell."

I saw the pain on his face. "Do you want to tell me more?"

He hesitated. "Suffice it to say, he gave us support when we needed it...but then took advantage of Vivienne's neediness."

I wanted to know more, but not at Tom's expense.

"Shall we go?" he asked. I nodded.

It was late enough now that the sun had finally set. But the air was soft and warm, and as the lights came on in the dormitories that lined the River Cam, the effect was magical.

"Point me in the right direction," he said, "and I'll see you home."

"Do you know Cambridge?"

"I know Oxford better, of course. But I was here in February and back for a speech in May. I've decided I like Cambridge better. It has a more interesting mix of people. Oxford seems rather boring by comparison."

Then he added, as if to reassure me, "But I still don't know that many people here."

I gave him the directions, and we strolled the way we used to, this time picking our steps more carefully on the old cobblestoned streets.

"Our place is right along the river," I said. "Margaret found an old canoe for the summer and taught me how to paddle."

"The weather is supposed to be fine tomorrow," he said. "What would you like to do?"

"I think I would like to go punting."

He stopped and turned to me, his face happy with surprise. "This is a new Emily," he said.

Yes, I thought, *this is your new Emily.*

"I've watched the boats go by on the river," I explained, "and I thought I'd like to give it a try."

"I don't think I'm up to that sort of thing anymore."

"You don't have to do the work. I've talked to my landlady. There's a place near the center of town where we can rent a boat and hire a guide. We could pack a picnic lunch and make a day of it."

"You've figured it all out, haven't you?"

"Well, only if you'd like to do it." I braced myself for disappointment.

"All right," he said, warming to the idea. "I'll be back bright and early in the morning."

* * *

The punt glided through the river like a whisper, the quiet broken only by the water running off the young man's pole and the laughter from the boats that passed on either side of us. Tom had made the arrangements before he came around to the Lings', contracting to pay the young man from Scudamore's what he would have earned for a day's worth of regular tours.

The young guide proposed heading to the weir near Grantchester, avoiding the tourists who were more interested in viewing the backs of the college buildings, pressed up against the river's edge. Mrs. Ling had organized a lunch—apples and cheeses and neatly trimmed sandwiches of cucumber and watercress fresh from their garden plot. She added a ground blanket to make the picnic complete.

I made half-hearted protests about abandoning Margaret, but she just laughed and shooed me away. She had plenty of books still waiting to be read.

It was a postcard-perfect day, the blue sky defined by a few high, puffy clouds that never seemed to block the sun. I was glad I had packed my umbrella to provide some shade on the open stretches of the river. I wished it was the kind of frilly parasol I had owned back in Chestnut Hill rather than the utilitarian brolly I always packed around England. But it would have to do. Like my umbrella, I was different now: older, more practical, better traveled. I had new priorities.

From my perch facing the rear of the boat, I studied our young punter. He was a local youth who introduced himself simply as "Hugh." He took pride in his work, seeming to understand that a job well-done might be rewarded with a larger tip from us middle-aged folks. I was glad Tom had chosen a quiet lad instead of one of the college men, eager to show off his knowledge of the trees, the birds, the local history. It was safer, too: There was little chance Hugh would recognize the famous poet in his boat.

But what did Hugh see? If any sparks flew between us, I suspected he would be oblivious to them. For now, he concentrated on picking his path carefully, avoiding other punts on the most crowded stretch of the river, and placing his pole carefully, then letting it slide gracefully through his hands.

Tom sat across from me, his eyes shaded by the brim of a straw hat. He had traded his tweeds for crisp summer whites, a loose shirt, and pleated trousers. He seemed relaxed and content. I was grateful we could still be that way, back in each other's company.

"What are you thinking?" I asked when we had pulled away from the fleet of younger couples.

He laughed softly. "I was remembering how seductive this is. I was thinking back to my college days, when I was still capable of steering a punt. I did it both here and in Oxford. Most of the fellows had gone off to war, and suddenly I was surrounded by young women. And there were dances and outings on the river....And the next thing I knew, I was married."

He looked at me sadly. "I'm sorry," he said. "I didn't intend to talk about that."

"It's all right."

We were silent for a moment. "Why didn't we ever go boating on the Charles?" I asked.

"It wasn't as pleasant as this," he replied. "The rowing was much more intense, more competitive. And the river was wider and rougher."

"Do you miss rowing?"

"Yes," he replied. "I miss the solitude of the river, I miss the rhythm of the stroke, the way it freed up my mind. I even miss the exercise, odd as that may seem. There is none of that now. Only work, and going home, and more work...and tending to whatever craziness I find once I get home."

"Would you like to give it a try, sir?" Hugh must have been listening after all.

"No," Tom said with a laugh. "I would probably fall overboard and you would have to rescue me."

As we drew near Grantchester, the river grew wilder, the college buildings giving way to open fields, and the banks scrubby with purple loose strife and forget-me-nots. Tom and Hugh began mulling potential landing spots, looking for a shady willow and a low place where the punt could be nosed up to the bank. Hugh turned toward land and at the last minute grabbed the coiled line and jumped onto the bank. Once the punt was secure, Tom offered me his hand, and Hugh helped me negotiate my way up the muddy bank.

Tom tossed Hugh a couple of coins, then checked his watch. "Go have lunch on us, then come back in a couple of hours. We should be ready to head back by then."

"Thank you, sir," Hugh said as he retreated with the punt. I stepped around under the tree, then snapped the wool blanket open on the softest, flattest spot I could find. I opened up Mrs. Ling's wicker basket and began unpacking the food.

Tom stretched out on the blanket beside me, resting his jaw in his hand so he could still take in the view of the narrow river.

I handed him a sandwich. "On a day like today, I can see why you wanted to become an Englishman..."

"...but you still don't fully understand it," he said, finishing my thought.

I shook my head. "What does your family think?"

He laughed. "I think they have given up trying to figure me out." He paused. "I'm not sure my mother actually knows I've done it. She is becoming frailer, and my brother and I agreed there was no reason to tell her."

I don't have the luxury of ignorance. I could well imagine how Tom's mother would react. Renouncing his citizenship was a rejection of his family, his friends, his past. Why did he keep drawing himself closer to Vivienne's world?

"I can't get over how quiet it is here," Tom said. "There is so little quiet in my life these days."

"But surely at your office," I suggested, "when you're writing or editing...."

"Yes and no," he replied. "It may be quiet, but the demands never stop. I must have sent out a dozen letters this week, and there will be a dozen more waiting to be written when I get back."

He polished off another sandwich, then laid his head down on the blanket. "I've given up on the notion of getting a good night's sleep. I come home from the office. I do some more work. I put my head down for a few hours, and then I get up and do some more work. And before I know it, it's time to go to the office again."

I finished off an apple, then wiped my fingertips on my napkin. I adjusted my position to rest my back against the slope of the tree trunk. "Come here," I said, "and put your head on my lap."

There was a long silence, a too-long moment in which I feared I had miscalculated badly. But then wordlessly, Tom inched his way closer to me and nestled his head in the soft pillow of my thigh.

As he closed his eyes, his jaw seemed to relax, his lips turning up in a smile. I exhaled deeply, then placed my hand lightly across his chest. I felt it rise slowly with each of his breaths, the time lapse between them growing longer as his fatigue finally gave over to sleep.

There was a time when I would have been annoyed if Tom had fallen asleep in my company. Now I closed my eyes and resolved to remember every detail of this moment. The warmth of the sun on my cheek, the dappled shadow of the tree, and Tom, all in white, his cheek against the crisp fabric of my skirt.

It would be heaven to remain here for hours. But what about tomorrow? What happened when Tom boarded the train, leaving me on my own again? Could I go on living like this?

But what was the alternative? Wasn't it better to know a few blissful moments, however short they might be, than the sterile life I was leading? Oh, that life was satisfying in its own way and certainly better than those first months after Tom got married. But would I ever be able to draw the boundaries, wrap up my emotions into neat little packages, and put them away when he was gone?

A breeze rustled through the trees, as if a spirit were whispering to me. *You've done it your whole life.*

When you were shuffled out of your home, when you were never quite sure which woman to call your mother, you learned how to protect yourself, to lock it all up inside. Because if you didn't, there was always the chance you would discover that no one really wanted you.

I felt Tom stir, readjusting his position. His eyes opened slowly, blinking at the sudden bright light. I wondered how long Hugh would be gone and wished that I could slip him a few more coins and ask him to stay away just a little bit longer.

"How long have I been sleeping?" he asked.

"Not that long," I replied. "I'm sure you needed it."

"Indeed, I did." He rolled over onto his side. "It was a very comfortable spot."

"I'm glad."

"Emily...."

The languid smile was gone. I could tell the grim penitent had returned, along with his guilt and the rules he had imposed on himself.

"Don't," I said. "Whatever you were going to say, just don't."

I pulled myself away and began packing up the remains of our lunch. The moment had ended, and up the river, Hugh came into view again, poling the punt back toward us. I closed my eyes and took a deep breath. *I can't keep doing this.*

Hugh drew up beside us, then tossed Tom the line but scrambled quickly to take charge of it. I supposed he saw "an old man," a man who moved slowly, not the boy who had skippered sailboats out of Gloucester, who knew which knot to use when securing a boat to a piling. Tom helped me fold the blanket and clean up the remains of our stay. Then we loaded the gear back into the punt and set off back down the river toward Cambridge.

* * *

We took a break before dinner, returning to our lodgings to shed our clothes, shower, and have a rest. This time, Tom had chosen a quieter spot to eat, a place with tablecloths and candles and a bit more privacy.

But even that was disturbed. A professor Tom knew caught sight of him and stopped by our table to chat. Introductions were made, but his name meant nothing to me. Tom apologized for not responding to his submission to *The Criterion*. He would track it down first thing on Monday and give him the answer he deserved.

"Everyone wants a piece of you," I observed as the professor retreated.

"Everyone deserves an answer," he replied. "I know how important it was when I was starting out."

"I think you have trouble saying, 'no.' But you always were a hard worker."

"It keeps me diverted," he said, his voice heavy with resignation.

"And what about your own writing?"

"Honestly?"

I nodded.

"I fear my best is already behind me. Oh, there are still plenty of words. But there is little poetry left. And that makes me sad."

I picked at the food on my plate, wondering what had happened to my appetite.

"What time do you have to leave tomorrow?" I asked at last.

"There's a train at two. I think I should try and catch that one." He hesitated. "I would like to go to church in the morning. Will you come with me?"

"Of course I will."

We finished off our desserts and lingered over glasses of sherry. And then it was time for him to walk me home.

"Thank you for humoring me today," I said as we crossed over Kitchen Bridge. "It was a very nice day. I will remember it for a long time."

"So will I," he said softly.

Somewhere along the river bank, an old song drifted out a window from one of the colleges. The recording was scratchy and showing its age, but that only added to its charms.

If you were the only girl in the world, and I was the only boy.

I remembered the song. It had been popular during the war, when Tom had disappeared and young men were heading off to fight. Back then it was a sad song, but tonight it was something totally different.

A garden of Eden just made for two
With nothing to mar our joy

I felt Tom's hand in the small of my back, pulling me into his arms. He took my wrist and guided me in a circle at the top of the bridge, oblivious to the other pedestrians. Our feet glided effortlessly despite the weathered surface of the bridge under our feet. After all these years, we still fit. *We still share the same rhythms, even if they have changed.*

The song ended, but Tom still held me close.

"That was nice," he whispered.

"I've missed dancing with you," I admitted, then felt vulnerable that I had.

"I have, too."

He let me go, and I gave my skirt a tug. We were back on the streets of Cambridge, a town filled with people who knew T. S. Eliot by reputation, even if they didn't recognize his face. We began walking again, and within a matter of minutes, we were back in front of the Lings' home.

"Services at King's Chapel start at 10:30," he told me. "I'll stop by a bit before that to pick you up."

"Good night, then."

"Good night, Emily."

I tiptoed in quietly, not wanting to wake Margaret. I was not ready to share the story of my day.

Moonlight pooled through the window of my bedroom, letting me find my nightgown without the jolting brightness of an electric lamp. The cotton felt cool against my skin as I settled onto the soft mattress and pulled the sheet up to my neck. I closed my eyes, imagining I was back on a picnic blanket, finding a comfortable spot on the tall grass.

I remembered the weight of Tom's head in my lap, the touch of his hand helping me into the punt, the moment when my old dance partner impulsively pulled me into his arms again. I stamped it as "a happy time" and resolved to bottle up the memory. Someday soon I would need it in Milwaukee.

* * *

No matter your faith, Europe's Gothic cathedrals could not help but take your breath away.

As we took seats just off the chapel's center aisle, my eyes drifted heavenward as the stonemasons had intended. The chapel was narrower than most of the cathedrals I had visited, but that only accentuated the extraordinary height of its ceiling, where the ribs spread out into an intricate fan design. Margaret and I had come before to listen to the choir at evensong, but this time my focus was on Tom as I tried to understand the puzzle of his conversion.

I did not doubt its authenticity. I could see the reverence in his face as his fingers dipped into the holy water and he quickly genuflected. I respected his rituals but felt no compunction to mimic them. I trailed him down the aisle, letting him decide where he wanted to sit. Then I took my place in the pew, my hands folded in my lap as Tom knelt in silent prayer for what seemed like a very long time.

My own thoughts wandered in a different direction. The Unitarians of Boston could be doctrinaire in their own way, but I had never believed there was only one right path to God. I had attended many kinds of services in many different settings. I never had the chance to satisfy my curiosity about the rituals of Judaism. But through funerals and weddings and christenings and baptisms, I had experienced most flavors of Christianity. I respected them all—as long as there was no hypocrisy.

And so even as Tom's newfound devotion puzzled me, I respected him for making the journey. Just as his mind had debated all those arcane philosophical questions back at Harvard, he had ruminated over the nature of God, of sin, of the possibility of redemption.

Yet I preferred just to let the spirit of the chapel wash over me, in the Bach harmonies now echoing from the organ or the shimmering colors of the soaring windows. They put my soul at peace.

The service began to unfold. I knew most of the music; the scriptures, too. It was a good place to be on a Sunday morning. But as the hour wore on, my mind began to wander. I thought of the prayer Lucia intoned every time she led a chapel service. "Help us to stand for the hard right against the easy wrong."

Was I settling for "the easy wrong"? Was it a sin to be here with a married man? Resting by the riverside, sharing intimate dinners, and dancing in the moonlight? Where did God draw the line between a loving friendship and infidelity? In His eyes, was the sex act the only thing that made it wrong?

I did not know the answer, but I did not have to find it today. The organist broke into the recessional, but we remained seated, savoring the wonderful music until the last chord died away.

"I don't get to concerts the way we used to," Tom observed as we walked back up the aisle.

"Nor do I."

We joined the line of congregants, murmured greetings to the rector at the door, then stepped out into the bright morning light.

"Where to now?" Tom asked.

"Wherever you like."

"I have to check out of my rooms. Let's head there and then find a place for lunch."

It was another warm summer day, but the mood had shifted. Two days ago, the hours had stretched before us with limitless possibility. Now we were only minutes away from the dreaded goodbye.

This is the price you have to pay for loving him.

He led us to a restaurant opposite the inn, giving me instructions while he retreated to fetch his bag. In the old days, I would have known exactly what to order for him. But he was a stranger now, a Brit following the breakfast customs of his adopted land. He specified a full English breakfast, complete with a sausage and *toe-mah-toe* on the side. I settled for a crumpet.

He returned just as our food arrived. He took his seat, then checked his watch. *Why can't we just be?*

Then he gazed at me intently. "When we were having our picnic yesterday, I wanted to tell you something, but you made me stop before I could say it."

I braced myself for whatever was coming.

"I've taken a vow of celibacy."

What was I supposed to say? Why did he feel he had to tell me? I was not some anonymous priest, hiding out behind a confessional screen. Nor was I the kind of woman who worked the docks of Boston or London, puzzled why my customer had suddenly gotten cold feet.

"What does your wife have to say about that?"

"She doesn't care," he said softly. "We haven't had relations for years."

I didn't need to know that, either.

"I'm sorry," I replied.

"Don't be. It has made things easier. It has helped me focus on my faith instead."

Anglican. Englishman. Celibate. *What was next?*

"I hope I haven't burdened you by telling you that."

"No. Of course not."

"It's just...it's just that I always felt you understood me, Emily. Everyone else...my parents, my professors, my friends, my wife...everyone was always trying to mold me into something different. You never did. And so I wanted you to know. Because, unlike all the others, I thought you would understand."

My heart soared at his affirmation. But still, I didn't understand. My gift to him was to accept him, not to argue or nag. But why had he told me? Was it the easiest way to make me understand the state of his marriage? Or had he feared I would demand something more for myself?

"I want to see you off at the station," I declared.

He looked startled but did not object. I had made up my mind last night, in the hours when I had lain awake. I could not bear to have him disappear again. So I needed to say goodbye the proper way—to shake his hand, put him on the train, and watch it pull away. It would resolve nothing, of course. But it would put a full stop, as the English would say, to this particular chapter.

And so we walked to the station together. I knew the train would not wait long, so if there were words to be said, they needed to be said now.

"When will you come back to England?" he asked.

"I don't know." It was the honest answer. My head was a muddle. I would have to check my accounts and see what I could afford. I had a job, students, and classes. But it was different here, and I loved it, even with all of my torments.

Down the track came a whistle, and then the chugging locomotive came into view.

"Please keep writing me," he said, his eyes turning earnest. "Your letters mean so much to me."

"I will."

He leaned over and brushed his lips against my cheek. My body remained taut and unforgiving. It was a public farewell, the kiss of a relative or a longtime friend. The show of affection between two celibates.

He opened the door of a coach and disappeared inside. There was no sign of him at a window. The whistle blew and the train pulled away, carrying him back to the life he had chosen.

* * *

"Did you have a good time?"

Margaret looked up from her book as I entered our sitting room, posing the inevitable question.

"Yes."

"Do you know when you'll see him again?"

"No."

The word hung in the air. Then she turned back to her book, signaling an end to the interrogation. "I was glad to get the chance to meet him."

I retreated to my room, thinking I, too, would try to read. But as I stretched out on the bed, my mind was still racing.

Around the faculty lounge in Milwaukee, we talked of Freud and Havelock Ellis and Margaret Sanger. I had read a few of the eye-opening novels that were making their way onto the best-seller lists. But what was the nature of desire? What did it mean for men and for women? My real knowledge was scanty, my sensibilities shaped by years in Boston rather than Bloomsbury.

If I were a bride approaching my wedding night, there were women I could turn to: Edith for one, Amy for another. But could I expect them to be honest about the men I knew so well? Would they even be honest about themselves?

And so, I had to admit, Tom's declaration brought some relief. He was not searching for a furtive romance or a late-night tryst. But I still remembered the weight of his head in my lap as we had rested on the riverbank. I remembered his gaze across the candlelit table. I remembered how he had pulled me close for our dance on the bridge. I remembered the intensity with which he murmured his words to God.

I pressed my fingers to my lips, recalling long-ago kisses. Then I reached between my legs, testing out the tender spots.

What else was there to remember?

I replayed the scenes over and over, but I still couldn't arrive at the answer.

* * *

Professor Brown blew into Cambridge near the end of our stay, and I invited her to camp out on our couch. We took her up to Grantchester, and she wore us out with the list of all the things she wanted to see. She was up at dawn, ready to visit two cathedrals and a garden in between. It was as if she had a long list and only a few years left in which to check off all the items.

After seeing her off at the train station, we collapsed back on the sofa in our sitting room.

"Is she always like that?" Margaret asked. "Back at school, I mean."

I nodded. "I feel like I need the Christmas break to recover from helping her with her pageant."

"Does she ever slow down long enough to actually read something?"

"What do you mean?" I asked, suddenly feeling protective of the older woman.

"Oh, she's mastered her Dickens and Hardy, that's for sure," Margaret replied. "The characters, the towns, the sites. But does she go deeper than that?"

"I've never sat in on one of her classes, but she does have a master's from Columbia."

"I think you're deeper than she is. If Emily Brown is the best your English Department has to offer, I think you could do better than that."

Her Seven Sisters snobbery surprised me a little. "But I don't even have a degree!"

"You know drama, Emily. I've seen you act, I've listened to you dissect every play we've seen over here. You've learned it all by doing it. You should consider getting out of Milwaukee." She smiled. "I daresay you could even be producing plays in England."

"And I think the summer heat has gotten to you!"

Margaret dropped the subject, but for the rest of our days in England, I could not shake the nagging memory of her words. We had shed our old selves when we had sailed across the Atlantic, but now I questioned whether I would be able to find my old self when I returned.

Speaking Out

MILWAUKEE

1928

THE FOUR CLASS YEARS AT Milwaukee-Downer were identified by the colors of the rainbow: green for the grass of the college's lawns, yellow for the dandelions of July, and red for the berries of the hawthorn trees, the bricks of the campus buildings, and the oak leaves of fall.

I had arrived the same fall as a new Purple class, and thus I had always thought of that color as my own, purple like the violets of spring or the nosegay Tom had brought me backstage at Brattle Hall.

My first Purple class had graduated in 1925; another would graduate next June. The years rolled by so quickly now. Four years, eight years. I had been at Milwaukee-Downer twice as long as I had been at Simmons, but the time, it seemed, had passed twice as fast.

If Tom's life read like a newspaper serial—each letter detailing the stresses of a new publishing deadline, a new medical crisis, a new apartment—my own life was entirely predictable. Nine months were strait-jacketed by the academic calendar. The school year began. The Mountebanks staged a play and Miss Brown ushered in Christmas with her annual production. Spring brought the Hat Hunt, May Day, and another maypole dance. The Mountebanks staged their second production, then the big final Commencement play, outdoors in the open expanse of the Hawthornden. Three months of vacation, and then it started all over again.

But my summer in Cambridge left me more restless than revived. I remembered Margaret's advice that it was time for me to move on. And I knew my heart was in England now, not on the banks of Lake Michigan.

* * *

As the years had passed, Lucia had grown as a college president—but not always in ways that I liked.

She was disturbed by all the changes around her: the smoking, the drinking, the frequent curfew violations. She decided to clamp down even harder. When the college codified all her new regulations, the rulebook was 20 pages longer than the year before.

There were new rules about who could have a radio and who could drive, what girls could do on Sundays, new procedures for checking out when they left the dorm. More rules, I argued, only led to more rebellion, but she was insistent. Standards had to be maintained, and violators would be expelled.

The miscreants' parents were outraged; the punishments usually outweighed the crimes. Tuition payments and family reputations were at stake. But Lucia remained firm—and the trustees backed her up.

I was glad I was no longer a dorm matron, forced to serve as Lucia's prison warden. What would she do if she found out I traveled to England every summer, hoping to spend a few hours alone with a married man?

But for now, she remained my biggest champion. *Theatre Arts Monthly* had put us on the map by including The Mountebanks in its annual list of established Little Theater companies. "It's high time we put something in the catalog about the drama program," she told me. So I tried to capture why I loved the theater so much:

"First, because in all of us lies inherent the love of 'make believe'; because the creation of anything is in itself thrilling; because even the work of that creation is a resource and a relaxation in our too highly organized, busy lives; because the elements of the drama demand the use of instruments we all possess, but allow to rust—voice and body; and because we learn and profit from the discipline of standards any art requires—intelligent, thorough application, sharpened perception, quickened imagination, sympathetic understanding, control of self, and a consequent freedom of self...."

How free did I really want to be? How much was I willing to risk? The rhythms of the academic year, once familiar and comforting, now seemed stifling. I missed Boston. I missed England and the rest of Europe, too.

And I now wanted the freedom to be there when Tom needed me, through all the seasons of the year.

* * *

Another Christmas pageant. Another Lantern Night of caroling to the orphanage, the hospital, the old persons' home. The dorms emptied out for the holidays. Professors and matrons departed for family celebrations, but this year I stayed behind. It was difficult to be alone at Christmas, but I wanted to save up my money.

Outside, the winter winds whipped up from the lake, but inside Johnston Hall, I loved the unusual quiet. There were others in the building—the cook, a janitor, a professor or two who, like me, had nowhere else to go. It was a good time to ponder where I should be headed.

I had become a professor. I had starred with the Wisconsin Players. I had mounted *Sherwood* with a cast of 125. The Mountebanks were a recognized theater troupe; they had been invited to perform off-campus this spring. What was there left to accomplish?

If Helen Keller and Robert Frost could make the rounds as professional speakers, I could do it, too. And now that even Edith was promoting herself as a guide for English garden tours, how could she possibly object?

It would be performing again, holding the attention of an audience, basking in the glow of their applause. Sharing my knowledge, marketing my skills. Positioning myself as an expert on something, even if it was Broadway instead of Bergson.

I could take the risk. I knew agents in London and Boston. I would write to them, get some dates on my calendar. I could become a woman of the world—the kind of woman Tom Eliot would want to marry if anything ever happened to Vivienne, if Tom ever became free.

I changed into my nightgown and climbed into bed, pulling the heavy blankets up tight to my chin. Their warmth provided comfort and confidence.

I would tell Lucia when the new term started—and steel myself now so that there was no chance she would be able to make me change my mind.

* * *

Lucia was not happy.

"How can you leave when everything we've worked for is finally in place?"

I had anticipated that argument. President Sabin had served for 30 years, and Lucia showed no signs of wanting to move anytime soon. She had become the complete college president, and there were only a handful of better opportunities for a woman.

"I need a change," I replied, straightening my back.

"Is there anything I could do to make you change your mind?" Lucia paused. "What if we changed your schedule so that you could do more acting?"

"It wouldn't make a difference."

"Do you have any speaking engagements lined up?"

"No," I conceded, "but I've made some good contacts. I didn't want to pursue them until I talked with you."

Lucia shook her head. "It seems very risky to me."

"There is some risk," I acknowledged. "But it's something I want to try."

Neither of us spoke for a moment. It fell to me to break the silence.

"I will never forget how you saved me, Lucia. You saw something in me and gave me a chance. I will always be grateful for that.

"But I'm like one of your students. It's time for me to graduate to a different life. I love teaching. I love directing. I love working with the girls. But I'm not committed to this life the way you are. Perhaps someday I will be ready to make that kind of commitment. But I know that if I stay here much longer, I'll grow stale and unhappy. And then I won't be doing the job you hired me to do."

Lucia paused. "I'm sorry you've reached that conclusion, but I appreciate your honesty. You realize, of course, that if your plans don't work out, I can't keep your job open."

"I understand."

The look on her face shifted then, from the sad gaze of an old friend to the impenetrable mask of a college president. "Very well, then. I think it best if we wait until the end of the term to announce your departure. I know the girls will be very disappointed. In the meantime, I will start putting out some feelers to find your replacement. If you have any suggestions, please let me know."

* * *

When The Mountebanks were admitted to the Wisconsin Dramatic Guild, the Woman's Club of Wisconsin asked us to present a program. There would be no stage or props, and we'd have to keep it short; the club still had business to conduct that day.

After much discussion, I came up with an idea. Three different balcony scenes: from *Pelléas and Mélisande, Cyrano de Bergerac,* and *Romeo and Juliet.* Seven parts in all; the cast would be able to fit into two cars for the trip across town.

"You should take a part, Miss Hale." Elsie Kraft, the club's vice president, was always quick to speak up. The rest of the girls agreed.

It had been years since I had done anything beyond Professor Brown's Christmas play. But as my students continued to plead with me, I realized this would be my "farewell" to Milwaukee.

"Which part should I take?" There was no obvious role for an older woman.

"Juliet," Elsie replied, waggling her eyebrows with delight.

The girls all laughed. "Perfect casting!" I declared. "I'm only 20 years too old!"

But the girls egged me on, and so I agreed. I chose Betty Jayne Biebler to play Romeo; I could count on Betty Jayne not to break down into giggles.

There was much to do, lines to coach, costumes to round up. But late at night, I still found time to study my lines, to try to remember what it felt like to be a young woman in love. And I knew now, more than ever, how Juliet must have felt, ignoring all those voices in her head, telling her that her love was doomed.

And all my
fortunes at the foot
I'll lay
And follow thee my
lord throughout the
world.

After Romeo and I had said our parting words, after the club women had applauded and plied us with tea and cookies, we piled back into our cars and headed back to campus.

"You were wonderful, Miss Hale," Elsie piped up. "I really believed you were a young girl in love."

I smiled. "You'd be surprised, Elsie, how much passion can still beat in an old heart like mine."

* * *

I made good on my promise to wait until Commencement to tell my students I was leaving, but my colleagues were another matter. Professor Brown insisted on organizing a farewell tea.

We swapped old memories and they wrote down my addresses, fighting back tears in between. It was different from when I had left Simmons. This time, I had become a peer in an academic sisterhood.

I postponed my packing as long as I could, grateful that I had not accumulated many things. Still, every item required a decision. There were the programs from the plays I had directed, photographs from the costume dramas. Father's dictionaries would still come along, as well as all my new reference books on the European theater. And then there were the poems and essays Tom had sent me, and the ever-growing box of his letters.

As I filled up the boxes, I came across the well-worn script. I scanned the notes I had written back when I had played Lulu Bett. It had taken me eight years instead of just two hours, but I had made a transformation of my own.

In the back I found the lines I had underlined:

I thought I wanted somebody of my own. Well, maybe it was just myself.

I was ready now to want myself.

Fantasy and Reality

IT WAS EXHILARATING AT FIRST. Returning to Boston, this time as Professor Emily Hale. Rejoining the old, comfortable networks of Cambridge and Chestnut Hill: Hales, Perkinses, Hinkleys, Halls, Briggses, and more.

In "the old days," everybody in the drama clubs was expected to sell tickets to our productions. Now I had to sell myself, even if Edith frequently mused that it was "not what ladies do."

First I managed to book a large meeting room at the Hotel Vendome for back-to-back weeks in November. I did the math; the deposit gobbled up most of my savings, but I had to make the investment. Uncle Philip and Aunt Irene lived there now, and the venue would provide a touch of class, not to mention a ready audience of relatives and neighbors. I picked the dates with equal care. I would wait until after Election Day but do it before Thanksgiving and December, when holiday parties would crowd everyone's calendar.

I picked my topics and titles carefully. I started with "The Popular Plays of the London Stage" and "Playhouses, Players, and Audiences of France and England." I was no expert, of course, and it had been more than a year since I had seen a play in England. But if I spoke with authority, I knew people would regard me as one. And if a "know-it-all" turned up in my audience, I would simply ask them to share their opinions.

Sarah Watters agreed to handle my ticket sales: $2 for one lecture, $3 to attend both. I made a list of old friends to approach to see if they would lend their name as a patroness. Edith registered her disapproval by demurring, but fortunately others did not. Aunt Irene signed on, and then Mrs. Hinkley did. After lunch with the Lefavours, the president's wife added her name. Mary Lee Ware was happy to support me, as were the Saltonstalls and Lucy Lowell, old friends from the Chestnut Hill church.

I had learned something about self-promotion from Lucia Briggs and Laura Sherry. All of my recent photographs showed me either surrounded by college girls or dressed for a costume drama. So I dug a bit deeper into my savings and made an appointment at the Bachrach studios. Wearing pearls and matching earrings, my hair sculpted into fashionable waves, I was pleased with how elegant I could make myself look.

The newspapers accepted almost anything these days to fill the society columns. So I took to my typewriter to tout myself to the rest of Boston:

"Miss Emily Hale, for eight years in charge of the dramatic work at Milwaukee-Downer College, Milwaukee, is to give two lectures....Miss Hale is the daughter of the Rev. Edward Hale, who formerly was assistant to the late Dr. Everett Everett Hale at the South Congregational Church in Boston and who later became minister of the Unitarian parish at Chestnut Hill."

The paper ran the names of all 26 of my patronesses.

When November 8th arrived, I was satisfied with the turnout. I managed to earn a bit more than my expenses. But I knew it wouldn't be easy. After the November 15th speech, I went back to my typewriter.

"In the Hotel Vendome this morning Miss Emily Hale gave the second of her two lectures on the Theater Abroad....Miss Hale made three classifications of French and English theater conditions, physical, social, and intellectual...."

The paper ran my story verbatim. I knew my talk was more entertaining than my news account suggested, but it was the best I could do. I needed to get my name back into the Boston papers, to resurrect as many of my old connections as I could.

In January, the Saturday Morning Club asked me to speak about the Irish theater, and the Massachusetts League of Women Voters asked me to play a part when they marked the 10th anniversary of the League of Nations. I played the emissary from Paraguay. It turned out to be one of the biggest roles, transcribed verbatim from the League of Nations' deliberations over that country's border dispute with Bolivia. Jessie Sayre, President Wilson's daughter, played the president of the League Council.

How far we had all come since women got the vote! It was hard to imagine I had once performed for the anti-suffragists, and now Jessie was running the state Democratic Party.

But despite all of my connections, it was hard to get speaking dates, and tougher still to get paid. The stock market crash had jolted everyone. I never had enough money to be comfortable playing the market, so my finances were still reasonably secure. But others were not so lucky. Friends were still buzzing about Beebo Bradlee. He had been an undergrad at Harvard with Oggie Perkins and Leverett Saltonstall and played halfback on the college's undefeated football team. Right out of school, he had landed as a runner with a bank, and within a few years was promoted to vice president. One day he was a rich man; the next day all his wealth disappeared. Word was he was now going door-to-door, trying to peddle the products of his old teammates.

In the Back Bay, of course, it was still important to keep up appearances. But even my wealthiest friends were more careful with their cash. Learning more about the European theater was one thing they could take a pass on if they had to.

* * *

For the next round of speeches, I moved to the Commander Hotel in Cambridge. "Fantasy and Reality" would cover the Shaw Festival at Great Malvern and the state of modern poetry. My audiences seemed to respond best when I read poems or did dramatic readings. Eleanor and Amy signed on quickly, along with many of our friends. Even Ada Briggs.

"I trust you're going to read some of Tom's poems," Eleanor teased.

"Of course," I replied with a smile. "People would think it odd if I didn't."

I saw less of Eleanor and Amy than I once did; their lives were moving in such different directions. Eleanor was trying to find backers to take her full-length script about Jane Austen to Broadway, now with the help of new best friend Eva Le Gallienne.

Amy, meanwhile, was playing the role of a Boston lawyer's wife. But she and Dick had failed to produce all the children the de Gozzaldis had expected. For now, the Cambridge Social Dramatic Club took the place of a family.

Unlike them, I had no choice but to keep trying to earn a living. Edith and John had invited me to go back to Europe this summer. This time we would visit Ireland, then head to Germany for the Bayreuth Festival and the Passion Play in Oberammergau. I had already lined up an agent in London and a few more engagements there.

I was moving into my own *Vita Nuova;* I would find out soon whether Tom was making any progress on his.

*   *   *

Margaret and Willard were getting married. It had taken them years to meld their academic careers, but at last they would be together in Princeton. They planned a small wedding in West Orange with the reception at the Farrands' home afterwards. Margaret had decreed there would be no attendants.

But the wedding was set for June 12, and we were already booked on a steamship three weeks before that. I was bitterly disappointed, but Margaret came up with a solution. Her parents were hosting an engagement party in April. Could I come and provide the entertainment?

I was happy to accept, and we fired ideas back and forth, discussing what poems I ought to read. I would have liked to include one of Tom's, but they all seemed too dark for the occasion. Certainly there was no ode to a happy marriage.

I had not been back to New Jersey since childhood, but the tree-lined streets of East Orange summoned up strange, happy memories. Playing with friends like Margaret. Keeping an eye on Billy. Mother singing around our kitchen.

But when I closed my eyes, the images faded. That time of happy innocence was much too long ago.

*   *   *

I liked Willard as soon as I met him. He was tall and broad-shouldered, with a shock of thick dark hair that required no brilliantine to keep it in place. He and Margaret made a handsome couple, their dark eyes flashing with private jokes and ongoing academic debates. Despite her parents' concerns, it was clear they were both deeply in love.

This is how it should be.

When the party got underway, Willard was gracious about squiring me around the room and introducing me to his Princeton colleagues. "Emily has been a friend of Margaret's since childhood. She was a professor of speech and drama in Milwaukee and Boston. Unfortunately, she'll miss the wedding because she'll be off to Europe again. She's a close friend of T. S. Eliot's."

I was certain the latter point heightened the status of both of us among members of the English Department.

"We're still waiting for his next great poem," noted one balding, portly man.

The professor might be an admirer of Tom's, but the wink to his colleague betrayed something else. It triggered something in me, something akin to the protectiveness of a mother bear for her cub.

"Lately Tom's been focused on criticism," I said. "I'm confident he will return to his poetry when he finds something he feels is worth writing about."

The professor's eyes widened.

"But I shouldn't presume to describe his plans," I added quickly. "We were friends when he was a student at Harvard. It's been some time since I last saw him."

I scanned the room for Margaret. "Now if you'll excuse me, I need to get ready for my reading."

I tracked down a maid carrying a tray of glasses and took one to wet my throat. *Be calm,* I reminded myself. *Take a deep breath.*

Margaret waved for me to join her by the window.

"Excuse me, everyone." She waited a moment, then found a spoon and gave her glass a forceful tinkle. This time the room quieted.

"We are so pleased that you could all be with Willard and me today to celebrate our engagement. We are particularly delighted that my oldest friend, Emily Hale, could also join us. We were sorry that she won't be able to attend our wedding because she will be in Europe, pursuing her career as a public speaker. But we are grateful that she could be with us today and share some poems that are meaningful to the two of us. Emily?"

The guests applauded politely as I took my designated spot. I remembered another parlor, another performance. Poems this time instead of songs and skits. But I felt the words so much more deeply now.

"Thank you, Margaret. I would like to begin with the work of a great female poet. She was a friend of Charles Kingsley, the focus of Margaret's dissertation. The words are particularly appropriate today because they express the love shared by two poets. Two lovers of literature like Margaret and Willard."

I paused, took a breath, then began to recite.

How do I love thee? Let me count the ways....

* * *

The summer was a busy one. We traveled to Paris, Munich, Bayreuth, and Oberammergau before we returned to England. I was lucky that Edith was still willing to pay my expenses, including tickets for the plays and concerts I wanted to see. The venues were filled with tourists, but I didn't feel like one. I was working all the time, gathering up programs, clipping reviews, making notes on performances, touring the backstages of theaters when they were open to the public.

Germany was unsettling, just as Italy had been on my first trip. Amid the *gemütlichkeit* of Bavaria, the enthusiasm of the Passion Play actors for their first new Christ in 30 years, there was an undercurrent of something more sinister. Of course, I knew that the script blamed the Jews for crucifying Jesus, but even so, I was shocked at how one-sided it was. There was an anti-Semitic edge to this production, and it frightened me. It made me long for a Barrie comedy.

Back in England, Edith had arranged to stay in the Cotswolds, in a newly renovated old home in Burford. It was a beautiful, quiet spot, close to the gardens and estates that she still wanted to explore. But there was a price to be paid for that tranquility. It was 20 miles to the closest train to London, and without a car of my own, it was easy to feel trapped there.

My agent had managed to arrange two speeches, one to the American Women's Club of London, the other to the Ladies' Lyceum Club in Piccadilly. This time, I would speak on contemporary American poetry. It was safer to talk about things that were many time zones away from my audience.

I had written Tom about my appearances, hoping he might be able to attend. I wanted to show him what a polished speaker I had become. But when the time came, I realized he would have stood out like a weed in my garden full of women. He did not need that kind of attention, even if I did.

He was more preoccupied than usual that summer. He and Vivienne had made another manic move, this time back to Clarence Gate Gardens. Too many of his friends and family members were visiting. I knew Rev. Rhodes Smith and his daughter, Abby Eliot, from my Boston days. They were followed by Lawrence Smith, Tom's former brother-in-law, and Samuel Eliot Morison, the Harvard historian. I would have enjoyed connecting with all of them, but Tom was still hiding me away.

Finally, a few weeks before I had to go home, he suggested we meet for lunch. If I could find my way to Oxford, he would take the train out to meet me. I told Edith I wanted to do some research at the Bodleian Library but that I could take the bus to get there.

Tom's train was on time, and his eyes lit up when he spotted me on the platform. But his body still slumped as if bearing all the cares of the world. We exchanged kisses on both cheeks, probably the same way he greeted his cousin Abby. This was Oxford, after all. We had to be careful.

He suggested a small, quiet restaurant a few streets from the station. The fall term had not yet started; the dining room was still nearly empty. After taking our orders, the proprietor was careful not to hover.

"How is Boston?" he asked.

"It's good to be back," I replied. "Eleanor sends her regards...."

"I owe her a letter," he muttered.

I hesitated. "I must admit it's been harder than I expected to get speaking dates. I have to be careful with my expenses. Edith and John have covered me this summer, but everyone is tighter with their money since the Crash."

"I've seen it, too," he said. "The market for first editions is disappearing."

"And you?" I asked. "What about you?"

He pulled out his cigarette case, offering me one this time. I declined, then he lit his. "Things are the same," he said, then shook his head. "No, worse actually. Vivienne has gotten completely out of control."

The proprietor brought our tea. Tom took a long sip.

"Our visitors try to ignore all the strange things that she says or does. We plaster smiles on our faces and talk about the weather. But I know I'm not fooling them."

He took a long drag on his cigarette. "Conrad was just here for a visit."

"I'm sorry I didn't get to see him."

Tom frowned. "He came to lunch, along with Gordon George, a friend of mine from church. Vivienne begged off. She had a massage scheduled later in the afternoon and said it would be easier to stay in bed.

"We were having a rousing conversation. And then Vivienne decided to join us. She began hurling food at Conrad and onto the floor, then scraped it up and began stacking the dishes. Gordon tried to ignore her and kept on talking. He made some comment about 'pure intellect,' and I said something to the effect that there was no such thing. Whereupon Vivienne began laughing hysterically and then started baiting me.

"I tried to keep calm. I thought that if I spoke to her quietly, she would eventually settle down. But every time I opened my mouth, she only got louder and angrier. Finally, Conrad slammed his fists on the table and said, 'Hear, hear,' and that seemed to jolt both of us into silence."

He buried his face in his hands. "I don't know what to do with her."

I sat quietly, stirring my tea methodically, long past the point where the sugar had dissolved. Even as a little girl, I had recognized the face of madness. Father's solution had saved my childhood, saved our lives.

I was free now, free to stay in England for as long as Tom wanted me to, free to come and go as I pleased, as long as I found a way to live frugally. But I knew I could not bear to live on the fringes of Vivienne's world. And as long as Tom wasn't willing to leave it, it was too painful to stay.

I looked up and found Tom gazing out the window.

"I had an epiphany this summer," I said at last.

"Oh?"

"When we were first courting, I always wondered why we rarely went out with your friends. I felt as if you were hiding me away. I worried that for some reason, I embarrassed you."

"You were special," he interjected. "I didn't want to share you with anyone."

It was a sweet thing to say, but he failed to convince me. "I felt that way again this summer. You could make time for all your other friends and relatives. You would schedule lunch with every young writer who wanted a critique. But you never seemed to have time for *me*."

I plunged on. "I was spoiled by that weekend we shared in Cambridge two summers ago. It was just a few days, but it was a magical time. You were there with me, in body *and* in spirit. You put all your thoughts of Vivienne aside, if only for a few days."

I chose my next words carefully. "I took a new path last year. I hoped it would give me more freedom, make it easier for me to be with you when you needed me. But I can't do this, Tom. I can't travel across the Atlantic and then wait for you to make time for me. If we are going to spend time together, no matter how short, you have to *really* be there for me. You can't be off in your other world, wracked with guilt about Vivienne."

I hesitated. "When I was a dorm matron, I had to enforce a rule book. I didn't like all the rules, but I learned that if the rules were spelled out clearly, it made things easier later on.

"I never asked you to abandon Vivienne or get a divorce. But here's my rule going forward: When I'm with you, you will have to *really* be with me. And if you can't do that, then I will go back to America. And I will go back to being 'your old friend from Boston.' And I'll still seek your opinions about poetry and theater....And I'll try to figure out how to spend the rest of my life without you. But...."

My eyes met his. "I think you need and want something more. I will give you my love. But only if you are really with me—in mind, spirit, and soul. If I am going to give up my life for you, you are going to have to give up Vivienne—at least while you are spending time with me."

I paused for a moment. "That may be too much to ask, but I have no choice. I have learned how to divide my life into compartments. There is a compartment that is still waiting for you. You have to do the same. You have to find a way to set aside the pain, the guilt, the regrets. You have to be there—all of you—just for me."

Neither of us said anything for a long, long time. Our food arrived, but now I wasn't hungry. I had delivered a threat, but I didn't know what I expected him to do.

"I understand," he said at last. "And I am sorry, truly sorry."

He took out another cigarette. He took his time lighting it, gaining the space to choose his words "I will never forget our weekend in Cambridge. I think back to it almost every day, especially when I am feeling low. When I fall asleep, I remember lying by the river with you. I pretend that my pillow is the softness of your lap. When I'm standing on a crowded subway train, I remember pulling you close to dance with me on the bridge. I was oblivious to all the people walking by. 'If You Were the Only Girl in the World.' Wasn't that the song? You are always there for me, somewhere at the edge of my consciousness.

"But I know I've hurt you far too many times. Somehow I am going to have to find a way to work this all out."

He checked his watch. "There's a train at two," he noted. "If I catch it, I can still get some work done today."

The afternoon was ruined, and it was all my fault. But I had no choice. I could become like Eleanor, the sympathetic cousin who was always there for him, ready to listen, never judging. But I was Emily, not Eleanor. I not could not play that role in this particular drama.

He paid the bill, and we walked back to the station. The next bus to Burford would arrive within the hour.

Another train station, another goodbye. I hated those memories.

"When do you go back to the States?"

"In October," I replied. "I have more speeches in Boston in November."

"And your topic?"

I smiled. "The German theater today. And modern British verse." I arched an eyebrow. "Do you know anyone whose poems I should read?"

He smiled, the tension broken. "I'll send you some ideas."

He reached into the pocket of his jacket and pulled out a tiny package. "I brought this for you." He placed it in the palm of my hand. "I wanted to give you a token to take back to the States. I wanted you to know how much you still mean to me."

I unwrapped the white paper slowly. It was a ring, a plain band like a wedding ring, fashioned out of a darker metal.

"I don't know what to say, Tom."

"You may not want it anymore, but keep it anyway. You don't have to wear it if you don't want to."

Down the track, the train whistled, jolting me as much as his gift had. As it pulled into the station, he took me into his arms and brushed his lips gently against mine.

"Goodbye, Emily."

"Goodbye, Tom."

He climbed onboard and found a seat on my side of the car. The train started up, and he gave a final wave.

I stared down at the ring, still cupped in my palm. It was simple, without ostentation. I slipped it onto my finger. It fit perfectly.

I took it off, rewrapped it in the paper, and slipped it into my purse. I knew I would wear it someday. And someday I would tell Edith he had given it to me. But today I was not capable of manufacturing a tale about finding it on the floor of the Bodleian Library.

* * *

In late October, we returned to Boston. And within a few weeks, another poem found its way to Edith's home. It was this year's Christmas poem, but a long way from the New Testament of the Magi. It was about a woman, a daughter named Marina.

There was sadness, regret, images of bodies getting older, breaking down.

> *What seas what shores what granite islands towards my timbers*
> *And woodthrush calling through the fog*
> *My daughter.*

Despite Tom's transformation into a Brit, I knew he was still homesick for the Massachusetts shore.

I carried his ring in my purse, still wrapped in the original paper. And sometimes, if I was by myself or surrounded by friends who knew our story, I would slip it on briefly, enjoying the feel of the smooth, cool band around my finger.

If Tom ever returned to the States, he would know where to find me.

Coming Home

BOSTON

1931

I RETURNED TO THE AMERICAN lecture circuit with a satchel full of notes and a handful of positive reviews.

I had met MacGregor Jenkins, the business manager of *The Atlantic Monthly*, when we had performed together a few years before. Now he agreed to supply a positive quotation for my new brochure.

Miss Hale has rare dramatic and interpretative ability. Her dramatic instinct has given her a keen insight into the problems and characteristics of the contemporary theatre.

In her dramatic rending of stories, poems and characters she is aided by a perfect sense of dramatic values and unerring taste.

—*MacGregor Jenkins*, The Atlantic Monthly

It was a bit of a stretch since his words had never actually appeared in the magazine. But desperate times called for desperate measures. In London, I'd met Cecil Armstrong and he heard my talk for the Ladies' Lyceum Club. He, too, was gracious about providing a short review.

Miss Hale illustrated her lecture with readings and extracts, all of which were beautifully recited. Indeed to one accustomed to judging elocution, this part of Miss Hale's programme afforded a pleasure as rare as it was real.

Cecil lived in London and had opinions. So I decided to identify him as "London critic and writer." It didn't matter if anyone on our side of the Atlantic actually had ever heard of him. I knew they would be impressed.

* * *

The Cambridge Social Dramatic Club called again, offering a wonderful role: The Actress in *The Guardsman,* by the Hungarian Ferenc Molnár. Lynn Fontanne had played the role opposite her husband on Broadway back in the twenties. Now, word had it, the couple was working on the movie.

Like every small business around us, the club was struggling to stay afloat. Memberships were down, Dick Hall explained, as were ticket sales. But we were determined to survive long enough to celebrate our fiftieth anniversary.

On the surface, *The Guardsman* appeared to be the club's usual comic fare: An insecure egomaniac of an actor tests his wife's fidelity by disguising himself as a Russian prince and setting out to woo her. Molnár, I decided, must know something about the topic because he had been married three times.

But there were deeper questions underlying the farce: questions about the nature of passion, attraction, and loyalty. How to sustain a relationship, through both long separations as well as the monotony of married life. Putting on one mask for the person you loved most of all and another for the rest of the world.

Robert Wallstein would deliver many of the key lines, playing the role of The Actor. I was shocked to learn that he was a Harvard junior, nearly 20 years younger than me.

"Don't worry," Dick assured me. "He's very talented."

I snorted softly. "It's going to take every ounce of my acting talent to make *this* believable."

The second act was staged in the anteroom outside of a box at the opera. The script specified *Madame Butterfly.* I remembered the tickets Tom had given me for Christmas and how the opera had made me cry. But there were also happy memories from those days. The club and Brattle Hall. *The Mollusc* and *Fanny and the Servant Problem.*

How our lives have changed! Back then, it was Amy who had played the beautiful star. Now the directors thought I had enough presence to portray The Actress, even in the shadow of the great Fontanne.

The play was scheduled for Valentine's Day weekend to help boost ticket sales for Saturday night. To save money, the club presented me with the same roses at my curtain call that The Actress had received in Act One. As I took a final bow and reveled in my standing ovation, I knew that if I couldn't be with my own Valentine that night, there was still nowhere else I would rather be.

* * *

Willard won the scholarship he had hoped for, and the Thorps would spend the next year in England. I longed to join them, but the Depression was tightening its noose. Even Edith and John were staying home this summer. I redoubled my efforts to find engagements, contacting the agents I knew from my days at Milwaukee-Downer. The principal at Miss Porter's School arranged for me to speak at one of their fundraisers. I landed one speech in Providence, another in Detroit. The competition for public speakers was not as stiff there as it was around Harvard and Radcliffe.

By summer's end, I had another fistful of good reviews.

We were all delighted with Miss Hale. Her lecture "Talkies or the Spoken Drama" was most interesting and of course her lovely voice and delightful platform manner added to the pleasure of the occasion.

Miss Hale's program was excellently balanced with sufficient variety to display her versatility and to hold the interest of her audience from beginning to end. Voice, diction, stage presence, all were admirable.

Her lecture, "A Play from Both Sides of the Footlights," was so admirably designed that we felt we had the theatre in the round, and her delightful manner of giving it would have made any subject persuasive.

The words, as always, lifted my spirits. Still, all the positive adjectives in the world were not going to pay my bills. Like it or not, I was going to have to find a regular job.

If I had learned one thing from my nomadic life, it was that I did, in fact, miss teaching. More precisely, I missed my students. Occasionally, I ran into one of the girls I had taught at Simmons or received a postcard from Italy from Mary Spicuzza.

But that was not enough. I missed coaching them on how to deliver their lines. I missed molding them into women who knew how to sit, stand, talk, and hold their hands. I missed being asked for advice, whether or not I could solve the problem.

I needed to feel needed.

I would stay in Boston if I had to, but I wanted something more. Dr. Lafavour suggested new schools I should contact. From London, the Thorps sent names of their friends. Lucia had never completely forgiven me for leaving Milwaukee-Downer; still she promised she would let me know if she heard of any openings. But times were tough, she cautioned. She had kept her own faculty together since the Crash, but she'd been forced to cut their salaries.

There was a new women's college out West, in the foothills east of Los Angeles. Scripps College had a generous benefactress and a drama program that needed attention. The Hollywood soundstages, the faculty feared, might prove too tempting to a coed who dreamed of becoming a movie star. I decided to write President Jaqua, summarizing my credentials while glossing over that pesky little detail that I still didn't have a degree:

I first began college dramatic work in 1916, when, at the age of 25, I went to Simmons College to assist the girls in the formation of a Dramatic Club....

I went on to describe my career, focusing on my promotions, my studies abroad, and my family's connections.

My forebears are of New England stock on both sides of the family. My father, a Unitarian minister, was for many years a teacher at the Harvard Divinity School, and my earliest associations are largely

*with Cambridge. He held a pastorate for many years at Chestnut Hill.
An uncle is Mr. Philip Hale of the* Boston Herald.

*I am fond of young people, of teaching and was keenly interested
in all student activities while at Milwaukee-Downer College. The
history of the theatre and the fascination of "make believe" evidenced
in college dramatics, are to me delightful, stimulating fields of and for
exploration.*

Claremont, California, was far away, but that was part of its appeal. If I had to start over, it was better to do it beyond Boston—even if I had to rely on my Hale connections to get me there.

* * *

As Christmas approached, the news swept along both sides of the Charles River. After 16 years of self-imposed exile, Thomas Stearns Eliot would be returning home. Harvard had appointed him to be the Charles Eliot Norton professor of poetry for the 1932-33 academic year.

I was speechless. Just as Tom had never told me about his application to Oxford, he had never written that Harvard was courting him again. He was embarrassed, he told me later, that *The Times* of London had announced he was leaving England before Harvard had formalized its final offer.

Only Harvard, I thought, could succeed in finally prying Tom Eliot out of England. Not a dying mother, aging siblings, or even a former girlfriend. Now his alma mater would confirm that he was a poet, not a philosopher.

Vivienne, he wrote, would stay behind in England. There was much to arrange before he could leave.

And what does it mean for me?

Should I try to find a job in Boston? But my applications had already gone out. And Tom would still be a celebrity at Harvard. He might be three thousand miles closer, but he was still a married man. And whatever had led him to accept the offer, he would not stay in the States forever.

* * *

We have been to a party at the Eliots' home.

Margaret had not lost her knack for surprising me.

Willard was very excited about going, but I felt very conflicted. I felt as if I was spying on your behalf.

The guests included some names you may know. There was Lady Ottoline Morrell and Robert Gordon George and Alida Monro, the owner of the Poetry Bookshelf. The evening was billed as a "party," but it was not at all what I had expected. The room was filled with rows of chairs. Tom read some poetry, another woman sang some songs and then they played some records. I had looked forward to some conversation, but it was all very stilted and scripted.

Of course, I was eager to meet Vivienne. I wondered, in fact, if the evening was organized so that she wouldn't do much talking. She is a tiny woman and did not look very well. She slurred her words when she spoke, and I wondered whether she was drunk or drugged. Tom also had too much to drink, and he seemed on edge the whole evening.

Willard enjoyed himself, mostly, I think, because he was thrilled to visit Tom at home. But I was happy to leave when the performances were over. We all pretended that everything was fine, but the Eliots are clearly not happy. I did not want to make Tom feel uncomfortable, but I'm not sure he really cared.

It was easier when Vivienne remained a vague abstraction. When Tom's wife was fleshed out—a "tiny woman," who "did not look well," or, as Eleanor had reported, someone with "sunken dark eyes," smelling faintly of ether—it made her come alive. She might be capable of bizarre behavior. But she was still a woman, with emotions of her own. A woman whose husband was about to disappear for a year.

So it was easier for me not to know her. "Tell me of Tom," I wrote back to Margaret and Willard, "and give him my regards when you see him. But please don't tell me about Vivienne," I said in closing. "It's better that way."

* * *

As the calendar turned into 1932, Scripps College came back with an offer: a two-year contract as "Assistant Professor of Oral English." They wanted me to teach Dramatic Interpretation and English Speech and Diction, and manage the drama program. They also needed a dorm matron; that would bolster my finances and surround me with students again. I would start in September, the same month Tom arrived at Harvard.

Sometimes it seemed that the Fates were conspiring to keep us apart. We were rather like trains, and whether on adjoining tracks or headed in opposite directions, the timetables of our lives rarely put us in a station at the same time.

But it *was* a wonderful offer, and I knew I was lucky to get it.

As I reread President Jaqua's letter, I noted the school's motto on the letterhead. *Incipit Vita Nova.* "Here begins new life." It was another sign: Dante, calling out to me again.

I wrote back that I was delighted to accept.

* * *

I took longer to share the news with Tom, wrestling with how to tell him that when he finally arrived in Boston, I would no longer be there. He wrote back quickly.

I was happy to learn that you had received such an excellent offer. But I'm also very disappointed that you will be so far away.

However, I am trying to arrange some lectures and poetry readings in other cities, and I would like to travel back to St. Louis to see my birthplace again. If you can advise me when you will be free, I will do everything I can to come visit you.

My heart soared. He was willing to carve out time for me. He was willing to come to California.

Citrus and Sunshine

THE FIRST THING I NOTICED was the sweet smell of citrus. Throughout my childhood, Edith had honed my sense of smell, along with my manners. Now, as I stepped out of the taxi, I paused to try to catalog the strange new scent. It was mostly oranges, I decided. Blossoms, but also the tang of juice. There must be a processing plant nearby.

The sunlight was also dazzling. I had always heard that the sun was different in Southern California, but I had dismissed the claim as Hollywood hyperbole. Now the light seemed astonishingly white.

And it was warm, too. Boston was turning into fall, but here it was still summer. Some of the leaves would change eventually, but their dusky green reminded me of the olive groves of Florence, not the rich dark green of Boston and England.

California was, in a word, different. And Scripps was, too. The ivy-covered red brick castles of my former campuses were now spanking-new Spanish haciendas with white stucco walls and red-tiled roofs. "Mediterranean Revival," they called it, or simply "California style." I wondered what Father would have made of it. Nevertheless, it was reassuring to know that there were still some American families with enough wealth to start a college or put their name on a new dorm.

Toll Hall, my new home, featured wood-paneled rooms, with fine Oriental rugs, overstuffed chairs, Gothic-style windows—and dozens of eager young women. But they sported deeper tans and more carefree attitudes than my students in Milwaukee and Boston. Scripps had only four years' worth of "traditions," and any good idea could still become one.

The faculty was evenly divided between men and women, a big change from the nunnery of Milwaukee-Downer. President Jaqua had been lured from the deanship at Pomona, just a few blocks away. But like most of the faculty, he was a transplant from the East. Paul Havens had joined the English Department from Princeton, where he had known Willard Thorp. His wife, Lorraine, had her hands full with a new baby girl but was hungry for female companionship. I was happy to provide it.

Ruth George was the only other woman in the English Department, the teacher of creative writing. I was grateful when she reached out quickly to help me navigate Scripps's unique version of academic politics.

Ellen Browning Scripps had died just a few weeks before. And as much as the college's elderly founder was grieved, her death seemed to free the campus from the weight of her strong opinions. We were all pioneers, joined together in building something new and exciting.

The drama program was clearly suffering. The first professor had left early on, and his successor had quit in mid-year. Nathaniel Stephenson, an older history professor who was a theater buff, had tried to keep the Siddons Club alive. The only direction the program could go now was up.

Gwendolyn Logan Seiler had been hired to direct *Pride and Prejudice* the previous semester. I was intimidated by her résumé—she had just played bit parts opposite John Barrymore and Loretta Young. But the British scriptwriter turned out to be friendly, sharing what she knew of the returning students and offering to show me around Hollywood after I settled in.

But there wasn't much time for that. Tom was arriving in only four months. I was determined to make my mark before then.

The department chairman had made it clear that my plays were as important as my classes. So I decided to start with a full-length production—and not just another drawing-room comedy. Walking across campus one night, inspiration struck: I would do Goldoni's *La Locandiera*.

When the curtain rose on opening night, the audience broke into applause at the sight of the set: a balconied inn, shimmering in artificial moonlight above a flower-bedecked courtyard. Backstage, I smiled; I knew everyone would be talking about the production long after the curtain came down.

* * *

As December approached, I was torn with indecision: What should I do with Tom once he arrived?

He could sneak into town; I could keep him hidden away if I had to. It would be romantic to rent a car and drive up into the mountains. Or we could head west and visit the Pacific beaches. We might never have another chance like this one.

But why did we need to hide? This wasn't Cambridge, Oxford, or even Boston. This was California, a college campus plunked down in the middle of orange groves. This was my domain, *my* Harvard, *my* Oxford. I was the professor now, a job I had earned without a stitch of help from Tom. And if Willard Thorp could drop Tom's name around Princeton, why couldn't I do the same thing at Scripps?

So I put his ring on my finger. I found a prominent spot for the leather frame that held the inscribed photos he had sent me. The autographed books and essays went on the shelves behind them.

From the depths of my closet, I pulled out the long robe I had purchased on a whim in London. The silk was cool against my skin, the Chinese dragons on the back made me feel exotic. I liked to put it on at night, the time of day when I let my fantasies take over. Dreaming of the stage. Dreaming of an affair.

And if a member of the Siddons Club dropped by to talk, I would pull out a letter from "my friend Tom" and tease them by reading some of it aloud. Not the most personal parts, of course. But enough for them to know that I had interesting stories, too.

The poet, I told them, was coming soon, and I hoped they would all get a chance to meet him.

* * *

Every Thursday night, students gathered in the dorm's Browsing Room to sip tea while a faculty member gave a talk. I signed up for December 6: "T. S. Eliot: The Man and His Poetry."

Tom was scheduling lectures all across the country, so I asked him to do one at Scripps. He quickly agreed and, "as a gift to you," he would not charge a fee. He decided he would talk about the comic poems of Edward Lear.

The choice surprised me, but I didn't object. For now, it was important that the girls appreciate the famous poet in their midst. I wanted no stupid questions or giggling.

Ruth George helped me choose the poems for my introductory talk. I did not want to scare the girls with Tom's darker images. I would read "Prufrock" and recall how we had discussed it when Tom was still in college. I was tempted to read "Mr. Apollinax" and recall the Fullers' garden party. But that was the cynical side of Tom. I fell back instead on "Journey of the Magi," "A Song for Simeon," and, finally, "Marina." It was easy to explain the literary works from which they were drawn.

The night of my talk, Ruth and Paul Havens dropped by to listen. As the tea cooled in my own cup, I warmed to my subject. I talked to them about "Tom," not Mr. Eliot. He was, I said, the product of many influences: a boyhood in St. Louis, his years among the elites of Boston and Harvard. "I know something of those same influences," I added with a smile. Arriving at Oxford just as a generation of Brits went off to war. His decision to convert, his decision to become an Englishman.

In summary, I said, "he is a man of extremes. He is a man of undoubted faults, but still a man of highest virtues."

I paused to take a sip of tea, then asked if there were any questions.

"Is he married?" a junior asked.

"He married an Englishwoman quite suddenly," I replied, struggling to keep my voice even. "Near the end of his time at Oxford. Unfortunately, she has never been in good health. I believe that's why it has taken him so long to return to America."

I paused, then added, "This will be the first time he has visited California. So I hope you will all join me in trying to make him feel welcome."

* * *

I could understand why Tom wanted to spend Christmas with his brother, but I was still disappointed. Our time together would be so special but also far too short. The train from New York would take three days to cross the continent, putting him in Claremont on December 29th.

I had booked a room for Tom at the Claremont Inn, the lodge-like hotel that Pomona owned and where many of its students took their meals. But then Mary Eyre contacted me. She was leaving town for the holidays. Perhaps Mr. Eliot would enjoy staying at her home?

I jumped at the offer. The inn was only a half-mile away, but Professor Eyre's house was even closer. It would be quieter and more private there, and Tom would like that. When Mary showed me around her place, I knew it would be perfect. There was a desk where Tom could write. I could stock the refrigerator, even splurge on some flowers.

I could pretend we were playing house.

As the day drew closer, I struggled to quell my anxiety. I had waited for this day for nearly 20 years, but even now, I had no idea what to expect—or, to be honest, what I even wanted.

My thumb played again with the ring on my finger. I wanted time, of course. Enough time to get past surface pleasantries, enough time for us to rediscover each other. As much time as we had, I knew it would never be enough. Tom would go on to USC and Berkeley, then to St. Louis, then back to his lectures at Harvard. Next summer he would return to London. Back to a job, back to his church, back to his wife.

Still, he *had* left Vivienne behind. Was it a test to see if he could actually do it? As each passing day lengthened the space between them, would he come to realize that he *could* change his life—if he only had the courage to do it?

And what about me? Could I ever give him an ultimatum? I tested the words out loud. "Don't come back, Tom, as long as you're still married."

But I was acting, and I knew it. That approach would never work. We both hated conflict. Tom might be able to eviscerate writers and critics with a stroke of his pen, but when it came to human relations, he was nothing but weary patience and politeness. And I, too, was shaped by a world in which pastors never told their parishioners what they really thought, and girls were taught to zip their lips.

Finally, the day came. The train was scheduled to arrive just after six in the morning. I knew the Havenses would be up early with their baby, so I asked Paul if he would drive me to the station. He had shared that he had met Tom during his own Rhodes scholarship year at Oxford. "Of course, he won't remember me," he said, "but I'd be honored to do it just the same."

The train was running late, not surprising considering the distance it had to travel. I pulled my coat tighter, crossing my arms to ward off the early morning chill. I was glad that Paul was still sleepy and not eager to chat. I paced the short stretch of the platform, noting the cheery flower boxes and brightly painted doors. The station would telegraph to Tom that this *was* different than the places we had shared before.

Suddenly, a whistle sounded down the track. I gave my coat a tug, then whisked out my compact to check my lipstick one last time. Then I remembered: Paul was watching. I still had to be careful; I had a job and a reputation to protect.

The train hissed to a stop, and one passenger stepped off slowly, a small bag in hand. He tipped the porter, then began walking toward us. Even four car lengths away, Tom's silhouette was unmistakable.

I skipped down the platform, leaving Paul behind. When I reached Tom, he put down his bag and took me into his arms. He held me for a long time, the weary embrace of someone in desperate need of comfort. And I clung to him for as long as I dared.

I was shocked when we drew apart and I could see his face. His chin was unshaven, his eyes heavy with exhaustion.

"I'm afraid I'm quite a mess," he said, stroking his chin sheepishly. "I haven't slept well since I got onboard, but I did manage to doze off for the last few hours. Fortunately, the porter woke me so I wouldn't miss my stop, but I didn't have time to shave."

"You're here," I whispered in his ear. "That's the important thing."

* * *

It was a short drive to Mary's home. Paul carried in Tom's bag, then excused himself to go home for breakfast.

"This is nice," Tom acknowledged as I showed him the rooms. It was, I realized with fresh eyes, the home of a woman, with a touch of chintz here and there. But every room was lined with bookshelves, and a comfortable chair was ready.

"Did you have anything for breakfast?" I asked. "I can make some coffee. Or perhaps you'd just like to lie down for a while."

"I think I might do that," he replied. "But just for a few minutes."

I put Mary's kettle on the stove. Our reunion now over, I realized I was actually hungry. I got out the bread I had stocked and put a slice in the toaster. I waited near the kettle, wanting to give Tom some space and to catch it before it began to whistle.

I turned off the stove, then tiptoed back down the hall. The bedroom door was open, so I peeked in. Tom had shed his jacket and shirt, but then seemed to have collapsed at an angle on Mary's bed.

I froze in the doorway, hypnotized by the slow rise and fall of Tom's bare chest. This was more of him than I had ever seen, an intimacy that we had never shared before. I could stand in this place for hours and be happy. And if Tom got the rest he needed, I was certain he could be happy, too.

There was a light yellow blanket at the end of the bed. I walked in and spread it carefully over his legs and bare shoulders. Tom murmured something, then settled into a new position and began, softly, to snore.

Oh, how I longed to crawl in next to him! But I tiptoed quietly back across the room. Before closing the door, I took one last look at his sleeping form. This was an image I wanted to remember.

* * *

Perhaps the rules of polite society dictated that I should leave Tom a note, walk back to the dorm, and wait there until he woke up. But I didn't want to follow the rules. What harm was there in making myself some breakfast and picking out a good book? Tom Eliot was a celebrity who deserved some hospitality.

I ran my fingertips over the books lining Mary's shelves, searching for an interesting title. Her collection was focused on child development, with many volumes by Freud and his disciples, some in German, some not. I pulled down a translation of Carl Jung's *Psychological Types*. I scanned the Table of Contents, read a few pages at the start. *Extroversion versus Introversion. Intellect versus Feeling.* Some of it was heavy going, but I was intrigued by the parameters of personality he described. It might come in handy in acting, not to mention teaching and collaborating.

Even communicating with a lover.

* * *

It was past noon when I heard Tom begin to stir. I set down the book and decided to organize lunch. I never had to do much cooking, but I could manage simple things, salads and sandwiches and such.

I heard the shower and imagined Tom, the water splashing against the planes of his bare chest. It was clean, ascetic. Would he have to worry about getting sunburned? Or would the warmth revive him, bringing back memories of the Gloucester coast? I shook away the images and went back to slicing tomatoes.

"I feel like a new man," he announced as he finally joined me in the kitchen.

I glanced over my shoulder. "You *look* like a new man," I said with a laugh. He had changed into a white shirt and pants like the ones he had worn the day we had gone punting.

"It's been a long time since I slept that well."

"I'm glad," I replied, focusing on the angle of my paring knife.

He came up behind me. I could feel his breath on my neck, but I didn't dare stop my chopping. Then I felt his fingers stroke down my arms, coaxing the knife to drop to the counter. He pulled me close to his chest and settled his chin on my collarbone.

"It's so good to be here, Emily. I can't begin to tell you."

I closed my eyes and reveled in the feel of him. I waited, wondering what might come next. But he did nothing more. He held me for a few more heavenly moments. Then he kissed the base of my neck and let me return to my chores.

"So what *do* you have planned for me?"

"First, I'll feed you," I said breezily, placing the sandwiches on plates and taking them to the kitchen table. "Things will be quiet until the students return after the first of the year. Your lecture is scheduled for a week from tonight. It's the night before you go to UCLA.

"I've received a couple of invitations from faculty members. The Havenses would like to have us over. They don't get out very much because of their baby. Paul has been very helpful to me, and Lorraine and I have become good friends. Paul may ask you to speak to one of his classes. But," I added quickly, "you can always say 'no.'"

I worried now that I had scheduled too much. I desperately wanted him to like it here.

"I've also accepted an invitation from the Stephensons," I continued. "Nathaniel's the head of the history department. He kept the drama club going until I arrived." I hesitated. "I wouldn't have accepted if I didn't think you would like them."

He smiled. "I'm sure I will."

"There's one other thing," I said slowly. "I thought it would be fun to have a small dinner party on New Year's Eve. I discovered some old friends from my Boston theater days are in Hollywood now, and I invited them to come. It's been nearly 20 years since I've seen them."

"Do I know them?"

"No," I replied. "I worked with them after you left for England." There was an awkward silence. "But your visit gave me a good excuse to reach out to them. I thought it would make for an interesting evening."

Tom said nothing.

"Why don't we eat?" I said quickly. "And then if you feel up to a walk, I can show you around campus."

We took our places at the kitchen table. It was nice, I thought, to actually cook something for Tom, to have time to linger over a meal in Mary's cozy house instead of grabbing a quick cup of tea in a forgettable English restaurant.

"Is there anything *you* would like to do while you're here?" I asked.

"I would like to attend church at some point."

Even on "vacation," Tom could not abandon his rituals. I forced myself to smile. "Well, the Congregationalists rule Claremont, you know. But let me talk to Lorraine. She probably knows a church where you would feel at home."

* * *

No matter how many years had passed, it never failed to amaze me how quickly we could pick up where we had left off. As we strolled around the now-empty campus, we talked of inconsequential things, falling into the rhythms of our long-ago strolls.

"How does it feel to be back at Harvard?" He had written me about his first impressions, but now I wanted to know more.

"Comforting, but also odd," he said. "They gave me a wonderful room that overlooks the river. The crews have disappeared until spring, but I still enjoy the view. There's a large library next door. It has comfortable chairs, and I can smoke my pipe in there. But like every building at Harvard, it's overheated."

I laughed. "You *have* become an Englishman!"

"I'm less impressed with the students," he went on. The two next door to me are particularly noisy, always playing the wireless and their gramophone. Some of the freshmen seem to think that Eliot House was named after me. My family's coat of arms is everywhere you look. I find it all rather embarrassing.

"But so far, it's a congenial place to be. Next semester, I'll be teaching modern English poetry. I decided I should make myself available to the students for at least an hour a week. So every Wednesday I open my door and serve up a big pot of tea."

"Does it make you wish you were a professor?"

"Not at all," he replied. "I've come to realize that I hate the performing. Oh, the quiet time for reading and writing is wonderful. And I don't mind working with young writers who actually have some talent. But I hate standing in front of a large group of people waiting for me to say something profound. I'm grateful it helps pay the bills, but I don't think I'll ever really enjoy it."

"Now you, on the other hand..." He stopped and turned to gaze into my eyes. "I can see how much teaching suits you. You're just acting on another stage."

"Ah, but the public wants to hear the famous poet, Thomas Stearns Eliot. As hard as I tried, I was never able to fill a lecture hall."

"The public," he said with a smile, "is clearly ignorant."

The afternoon was pleasant, and the fresh air seemed to have energized Tom. So I led him across the street to the Graduate School campus and then down College Avenue to Pomona.

"The founders didn't want to duplicate what the Stanfords did," I explained. "They wanted to create a collection of small colleges. They wanted to create another Oxford."

Around us, the red-tiled roofs shimmered in the afternoon sun.

Tom smiled. "I think they've still got their work cut out for them."

* * *

I had rarely celebrated New Year's Eve since I first left Boston. Even after I returned, most of my old friends had moved on, to new cities or social circles, to lives as married couples or parents with children.

But the theater world was like a family, and it turned out Gwendolyn Seiler knew Oggie Perkins now that he was working in Hollywood. He had just wrapped up the role of Johnny Lovo in *Scarface*, and when I finally phoned him, he was eager to reconnect. As much as he loved the theater, he explained, the movies provided a more regular paycheck.

"You probably have lots of invitations for New Year's Eve," I said impulsively. "But a friend is visiting from England, and I wondered if you would join us."

"I'll have to double-check with Janey, but I'm sure we're free....As long as you don't mind if we bring along our little boy."

"Of course not. What's his name?"

"Anthony Richard Perkins."

"Anthony," she repeated. "I like it."

They chatted on. Clifford Pember, their old set designer, was also in town. And so was Hamilton MacFadden. Oggie had met him on Broadway when they both did *Beggar on Horseback*, but he had actually gotten his start in the Social Dramatic Club. Now he was directing Charlie Chan movies.

Before I could change my mind, Oggie offered to invite them all.

"Tell me more about your visitor," he said.

"I knew him before you and I met. He also acted with the Cambridge club." I hesitated. "You've probably heard of him. His name is T. S. Eliot."

* * *

I was surprised when everyone said they could come. It was one thing to host Oggie and his wife and their toddler, quite another to plan a dinner party for eight. Gwendolyn couldn't come, but she provided useful advice: It's all right to keep things informal, even for New Year's Eve.

I made sure Tom was well rested; I wanted him to have a good time. But as I put out Mary's china and readied a roast for the oven, I knew there was more at stake. Tom was a member of the English literary establishment. But I had famous friends, too. Actors who had played on Broadway and starred in the movies. Set designers and directors. Scholars and authors. In the end, of course, he might still turn up his newly minted English nose. But my friends were somebodies, too.

The Pea Green Boat

NEW YEAR'S DAY, 1933. AS I opened the door of Mary's house, I surveyed the detritus left from the night before. A dining room table covered with unwashed plates, a living room littered with near-empty glasses and discarded party hats.

Happy New Year.

I was relieved that Tom was still sleeping. There would be no trip to church this morning. I moved slowly to clean up the dishes, taking care not to clatter the plates. I enjoyed pretending to be a housewife, puttering around in Mary's kitchen in the mid-morning light.

The party had turned out to be a success. The conversation had been lively, as we all shared news about our mutual friends and the challenges of making a living as an artist. Tom had mostly listened. He acknowledged that he rarely went to the movies and had little time now to get to the theater.

When midnight arrived, we toasted the New Year with a drink I had mixed up out of orange juice and soda water. Prohibition was on its way out, but it was still the law of the land. I thought someone might have brought along a bottle of something, but I knew it was harder to find in California. Tom complained that he hadn't had a real drink since his train had left New York City.

The party broke up a short time later. It was a long drive back to Los Angeles, and little Anthony had awakened from his improvised crib in the back bedroom. There was an awkward moment when my guests were not sure where I was staying. Then Clifford offered to drive me "home."

"Leave the dishes where they are," I told Tom. "I'll clean them up in the morning." He gave me a quick kiss goodnight, then I left to join Clifford in his car.

It was a short drive back to the dormitory. "It was wonderful to see you again, Clifford."

"I hope we can do it again sometime. And if you make it back to England, be sure to look me up."

"I will."

I started to open the door, but Clifford had something more to say. "I remember when we worked together back in Boston. How could we ever forget the day the *Lusitania* sank?"

"I know I never will," I replied.

"But I remember something else about that time. You were waiting for someone. Your heart was in a different place. It was so obvious to all of us. You tried to throw yourself into the play, but—what play were we doing?"

"*Eliza Comes to Stay.*" I remembered it so clearly.

He paused. "You were waiting for Tom, weren't you?"

I nodded.

He reached over and gave my leg a brotherly pat. "I hope you have a happier ending this time, Emily."

There was reason for me to hope this New Year's Day. The man I loved was not on the other side of an ocean. He was sleeping in a room down the hall. This time we had more than just a few stolen hours. To be sure, ten days was not exactly eternity. But as another year of my life ticked away, I was reminded just how precious time really was.

I had placed the last of Mary's fine china into the drying rack when Tom emerged from the bathroom, toweling off the last of his shaving cream.

"It seems my timing was perfect to avoid helping with the clean-up," he teased.

"I didn't mind."

"I'm sorry I didn't walk you home myself last night."

"That's all right. Clifford and I had a chance to talk."

"It was a nice party."

"You were so quiet at times. I worried you weren't having a good time."

"No, I rather enjoyed just listening for a change. Since I arrived in the States, everyone is always clamoring for my opinion. And I enjoyed recalling the old days in Boston and Cambridge."

He paused. "It's too bad that some of your friends have been forced to abandon their theatrical careers to churn out movies for the masses." Then he chuckled. "I suppose I should go see one of those Charlie Chan movies so I can fully appreciate how awful they must be."

"Did you make it to New York to see Eleanor's play?"

"I had hoped to," he replied. "But it closed almost as soon as it opened."

"I was sorry when I heard that. She's been working on her Jane Austen material for so long."

"Yes," he said, "since we first met...." His eyes caught mine. "I often think back to that night."

"So do I." I was wary of returning there. "Do you remember Tracy Putnam?"

"Was he in our skit?"

I nodded. "We were in a play together last February. I hadn't seen him for years. He's a neurologist now, doing research on seizures."

Tom's eyes darkened. "And did you wonder how your life might have turned out differently...?"

"He's married now," I responded quickly. "To another doctor." I hesitated. "But since you ask, yes, seeing him again did make me ask, 'What if?' Life is full of choices, big and small. Some things you can control and some things you can't. But I learned a long time ago that there's little point in ruminating over the 'might have beens.'"

He took a long sip of tea. "I wish I had learned that."

The words hung over us like a thick cloud of regret. I could find a way to dispel it, with the cheeriness of a hostess or the bustle of an efficient housewife. But no, I wanted him to feel what I felt. I wanted him to know that loneliness, too.

"Speaking of plays...," he said at last. He rose from his chair and disappeared into the bedroom. He returned, pulling a slim volume out of a large envelope. "I wanted you to have this. You can put it on your bookshelf."

I read the odd title out loud. "*Sweeney Agonistes: Fragments of an Aristophanic Melodrama*." I flipped through the pages. "It's a play!"

"My first," he replied. "I've been working on it for years. Since that first time we saw each other in London, actually. It's not really finished, but we decided to publish it anyway. I'll be eager to find out what you think."

"I'll treasure it," I said, pressing it to my chest. "I'll try to finish it... before you leave."

"Yes," he acknowledged, "before I leave." He took another sip of tea, then placed his cup carefully back into its saucer. "You've packed my days full of talks and dinners, it seems." He looked at me intently. "Is there any chance we could get away? Just the two of us?"

The words I had longed to hear. Then finally, I spoke.

"Let me see what I can do."

* * *

The students returned the next day. Tom's formal lecture was scheduled at the end of the week. But Scripps was more than ready to heat up a pot of tea for him and start pouring. And so I was asked to organize a gathering in my dorm so that a few of the girls could talk with the famous poet.

I was amused to see their reactions when they finally caught sight of Tom. He was not their image of a "famous English poet." He was not Lord Byron or Shelley or Tennyson. He looked like a banker. He could pass for a father. *Where in his brain does he find all those images?*

I had begun reading *Sweeney* the night I received it. I did not get very far. As a drama, it clearly needed work. The characters did not talk like real people. But I was more disturbed by the plot. Had Tom spent time with prostitutes when he was young? I knew it was the norm among some circles at Harvard. But what about the new celibate Tom? How did Vivienne fit in with this? Why did he feel compelled to write it now?

The students had filled their cups and taken their seats. It was time to begin.

"We have a very special guest tonight," I began. "The poet T. S. Eliot. Tom and I have known each other since we were your age, and I'm delighted that he was able to come out to Scripps during his fellowship at Harvard this year. He will deliver a formal lecture Thursday night, but we're pleased he was willing to meet informally with some of you. So without further ado, let me present my friend, Thomas Stearns Eliot."

The girls applauded politely.

Tom set down his cup. "This is my first trip to California, and I must admit I am experiencing a bit of culture shock. I have never been this far west before. Although my family comes from New England, I was actually born in St. Louis and spent most of my childhood there. Coming here reminds me of how out of place I felt when I first traveled East to attend Milton Academy. I was annoyed that I had been born in St. Louis." There was laughter around the room, and Tom seemed to relax a bit.

"My lecture later this week will focus on the poetry of Edward Lear. In preparation for that, I'd like to talk a bit tonight about Lear and another English poet, Lewis Carroll. Lear was a brilliant poet. But because he wrote mostly humorous poems, I don't think he is appreciated as much as he should be."

"I'm sure many of you learned this poem in school:

The Owl and the Pussycat went to sea
In a beautiful pea green boat...."

Is there any chance we could get away? he had asked. *Just the two of us?*

We can't just disappear, I thought. Too many people know he is here. Hollywood actors do that sort of thing, but not the Congregationalists of Claremont. There would be gossip; my reputation was at stake.

What about a chaperone? Paul and Lorraine would never be able to arrange a babysitter. The Stephensons were too old. I couldn't ask Ruth George.

What about a student? Was there a girl I could trust?

I looked around the room and spotted Marie McSpadden. "McSpad" was a model of a tall, tanned California girl. She had played the cavalier in *Locandiera*, but more importantly, she was reliable; she had helped to round up props and return them when the play was over. She knew her way around Los Angeles, and better yet, she had a car.

"I've written some light verse myself," Tom was saying. "But I usually just send them to my old college friends."

Was it appropriate to ask Marie for help? I was just giving a talented student the chance to spend more time with a distinguished poet, something she could tell her children about some day.

But what about the other girls?

The students were now applauding. Tom had wrapped up his remarks, refilled his teacup, and was now encircled by a small group of admiring young women.

"Marie," I called out before I lost my nerve.

"Yes, Miss Hale?"

"I was wondering if you could help me," I began slowly, choosing my words with care. "Mr. Eliot asked me if he could take a break away from campus. Since you grew up around here, I thought you might have an idea of something we could do together."

I watched Marie's face. My question was innocent enough, a request for travel advice, not an invitation to become a co-conspirator.

She smiled. "Actually, I have a great idea. The weather's supposed to be sunny and warm this weekend. My family's got a cottage on Balboa Island. Why don't we all go to the beach?"

It was an audacious idea, more exciting than I had expected. Did I dare accept?

"Mr. Eliot is scheduled to lecture at UCLA on Friday afternoon," I said, worried now that it was all falling into place too easily.

"That's perfect," Marie replied. "I have an early morning class, and then I could drive us all to the lecture. We could head to the island after that. When do you have to be back?"

"By Saturday night. We've made plans to go to church with Professor Havens and his wife on Sunday morning."

"Then we can stay over on Friday and come back Saturday night. My family has a boat, and if the weather's warm enough, you may want to go to the beach."

The fantasy sounded wonderful. "That's a very gracious offer," I replied. "Let me discuss it with Tom and I'll let you know tomorrow."

"I'll double-check with my parents, too."

Marie returned to her friends, leaving me with too many questions. Who would sleep where in the cottage? Marie didn't seem worried, and she was a level-headed girl, the kind who always got back to the dorm by curfew. If there were only two bedrooms, she probably figured she would share one with me.

But the prospect of time away with Tom! Four months in California and I still hadn't been to the coast. I missed the sweet tang of an ocean breeze.

I yearned for the room to break up so I could share the plan with Tom. But he continued to chat politely with the girls, even as I could see that all the conversations were wearing him down.

Finally, I intervened. "You'll have another chance to hear Mr. Eliot tomorrow night, girls. I think it's time we let him go."

They said their goodbyes. The Browsing Room was a mess of abandoned tea cups, but I wasn't ready to do the clean-up.

"Let's go for a walk," I said.

The sun was just setting, the nighttime chill had not yet settled in.

"I talked with one of my students," I began as we strolled down the walkway. "Her family has a place on Balboa Island. It's in the harbor, near Newport Beach. She could take us to UCLA and then we could stay there Friday night. We could get back by Sunday morning."

He turned, his mouth widening into a smile, his eyes brightening. When he spoke, his voice was determined.

"Let's do it!"

* * *

Marie proved to be a good tour guide as we headed west toward the coast. She noted points of interest but refrained from chattering too much. We stopped in at the Brown Derby for a late breakfast but didn't spot any stars.

Tom shook his head in dismay when he saw the restaurant.

I laughed. "You should have worn *your* bowler."

We headed next to UCLA. The campus was slowly taking shape in Westwood. It was dominated by Royce Hall, its stunning Italianate architecture even more incongruous than the stucco buildings of Claremont.

Tom left us to go find the organizers of his talk. The auditorium was cavernous compared with Balch Hall at Scripps, and I worried whether Tom's voice would be able to fill it. But I knew better than to fret over such things; it would only make him more nervous.

We settled into two seats on the aisle, not too close to the front.

Marie broke the silence. "The other night you said that you had known Tom since you were young. How did the two of you meet?"

I hesitated. It was odd to hear a young person call him "Tom," instead of "Mr. Eliot." But I knew Tom would encourage it. I owed Marie some of our stories. But what should I share? How much was too much?

"I went to school with his cousin. We think we first met at one of her debutante parties. The time we do remember was when Tom was getting his master's at Harvard. Eleanor drafted some of us to perform in a little show she organized to raise some money for charity."

"What did you do?"

"Tom and I were in a scene from *Emma*. Eleanor also asked me to sing." I smiled at the memory. "The songs were so different back then...."

"You are a woman of many talents, Miss Hale."

I cocked my head. "If you're going to call Mr. Eliot 'Tom,' then I think you should call me 'Emily,' don't you think? At least while we're away from campus."

"All right, Emily."

I hesitated. There was more I could tell Marie. How Tom had gone off to Europe. How I had expected him to come back. How he had gotten married and become a famous Englishman. But Marie could figure that out for herself if she tried.

I took a different tack. "Back then I dreamed of becoming a professional actress. I took on every amateur role I could find. But eventually I had to earn a living. So I began directing and teaching. And I discovered that it was enormously satisfying."

The hall had filled up around them, and a man stepped out onto the stage. He was probably the head of the English Department; I did not catch his name. "It is my distinct honor," he said, "to introduce one of the foremost English poets of the 20th century, T. S. Eliot."

The audience applauded enthusiastically. The great man had come to UCLA, another step toward putting their university on the academic map.

Today his topic was "The Development of Taste in Poetry." I listened carefully, learning more each time I heard Tom speak. This talk was not as esoteric as some of the essays he had sent me. He outlined four stages in the formation of taste, beginning with childhood. I thought back to Robert Frost's poems and how much they had appealed to me when I was young. Tom and Frost were great poets, but they would never be great public speakers.

"I do not affirm," Tom was saying, "that what I like in poetry is good. If one is sincere he will not enjoy a thing because he is told it is great. He must be true to his own feelings. Self-knowledge is the most important factor in knowing what we really feel."

There was much of Tom's poetry I didn't like. I didn't like the violent images, I didn't like Sweeney's crude language in his new play. But I never told him, and he never asked. He no longer seemed to care what the critics thought.

I longed to be out of the elegant hall, filled as it was with puffed-up academics, and off to Marie's island. But the audience expected some poetry, and Tom had to satisfy that hunger. He was more comfortable reading his own words, knowing exactly how he wanted them to sound. He read a section of "The Waste Land" and another poem I didn't like. And then he turned to "Ash-Wednesday."

The poem was published three years ago, but he had never sent me a copy. I supposed it was because it was dedicated to Vivienne.

Most authors, I mused, dedicated their first or second work to their spouses. Tom, on the other hand, had waited 15 years.

I wondered if he regretted it now.

* * *

It was late afternoon before the reception wrapped up, the last autograph signed, the last fawning scholar dispatched. As we descended from the hills and Newport Harbor came into view, Marie explained her plan. There was a ferry to Balboa Island, but it would be faster to stop by the Yacht Club and pick up her family's boat for the quick run across the harbor.

We loaded our bags and supplies into the sleek, wood-paneled motor boat. Tom stepped up to help Marie with the lines, but it was clear she knew what she was doing. "When I was growing up," she said, "I was an officer in the junior yacht club."

The island had bounced back, she explained, since the twenties, when a developer had gone bankrupt. But the Depression had still left its mark. There was no money to dredge the harbor, and boaters had to pay close attention to the markers to avoid running aground. There was less time to enjoy a vacation cottage these days—unless, of course, you were financially independent.

I settled into a seat in the stern, while Tom stood next to Marie at the wheel, taking in all the sights and smells. The sun was setting in the west, but still felt warm on my arms and face. Marie throttled down, and the wind freshened on our faces, strong enough, finally, to muss Tom's slicked-back hair just a little.

He turned around to smile at me and then began reciting, loudly enough to be heard over the noisy hum of the motor:

"The Owl and the Pussycat went to sea in a beautiful pea green boat."

Marie smiled and continued the verse. "They took some honey and plenty of money wrapped up in a five-pound note."

I laughed as Tom struck a dramatic pose. "The Owl looked up to the stars above, and sang to a small guitar. 'O lovely Pussy, O Pussy, my love, what a beautiful pussy you are, you are. What a beautiful pussy you are.'"

He stopped and smiled at me.

"Keep going," Marie egged him on.

I knew where the poem went next, and I knew Tom did, too. I began to recite my part:

"Pussy said to the Owl, 'You elegant fowl! How charmingly sweet you sing! O let us be married! Too long we have tarried: But what shall we do for a ring?'"

My thumb found the slim band on my fourth finger; my eyes posed the question.

Tom spoke up. "They sailed away, for a year and a day, to the land where the Bong-tree grows." But he stopped there, before the ring was purchased, the marriage consummated, and the dance begun. The question could not be answered. And I was grateful that either Marie did not know the words or was too focused on navigating the sandbars to fill in the rest of the lines.

She slowed the boat as we approached a dock and gave Tom crisp instructions on what he should do. I knew my instincts had been right. Marie was a take-charge girl, a girl who could be trusted.

We unloaded our gear, then headed to the cottage. The houses were small and tightly packed but well-maintained and freshly painted. I could see why a family would enjoy coming here.

The McSpaddens' place was cozy, but large enough for a family, particularly if you planned on spending most of your time on the water. Marie gave us a quick tour, then directed Tom to take her parents' bedroom. I was grateful to discover I would have my own space.

I closed the door of the tiny bedroom, kicked off my shoes, then stretched out on one of the twin beds. Marie had suggested Tom be the first to use the bathroom, and I listened as the water came on and the shower walls began to rattle.

It was Friday night, and Tom would be off again on Monday. Where had all the time gone? Why hadn't I guarded it more?

We had managed to get away, but I could not ask Marie to disappear. We were lucky to be here at all. We would have to make the best of it.

* * *

Saturday morning dawned warm and bright, and Marie was up early to organize breakfast.

"It's going to be a beautiful day," she said when both of us emerged from our rooms. "I could take you on a boat ride around the island. Then I could run you down to the beach at Corona del Mar, and you could have some time alone there."

"Wouldn't you like to go to the beach, too?" I asked.

"Of course, I would," Marie replied. "But my mother has some things she wants me to take care of here. And my professors," she added with a wink, "have already loaded us down with reading for the new semester."

Ninety minutes later, we found ourselves on the beach with a blanket, an umbrella, and a basket packed with our lunch. I had brought my swimsuit, but Tom had left his in Boston. When we began walking across the sand, Tom took off his shoes and socks and rolled up his pant cuffs.

"I grow old....I grow old," I began reciting in jest. "I shall wear the bottoms of my trousers rolled." Then I improvised: "I shall wear white flannel trousers and walk upon the beach."

He took my hand. "Come on," he said, "let's find the perfect spot."

We decided to stretch out our blanket a ways down the beach. It was close to the water's edge, but not so close that we would have to move when the tide came in. It was beyond the noise of the frolicking children. I usually enjoyed watching them, but today it was suddenly painful. There would never be any children for either of us now.

We propped up the umbrella and I shimmied out of my slacks. I sat down on the blanket, and then Tom sat down beside me, stretching his long legs toward the water. Once again, he settled his head into my lap and closed his eyes.

There were so many questions I hadn't asked him yet, but I was afraid I would destroy the mood. Still, it was easier to ask them now, rather than writing a letter and worrying about how Tom would respond.

"How does it feel to be back in America?"

He hesitated. "It's been good," he said. "Strange in some ways, but still good.

"I've enjoyed reconnecting with old friends in Boston. But most of all, it's been good to be back with my family, with people who knew me when I was young." He opened his eyes and gazed up at my face. "That applies to you, too, of course, but in a different way."

"But," he said. There was always a "but" with Tom, I thought, waiting to hear what this one would be. "But despite all that, I'm still homesick for England. I'm not a celebrity there the way I am here. I can disappear into my work and my writing. But I've also discovered that I miss the green of England, the rain, the ancient buildings, the traditions. I'll be ready to return when my fellowship is over."

I'll be ready to return. What did I expect? He's a British citizen now.

He propped himself up on his elbows so he could see the harbor and the deep blue of the Pacific beyond it.

"I'm sorry I never took you to Gloucester," he said. "I've really missed that. That and sailing up the coast to Maine."

"Do you ever get to the English coast?"

"Not like I used to. We went to Eastbourne for our honeymoon. But things did not go well, and we left early."

He sat up then, his back facing me, his face now hidden.

"I know you've asked me not to talk about Vivienne when we're together. But I've come to a decision, and it's important for you to know about it."

He took a deep breath. "I've made up my mind that Vivienne and I have to separate. I have been thinking about it for several years, but Harvard finally gave me the space and time I needed to make up my mind. The time I've spent with you has only made me more determined to do it.

"When I get back to Boston, I'm going to write my solicitors and have them prepare the separation papers. I don't know how Vivienne will respond, but I no longer care. Things will only get worse if we stay together.

"I've had reports from friends who've checked in on her while I've been gone. Unfortunately, she is so needy and erratic that they can't bear to spend any time with her. But I'm determined to see this through. I will continue to support her financially. It won't be easy, but I can manage it. And if I have to, I'm prepared to hide from her. I can't put it off any longer."

I closed my eyes and let out my breath. It was nearly 20 years since Tom had gotten married. I had come to believe that I would never see this day.

"Of course, divorce," he went on, "is out of the question."

I hesitated. "I know that," I said softly.

I did not tell him about the odd dream I'd had last night. I was back in Christ Church, but this time, Tom and I were the ones getting married, not Amy and Dick. As we strolled down the aisle together, I saw Mother and Father and all our family and friends, turning to watch us from their pews. But as we processed toward the altar, the faces disappeared, turning into roses, beautiful, but still.

The waves broke on the shore; a motorboat chugged past. Down the beach, a child cried out for his mother.

At last, Tom broke our circle of silence.

"I can't promise you anything. I hope you understand that. Nothing but the love and affection we have always shared. I will still be constrained wherever I go. I hope, as always, you will find your way back to England. I will try to see you as much as I can if you come. But you will have to decide for yourself what you want to do."

My fingers found the warm sand off the edge of our blanket. I sifted idly through the grains, letting them fall as if in an hourglass. Summer would be coming again, and the summers after this one. It would have to be enough. What choice did I have?

"There is time," I said at last. "There has always been time for me to decide. But we have the gift of a beautiful day today. And the two of us are alone right now, away from Harvard and away from Scripps. Away from theaters and lecture halls. We are two middle-aged people that nobody recognizes." I smiled. "And two people who are so pale and out of place on this beach that no one would want to stare at us for long.

"So for now," I said, reaching out to push back a strand of his hair that had fallen across his forehead, "why don't we just try to enjoy the rest of our day?"

He took my hand and slowly lowered me down alongside of him. We clung together, holding each other more tightly than we ever had before, our curves matching as if we were an old married couple who did this every night. I closed my eyes and tried—very, very hard—not to cry.

* * *

And then, just as quickly, it was over.

Marie returned at the time she had promised. I spotted her first, a small wooden boat in the distance, growing closer and closer. I wanted to will her to stop, for the boat to go aground or run out of fuel. But like the young punter in Cambridge, Marie was too reliable. We packed up our lunch basket, folded up the umbrella, and shook the sand out of the blanket. I pulled on my slacks and buttoned up my blouse, covering up my bathing suit for the long drive back to Claremont.

We didn't say much on the trip home. The sun and the sand had left me sleepy, and Marie concentrated on the road. Up front, Tom watched the passing scenery, then let his chin fall to his chest as we headed to the east.

Mary Eyre had arrived home, reclaiming the role of hostess to a great literary figure. We made polite small talk for a while, then Tom said he was tired and would like to head to bed.

"I'll be back at 9 tomorrow morning," I advised him. "The Havenses are taking us to church."

Lorraine drove us to the Episcopal church in Upland, the best place she could find for an Anglican amid the orange groves of California. And then it was time to say goodbye. Tom was lecturing about Edward Lear again tomorrow, this time at USC. Then he would head north to Berkeley. And I had my own classes to teach and the first meeting of the term of the Siddons Club.

It was never easy to say goodbye, but this time, it was even harder. I had glimpsed what our life could be like—conversation over eggs and bacon, dinner parties with old friends, heady talk among brilliant academics, playful days together at the beach. And now there was a glimmer of hope that someday we might share it for longer than a fortnight.

Perhaps Vivienne herself would decide to move on. Perhaps their marriage could be annulled.

This time, we went alone to the train station. Another station, I thought, another destination down the tracks. We held each other for a long moment when the train to Los Angeles finally came into view.

"I'll write you," he said, "and tell you what happens."

And then, once again, he was gone.

* * *

I never told Marie not to talk about our trip. To do so seemed to suggest that there was something she needed to hide. We began planning the sets for *The Dragon*, and Marie went back to calling me "Miss Hale." As far as I could tell, she never betrayed my secret.

But later in the spring, she stopped by my room, eager to show me what had arrived in the mail that day. It was a package from T. S. Eliot. It was not, I was relieved to see, an autographed copy of that dreadful *Sweeney Agonistes*. It was a poem, a few short lines that recalled the joy of being on the water, and the rediscovery of a long, lost daughter.

The poem he had titled "Marina."

* * *

Once again, the letters had to suffice. Tom wrote that he enjoyed visiting St. Louis and was stunned when 900 people turned out for his speech. His calendar was booked solid with lectures now, and his class on contemporary literature required him to study new works. Hallie Flanagan, the head of the drama program at Vassar, was mounting a production of *Sweeney* and sought Tom's advice on how to end the play. The University of Virginia had commissioned him to do a series of lectures. Columbia was giving him an honorary degree.

He had traveled down to Princeton and squeezed in lunch with the Thorps. No one, Margaret wrote me, had dared to ask about Vivienne over sandwiches and tea. Nor did Tom in his letters. I wondered if his courage had failed him, if he would skulk back across the ocean and resume his hopeless life.

But then, just as quickly, that cloud lifted. Tom decided to stay just a little while longer. He had visited Edith and John, and a friend had invited them all to visit her home at Woods Hole. His family was going to vacation together in New Hampshire for a week. And Milton Academy wanted him to give its commencement speech.

Would I come back East to join him?

With my family. With his family. Out of the shadows at last.

I bought my train ticket that afternoon.

* * *

Dorothy Olcott Gates had graduated from Smith a year ahead of Margaret. Smith was where, I concluded, they must teach gracious hospitality alongside English literature. She welcomed us to Olcottage and made clear we could do whatever we wanted. She apologized for her five noisy children and her husband's absence; he never seemed to be able to pull himself away from his medical lab at Harvard.

I was happy that Tom had drawn closer to Edith and John. There had been many invitations to dinner, and he had spoken to Edith's women's group at King's Chapel. As a favor to John, he had spoken to the Association of Unitarian Clergy. He was becoming, I thought, the son they never had.

And as I slowly tested the limits of my family's rectitude, I was relieved that no one seemed to care that Tom was still married. We were free to disappear for long walks on the beach, with nothing more than a "Be back for dinner at 5."

Dorothy planned to attend the 20th reunion of her class at Smith and had made arrangements to stay in a big home in the Berkshires. "Why don't you come with me?" she urged us one night over dinner. And no one came up with a good reason not to extend the party.

Before Tom and I left for New Hampshire, Edith pulled me aside.

"Something has changed," she pronounced. Her eyes demanded to know what it was.

I knew I could trust Edith with Tom's secrets. "He's going to seek a formal separation from his wife."

She searched my face intently. "You've never stopped loving him, have you?"

"No."

"Did you visit him while we were in England?"

"A few times. Yes."

"So what happens now?"

I sighed. "He goes home, the lawyers prepare the papers, and he hopes that she goes along with it."

"But there's no possibility of divorce, is there?"

"No."

"What are you going to do?" She was relentless.

"Go on, as I always have. What choice do I have?"

Edith hesitated. "I've lived a long time, Emily. And when you're married to a pastor, there's little that your eye misses. It's been obvious that you are still deeply in love with Tom. And it's equally clear how happy he is when he can spend time with you.

"I'm old enough to know that love can take many forms. Some of them are sanctioned and some of them are not. But I also believe that God wants us to err on the side of loving. Still, I worry that there can be no happy ending for you."

She paused, then said, "We're going back to England this summer. As always, you're welcome to join us."

* * *

At first, I was wary about vacationing with the Eliots. I knew Tom's older sisters doted on him, particularly now that their mother was gone. I liked Tom's brother Henry immediately and felt a kinship to his wife. Of course, Theresa and I were both Eliot outsiders. But I knew that Henry and Theresa had visited Tom and Vivienne in London, and as the days went by, I learned that Henry was still receiving frantic, rambling letters from Vivienne, demanding to know where Tom was and when he would return home.

But no one talked about that. They all put on their "Eliot faces" and pretended that nothing was amiss in their isolated little world.

And I realized I felt comfortable in that world, too, the universe of Harvard and Cambridge and Unitarian forebears, of spinsters filling their days with reading and needlework, hanging on every word uttered by their celebrated little brother.

The days were lazy ones, spent rocking on the porch, snapping beans, or peeling apples gathered from the orchard. I explained how I had learned to peel an apple while playing Lulu Bett, and the sisters listened politely. If they believed that the stage was no place for a proper woman, they kept their opinions to themselves.

My heart soared with the views of the mountains. I slept soundly at night, my window open to the cool, crisp air. Tom and I found an old swing hanging from a distant tree and took turns pushing each other, giggling like we were children again instead of middle-aged adults.

And then it was time to head back for one final speech.

Tom now regretted he had accepted the invitation—he felt he was "all talked out." But it was an important anniversary for Milton Academy, and he was a "distinguished alumnus." He could hardly back out at this late date.

When we met up with Edith and John, Edith seemed to be wound as tight as a drum, and my uncle was strangely silent. Edith waited until Tom was out of earshot.

"It's so terrible," she said, struggling to control herself. "I would have called if I had known how to reach you."

"What is it?"

"Fred Gates. He was working late in his lab two nights ago. They think he fainted and hit his head on one of the tables. His skull was split open. They got him to the hospital when they found him. At first they thought the wound was only superficial. But he died earlier today."

I gasped.

"His colleagues had trouble locating Dorothy. Finally, they tracked her down in Northampton. She managed to get to the hospital before Fred died, but only barely."

"How old was he?"

"Forty-eight," Edith replied. "And five young children left behind."

Only four years older than Tom.

Tom was taking the stage now as his own family and all the students' families began clapping around me. I mimicked their motions, unable to feel anything.

"Twenty-seven years ago," Tom began slowly, "I sat here with the graduating class—not in this hall, we did not seem to need so much room in those days—and somebody then got up on the platform and made the sort of speech that I am supposed to make. At least, I believe someone did. I really do not remember."

I tried to focus on Tom's words, but I knew that I, too, wouldn't remember what he said this time.

"The reason of this extraordinary and periodic lapse of memory must be that none of us ever listen. There are too many other things to think about at the moment, more pressing and more interesting. The immediate future, the next day, the summer, and the next year at college are all more interesting things to think about than what you hear from some old duffer who gets up on the platform when you are anxious to get away."

The next day, the summer, the next year at college. There was always the future. And then there was Fred Gates. Gone in a moment, doing the work that he loved.

There would be no wonderful summer at Woods Hole. With a phone call in the middle of the night, your life could change in an instant.

Tom was recalling his 17-year-old self now. "I have always wanted to say something to him and I have a number of grievances against that character. I should like to face him and say: 'Now look at me. See what a mess you have made of things. What have you got to say for yourself?'"

Yes, you have made quite a mess of things.

My mind wandered as he recalled all the jobs he had held: teacher, banker, editor.

"There are always some choices sooner or later which are irrevocable, and whether you make the right one or the wrong one, there is no going back on it. 'Whatever you do,' I wish someone had said to me then, 'don't whimper, but take the consequences.'"

I knew Tom dreaded the choices that lay ahead. There would be meetings with the solicitors, struggles with his finances, and, it seemed likely, hiding out from Vivienne. But there would be no more whimpering.

"And the third thing which I have learned is this: Don't admire or desire success. Admire and desire the qualities, moral and mental, which go to make success. Admire the end of any successful career, if it has been a good end to pursue, but never admire the success itself."

Tom had yearned for his success, turned his back on everything that was safe and comfortable from his early years. Now he had fame and he had celebrity—and a wife who had been a burden for most of their married life. And, from the reports filtering back from London, a wife who was not about to disappear, even if he wanted her to.

In the Garden

IT DID NOT TURN OUT to be a good summer to be in England. Any hopes that Vivienne would make things easy were dashed as soon as Tom arrived home. He was working from a farm in Surrey, fearing that she would confront him at his office and throw his life into turmoil. He and his lawyers were sending clear messages, but Vivienne was refusing to hear them. He told me to mark my letters "PERSONAL," and send them to his office at Russell Square. He would get them there eventually.

Edith and John had rented a home in Gloucestershire, and Tom managed to visit us twice. But his nomadic life had left him stressed and weary, and it was impossible for him to relax. I appreciated Edith's emotional support. I also felt the weight of her constant scrutiny. It was a relief, in a way, when it came time to return to the sunny freedom of California.

* * *

When I heard that the Claremont Community Players would be doing *Hay Fever* in January, my heart soared. I had loved playing Judith Bliss back in Boston. Noël Coward was replacing James Barrie on American stages, and Judith was replacing Alice Sit-by-the-Fire as the middle-aged mother whose children were leaving the nest. I knew the script backward and forward and had perfected my English accent. True, I was getting older, and the gray was starting to show in my brown tresses. But the role called for a presence, not a beauty, and I knew how to sashay across the stage if it was called for.

When the auditions were over, the part was mine.

The play was largely plotless, turning on the chaos that ensued after four members of a dysfunctional family each invited a different house-guest for a weekend in the country. Now there were so many familiar touchstones for me. Judith's husband, David, was a writer, lost in his work, hungry for approval. There was talk of punting and drinking too much tea and heading to Italy to escape the depressing October weather. And there was an attraction to a male visitor, "so gallant and chivalrous, much more like an American than an Englishman."

We did two performances in Holmes Hall at Pomona. The set was simpler than the one we had in Boston, making our acting more critical. Afterwards, like Judith, I could revel in my reviews.

"Miss Emily Hale was easily outstanding in point of acting promi-nence, both because she had the most insane part and because she was able to carry it off with the perfection of enlightened understanding and technique."

Meanwhile, the *Pomona Progress-Bulletin* said that my "delightful work...would grace any professional stage." My "breeziness, her drawl and pseudo-aristocratic manner are captivatingly done."

I was pleased that—this time—a critic appreciated the way I spoke.

I clipped out the reviews and filed them away, along with the sweet note from the director, Louise Padelford.

Emily dear,

Even if you weren't an actress combining "marvelous looks, marvelous clothes, marvelous brains—oh God!" and incalculable talent, I should have thanked you for doing Judith (under is hardly the word!) over me and is so far over me that it was a rare treat for me to work with you and learn from you. My only regret is that your health may have suffered from the ordeal.

We all thank you for the great pleasure you and your acting have given us....Something I treasure even more than your excellent play-ing is your subtle understanding and sense of "playing the game" as well as "the comedy," if you know what I mean. And if you don't, let me explain to you someday how much real affection this quality in you inspires. Primarily in your humble director.

In the middle of the note, Louise shared a conversation she'd had backstage. The prompter, Hannabelle Grant, had told her, "Miss Hale should be on the professional stage!"

"If," Louise mused, "we could only lure Edward Everett Horton (her brother) and his director out to see you!"

Hanabelle Grant. The sister of a great comic actor.

If only, I thought. If only. Or as Noël Coward had put it, "Nothing can be helped. It's fate—everything that happens is fate."

* * *

Summer was approaching again, and Edith was making more plans. They had a rented a home in Chipping Campden and planned to stay longer this time. There was a cottage next door, and they would rent it for me if I wanted to come.

They make it too easy, I thought.

But I was building a full life for myself in Claremont—close friends, devoted students, new productions, glowing reviews. What was to be gained by heading back to England?

And then the letter came. Tom wrote at least once a week now, sometimes twice. His own life was settling into a more regular rhythm. He had moved back to the city; it would be easier now for the two of us to be together.

I miss you so. I miss the time we shared last year. I long to see you again, to walk with you and talk with you. Please come back if you can.

Did I dare ask President Jaqua for a sabbatical so soon? But I finally screwed up my courage. And he surprised me by saying yes. He would keep my job open for a year.

It's fate, I reminded myself. Everything that happens is fate.

* * *

I put my belongings into storage, including Tom's letters, now overflowing into yet another box. The girls of Toll Hall arranged a harpist and pianist for a final tea, and the Siddons Club organized a barbecue. There were tears and hugs and promises to write. And then, on the 15th of July, I left for England.

Edith and John were already installed at Stamford House. Its owner, Miss Sunderland-Taylor, went to Yugoslavia for the summer, and it suited their needs, close to the gardens Edith wanted to visit. There were older houses in town, but by American standards, one dating from 1705 was old enough. It was built with the same luminescent limestone as the rest of the town and was pressed up against High Street, the wide road whose larger homes telegraphed the wealth the local landowners had once enjoyed from their crops and their sheep.

Their home was flanked by two cottages like a mother house guarding two small children, and they had rented one of them, Stanley Cottage, for me. I could stay for a year if I wanted. I hated that in my forties, I was still bound to them financially. It meant Edith could still be in charge, including sending invitations to Tom. He was coming next weekend. It was a good sign. I had taken a gamble, left my old world behind. Perhaps this time, he was finally ready to meet me more than halfway.

* * *

Thirteen months. Each time I saw Tom again, I calculated how long it had been since the last time. By our standards, this absence was not very long. He arrived in time for dinner, and we lingered in a warm embrace. He seemed happier and healthier now. He flirted some with Edith, laughed readily at John's corny jokes, ate heartily, and savored a glass of sherry at the end. We stayed long enough to make Edith happy, then I noted that the hour was late and begged off to help Tom get settled in.

"This is very nice," he said as we entered under the cottage's flowering bower, and I showed him his room upstairs. "Much cozier than the rooms I've taken with the priests." A while back, he had written that he had moved to the clergy house at St. Stephen's Church in Kensington to try to save his money.

He set down his valise, hat, and umbrella, then we went back downstairs to the tiny parlor in the front. The old stone fireplace beckoned. It was a summer night, but the sun had gone down, leaving a misty chill behind.

"Would you like me to light a fire?" he asked.

"That would be nice."

I busied myself bringing out two glasses and opening another bottle while Tom arranged the wood and sacrificed that morning's newspaper to the cause. The dry logs flared up quickly. The fire would not last long, but it would be long enough. It cast a warm glow over the dark wood of the room—and over all of our old memories.

We sat side by side on the sofa, staring at the flames and sipping our sherries. Tom offered me a cigarette, but I declined. He lit his own and took a long draw.

"You *are* looking good," I said at last.

"It has taken me a long time," he acknowledged. "But I finally feel liberated. I have accepted that Vivienne is not going to sign the separation agreement. It's further proof of her delusions. But I have worked out a routine, and it suits me very well. And if she tries to show up at the office, they know how to cover for me."

How long will we go on this way? I was afraid to know the answer.

I changed the subject instead. "I was excited when you wrote me about your new play. How did it go?"

"Well, the bishop was happy. The production managed to raise quite a bit for the diocesan building fund. They provided me with the story line and the scenes, so all I had to do was fill in the words." He took a long drag on his cigarette, staring into the fire. "Still, I realized it felt good to be writing again. Something other than lectures and essays and polite rejection letters to mediocre writers. It was good to have a vision, a deadline, a project...even if it was not the same kind of challenge as coming up with an original idea."

He rose, stretching his back and his legs. "I quite liked Martin Browne, the fellow who directed it. I liked the give-and-take with him. It made me realize how much I missed the old days when Ezra and Conrad and I would criticize each other's poems. Now Martin and I are working on a new project for the Canterbury Festival."

He was becoming alive again; I could see it in his eyes and how quickly the words tumbled from his lips. It was the Harvard student I had known, a young man with so many ideas, he couldn't get them all down on paper. He was not the overworked editor, the depressed husband, the tired traveler stepping off another train at a crossroad in our lives.

Theater was something I knew, something we could share. "Tell me more," I prodded him gently.

"It's the story of the assassination of Thomas à Becket and his conflicts with Henry II. I've discovered I've got something I want to say about that story."

I smiled. "And you'd be staging it right where it happened. That should make the sets easier."

"I've been jotting down my ideas," he went on. "I've even got a working title. *Fear in the Way.*"

I scrunched up my nose. "I think we can work on that."

He realized I was teasing him. He smiled and sat back down beside me. "Enough of that," he declared. "I'm just so glad to be here."

"I am, too."

"How long do you have?" he asked. I had avoided that detail when I had written, fearing he would view it as an ultimatum.

"A year," I replied. "I was grateful they gave me any kind of sabbatical."

He reached out and took my hand. "It's clear they recognize how wonderful you are. Just like I do."

I needed nothing more than this, to sit by his side and share in his life, to feel wanted and adored. Some women might need a wedding ring, but I didn't. Oh, it would be wonderful if it happened, but I couldn't wish for Vivienne to die.

"I'm sorry," he said, "but it's been a long day. I think I would like to go to bed."

"That's all right," I said. "We have plenty of time."

We rose from the couch. I picked up the empty glasses, and Tom spread the ashes so they would die. Then we climbed the narrow staircase to the bedrooms. He gave me a lingering kiss. Then he reached for the knob of his bedroom door.

"Good night," he said.

"Good night."

* * *

Tom visited as often as he could, and as he began to feel more at home, he started leaving things behind. I loved finding them when I straightened up his room; it was a sign he planned to come back.

When I found a jacket or a sweater (a "jumper," he was calling them now), I would press it to my face, searching for a reminder: the scent of after shave or tobacco, a lozenge left in a pocket after a poetry reading.

In between, I devoured the books that lined the cottage's shelves and wrote letters to my former students and colleagues. I supposed I should think about what plays the Siddons Club should do in the coming year. But would there be a next year? I still wasn't sure.

In July, Jeanette McPherrin came for a visit en route to a year in France. Jeanie had graduated from Scripps before I arrived but had stayed on in Claremont to get her master's. I was happy to see her again, but I was also jealous of my precious time with Tom. He seemed to enjoy Jeanie's company and bantering with her in French. He was full of advice on places she should visit or where she could find a job as a translator. She might be more mature than Marie McSpadden, but she was still 20 years younger than Tom.

I am getting old. And men will always enjoy the company of a younger woman.

We joined Edith in another pilgrimage to the gardens at Hidcote and explored the length of Chipping Campden. But eventually the time came for Jeanie to leave for France. And the next time Tom came, I had him all to myself again.

There were many good walks to be had in the Cotswolds. During the week, I scouted the options. There was no more beautiful time of year than late summer, and the countryside seemed to bolster Tom's spirits. It was enough just to walk and talk, the way we had when we were young.

I was still in awe of his intellect and drawn to his quiet reserve. It infuriated me but still held me captive. There *was* something to be said for men who could make up their minds quickly and carry out their plan. I had known them at my schools: the presidents, the department chairs, the businessmen who served as trustees.

But that wasn't for me. That wasn't my Tom.

* * *

The village postmistress told me about the old manor house. About two kilometers out of town, off the road to Stratford. Built by Sir William Keyt in the 1700s as a place to delight his mistress. But then she left him, and on one drunken night in 1741, he set the place on fire and died along with his dreams.

"They built a new home on the site of the old one," the postmistress explained. "And that's why they call it Burnt Norton."

It was privately owned, she explained, but no one lived there now. "So there's no one to stop you from visiting."

There was a garden, too, but Edith wasn't interested. "I've heard of it," she said. "But my friends say there's nothing to see there. It's overgrown and abandoned."

Tom was coming that weekend, and I wanted to find a new place to explore. It was warm for September, and the trees and flowers were showing the stresses of drought. It was close enough, I figured, that we could probably cover the distance on foot. But I knew the day would grow warm. It might be nice to drive there, pack a lunch, take a blanket, and enjoy what was left of summer.

Tom was tired and distracted when he arrived, happy to let me take charge of the plans. He said he was up for a walk—as long as it steered clear of livestock. I admitted I was not sure what we would find there. But I liked breaking out of our routines. I always enjoyed a surprise.

I rose early and headed down High Street to pick up some cheese and fruit, a freshly baked loaf of bread, a bottle of wine. Tom was just rising when I returned, but there was no need to rush. I fixed myself a cup of coffee and an egg, glanced quickly at the paper. There was more worrisome news out of Germany, but I didn't want to let that spoil our day. I pushed the paper aside, gazed out the window, and listened to the whine of the cottage's ancient plumbing as Tom lingered in the shower.

"Did you sleep well?" I asked when he finally emerged.

He smiled. "You know I always do when I'm here."

He fixed some toast and tea, did his own quick read of the headlines. Then we headed out of town, driving slowly, as the postmistress had suggested, so we wouldn't miss the turnoff onto an unmarked dirt road. We pulled in, then decided to park as the road narrowed and the unmown undergrowth threatened to swallow the car. We divided up our gear and began walking slowly down the long, curving dirt path.

There were no remnants of tire treads or footprints, just a shuffle of leaves, now drying at the end of the hot summer. No sign that anyone had ever lived here, no sign there was anything worth visiting. As the sun rose higher, I wondered if I had made a mistake choosing a road to nowhere.

"It's so quiet," Tom said. "You can't hear any traffic."

I stopped and tuned my ears. Several hundred people lived in the nearby town, but it felt as if we were on a new planet. The only sound came from two birds, calling back and forth with distinctive tunes.

"Do you recognize the birds?" I asked. The songs were different here in the country.

Tom listened. "I think they are thrushes. They're small and hard to spot."

But the birds seemed to urge us on, leading us around yet another turn. And there we found it, an archway, sad with neglect, leading into the garden we were seeking.

The path was lined with rose bushes, overgrown and untamed, their perfume suddenly overpowering. As we walked side-by-side, I felt I had been here before, even as I knew that was impossible.

Then the memories converged. My feet froze, I let out a gasp.

"What is it?" he asked.

Should I tell him?

"I felt as if I had been here before," I said quietly. "And then I remembered. It was like a very strange dream I had, back when you came to California. I dreamt I was getting married. In Christ Church, where Amy got married. And as I walked down the aisle, all the faces of my friends and family turned to flowers. Like that scene in *Through the Looking-Glass*. Remember? You were lecturing about it then."

I went on. "And when the breeze blew up, the roses all turned to face us—and watched us walk down the aisle."

I must sound crazy. The last thing he needs is another crazy woman.

But Tom took my hand and threaded it through the crook in his arm. "Why don't we pretend?"

And so we strolled down the grassy path, following the line of rosebushes, processing to an insistent cacophony of birds. The path emptied out into an odd expanse of garden. There were two pools, both of them empty but edged with green moss. The larger one was rectangular, the smaller one a semicircle with a platform in the middle where a statue must have once stood.

The manor house was in the distance, lonely and in need of repair. For a moment, I could imagine an elderly woman, watching from a second-floor window, but then shook away the vision. In the other direction was a stone railing, offering a breathtaking view toward Wales, and another pathway, this one lined with trees.

We said nothing as we took in the view and the stillness. Then Tom spoke up. "Why don't we spread our blanket over there, beneath that big sycamore tree?"

We worked together to place the blanket, straightening out the corners, smoothing the bumps and wrinkles. Then I busied myself, setting out lunch. I felt that my heart would burst if I tried to speak; it was easier to pretend that there was nothing important to be said.

Tom uncorked the bottle of wine, poured each of us a glass, then took a sip from his.

"I was so foolish not to ask you to marry me."

How long had it taken him to realize that? What made him say it now?

"I've thought about that so many times over the years," I began. "We were both so young and foolish."

My words drifted away with the late-summer wind, and then I spoke again. "I was so confused and hurt when you were going away. I didn't want you to leave, but I knew I couldn't hold you back in Boston. You didn't know what your future was, but I knew you had to find it."

"You were right about that," he acknowledged. "But when I left, I did plan to return."

I took a long sip of the wine.

"When I came back two years ago," he said, "I remembered what it felt like when I left home that summer. I felt liberated when I arrived in Europe. I had escaped my family's expectations. I had escaped Boston and Cambridge. I had escaped the philosophy department at Harvard...."

"You escaped me."

"I never felt that way."

"But I was part of all those other things. Your old, conventional life."

He hesitated. "I suppose you are right." His lips formed a thin smile. "I must say that that conventional life can look very attractive right now."

"In some ways, you are living it. Going to your office every day, living with the priests."

I heard the sarcasm in my voice, but I didn't regret it. I could tell when the specter of Vivienne was about to descend again, blackening his mood.

But this time, he stopped himself. "I wonder if children ever played here."

I glanced around the formal garden. "It's hard to imagine."

"I've been spending more time around children since I returned to England. I'm surprised how much I can enjoy them, particularly the bright ones."

"It's odd," I said, "but I don't think I've ever regretted not having children. Perhaps it's because I always had my students."

"As I get older," he said wearily, "I find that I regret I will never have any children."

*As I get older....*I stretched out on the blanket, feeling sleepy from the wine. How long would Vivienne live? How long would I have to wait? How many more regrets would we have?

I had known the flutter in my heart when I was young, but there was still more that I might never know. Didn't I deserve that? Would he be willing to help me find it?

I thought of the women I had portrayed, of Judith, and The Actress, of Roxane and her word dance with Cyrano and Christian. What would they do now?

What had Vivienne done to make Tom's head spin? Did she tell him how strong he was when they went punting? Did she talk about the other men she had known? Did she laugh in his ear or press her body up against his when they went dancing?

Did she lie down on a picnic blanket and part her legs, inviting him to enter?

The bird calls had given way to the measured sound of Tom's breathing. I closed my eyes and reached out for his hand and placed it gently on my breast. When he did not recoil, I reached up to begin unbuttoning my blouse. I moved slowly, deliberately, waiting after each button. If he flinched, I could still pretend that the day had grown hot and I needed to feel the breeze.

But he did not move his hand away. Instead, he began to stroke my breast, his fingers warm through the flimsy fabric. He could take the next step, but I knew that he wouldn't. This was Prufrock after all. A man who lurched between paralysis one moment and impulse the next. A man who had drawn a line around celibacy and declared his vow to all who needed to know.

But how did he define that? How did I define virginity? Had we already crossed over into infidelity?

I thought back to the cottage and lying awake at night in my bed-room, thinking of Edith and John next door, and beyond them the vil-lagers, starting to gossip about the famous Londoner who visited on weekends. But here we were alone, away from the vigilant ears and the prying eyes. With only the birds as our witnesses, preoccupied with their own mating dances and songs.

I arched my back and reached behind to slip off my bra. For a mo-ment I reveled in the warmth of the sun on my bare nipples, and then Tom lowered his face to take one of them in his lips. I felt my blood race, my breath quicken. I pressed my hips to his, and he slipped a hand below.

And then, in a matter of moments, I knew what the others had known and what I had been waiting for.

* * *

We had fallen asleep, our arms entwined. The sun had shifted lower in the west, dropping below the canopy of leaves. We should be getting back; Edith was expecting us for tea. But I didn't want to move. I relished the sense of happy languor in my limbs, the hope that had taken root in my heart.

I blinked my eyes open and looked around, trying to take it all in. How the shadows dappled across the blanket, how the moss around the pool had darkened in the late-afternoon light. The sight of a brilliant blue-plumed bird—could it be a kingfisher? I wanted to remember it all.

We will not come back, I realized with sadness. You cannot recreate a magical moment like this. The next time would be too hot, or the sun obscured by darkening clouds. There might be flies buzzing or the stench of decay. A twisted ankle on an uneven stairway.

No, it was best to bottle it up and preserve the memory as best as I could.

Beside me, Tom began to stir. What would he think? What would he say? Would he manage to find a way to ruin it?

I sat up and began putting myself back together, wondering whether Edith would sniff out the difference.

He reached out his hand and began to stroke my back. "Will you be surprised," he began, "when I say that was all new and different for me?"

My heart leapt with joy, but I kept my voice even. "No," I replied. "And it was the same for me, too."

He sat up beside me, his brow furrowed, his eyes darkening. "It was a wonderful day. But it also made me sad. There is so little left of me." He paused, then went on. "I wish I could do more. I wish I could love you better. But I am burned out and empty. I doubt I will ever be able to recapture it."

"I hear it can come with age," I said, trying to reassure him.

"Perhaps," he said. "But if any moment should have made me come alive, this one should have."

We would not come back. Now I was sure of it.

"We ought to be getting home. Edith will be expecting us."

We packed up the dishes and folded up the blanket. Tom took one final long glance around the grounds, and then we headed back through the bower of roses.

"What will you tell Edith about the garden?" he asked when we reached the car.

I thought for a moment, then replied slowly. "That it was sad and abandoned. And that she made the right decision not to come."

* * *

As always, Tom sent Edith a gracious note when he returned to London, thanking her for her hospitality. And as the weeks went by, he began sending me fragments of his play. I could tell that he was energized, inspired by his new literary challenge. And I was thrilled that he wanted my opinions.

I tried to review the script with a director's eye, thinking how the actors would move across the stage, where the audience's attention might lag. But I also read the poetry, looking for deeper meanings. I came back, again and again, to a short passage in Act One, when the First Tempter urges Becket to stop fighting the King, to try to rekindle the camaraderie of their youth. But the Second Tempter interrupts:

Time present and time past
Are both perhaps present in time future,
And time future contained in time past.

I was disappointed when he wrote that Martin Browne had persuaded him to trim the lines. "But," he said, "I can't let go of them. And I'm beginning to think that I may still have one more poem left in me."

Vivienne and Virginia

WE NEVER RETURNED TO THE garden. And we never spoke about that day again.

On the surface, nothing had changed. Tom kept coming for the weekend, Edith kept playing the solicitous hostess, John was happy to retreat to his books. At night, we would return to my cottage, light the fire, enjoy a sherry.

And head to our separate bedrooms when it was time to go to bed.

I remembered the agonized whispers of my charges in the dorms.

"Did I go too far?"

"What will he think of me now?"

I worried that I had, in fact, crossed some unspoken boundary and that things would never again be the same.

Why did Tom never invite me into his bedroom? Couldn't we just lie there together, warming our bodies, sheltering ourselves from the rest of the world? I didn't need anything more than that.

Girls had shared their tales of fighting off too-amorous suitors, but Tom had never been like that with me. He had always been polite, respectful; I had always liked that in him.

But I wanted something more now. I found myself wondering: Was it him or was it me? Had I grown too old to stir his desire—or had he never really felt it at all?

Alone in my room, my mind wandered back to California. If I were there now, I would be somebody. I would be the assistant professor of English, planning my next lecture. I would be the celebrated director, figuring out how to top last year's production of Milton's *Comus*. I would be the actress, wowing the critics of Claremont.

But instead I was alone, with no one to provide the applause. From Boston came the shocking news that Uncle Philip had died, apparently from a cerebral hemorrhage. The memorial service was quickly arranged; Serge Koussevitzky and the rest of the Boston musical establishment attended, but there was not enough time for us to make it back from England.

Since I was a little girl, Philip had been the source of all the art in my life. He had given me music and theater and ballet. Tom could still bring me that, of course, but with Tom, there was always Vivienne. And he was still incapable of breaking free of whatever had enchained the two of them when they met. I was caught in Tom Eliot's version of Limbo, and the state of unknowing disturbed me more than ever before.

My jaw ached. I had trouble keeping meals down. I traveled into London to see high-priced doctors and dentists in Kensington. A dentist found an abscess, but the doctors, nothing more. It was, they told me, "all in your head." And I feared that indeed they were right.

I met Tom for lunch when he could get free, but he never took me to his office. I yearned to see his warren there, to help me visualize how he spent the long days in the city. I wanted to meet Mr. Faber and the secretaries and even the office cats. But Vivienne still showed up without warning, wild-eyed and demanding. The secretaries knew the protocol, to keep her occupied while Tom sneaked out the back door. But if Vivienne were to find out about me...well, he had explained, his voice full of regret, there was no telling what the woman was capable of doing.

* * *

I owed Dr. Jaqua an answer: When *was* I returning to Scripps? But as the new year approached, I still waffled. I could return to that life, but if I did, I might lose Tom forever. He would never come back to California; I knew now that he had hated the place. And his own finances were still strapped by the bills that Vivienne was racking up all over London.

In Chipping Campden, I was a different kind of "kept woman," dutifully doing whatever Edith wanted in exchange for a house and food and travel to England. But here at least, I could know Tom, the warmth of his hand, his lips on my cheek. I could be close enough to measure his moods, to wait patiently for the day when he could finally change his life.

So I wrote President Jaqua and asked him for another year. He wrote back quickly, pleasant but firm. The college could not wait forever. He had already hired my replacement. They appreciated everything I had contributed to Scripps. He wished me nothing me but the best.

From the president's letterhead, Dante's words mocked me now. *Incipit Vita Nova.* Here Begins New Life.

* * *

This time it was Jeanette who rescued me from the long darkness of the English winter. She was cobbling together a trip to Italy over her semester break. It wouldn't be fancy—her money was tight. But if I wanted to join her, she would love to have my company.

And so I found myself in Rome, where even on a cold day in December, the sky was a brilliant blue. The streets teemed with priests and nuns, soldiers and cyclists, and, more ominously, the fascists, strutting about and saluting each other, some in drab green, others sporting black shirts and fezzes, daggers slung on their hips.

Then we headed to Florence, where our finances forced us to stay further out of town than I did when Edith was paying the rent. Still, our rooms were in a villa, with a wonderful view of the Cathedral. Olive orchards in the foreground, cypress trees in the foothills, and farther still, the snow-covered Apennines. It made me homesick for California.

Back at Scripps, the academic year was coming to an end. The Siddons Club would be mounting its final production, another senior class would be leaving its mark on the Graffiti Wall and exiting under the archway. Former students were moving into more exciting lives than mine. Marie McSpadden, someone wrote, had gone to work for Mrs. Herbert Hoover, now that the former First Lady had become president of the Girl Scouts.

But even sharing a room with Jeanie, I was overcome with loneliness, a desperate feeling that I had risked far, far too much.

I found a typewriter and some carbons and tapped out a letter to my California friends. I recalled the Duke of Kent's wedding last fall, the reception where I had met the Prince of Wales. I forced myself to be cheery and optimistic. And then I brought it to a close:

I had hoped very much that I would see you all next autumn, but as you probably know, I am not coming back; this makes me all the more eager to hear from any of you who can write, or better still see any of you, be it in England this summer or at home, wherever that is going to be; a hearty welcome waits for you in either case. A happy last six weeks to you, if I may dare say happy in the face of examinations.

* * *

There was a change in Tom, a change that puzzled and distressed me. For the first time in our long relationship, he was telling *me* what I should do.

It began when Jeanie and I were heading back to England. "Don't go back to Chipping Campden," he told me. "I can find you rooms in London."

But Irene had come to visit us, and I couldn't expect Edith to manage the grieving aunt from Father's side of the family. When Tom came back out to visit, he was all wit and politeness, ever the gracious guest. But when we left my relatives at the end of the evening, he let down that pretense.

"You need to get away from them."

"Why?"

"Because Edith wants to control you. And you are letting her do it."

"But I owe her so much." If not for Edith, I would never be able to come to England.

"They are breaking your spirit. There is nothing but decay around them, and Irene only makes it worse. If you don't try, you will never be able to escape it."

I lay awake that night, mulling his harsh judgments. Was he right? Was I turning into Lula Bett after all these years? An aging spinster controlled by my family? Or was Tom the one who was breaking my spirit? I remembered his days at Harvard. There were never any parties, never any group outings. We enjoyed long walks together, but I rarely met his friends.

On our walk down High Street the next day, I found the courage to confront him.

"Why don't you ever introduce me to your friends?"

He did not have a ready answer. "I had thought it was better to be discreet. Some of them are still in touch with Vivienne. I did not want to put them in an awkward position."

"From what I've heard around London," I said archly, "there is little that your old friends find awkward."

* * *

Murder in the Cathedral had been well received in Canterbury and was moving on to the Mercury Theatre in Notting Hill Gate. Tom was preoccupied with tweaking the production and the Perkinses were preoccupied with returning home. King's Chapel was celebrating its 300th anniversary in the coming year, and John, as minister emeritus, was going to play a major role in the celebrations.

Tom was unusually quiet when he arrived on that chilly November weekend, but John took up the slack, fueled by a few early glasses of port and the prospect of being important again. But when we were alone at last, Tom held nothing back.

"Vivienne finally tracked me down."

"What happened?"

He lit a cigarette, as if steeling himself to remember. "It was so embarrassing. It was at the *Sunday Times*'s book fair, at a hall in Lower Regent Street. Of course, my appearance was publicized in advance. I had heard from friends that she had joined the fascists and that she was going about town wearing some sort of black uniform. She was wearing it when she showed up. And to make matters worse, she brought our dog to the reading.

"I didn't see her at first, but my secretary did. She tried to divert her, but Vivienne elbowed her way to the front. As I was about to start, she called out my name. I was afraid she was going to make a scene, so I decided I should shake her hand and try to be civil. I think I said, 'How do you do?'—I don't really remember. And then I proceeded to the podium to give my talk.

"I'm not sure how I got through it. When I finished, she pushed up to the front of the crowd again and let go of Polly's leash, and the dog ran and jumped up on me. Then she climbed up on the platform and dumped three books on the table. She asked if I would come home with her—there in front of the audience and the editors. I told her I couldn't talk to her then. I signed her books as quickly as I could and left. Fortunately, one of my authors was there and helped me get out the door."

He buried his face in his hands. "It was a nightmare."

I reached over and touched his knee, feeling powerless to protect him. He shook his head. "I thought I could escape her, but I never will."

I said nothing for a moment. I reached for a cigarette, lit it, and took a long drag. I had arrived the summer before with such hope in my heart. Things would be different this time. Tom would make changes. And on one afternoon, I had known true joy—and the hope that we might achieve a new understanding.

But a year had passed. We were still stuck in Tom's marriage. And when December came, I would sail back to Boston with Edith and John, with no job or prospects—or any kind of commitment from Tom.

"Well, enough of that," he finally said. "It reinforced for me that I had made the right decision. And it strengthened my resolve to continue to hide from her. But it is no way to live.

"So," he said, his voice brightening a little, "I'm trying *not* to live that way. Virginia has invited me to tea on the 26th. And if you can make it to London, she would like you to come, too."

* * *

It had thrilled me to curtsy to the Prince of Wales. But as we hurried across the tree-lined paths of Tavistock Square, I was even more excited to be visiting the Woolfs.

Tom, of course, had been there many times. He owed his fame to Virginia. Who else would have published "The Waste Land"? She had welcomed him into her circle; Vivienne, too. But over the years, he explained, things had changed. Ever since he had become an Anglican, he was no longer her pet.

A set of stairs led past the publishing business to their residence upstairs. Tom knocked, and a charwoman opened the door. We climbed another flight of stairs and paused to shed our coats and catch our breaths. "Only one more flight," he reassured me.

The Woolfs were waiting in their dining room, chatting with another male guest. Virginia rose to greet us. She was much as I had imagined her: tall and slender with deep, soulful eyes, the most dramatic feature of her long, angular face. Her graying hair was coiled up at her neck, tied back with a narrow ribbon. She wore a nondescript dark dress covered with a short velvet cloak.

Introductions were made. The younger guest was Stephen Spender. I had read some of his poems and knew that Tom respected his work. Virginia invited Tom to sit at her end of the table, where the three of them could focus on their publishing plans and the latest gossip about their friends.

"Here," Leonard said to me. "Why don't you sit next to me?"

The maid brought in tea and a honeycomb from their country place. There was a cake left over from Leonard's birthday the day before. His mother always sent one, he explained, and they needed help finishing it.

He was shorter than Virginia, with a sad sort of face that was just as long as his wife's. Still, he seemed to be trying to make me feel comfortable, no matter what his wife did.

"I don't get the chance to meet many Americans," he explained, "and I have so many questions."

"You could always ask Tom," I replied.

Leonard smiled. "Tom is no longer an American."

He proceeded to quiz me about the state of the economy, about Roosevelt's chances for reelection, about the novels that were taught in American schools.

"There's something else I'm curious about," he mused. "Are your American Indians mingled in your good society?"

The question took me aback. "Well, no," I replied. "Although the first Thanksgiving was held close to Boston, we don't actually see them there."

On the other side of the table, Virginia huddled with Tom and Stephen. Tom acted like a college student, flirting with her, trying to make her laugh. He *was* very good around women, I thought. It was the same with Aunt Edith, even Jeannette and Marie McSpadden. Tom had an instinct for telling a woman what she wanted to hear.

And after more than 20 years, he knows how to play me, too.

As we finished our tea, the Woolfs suggested we move downstairs to the living room. We followed them down and Virginia took a seat at one end of a long sofa. She motioned for me and Stephen to join her there.

"So tell me about your work," she said.

I hesitated. I wanted to say the right thing, to earn her approval, to fit in like Vivienne must have when she was young. But what could I possibly say that would impress Virginia Woolf?

"I'm between jobs actually. I have taught vocal expression at a number of colleges back in the States. Most recently at Scripps College in California. Perhaps you have heard of it?"

She took a long draw on her cigarette. If she had, she was not going to acknowledge it.

"I've also lectured, here and in Boston," I went on. "I've studied the state of the theater. English, Irish, French, German. I spoke to the American Women's Club in London a few seasons ago."

"How very interesting!" Virginia replied, then turned her attention back to Stephen.

I looked around the room, cataloging the details to try to quell my nerves. The furnishings were an odd mix of styles and pieces, set off by large panels on the wall. I squinted to see the name of the artist. Of course. Virginia's sister Vanessa. It was the home of people who wanted to be comfortable, people who *were* comfortable with each other. I looked at Leonard, then glanced back at Virginia. How wonderful, I thought, to have such a partnership. To share in a business, a creative venture.

How wonderful it must be to have a husband who was there for you.

The maid ushered in two more guests. They spoke rapidly in French. I did not catch their names, but I managed to pick up that they were connected to some literary journal. Virginia spoke to them in French, making no effort to translate for the rest of us.

The mood had changed. There seemed little reason to linger. I caught Tom's eye across the room and was relieved that he, too, was ready to leave. "We should be on our way," he said, rising from his chair.

"So early?" Virginia replied, but it was clear she didn't really care. We said our goodbyes, made half-hearted promises to get together again soon, then we headed back down the stairs and out into the chilly November night.

"What did you think?" Tom asked.

"They're a very interesting couple," I said slowly. "But I don't think she liked me."

"Don't be silly," he replied. "She treats everyone that way."

And so I tried hard to be gracious. I wrote Virginia, thanking her for inviting us to tea. I noted that I had failed to mention how much I had enjoyed her books, and that my old colleague, Ruth George, was a great admirer who had taught her work in her advanced English seminar at Scripps.

But I couldn't shake the feeling I had done something wrong. Had I made a grammatical faux pas or held a teacup incorrectly? Or perhaps my only offense was becoming Tom Eliot's new lady friend. But whatever it was, the air of disapproval had lingered on after we had left. And years later, I acknowledged, a second invitation never arrived.

The Waste Sad Time

THE ANCIENT HALL CLOCK IN the massive home on Brimmer Street began counting down to midnight. Miss Ware had gamely offered to try to stay up as late as she could, but I was not surprised when the clock struck ten and she wished me Happy New Year and slowly hobbled upstairs to her bedroom.

I could have found a party somewhere, but I preferred to stay here, nursing a flute of once-forbidden champagne. Alone except for a few servants, checking their watches and eager to lock up the place for the night.

What a difference three years makes! Three years ago, I was holding court at a dinner party, laughing with old friends, enjoying the warmth of a winter night in southern California. Kissing Tom when the clock finally struck midnight.

But my gamble had failed. Now I was stuck, stuck back in Boston with no job, no future—and no one to give me a celebratory kiss.

* * *

I was happy when Mary Lee Ware had invited me to move into her home. It was easier than staying on with Edith and John, and she was an interesting dinner companion—when she was able to stay awake. We could share memories of Italy and Florence. The old woman loved talking about the Botanical Museum and the glass flowers her family had commissioned from the Blaschkas in Dresden. But she was getting up in years—close to 80, I guessed. And so I learned to smile and nod politely when I heard the same story for the third or fourth time.

Miss Ware actually liked reading poetry, and some evenings we would sit by the fire and share our favorite poems. But, she made clear, she did not like those "modern boys." And as for "that Thomas Eliot," he had abandoned his elderly mother, his Harvard mentors, his denomination, and his country. On top of that, she didn't understand a word of what he was trying to say.

So I kept those poems to myself and sequestered Tom's letters when they found their way to Miss Ware's mailbox.

I knew I had to find a job, but it was even harder now than before. Every college, especially those for women, was struggling to keep its doors open. The schools around Boston could be fussy about who they hired: They expected their professors to have doctorates, and I had still never mustered the time or the money to earn a degree.

My long list of productions and the glowing reviews were all very interesting, I was told again and again. But the colleges could survive, if they had to, without a drama club or a speech instructor. They needed professors who could teach both French and German or cover both chemistry and physics.

Tom Eliot was still the darling of Harvard, but Harvard wasn't about to hire me. Tom's brother-in-law taught at Wellesley, and Tom had another good friend in the English Department there. But even Wellesley expected its professors to have master's degrees.

President Lafavour had retired from Simmons, along with most of my old friends. Paul Havens was being considered for the presidency of a small college in Pennsylvania, but a final decision had not been made. Margaret and Willard were trying to use their connections at Smith, but so far nothing had materialized.

Amy and Dick Hall nagged me to try out for the next production of the Cambridge Social Dramatic Club, or at least come help with the props. But I didn't have the energy. The doctors could find nothing wrong. I was going through "the change of life," they said. When I rode out to Belmont to visit Mother, I wondered if I, too, might be destined for the hospital someday.

Tom's letters kept arriving like clockwork, at least one a week, sometimes two. He encouraged me to take an acting role, look for a job, get away from Beacon Hill and Cambridge. But I didn't have the energy to send a reply. What difference did it make? Nothing had really changed.

In England, though, it was different. The king had died and the Prince of Wales had ascended to the throne. Now even the Boston papers were abuzz over who the bachelor would take as his queen. Princess Frederica-Louise, the granddaughter of Kaiser Wilhelm, and Princess Alexandrine Louise of Denmark seemed to be the most likely candidates.

I read Miss Ware the story, then told her about the time I had met the prince. Then I folded up *The Globe* and smiled. "It appears, however, that I have missed my chance to marry Edward."

* * *

It was Edith who suggested I visit Senexet. The Unitarians had just opened the retreat center and our old friend, Velma Williams, was running it.

It was easier to go along with Edith than to put up a fight. I knew she was worried about me, almost to the point of exasperation. But if she was willing to pay the fee and arrange for a car, there were certainly worse ways to spend a weekend than to visit the Connecticut woods.

And it *was* good to get away, I acknowledged as I headed south out of Boston. I enjoyed driving when I got the chance. The traffic was light, and I could let my mind wander.

I knew Tom loved going on retreats, but I was dubious whether I would be able to find the kind of peace he did visiting the priests at Kelham. Still, I was sure that Senexet would be a cozier place to stay. Velma and her friends had been looking for a rural spot somewhere between New York and Boston. The rambling Victorian cottage sounded perfect—large enough to provide the rooms they needed and situated in the middle of a pine forest, a buffer from urban cares. As I navigated my car up the muddy winding road, I felt I was entering another cathedral, the tall evergreens taking my eyes skyward to the clouds the same way the flying buttresses of King's Chapel had.

I found Velma in the front hall. She gave me a hug, then directed me to my room upstairs. She was like a Mother Superior, but this was no dreary convent. The rooms sported vases filled with flowers and tasteful arrangements of pine cones, branches, and grasses. The walls were lined with watercolors and woodland photographs, my narrow bed covered with a handmade quilt.

I unpacked my bag, then went back downstairs. The day had turned unseasonably warm, and I found Velma on the porch, watching her guests begin to explore the grounds.

"It's beautiful here," I said. "You've done a wonderful job."

"Thank you. It's given me a great deal of joy."

"Your husband was a good friend of my father's. I remember meeting him when I was a girl."

"They were both good men," Velma said, "and they both died too young."

"Ah, but your husband left behind some great hymns. 'Glory be to God on high,' I began to sing. 'Let the whole creation cry.'"

Velma smiled. "I often hum that one when I'm walking around the grounds. 'Creatures of the field and flood. Earth and sea cry "God is good."'"

We were silent for a moment, each of us lost in our thoughts.

"I feel my husband's spirit with me here," Velma said at last.

"I can see why," I replied.

"What are you looking for?"

The question startled me. "I'm...I'm not really sure." Then I was embarrassed, feeling the weight of all my Unitarian relatives. "I'm sorry. I should have a better answer than that."

"Nonsense," Velma replied. "I would be more worried if you had a pat one."

* * *

It was a congenial group, and Velma worked hard to make everyone feel at ease. The food was good, the conversation around our large table was lively and fun. When it was time to go to bed, I felt a sense of happy fatigue, so different from the restless hours I lay awake back in Boston. As I drifted off to sleep, I listened to the murmur of the wind in the pines, telling me: "It will be all right. It will be all right."

In the morning, Velma began her program. She read some poems and posed a few questions. We could choose to discuss them or spend time in personal meditation. I debated whether to stay inside with the others, but I was tired of putting on a smile and making small talk. I needed to try to find myself.

My thoughts wandered along with my feet, following the path down to the lakeshore, now shimmering in the late-afternoon sunlight. I thought of Father and singing in his sanctuary. I thought of Tom and how he had changed over the years. I still did not understand how a cynical Unitarian, a young man who had dabbled in Eastern religions, could become such a rigid Anglican. It was all because of Vivienne. Would he ever overcome the guilt he felt over what had happened to the two of them? Others moved on with their lives, got divorces, took lovers. But the two of us seem fated to keep struggling to meet others' expectations—and be miserable in the process.

I am not going to let him suck me dry!

Where had that come from? From my font of memories? Or was "the Spirit," whatever that was, trying to tell me something?

I knew how to live. I had been here before. There were four ways the story could play out, and I controlled none of the endings. I could die or Tom could die or Vivienne could die first. Or Tom could change his mind and get a divorce. I smiled. There *was* one other ending. We could run away to a faraway island. Balboa Island would do in a pinch. And we could live happily ever after.

Somehow the other endings seemed much more likely.

I checked my watch. It was getting late, almost time for dinner. I headed back to the house, now glowing with warm lamplight. It was quiet when I entered, except for a bustle in the direction of the kitchen. I wiped my muddy feet on the rug and hung my coat on an empty peg.

Off to one side was "the chapel." Candles were lit on the makeshift altar, and I felt drawn to them, not understanding why. I remembered sad Christmas Eves and painful Christmas Days. I remembered Miss Brown's Christmas pageants. I remembered singing carols on Lantern Night and in the courtyard at Toll Hall. I remembered the sad memories of Tom's aging Magi.

And then I began to cry. I was not exactly sure which memory had triggered the tears. But as I knelt there, I realized I had held them in for too long. And now it felt so good to be in this protected place and let them flow as long as they had to.

* * *

In the end, Smith College came through with an offer. I figured that the Thorps had twisted every arm they could but spared me from the details. I survived the interviews and was deemed an Assistant Professor of Spoken English. Now all I had to do was find a place in Northampton and get to work.

But it still seemed overwhelming.

I still felt tired and out of sorts. Edith said I should move back in with them. She was worried about my health. She thought I needed fresh air, a better diet. There were too many ways I could waste my time if I stayed at Miss Ware's house. So I gave in again, and on a sunny Saturday morning, a hired hand helped me move to the Cambridge side of the river. The air there might be more rarefied, but I doubted it was any cleaner.

* * *

On a late day in August, Edith knocked on my bedroom door. "I have a surprise," she said. "Tom is in town. I invited him to come over this afternoon."

I scurried out of bed, checking my hair self-consciously. *When had I last washed it?* "Why didn't he tell me?"

"He was worried about you. He wrote me that you weren't responding to his letters."

I knew that was true. I would start a letter but could never finish it. "I've been busy," I protested. "There's so much to do to get ready for this fall."

"Well, you can explain that to him. He's staying at his sister's. I invited him for tea." She scrutinized me from head to toe. "You've got a few hours to try to make yourself presentable. I suggest you get started."

* * *

Tom came right on time, dressed, as always, as if he were still a banker. I watched from the parlor as Edith greeted him in the entry hall. He kissed Edith on both cheeks, then handed her his hat. She ushered him into the parlor, asked the maid to bring in tea. He kissed me chastely on the cheek, then joined me on the sofa. Edith fussed over the tray, then backed out of the room. "I'll leave the two of you alone now." She closed the pocket doors as she left.

Neither of us spoke for a moment. "How are you taking your tea these days?" I asked at last.

"The same as always," he replied.

"And what brings you to America?" I asked archly as I filled his cup. "Another honorary degree perhaps?"

"I wanted to visit my family," he said quietly. "And I wanted to visit you." He hesitated. "I'm been worried about you."

"So Edith told me."

"You haven't been answering my letters."

"They're hard to keep up with. You write much more quickly than I do." I took a sip of tea. "Besides," I said, "I don't have much to say. There's not much happening in my life. And nothing has changed for you, has it?"

"No," he said. "It hasn't."

"Then what's the point?"

"The point, Emily, is that I still love you. I worry about you. I want you to be happy."

Did he really?

"Edith said you've gotten a post at Smith," he said. "That's wonderful news. I think you'll be happy there. But you have to try to recapture your old self."

"That's easy for you to say."

He was quiet for a moment. "I've started working on a new play. I'm having some trouble with it. It's about a family, and a son coming home after a long time away. I'm trying to work out a lot of things that are inside of me." He paused. "I was hoping that you'd be willing to read it and give me your advice...as a director, of course."

"If you want me to...."

"I've also written a poem. I think it's the best thing I've written in a while. I hope you'll agree." He pulled out an envelope and slid it across the table.

He went on. "I hope I didn't shock you by showing up unannounced. I'll be here for a few weeks. I'm staying at my sister's on Madison Street." He hesitated. "I'd like to come by tomorrow if it suits you."

"All right."

"About two?"

I nodded.

"Then I'll see myself out."

We rose from our chairs, but before he turned to leave, he took my hands and drew me close. He lifted my wrists to his lips, kissing each pulse point in turn. Could he feel my pulse race? This simple gallant gesture, breaking through my hardened shell?

He left me then, alone with a half-finished cup of cooling tea and a stark white envelope labeled "Emily." I snatched it up quickly and headed out the door.

I ran into Edith hovering outside. "How is Tom?" she asked. She was never far away.

"He's well," I replied. "He'll be back tomorrow."

"That's nice."

I retreated up the stairs, closed the bedroom door, and took a seat by the window. I remembered the first time I had read "Prufrock." I remembered my excitement when each new poem or essay arrived in the mail, inscribed with my name. The inscriptions were circumspect, never passionate. Still, they told the world that I was Tom's special friend.

I did not like to admit it, but I knew Tom gave me status. Status that might come in handy when I started teaching at Smith.

At last, I opened the envelope. I gasped when I saw the title.

Burnt Norton.

It began with the lines I had seen before, the ones he had trimmed from the Canterbury play. They seemed to fit here. The poem went on, filled with longing and sadness and memories.

Ridiculous the waste sad time
Stretching before and after.

The waste sad time. Yes, that was an apt way to describe these last years together.

I read the poem again and again, trying to decide what Tom was trying to tell me. That we could never recreate the past? Or were his vivid memories a sign that he still believed we could?

For now, at least, I was touched that he remembered the birds and the roses, the empty pools, the dappled sunlight. The quickening of our love as that afternoon drew on.

I was happy he remembered it at all.

* * *

I couldn't deny that it was good to have Tom in town. Nothing had changed, of course, but he had a gentle way of teasing me that always left me feeling happy. To spend time with him, to talk with him, it all renewed my confidence that I could still be a successful teacher.

We both were itinerants, I realized, itinerants who had learned to travel light. Tom had the luxury of an office, but Vivienne still controlled most of his personal effects. I had no furniture to speak of, no fine china, no paintings. I had a few photographs and programs from my plays. And I had the letters, the one thing I would never part with, even as the boxes got bigger and heavier and harder to move.

"I've saved all your letters, you know," I told him, as I worked on packing up for Northampton.

"I've saved all of yours, too."

I hesitated. "I've been wondering what will happen to them after I'm gone."

"That's not a very cheery thought!"

"Seriously, Tom, you're an important person now. Your letters should be preserved. Scholars will want to read them some day."

"I don't like the thought of other people pawing through our letters. It's bad enough the kinds of things that critics are trying to read into my work. Most of it is hogwash."

I said nothing for a moment. "Your letters are the most valuable thing I own, Tom. No matter what you think, I'm going to find them a good home."

* * *

Twenty years before, I had traveled to Smith as a star, playing Olivia in *Twelfth Night*, with Margaret there to cheer me on. Now I went as the most junior member of a department that, I quickly observed, was not particularly high on the college's academic pecking order.

And Smith was so much larger than the other places where I had taught. At Scripps and Milwaukee-Downer, all the faculty members could fit on the front steps for our yearbook photo. But here there were more than a hundred, and everyone, it seemed, held a doctorate.

I still felt shell-shocked, but it helped that Tom was staying on until October. He had committed to making one speech at Wellesley, and I debated whether I should try to arrange for him to talk at Smith. But I didn't know how to begin. President Neilson was surrounded by layers of protective secretaries, and Tom already had a distant cousin in the English Department. It would be presumptive of me to propose it. And Tom wouldn't want to do it anyway.

His family was returning to New Hampshire in late September, and he asked me to come along. I was able to get free for a long weekend and made the trip north by train.

It was good to be back among the Eliots. Tom was relaxed and funny, basking again in the adoration of his older sisters. I enjoyed spending more time with Theresa, quietly observing Tom's sister-in-law as she huddled over her sketchbook, trying to capture the essence of each member of the family in her portraits.

I envied Theresa's marriage. She and Henry were deeply in love, but also each other's best friend. She brought out the best in him and had a calming effect on Tom. I knew she corresponded with Vivienne and had visited her, but she kept those confidences to herself.

This is what family feels like, I thought, as the long weekend drew to a close. I had tried to find one wherever I lived, but it was hard to build one from scratch. The Eliots provided Tom with a warm cocoon of acceptance and siblings who still welcomed him home, even if he had rejected everything they stood for. It was not the same as a judgmental aunt, a distracted uncle, a barely functioning mother.

"You are good for Tom," Theresa observed, as we sat on the porch the last night of my visit. "He is happier when you are around."

"I hope so," I replied.

"I wish it could be different," Theresa said. "I wish he were free. I think he would marry you if he could."

I smiled wanly. "But he can't, can he?"

"No, he can't," she agreed.

Summer was ending, and the nights were growing cool. Tom would return to England and I would go back to Smith. We were always saying goodbye at this time of year, when there was a hint of frost in the air and the leaves were starting to fall. The premonition of another winter of emptiness.

"Promise me you'll write," Tom said as we waited at the train station.

"I'll try," I said.

"Will you come back to England next summer?"

"It's too early to say."

But what was the point, I wondered? My thumb found the ring on my finger, and I played with it distractedly. It had been four years since Tom had given it to me, but nothing had changed. Once again I could cross the ocean, passing another summer waiting for Vivienne to die. But what kind of a life was that?

"You still give me hope," he said, drawing me into his arms.

One more train station, one more embrace.

He whispered the words again. "You still give me hope."

* * *

At other schools, the young women had taken my classes to learn how to speak in public, to build their poise and their confidence. In Milwaukee and Claremont, my Boston accent was considered exotic, something to be mimicked.

But Smith was different. The girls came from all over the country, most from wealthy, well-educated families. They were not easily impressed. In fact, it was considered fashionable *not* to be impressed.

And my classes were different, too. There were still the girls who wanted to be teachers or whose fathers were pushing them into business careers. But everyone at Smith was expected to speak properly, and everyone was screened as soon as she arrived. If a student had a stutter or spoke with too much "nasality," she was told she had a handicap that she had to overcome. It was a terrible way, I thought, to start a new subject. There were girls who did not realize they had a "problem" until Smith College told them that they did.

I was used to teaching the class presidents and the best actresses. Now I got the girls whose confidence was shaken, the girls who had made it into Smith only because of their last name, girls who knew their grades weren't really good enough.

I tried to inspire them and to be a friend. But I still was careful to keep them at a distance. When I read the long list of the faculty members and the advanced degrees that were attached to their names, I felt as if I were one of the stutterers. It would be too easy for those lagging students to drag me down, too.

* * *

It turned out that the King of England did not have his eye on a European princess. Instead he was cruising the Adriatic with an American, Mrs. Ernest Simpson. "Wally" was, according to American press reports, "vivacious," "dark-eyed," and "dashingly attractive." The king had booted his widowed mother out of Buckingham Palace and her role as his official hostess. And Mrs. Simpson was about to divorce her second husband.

Around London, it was known that Edward definitely had an eye for the ladies. I studied the newspaper photos critically. Wallis Simpson, I decided, was not a great beauty, but she made the most of what she had.

Would the king make her queen? Could a divorcée become queen? Would the Church of England ever allow it? The girls at Smith were abuzz about the possibilities, while the Boston papers tracked each new chapter of the soap opera. From Cannes, Mrs. Simpson issued a statement saying she was ready to give up the King. The King, however, would not relent. It was suggested he would resign and run for prime minister. Just like the plot of that Shaw play I had caught in Malvern a few summers before.

And then in mid-December, the crisis ended with astonishing speed, and the full story was finally shared with the English people. The King had decided to abdicate his throne so he could marry Wallis Simpson.

His radio address was broadcast around the world, and as I listened alone in my room, I was surprised how clear the reception turned out to be. Edward's voice did not falter, but he still sounded very, very tired, the way Tom often did. I wondered if Tom was listening. It would be hard, I knew, to escape the broadcast.

But you must believe me when I tell you that I have found it impossible to carry the heavy burden of responsibility and to discharge my duties as King as I would wish to do without the help and support of the woman I love.

I gasped, even though the outcome was ordained. He was putting Wallis Simpson before his country, his crown. Even the Church of England.

If only Tom Eliot could see *his* choices the same way.

It may be some time before I return to my native land....

Did I hear a choke in Edward's voice? Where did Tom's heart belong now?

If there remained any doubt over how the Church of England would come down on the whole matter, the Archbishop of Canterbury took care of that two days later. "Church Censures Edward; Archbishop Voices Rebuke as Windsor Reaches Exile; Ex-King's Social Set Denounced on Radio," *The Globe's* headline read.

"Strange and sad it must be," said the Archbishop, "that for such a motive, however strongly it was pressed upon his heart, he (Edward) should have disappointed hopes so high and abandoned a trust so great.

"Even more strange and sad it is that he should have sought his happiness in a manner inconsistent with the Christian principles of marriage, and within a social circle whose standards and ways of life are alien to all the best instincts and traditions of his people."

I was confident that somewhere in London, Tom was saying a prayer for the soul of the former King of England.

* * *

There was a drama program at Smith but no suggestion that I should be a part of it. And once you had been a director, it was hard to go back to managing the props. So I stayed on the sidelines. Tom was hard at work on his new play, and this time, he made clear, he really *did* want my input.

Follow the Furies needed work, including, I thought, a better title. I was amused that he had set the play in an English country home, but it was certainly not another parlor comedy by Barrie or Coward.

I was cautious about making suggestions. I wished I could recruit some friends to read the parts out loud and try blocking the scenes. It was always hard to evaluate a script by reading it silently. His chorus of Furies provided a new staging dilemma.

But there was another reason I had to be careful. The script, it was clear, grew out of Tom's marriage. It was more accessible than *Sweeney Agonistes* but still shocking in its own way. Harry was returning to his family after eight years away, tormented by the conviction that when his wife had fallen overboard on an ocean cruise, he was the one who had pushed her.

And what of Mary, I wondered, the younger distant relative that Harry might have married? The character was critical to the structure of the play but still needed more development. But was I critiquing a character or the part I had played in Tom Eliot's life? It was hard to separate the two.

I was relieved to learn that Tom was seeking input from others, but proud that he still valued my opinion. But would he incorporate my suggestions? Or was the play just another confession, different from the kind he made to his priests?

I sharpened a new pencil. It was time to play the director and try, yet again, to bury all those other old emotions away.

* * *

The second year at Smith seemed easier. I knew my way around campus and had lesson plans in place. And then I picked up *The Globe* one day in late September and was shocked when I saw the headline:

"Osgood Perkins Is Dead, Show Goes On."

Oggie had just opened as the lead, opposite Gertrude Lawrence, in *Susan and God* at the National Theatre in Washington. He had died of a heart attack in his hotel room just a few hours after drawing rave reviews.

Osgood. Dead at 45, younger than I was. His body already cremated, his ashes bound for Forest Hills Cemetery in Jamaica Plain.

I remembered New Year's Eve, the laughter and gaiety, little Anthony sleeping in Mary Eyre's bedroom. Now he was five, attending school in

New York. I closed my eyes, not wanting to imagine how he learned his father had died.

I moved through the next hours in a daze. The campus was ablaze with fall colors, but I saw none of them. It was so cruel, so unfair. What kind of a God would strike Oggie down only hours after his biggest success?

It was weeks before I worked through my rage, cried some tears, sent Janey a painful condolence note. I thought of reaching out to Tom for comfort but feared I would receive the chill of his perfect piety instead. I was left instead with my memories of Oggie and how he had bolstered me when we performed in *Eliza Comes to Stay*. After that, he had signed up to drive ambulances in France. When America went to war, he had enlisted in the Army. A career on Broadway, movies in Hollywood. A husband, a father. He had lived his life to the fullest.

What was I doing with mine?

* * *

Christmas was coming, with more bittersweet memories. Perhaps if I found my way back to the church, that would help. Nothing else seemed to.

On a whim, I stopped by the office of the college chaplain. Burns Chalmers was a Quaker, recruited by President Neilson to teach religion and biblical literature. Chapel services were no longer compulsory, but the college still held a special service at the end of the fall term.

"I wondered if you could use any help with the Christmas service?" I asked.

A smile lit up his long face, and behind his wired-frame glasses, his eyes twinkled. "I must admit I don't have a long list of volunteers clamoring to join me."

"You probably have it planned already," I added quickly. "But I've helped with the vespers and nativity plays at the other places where I've taught, and so I thought I would ask."

"I can always use new ideas."

Burns proved to be a good listener as I talked about Father and shared old programs. He liked the idea of using a mix of scripture and poetry, and moving beyond the manger scene. He asked me to suggest some poems, and better yet, to help him read them.

It was good to have an assignment and another speaking role. I pored over my own books, spent more time in the library. I found two poems I liked from *The Home Book of Poetry*. Tom would roll his eyes, but I didn't care. Chesterton had died the year before, so it seemed fitting to include his poem about the wise men. Burns readily accepted my suggestions.

The final section of the service would be entitled "The Light of the World." I had another suggestion to make from one of the choruses of Tom's first play. A section entitled "O Light Invisible." I began reciting from memory.

> *...In our rhythm of earthly life, we tire of light. We are glad when the day ends, when the play ends; and ecstasy is too much pain....*

"I like it," Burns said when I finished. "Who wrote it?"

"T. S. Eliot," I replied. "He's a friend of mine."

* * *

But I kept Tom a secret from most of my colleagues. It was not like Scripps, where he had met all of my friends and they had lobbied me for some small piece of his time. The letters still came, week after week, but now I read them alone in my apartment.

I took my meals with the residents of Laura Scales House, but I had little in common with the girls assigned to my table. Europe was on the brink of disaster, yet their preoccupations seemed so frivolous: The parties back home at the country club, the dance next weekend at Amherst. I chewed my food slowly and was always careful to set down my silverware in between the bites. I ignored the girls' impatience, their eagerness to be dismissed.

Still, I yearned to connect with them. And deep inside me, the heart of an actress still burned. When Valentine's Day approached, the dorm laid plans for a costume party, with everyone expected to come dressed as a book. I mulled the possibilities for days before coming up with my inspiration. Edith lent me a favorite gown from her youth, an Edwardian silk dress, a vision of green, along with a necklace and earbobs. I found an old silver mirror in a store downtown and swept my hair up like a latter-day Gibson Girl.

As I walked down the stairs, I stared into the mirror, held at arm's length in front of me. I heard a few admiring "oohs" from the girls gathered at the bottom but did not let it shake my haughty gaze. "*A Backward*

Glance by Edith Wharton," the emcee announced, and the girls broke into applause.

I relished that sound, wherever I found it. There were places that had treated me like a celebrity: smaller colleges, amateur theater companies. But I lacked the courage to do more than that. I had made my choice, cast my future with Tom. He would always be the star.

* * *

We returned to England that summer, but the leisurely country walks and gay outings to the London theater now seemed like a distant memory. Across the Channel, Hitler was flexing his muscles, annexing the Sudetenland and harassing the Jews. I remembered the black-uniformed fascists strutting through Rome and Florence with exaggerated self-importance. But here in England, the memories of The Great War were still too fresh. No one wanted to contemplate another.

In the meantime, Tom had finished *The Family Reunion*, a more marketable title, I agreed. He had incorporated some of my other suggestions, too. I had hoped he would develop the character of Mary more, but it was clear he was more interested in Harry, his struggles and his guilt. Mary was just a plot device, not a flesh-and-blood woman. For now, she did not interest the playwright.

* * *

In July, we went north to Swanwick, where the Student Christian Movement had invited Tom to speak at its conference. He was in a foul mood; his voice was scratchy, his neck stiff. He asked me to bring him one glass of water after another to wet his throat. He did not bother to introduce me to the eager young woman in charge, but I figured it out for myself. She was Mary Trevelyan, a member of a prominent family of clergy, diplomats, and professors. She was rather like Edith, I thought: efficient, but just a little bit bossy. She filled the room with her tall frame, loud voice, and hearty laugh. She welcomed Tom but did not fawn over him. She had a conference to run, and he was just one of her speakers.

And what does she make of me? *Am I his wife? His friend? His mistress?* As always, I took a seat in the rear where I wouldn't draw attention.

They had invited Tom because of his faith, but what they really wanted was his poetry. He recited a few poems, but his voice was a monotone. I knew his heart wasn't in it.

But Mary helped to cover for him. She gently guided Tom back to the podium, urged the students to show their appreciation, and signaled them to applaud longer and louder.

In a flash, I remembered another night, a rainy night in Milwaukee, when I had escorted Robert Frost out onto the stage and confidently introduced him to a hall full of people.

I had relished playing that role for a famous poet. And now, I observed, Mary Trevelyan did, too.

* * *

Sometimes Tom stayed long enough in the countryside that he made arrangements to receive his mail there. We had planned to go for a walk that day in mid-July. But when he returned from the post office, I knew from the look on his face that it was not going to happen.

"What is it?" I asked.

He handed me the opened envelope. I glanced at the return address. It was from Vivienne's brother.

"Vivienne was found wandering the streets at five in the morning," he recounted. "She was ranting and raving. Someone got her to the Marylebone Police Station. The police told Maurice that if they hadn't reached him, they would have placed her under observation. She said she was hiding out from mysterious people and asked Maurice if I had been beheaded. Maurice has made an appointment with a doctor tomorrow. He asked whether I would come into town in the morning to go with them."

I hesitated. "Will you?"

"No," he replied wearily. "There would be no point. And Maurice seems to have it all under control."

He tucked the letter inside his jacket and replaced his hat. "I'm going out for a bit," he announced. "I need to do some thinking."

* * *

A month later, the second letter arrived. The deed was finally done. Vivienne had been committed, Maurice wrote, to a place called Northumberland House, an asylum in London. He had met with the doctors, heeded their recommendation, and gone before the magistrate to get the order approved. He had arranged for a doctor and two nurses to fetch her. They had arrived in late evening and reported that after some discussion, Vivienne had gone with them quietly. She was settling in to the place, sleeping and eating well, doing a bit of reading. Actually, Maurice said, she was acting rather cheerful.

It was exactly what Tom would want to hear. I wondered how much of it was true. The committal order would have required the signatures of two friends or family members. I wondered who had provided the second.

Vivienne was finally locked safely away. There would be no more wandering through the streets, stalking their friends, showing up at Faber's, or surprising Tom at book signings. She could no longer hurt herself. She could no longer hurt Tom.

Still, Tom *should* have been more involved. Despite their separation, he was still helping Maurice manage the Haigh-Woodses' estate. It was cowardly to abandon Vivienne's brother at a time like this.

But that was Tom Eliot. He had relied on Eleanor to break the news of his marriage. He had left it to his solicitors to tell Vivienne he was leaving. He could adopt a new religious faith if it saved him from pursuing a divorce.

He was a man who hated face-to-face confrontations. And time and again, he had done everything he could to avoid having to have one.

* * *

I was troubled as the summer drew to a close, but I found I could not give voice to what was troubling me. Tom seemed happier now that someone else was managing Vivienne. But if he could put his wife in a box, could he do the same thing to me? Would things change now between us, or did I suit his needs for now: a woman who would listen, a woman who would re-enter his life every summer, then conveniently disappear at the end of it?

Before I left once again, he told me he had arranged a surprise. He took me to a kennel, where, it turned out, he had picked out a dog for me. It was an elkhound, a ball of gray fluff, whose ears perked up when we stopped by his cage. "His name is Boerre," Tom informed me. He pronounced it like a shiver.

The dog was sweet, but I was not sure I wanted him. Could I even take him with me on the ship back home? And once I got him there, would he just become one more complication and expense? Could I even keep him in my rooms back at Smith? Was Tom trying to make it harder for me to leave home while he sorted out the mess of his life?

But after I arrived back in Northampton, I discovered I liked having Boerre around. When I took the hound for a walk, I would talk with him, pretending he was Tom. At night, the dog cuddled by my feet while I reread Tom's latest letter, and when I went to bed, I let him settle in beside me. His love was full, uncomplicated. And that, I found, was nice for a change.

The Big Pond

EACH DAY THAT FALL SEEMED to bring another piece of terrifying news. Sometimes even close to home.

In late September, a massive hurricane blew out of the Atlantic, farther north than the forecasters had ever predicted. At Smith, we hunkered down in our dorms and apartments. The girl from Florida retold the stories of the terrible hurricane that had hit the Keys a few years before. Don't venture out, she warned, when the eye passes through. Boerre trembled as he sensed the barometer dropping; we camped out in our halls and stayed away from the windows.

I remembered living through the flu epidemic at Simmons. At least this time, we could clutch each other tightly, huddling together as the winds raged around the buildings, reminding me of the fury of God. But when the winds finally dissipated, the damage had been done. On the beautiful campus, more than 200 trees had come down. Across the expanse of New England, the reports were all the same. Floods, mayhem, destruction. The forestry departments at Harvard and Yale woke up the next day and discovered they no longer had forests.

But in Europe, the news was even grimmer. By the end of September, Neville Chamberlain had returned from Munich, declaring that he had reached an agreement with Hitler to achieve "peace for our time." Still, the Sudetenland had been annexed by Germany. Two months later, Hitler's followers ransacked synagogues and shops owned by Jews.

In his letters, Tom wondered whether his adopted country still had any backbone left. In Northampton, President Neilson and Professor Kraushaar organized a rally to protest *Kristallnacht,* and I went down and joined the crowd. It made me feel good to do *something*, but I suspected that the *Führer* wouldn't notice.

The following spring, *The Family Reunion* finally premiered in London. It was not a good time for a play to open on the London stage, and the critics echoed the city's anxious mood. They were puzzled by what Tom was trying to say and the odd juxtaposition of the English drawing room and the threatening Furies peering through the window. The play ran for only five weeks. And when I arrived with Edith and John for one more summer vacation, Tom was still stewing over his artistic failure.

I was free to visit his office now. I got to know the secretaries and all the cats that roamed the place. One of them, named "Morgan," even composed some verses for me.

"Mr. Eliot," he said, had encouraged him to try his hand at poetry, because he was "too fat for mousin' and too old for fightin.'" Tom had suggested he write a "birthday oration" for "Miss 'Ile" and told him he'd pay him a kipper per line.

She's the one ol' Morgan would most like to see,
Be it winter or summer, in snow boots or slippers,
At breakfast or luncheon, at dinner or tea:

This was what I had always yearned for: simple, straightforward affection. No troubled Prufrock. No Sweeney or Harry. Just to be the one Tom (or Morgan) most wanted to see.

It would be nice to hear it directly from the man rather than from a cat, and a Cockney one at that. But then I recalled owls and pussycats, a trip to Balboa, and breakfasts and luncheons and dinners and tea.

There were simple pleasures still to be shared.

But there was no change in the pattern of our lives. Vivienne might be confined to an asylum, but she was still Mrs. T. S. Eliot. And that anxious summer of 1939, like all the ones before it, eventually came to an end. We sailed away on a ship bound for Boston. And in the middle of the Atlantic Ocean, we learned that Germany had invaded Poland.

* * *

Alone in my cabin at night, I found it impossible to sleep. In "the old days," I had always used the voyage home to savor my memories of times with Tom, the summer walks, the late-night talks in front of the fire, teasing him relentlessly about his stodginess. I wanted to organize each moment like a card in a library catalog drawer, making it easier to retrieve it from my brain when I needed it in the long empty months alone.

But this trip was different. This time, as we zigzagged a route through unknown terrors, my memories were heavy with fear. I remembered worrying about Tom when he was stuck in Germany. I remembered the U-boat raids and the *Lusitania*. I remembered the vast, dangerous ocean that had kept him from coming home.

Kept him in England with Vivienne.

Back then, I had been a powerless young woman. Now, I acknowledged, I was a powerless old spinster.

* * *

Smith College was in turmoil, too. After 22 years, President Neilson had retired, and in every corner of the campus, the politicking had begun over who would replace him—and what it would mean for our departments. The trustees drafted one of their own, Elizabeth Morrow, to serve in the interim, and she was a popular choice: an alumna, a senator's wife, and Lindbergh's mother-in-law to boot. But she was simply the "acting president," because everyone knew the college wanted to find a man for the job.

And eventually they found one. Like Neilson, Herbert Davis was a professor of English, this time out of Cornell. My colleagues respected his academic credentials but were not sure he knew anything about running a university.

My own dramas seemed so insignificant compared with the stories coming out of Europe. Burns Chalmers had left for southern France, hoping to help Jewish refugees escape the country if they got that far. Meanwhile, my Unitarian friends were buzzing about the pastor from Wellesley Hills. He and his wife had left their children behind in the States to do the same kind of dangerous work in Eastern Europe.

As for Tom, he had written that he had moved to Surrey to escape the terrors of the nightly bombings of London. But he returned to the city two days a week to volunteer as an air-raid warden. He checked on his neighbors, then stood watch at his office or on a rooftop in South

Kensington, waiting as the hot ash drifted down through the night sky, threatening the roofs of tinder-dry houses.

It was odd, I thought. Unlike most of his generation, Tom had managed to stay out of The Great War, a combination of one medical condition after another, or of being an American stuck in a foreign land. But now, when he was old enough to escape the call, he had chosen to step forward for King and for Country.

I wondered if some part of him yearned to die gallantly, to rise above the humdrum meaninglessness of the publishing industry. And I wondered, too, about Vivienne. She was still in London, locked up in an asylum, a place that could just as easily be hit by a wayward bomb or falling, flaming debris. Did Tom worry about what could happen to her? Or would it solve all of our problems if she became "a casualty of war?"

Amid all of the chaos, he *was* finding time for his poetry. A new poem, "East Coker," arrived in the mail. I recognized the name of the town in southwest England from where his ancestors had left for the colonies. He had written me of his visit there back in the summer of 1937.

In the beginning is my end....

There was no Greek or Latin to decipher, just a bit of Old English. It was a sad poem, written by an aging man, with a few lines about a man and a woman dancing.

It had been so long since we had danced.

* * *

"This is London," Edward R. Murrow always began his reports.

As the 1940-41 school year started, London was still enduring a shower of bombs. The Woolfs' home on Tavistock Square had taken a direct hit. Fortunately, Tom wrote, they had moved to the countryside before it happened.

Every night, I turned on my radio to listen to Murrow. The backdrop of whizzing noises and distant explosions only fueled my anxiety. But they also made me feel closer to Tom. And Murrow was a calming presence. He spoke slowly, clearly, masking his emotions. He must have studied with a very good speech teacher.

He described the scene around him, drawing his audience into the terror-filled lives of the English people. Then he ended as he always did: "Good night and good luck."

I made a note to assign my classes to listen to one of his broadcasts. They might learn something about public speaking. And, more importantly, they might learn something about the chaotic adult world they were about to enter.

* * *

In April, Tom's cruelest month, another shocking tragedy unfolded in newspapers on both sides of the Atlantic. Virginia Woolf had gone out for a walk and had disappeared, her hat and cane left on the banks of the River Ouse near her house in Sussex. A few days later, Leonard shared the suicide note she had left behind. And then, after three weeks of waiting, her body was finally recovered.

I couldn't reconcile my memories of the magisterial woman, coolly serving up tea to her salon of admiring poets, with a woman who was so depressed that she could write her husband a farewell note and walk into a river. Her letter had been shared at the coroner's hearing and reported by all the papers. "I have a feeling I shall go mad," she had written Leonard. "I cannot go on any longer in these terrible times."

When Tom's letter finally arrived, he was still struggling to make sense of Virginia's death. Even though they were not as close as they once had been, it felt, he wrote, as if he had lost a family member. Now he was sorry that he had agreed to write an essay about Virginia for the *Horizon*. Whatever he wrote, he said, would come out all wrong.

He shared a few more of the details. How Virginia had put rocks in the pockets of her coat. How Leonard was angry that the papers were blaming her suicide on the war. Who wouldn't be distraught if their home disappeared into a pile of rubble? But Virginia, he explained, had struggled with her own set of demons since childhood. She had simply been very, very good at keeping them buried inside.

Did Tom worry now about Vivienne? And what about Mother? I knew there were suicides at McLean, try as the staff did to prevent them and keep them hushed up. Still, I did not think Mother was capable of doing that. Vivienne, however, was quite another matter.

* * *

A summer in Europe was definitely out of the question. A summer in Northampton would only remind me of my academic deficiencies. There was no time or money to earn a degree now, but perhaps there was some way I could burnish my *curriculum vitae* beyond acting schools.

The Speech Department at the University of Wisconsin, I learned, was offering graduate degrees—and summer courses. Now I yearned to go back to Milwaukee, to see my old students and colleagues, to walk through the Hawthornden and see a play at the Pabst Theatre. When I sent in my application, it was quickly accepted.

The term ran six short weeks, but I tried to make the most of it. I took three courses and was on my way to an "A" in all of them. I worked hard on my thesis for Gertrude Johnson's graduate course: "Criticism and Its Function for the Teacher of Interpretation." I considered sending a copy to Tom but feared it was not up to his standards.

And I was acting again—for the first time in years. The Union Theater had opened on campus just a few years before, its sleek Art Deco design such a contrast to the classic playhouses I had known in Boston and Milwaukee, much finer than the rented halls of Claremont and Cambridge. I loved to walk along the lakefront on nights when a performance was taking place, pausing for a moment to savor the sight of the lights glowing through the lobby's tall windows.

Zona Gale had died, Laura Sherry had retired. The old Wisconsin Players were now situated at the university, with four plays planned for this summer. I decided to try out for the drama set in Salem in the early 1800s, Maxwell Anderson's *The Wingless Victory*. Anderson, I learned, was the same age as Tom, but he'd had a different kind of early struggle, a penchant for angering his employers and getting fired. But he had finally made it as a playwright and screenwriter and been recognized with a Pulitzer Prize.

I was older than most of my classmates, so I knew I was best suited to play Mrs. McQueston, the hard-bitten mother of three squabbling sons. It was a challenge, though, unlike anything I had ever done before. She was the most unlikeable woman I had tried to play since Eleanor had cast me as Mrs. Elton. Like Tom, Anderson wrote his plays in verse. But the crisis of *his* family reunion, set off when a seafaring son returns home with a dark-skinned wife, made more sense to me than Tom's had.

Professor Lane was directing—he did most of the campus productions now. Rusty was younger than I was, but I respected his approach. He gave clear instructions and tried to help his nervous actors relax.

When I finished reading Mrs. McQueston's long speeches in Act One, he commended me for a job well done.

I realized then that I had met him before: We had served as judges in a college dramatic competition when I was at Milwaukee-Downer and he was teaching at LaCrosse State. His long face and bushy eyebrows made him hard to forget. When I shared our connection, he asked me to stay until he finished the auditions so we could talk privately.

"You have a good memory," he said when we sat down in a row at the rear of the auditorium. "That was what?—more than a decade ago?"

"I remember we had some good conversations about the plays we were judging."

"It's coming back to me now," he said. "I think we were both proud of the work our schools were doing, but still itching to move on." He paused. "Weren't you about to go back East and become a public speaker?"

I nodded.

"What happened?"

I smiled. "I did it for a while. But it didn't pay the bills. I eventually found my way back to teaching. I teach public speaking now at Smith." I glanced around the spacious auditorium. "It looks like things worked out all right for you."

He nodded. "I came here about the same time you left. I've enjoyed it, particularly after they built the new theater." He hesitated. "But I still wish I could make a living as an actor."

"Don't we all?" she replied.

"As you so wisely observed, 'it doesn't pay the bills.' But at least it makes life more enjoyable." He rose from his seat. "Take your script home and start studying. You're going to be my Mrs. McQueston."

* * *

I had not lived the life of Mrs. McQueston, but I knew women who had: The widowed mother of a minister, lonely, rigid, angry. Loving her prodigal son, but shocked that he would return home "enamoured of black flesh." The bigoted words were hard to say out loud. But I knew they were critical to creating the judgmental Christian community in which the play unfolded.

I tapped into the well of my old emotions, remembering the loneliness of my separations from Tom, wondering whether I would ever see him again. "Seven years," the Salem mother mused. "Seven years without a word." And yet she could forgive him. "Where did you think to find a welcome if not here?"

Most of my lines were in the first act, but I loved lingering in the wings, listening as the mixed-race couple expressed their passion for each other. I remembered a deserted garden, empty pools, and a late summer day in England when my heart was filled with love.

And when the play was over and the reviews were delivered, they helped, once again, to warm my heart: "Characterizations which will live long in the annals of the campus theater were those of Charles Avery as the Rev. Phineas McQueston, and his mother, played effectively by Emily Hale. These hard-bitten characters came alive and were made real at the hands of these capable actors."

* * *

At the end of the summer, I headed back to Massachusetts, my bags packed with a copy of my thesis and the program of my latest dramatic triumph. And I carried a few more of Tom's letters, destined for the complete collection in Northampton.

What would it be like, I wondered, to cut the tether of our correspondence? My summer at the graduate school, my time back on the stage, had given me a vision of a new and different life. Still, I never seemed capable of breaking free of my past. I was always "the good girl," the patient girl, the girl who did whatever Edith told me to do, the girl who would always wait for Tom.

And back at Smith, a new group of girls would also be waiting for me to correct them—the girls who were afraid to speak, much less to speak out.

* * *

I didn't always make it out of bed on Sunday mornings. The Unitarian church on Main Street was struggling these days, and when I walked through its doors, I always feared I would get roped into doing a project or serving on some board. But on that cold, crisp December morning, something compelled me to roust myself up, walk the few short blocks, and take a seat in the pews. And by the time the service ended, the word was spreading from neighbor to neighbor, across Northampton and over the air waves: The Japanese had bombed Pearl Harbor.

The next day, President Roosevelt made it official: The United States was going to war.

All across the Ivy League, the boyfriends and brothers of the Smith girls were heading to recruitment offices. But from coast to coast, women wanted to contribute, too. The Alumnae Council at Smith scrambled to reorient its February conference to reflect the war effort, and I volunteered to talk about how the lessons they had learned in their old speech classes would help them organize their neighbors or sell war bonds.

By summer, Congress had forced the Navy to start accepting women into its ranks. They had even come up with a clever acronym: the WAVES, Women Accepted for Voluntary Emergency Service. President Davis had succeeded in getting Smith designated as one of the training sites; Mildred McAfee, the president of Wellesley, was taking a leave of absence to run the whole operation.

But the war hadn't slowed down Herbert Davis from pursuing his vision for Smith. He wanted to spark an artistic renaissance in Northampton with a brand-new Theater Department. And he had found just the right person to lead it.

Everyone in the Speech Department knew about Hallie Flanagan. Roosevelt had recruited her to run the Federal Theatre Project during the Depression. She had valiantly defended it from Congressmen who claimed it was harboring communists. Then she had retreated to Vassar to direct that college's own innovative theater.

But I knew more. Hallie had been Eleanor's classmate in the 42 Workshop at Harvard. Eleanor had liked her but was jealous of the way Hallie had quickly worked her way into becoming Professor Baker's trusted assistant, the person who kept him on track.

And I harbored some jealousies of my own. It was Hallie who had brashly offered to mount *Sweeney Agonistes* the year Tom was at Harvard. The two of them had corresponded about the play, but in the end, Hallie had rejected most of Tom's suggestions in favor of her own vision of how to end it. And Tom acknowledged that Hallie had, in fact, been right.

But now our department was in turmoil. President Davis had chosen Hallie without consulting the faculty. We first learned she was coming when we read it in the newspaper. And even more inexplicably, a woman who didn't have an advanced degree was going to be dean of the whole college.

Among my whining colleagues, I held my tongue. I wanted to like Hallie Flanagan. She had been widowed twice and had lost a child. Now she was arriving in Northampton as a single mother with two young stepchildren in tow. She had overcome so much to achieve her dramatic successes.

But word spread quickly that President Davis was already in her thrall. Hallie had been rewarded with a big home on the lake, and over the summer, workmen could be seen adding on a guest room, transplanting trees, and grooming the flower beds. When I went out for a walk on a cool evening, my feet led me to the lakeshore. I enjoyed the sight of the rowboats on the water, but I also watched as Hallie's house took shape. I looked for signs of life inside and wondered whether its future owner would end up deciding my own future.

* * *

The new dean began by hosting parties for the faculty. She could not invite everyone at once, so she began with the class deans, the department chairmen, and then the tenured professors. I did not qualify for an invitation, but I heard reports from those who did. Hallie actually was a gracious hostess. She served the tea that everyone expected but also put out a pitcher of rum to keep her male colleagues happy. She swept through the public spaces of her home, flattering her older peers with her knowledge of their publications, rounding up the introverts to make them feel at ease. A few professors had found outrageous notes in their coat pockets when they returned home. The culprits were thought to be Hallie's stepchildren, who seemed to have free run of the place.

Word went out that the new dean wanted to meet with as many faculty members as she could, starting with the speech department. My appointment came two weeks later.

The dean rose to greet me as I entered her office. "Miss Hale," she acknowledged.

"Please," I said, struggling to control a rare case of stage fright, "call me Emily."

"Very well," she replied. "And please call me Hallie."

She was tinier than I had expected. She wore her hair short, with crimped waves and bangs that framed a set of piercing eyes. There was probably little that those eyes missed. She looked down at a folder on her desk; on the top, I saw the résumé I had prepared when I applied for my job.

"Tell me a little about yourself."

I took a deep breath. "I've been an assistant professor here since 1936. I work mostly with the students who need help with their diction or speech impediments."

That was not likely to impress Hallie Flanagan.

"But before I came to Smith, I led the drama programs at Scripps College, at Simmons, and at Milwaukee-Downer College. I also did quite a bit of acting. Amateur productions, of course."

"Why did you leave those posts?" she asked.

I hesitated. "I wanted to travel and spend time in Europe. I studied the theater there and lectured about it when I came home."

"I spent time in Europe, too," Hallie replied with a smile. "Who knows, maybe we attended the same performance." She paused, then asked more pointedly. "What did you learn while you were in Europe?"

I swallowed hard. It had been years since I had reviewed my notes. My lectures seemed so superficial now. They were little more than travelogues for women's clubs, not the kind of critiques I had tackled in my coursework last summer.

"I focused mostly on England, Ireland, and Germany. This was back in the early thirties. I spoke about the playwrights who were coming to the fore on the continent. I was careful not to impose my own judgments."

I sensed that was the wrong thing to acknowledge.

"What kind of roles do you like to play?"

"I started with light comedies; they've always been a favorite. I like to hear laughter. I did a lot of Barrie when I was young, and then moved on to Coward." I paused, remembering this was the woman who had directed the premiere of *Sweeney Agonistes*. "But I did *The Wingless Victory* last summer at the University of Wisconsin. That was a good challenge."

"Tell me what you like about directing."

I relaxed a little. "I love pulling it all together. I love working with the actors. They were almost always young women, and I loved helping them develop their roles and watching them grow. And," I concluded, "I must admit that I loved it when we got a good review."

"Is that the most important thing?"

"No," I replied. "But it still was satisfying."

The dean remained friendly but noncommittal. My time was coming to an end. I had resolved not to drop the names, but now I felt I had nothing to lose if I did. "I think you may have crossed paths with some friends of mine in the course of your career."

"Oh?" Hallie arched an eyebrow.

"I think you were in the 47 Workshop with Eleanor Hinkley. She's been a close friend since our school days."

"Yes, I know Eleanor. But I haven't seen her since her play opened on Broadway."

"I also know Eleanor's cousin, Tom Eliot. I know you've worked closely with him....We are...longtime friends."

Hallie drummed a pencil on the folder. *Was she putting the pieces together?*

"I'm a great admirer of his work," she said. "*Murder in the Cathedral* was the last play I did before I left Vassar. It opened the night before Pearl Harbor, which turned out to be brilliantly prophetic. Unfortunately, it also meant that for the rest of the run, people had more important things to worry about."

She said nothing for a moment. "I'm going to be very honest with you, Emily. As you probably know, President Davis recruited me to rebuild the Theater Department. I've got the authority to hire the best people I can find. And that probably means letting some of the current staff go.

"I think Smith could keep you on, but I don't think you would find it very satisfying. You could go on teaching students how to speak, but I think your heart is really in the theater. That said, I think we have very different tastes in drama, and it would be hard for me to find a place for you. I've already got two strikes against me because I don't have a doctorate; you've managed to survive without any kind of degree at all. I can't give you the kind of job that I think you really want and deserve."

I tried hard to focus on what she was saying, willing myself not to break down and cry. So odd, I thought, to have to summon tears for a performance, and now to have to struggle so much to control them.

Was Hallie right? What was most important: to have a salary, a credential, or a passion? Tom wrote his poetry as a banker, his plays as an editor. Diction classes paid my bills, but did I need to find a way back to drama?

"I'll give you a piece of advice," Hallie said at last. "But I'll also understand if you don't take it."

"Go on," I murmured.

"In my short time here, I've learned that Smith is a political snake pit. I've led the Federal Theater Project, I've fought members of Congress. None of that fully prepared me for what I've encountered here. I know I got off to a rocky start, and some of that is beyond my control. Still, I'm determined to survive and succeed.

"But in the process, I've learned that nothing makes me happier than running my own little theater company. And I suspect you feel the same way. So, if I were you, I would try to find another drama program I could manage. It may not be at a college. The best high schools are starting to appreciate the importance of theater. You could have the satisfaction of building another program." She paused, then added, "And I would do what I could to help you find one."

"Thank you," I murmured. "I appreciate that."

She checked her wristwatch. "I'm afraid I have to move on to my next appointment."

"I will think about what you said."

It did not take me long to make up my mind. I could hang on at Smith, going through the motions of teaching speech and keeping my head down as the battles raged around me. There was much I could learn from watching Hallie Flanagan direct her plays and manage her complicated life.

But I knew Hallie was right. I missed directing and being in charge. I had skills, but I did not have the kind of vision—or connections—to premiere *Sweeney* or defend the theatrical arts before Congress or battle through academic politics. The pond of Smith College was too big for me now. I would never be in charge the way I had been at Simmons or Scripps.

So I told Hallie I would resign when I found a new post. In the meantime, I would do whatever Smith wanted me to. I would coach the lisping freshmen and calm the girls with stutters. I would work with the students who were chosen to speak to parents and alumna groups. And if Hallie Flanagan needed someone to manage a prompt book, all she had to do was ask.

But I still needed more—and I was determined to find it.

* * *

Every time I moved, I fretted about the letters. They were jammed into eight boxes now. Would I have enough closets to store them? What would happen if a pipe burst or a window leaked?

Tom never liked talking about them, so I turned to Willard and Margaret for advice. The correspondence was valuable, they agreed, and it would be best if both sides of it ended up in the same place. Surely Tom would eventually make some provision for preserving his papers, probably at Oxford.

"But what do you do in the meantime?" Margaret asked.

In July 1942, I received a letter from Julian P. Boyd, the director of the library at Princeton. "I understand that you wish to protect the Eliot letters by placing them in a safe repository until they can be transmitted to their permanent home, which I assume is to be the Bodleian Library."

Princeton, I knew, would protect Tom's letters from the perils of fire, leaking pipes, even mildew and silverfish. It was tempting to send them there now. But when I mulled Mr. Boyd's letter, I knew it was still too early. I wasn't ready to part with them yet.

The Hollow Man

IT TOOK LONGER THAN I would have liked to find my way to Concord Academy. But once I was there, I felt I was home.

I detoured first to Dutchess County, New York. Bennett Junior College was a hulking former luxury hotel that had been converted to a girl's school and then to a college for women. But the spring of 1943 blew up cold and dreary along the banks of the Hudson River, and when a job opened up at the academy, I jumped at the chance to return to Boston.

I was teaching high school girls, and that *was* a comedown. In their eyes, I was truly a matron now. Some even called me "Mrs. Hale," but I set them straight. "*Miss* Hale, if you please," I said. "As yet I have not accepted the hand of any man in matrimony."

Still, the girls were not unlike the students I had coached at Simmons. Two World Wars and a Depression had made young women grow up faster. Their older brothers were off fighting the war; their beaus could be drafted at any moment. Older sisters and cousins were taking jobs in factories and offices; their mothers were managing rationed households.

The war was all around me, yet I felt oddly isolated from it. London had survived the Blitz, and Hitler had turned his attention to Moscow. Americans headed for the airfields of England and set sail for the South Pacific. Smith was churning out WAVES, and Jeanie McPherrin had joined the Navy. But most of the men I knew were too old to be drafted. Rusty Lane, I'd learned, was now producing plays for the Red Cross in Europe. But Maxwell Anderson was bringing him home to direct the premiere of *Storm Operation* in Pittsburgh. If Rusty managed to survive life in a combat zone, the war would probably boost his career.

If I had gotten married, I might be worrying about a son. But none of my closest friends were dealing with that. Ollie Gates, Dorothy's oldest son, had enlisted, but he was in the Coast Guard, far from the most dangerous action. Margaret, Eleanor, Amy—none of them had children. Nor, for that matter, did Tom.

So I did what every loyal American did—I focused on my job, I purchased war bonds, I managed my ration coupons. And on Sundays, I went to church and prayed that it would all be over soon.

* * *

The war, it seemed, *had* helped Tom focus on his writing again. Out of the stresses of wartime London, new poems had flowed. "Burnt Norton" and "East Coker" were followed by "The Dry Salvages." I knew the rocks off the coast of Cape Ann, even if I had never sailed by them myself. Finally, he published "Little Gidding." That spot was more obscure, but Tom had told me about the pilgrimage he had made in 1936. A religious community there had sheltered Charles I during the English Civil War. Now only the chapel remained.

He had sent me each poem as it was finished. Now they were published together as the "Four Quartets." Late at night, I would delve back into them, trying to parse what Tom was trying to say. I felt like a Benedictine monk practicing *Lectio Divina*. Each time I read the poems, a new phrase called out for further contemplation, depending on my mood or what had happened that day.

More than anything, I decided, the poems spoke to time and memory. I loved the words he had set down near the end of "Little Gidding":

We shall not cease from exploration
And the end of all our exploring
Will be to arrive where we started
And know the place for the first time.

Someday the war had to end. Someday Tom would have to come back to his family.

Before turning off the light each night, my memories returned to Burnt Norton. It always helped keep the nightmares away.

* * *

I liked living in Concord. It was quieter than Boston, but it was still easy to travel into the city to visit friends or go to the theater. I took comfort in the world of Emerson, Thoreau, and the Alcotts, where my students' ancestors had first confronted the Redcoats. I was still nervous about my finances, but I was able to find a few rooms in an old home and put all of Tom's letters and books into storage. I wanted to be ready when the war finally ended. And I wanted to be ready for the day Vivienne died.

The academy was small, but its headmistress, Josephine Tucker, was determined to shore up its reputation. I survived my first semester, and my contract was extended. Now it was time to do a play.

But where to start? How many good actresses could I find in a class of 20 girls? I started with Barrie again: *Quality Street*, about a school for genteel young women. The sets would be easy; the girls could play themselves. Some might have even seen Katharine Hepburn in the movie version. Hallie Flanagan, I knew, would roll her eyes at the choice, but this was Concord Academy, not Smith or Vassar.

I had to scramble to arrange the costumes and props. I let Fanny Tomaino wear my satin peignoir, styled for the era of Napoleon. When the curtain came down and Fanny returned it, I was stunned when I saw the sweat stains she had left. "Oh dear," I said, "it can never be worn again."

Then I saw the sad look on Fanny's face. Who was I kidding? I had purchased the sexy nightgown to fuel my own secret fantasies, but no man had ever seen me in it.

"Never mind," I consoled Fanny. "The play is more important than any old nightgown."

* * *

The long-awaited announcement came on May 8. It was President Truman's birthday, and we hurried the girls into the gymnasium to try to catch his radio broadcast.

"This is a solemn but a glorious hour. I only wish that Franklin D. Roosevelt had lived to witness this day....The flags of freedom fly over all Europe."

The girls erupted in cheers; we tried to shush them to hear the rest of the president's solemn speech. Sunday, Truman declared, would be a national day of prayer.

Around Concord, the church bells began to ring. I knew Miss Tucker would let everyone out early—we had all waited so long for this moment. There had been the anxious suspense of the D-Day invasion, the slog across Belgium at Christmastime, the slow march to Berlin. At last the war in Europe was over.

Now there was nothing to keep Tom and me apart.

*　*　*

Across town, in a storeroom, were my most prized possessions. The books fit into two boxes, more than two dozen first editions, poems, essays and plays, all autographed in one form or another by the poet T. S. Eliot. The latest arrival was "What Is a Classic?," a speech Tom had made to the Virgil Society the previous fall. Faber had turned it into a 32-page booklet, and Tom had sent me a copy. "To Emily Hale from T. S. Eliot 7.ii.45."

I would have liked him to say more, but I cherished the inscribed works all the same. I knew they were valuable. What would happen to them if I died? What if some idiot threw them away, not realizing what was boxed up among the old furniture and clothes?

As the weeks went by, I mulled what I should do. There was Princeton, of course. There was also Harvard. It was Tom's alma mater; they would know how to preserve the books. But would they be special there? Harvard received everything: centuries worth of documents, letters, photos, and memorabilia. The books might disappear into another storeroom, catalogued but forgotten. Who would care about a gift from someone named Emily Hale?

And then I thought of Scripps. It was smaller, younger, still filling out its library. I had been somebody at Scripps, Tom had visited there. People would remember us. And I remembered Ruth George and how Ruth had loved English literature. I could make the gift in honor of Ruth, and Scripps would make the collection special.

When I wrote the new president, I recalled Tom's visit and how Ruth had met him and continued to teach his works. "I feel that the contribution of these facts, as I have told you of them, makes the beautiful Scripps College library a fitting place for the collection—a reminder always of the distinguished man of letters who saw the campus himself, and of a beloved teacher and interpreter of the humanities, herself a writer with so much to give."

President Hard was amenable, but I realized I had confused things. I would not be able to retrieve the books from storage until the weather improved. In the meantime, I hoped the college might arrange a little ceremony to receive them. It would be nice to paste a special bookplate in each book. I had some ideas about that, too.

I was making a bequest. I was about to become "a donor." And, I was surprised to discover, it brought me a measure of happiness.

* * *

The phone call came on a dreary February day in 1946. It was Edith, and even over the telephone, I could tell my aunt was struggling to choke back her tears.

"It's your mother," she said. "She died this morning."

There was no need for a fuss, Edith explained. She had it all arranged. Emily Jose Milliken Hale had no friends, no life that needed to be recalled or celebrated. Edith would arrange the cremation, the spreading of her ashes near Father's grave at Mount Auburn. Could I do it on Saturday?

I was numb as I hung up the phone. It was over now. No more sad visits to McLean. No more strangling guilt over how infrequent those visits were. Now I was truly on my own.

I tried to feel happy for Mother. After 77 years, her painful life had finally come to an end. She would be reunited in heaven with her dead little boy and her minister husband. I did the math quickly in my head. Twenty-eight years since Father had left me. Could it really be that long ago?

I knew I should resent Edith's take-charge efficiency. This was *my* mother, after all, my decisions to make. But I was grateful Edith was still making those decisions. Suddenly I felt so tired. I grieved for Mother. But more than anything, I grieved that I had never really had a mother.

* * *

There was no time for sadness, even if I had been inclined to wallow in it. The Academy's production of *Hay Fever* was opening in three weeks. Two performances this time, with the proceeds designated to support the American Friends Service relief efforts in Europe. There were rehearsals every day and sets to be painted. I dispatched the extroverts into town to locate the props we still needed and beg the merchants to buy advertisements in the program.

It would not be as good as the production in Claremont, but it would be good enough. And when the review appeared in the local paper, I clipped it out and added it to my files.

"The auditorium was filled to capacity both evenings, in itself a tribute to the reputation of the Academy's productions, and indeed expectation was not disappointed, for the amusing play was a most happy selection and was exceptionally well presented....There was a refreshing absence of that self-conscious paralysis which so often assails amateurs on the stage, causing them to move like wooden dolls in a trance while they gaze hypnotized at the floor, addressing their lines exclusively to the carpet at their feet, to the sad discomfort of their audience....

"The cast must be sincerely congratulated on its excellent performance, while to Miss Hale, under whose direction the play was presented, is due the very warm appreciation her work deserves."

* * *

Tom was coming home again.

There was no longer a war to keep him in England or a sickly wife requiring his care. He missed his family, the Gloucester coast, the world of St. Louis. Ada, his dear oldest sister, had died two years before, and the war had kept him from making it back for the funeral. Ada had died at 74, and he knew none of his siblings was getting any younger.

And yes, he wanted to see me, too.

But what woman did he hope to see? When he looked at me now, did he still see the young woman from Chestnut Hill, the minister's daughter, the girl who became shy around the Harvard philosophers? Or did he see a woman in her mid-fifties, whose hair was rapidly turning gray, whose laugh lines were beginning to deepen? Did he see a woman who could critique his plays, lecture on the theater, move on with her life?

I knew from his letters that his own life had changed. He had taken an apartment with John Hayward, a third-floor flat with a view of the Thames. He had been friends with John for years; owed him much, he said, for the help he had provided with the "Four Quartets." John had been wheelchair-bound for more than 20 years, but he was a witty roommate, and the slower pace of his life seemed to suit Tom perfectly now that the war was over.

And then there was Mary Trevelyan. I tried not to be jealous, but Mary's name kept turning up in Tom's reports on how he spent his days. They had become friends, he explained, since that first meeting in Swanwick eight years before. Mary provided good company, the set of legs that John Hayward couldn't, and the kind of nagging Tom now seemed to need about his schedule and his health. I was glad there was a "Mary" to look after him, even as I yearned to play that role myself.

But summer was coming, and I would get another chance. I was still there for him, still waiting, still available. But I did not want to appear to be desperate. He had seen me at a low point, helped to coach me back to my old self. I was no longer teaching at the college level, but I was still proud of my work. And I wanted Tom to be proud of me, too.

I planned to produce *Richard II* next March. With 30 roles, it would be the most ambitious play I had tried to mount at the Academy. And I was going to rewrite some of the speeches to help the girls—and the audience—understand what was happening. Tom could give me some help.

And I had another surprise in store. There was a good summer theater in Dorset, a few hours away in southern Vermont. It was doing Noel Coward's *Blithe Spirit*, and I had won the lead. I hoped Tom would come see me perform. It was a farce, but still a farce about a man who is haunted by the ghost of his first wife. And when she reappears, it disrupts his relationship with his new spouse. I would never point out the parallels myself, of course. But Tom Eliot was nobody's literary fool.

* * *

Another summer. Another city. Another train station. We had been here so many times before. But this time, it had been so much longer since the last visit. Still, I could always recognize Tom's silhouette, even at the far end of the platform. I called out to him and waved but did not run to greet him. I was beyond the age of running in high heels.

His hat was still in place, the handkerchief in his pocket. But he moved more slowly. As he drew closer, I was shocked by how the war had aged him. He wore a fine suit, but it seemed to hang on his bones. It was summer, but his skin was pale. The cheeks of "The Hollow Man" were indeed very hollow.

But when Tom saw me, his face broke into a smile. I remembered that face. I remembered that man, bringing me a glass of punch on an icy night more than 30 years before. He was still my young man, and my heart soared at the sight of him.

"Emily!"

He put down his satchel and took my hands, his eyes taking their own inventory of how *I* had changed. Then he took me in his arms and pulled me close to his chest.

"Where have the years gone?" he whispered.

* * *

It felt so good to have Tom back, but our time together, as always, was much too short. He was determined to spend time with his siblings. But they invited me to join them again in New Hampshire, and I went along for a weekend. And Dorothy Gates Elsmith—she had divorced her second husband, but hung onto his name—insisted we visit her home at Woods Hole.

It was hard to get Tom to shed his tweeds, that air of formality that followed him from London. His family could get him to do it—it was tough to be stuffy around those who knew you from childhood. Tom could laugh and share a story, enjoy his cigarettes and his gin. But it was difficult for him to truly relax. He wore his suit like a turtle wears a shell—afraid, it seemed, that if he took it off for just an evening, he would forget the man he had become. He would no longer be an Englishman, the man who had taken his austere Anglican vows. He might instead be the little boy, fascinated by the sailboats turning into the wind off of Cape Ann. A boy who longed to be a different person in a new and different place.

* * *

Winter blew into England late that year with a ferocity the record-keepers said had not been seen for 300 years. The snow piled up, blocking roads and rail lines, forcing power plants to shut for lack of coal. The British huddled together, seeking warmth where they could, managing their rations of food as the root vegetables froze in the ground.

I had not heard from Tom in several weeks, and that worried me. Usually the letters arrived like clockwork every other week. Sometimes if he was busy, the message would be short. But the letters would still arrive, the lifeline of our relationship.

But this time was different. As each day went by, I dreaded checking the mailbox. Had Tom been taken ill? Had he had an accident? Could he have died? No, that would certainly have made the newspapers. Theresa and Eleanor would tell me. There had been another big storm in late January. Perhaps that had disrupted the mail service or thrown his old routines into disarray.

And then, near the end of February, a letter finally arrived.

Dear Emily,

I write to share the news that Vivienne died on January 23rd. Her doctors said it was heart failure; it was very unexpected. John was home when Maurice called, and he was the one who broke the news. Maurice and I arranged for her to be buried close to her mother, in the cemetery in Pinner. It was a cold and miserable day. The Fabers were kind enough to travel out with us, and as we gathered at the gravesite, the snow continued to fall.

I could not exult in the death of anyone. Still, I could not quiet the emotions that rose from my heart. *Tom was free now. We could finally be together.*

But there was more.

I must confess that her death has hit me very hard, harder, I feel, than if she had died 15 years ago, when we first separated.

I scanned the rest of the letter quickly. There were no words of love, no promises for the future. Of course, it was much too soon for that. His world was filled with bleakness—winter cold, hunger, financial struggles, loneliness. There was little I could do to dispel any of that.

I have taken sick since then. I developed a bad case of bronchitis and spent 10 days in the hospital. As you know, I was supposed to undergo an operation on my hernia, but it has now been postponed until sum-mer, when they hope I will be stronger.

Meanwhile, I received word from Theresa that Henry has been diagnosed with leukemia. The doctors say he does not have very long to live. I am trying to come as quickly as I can, but I have to arrange some speaking engagements first to help cover my expenses.

Henry dying? I could not believe it. I thought back to the previous summer, searching for any sign of his cancer. Of course, we were all growing old. Our hikes were shorter; we no longer tried to climb as high as we once did. We went to bed early and sometimes woke up and rambled about the house in the middle of the night.

And Theresa! I closed my eyes for a moment, my lips pursing with a silent prayer. I remembered the joy in Theresa's eyes as her pencil moved quickly across her sketchbook, laughing and talking as she captured another moment of Eliot family life.

Why was happiness so elusive?

I set out to compose a note to Henry and Theresa, trying to summon words of comfort and encouragement but falling back on proper, time-worn clichés. I told her I would continue to hold the two of them in my thoughts and prayers.

Tom, however, was a different matter. I started one letter after another, crumpling each one into a ball before I finished. I tried to express my sympathies but could not find my voice. What about *us?* I wanted to ask. *What does Vivienne's death mean for the two of us?*

But Henry had to come first. What would Father say at a time like this? From the recesses of my brain came a memory, a sermon I had heard him preach after a young woman in our congregation had fallen off her horse and died.

"When words fail you at a time like this, look around you. There is always something you can do to help."

And there was. Tom needed speaking engagements to support his time in America. It was the Academy's twenty-fifth anniversary. The daughter of the governor would be graduating. This year, more than others, the school would want a celebrity to deliver the commencement address.

Miss Tucker said my idea was "brilliant."

"We could offer him an honorarium," the headmistress thought out loud. "But how would we contact Mr. Eliot?"

"He is a friend of mine," I replied. "I think it could be arranged."

* * *

Tom arrived near the end of April. I had dreamed of this moment, unlimited time together, joining new friends for dinner, accompanying him to his speaking engagements, taking a seat in the front row. This time without any fear of scandal or gossip.

But it did not take long for that bubble to burst. For starters, I still had classes to teach, and Tom's schedule was crowded with speeches, readings, and now a crowning glory—commencement ceremonies at Harvard, Yale, and Princeton, all of which were giving him honorary degrees.

His first appearance was at Wellesley. Jeanie McPherrin was a dean there now, and she had volunteered to drive Tom from Boston. I was pleased that Jeanie and Tom had remained good friends, but I wished Tom had invited me to go along.

He was then off to New York for a talk about Milton at the Frick Museum. Henry died two days later. Tom was scheduled to deliver a poetry lecture at Harvard, but the organizers agreed to delay the program. Henry's funeral was to be small and family-only. This time, I was not included in that circle.

It was a difficult time; I appreciated that. And yet, I felt as if Tom was trying to avoid me, retreating into the homes of his siblings or former colleagues, or begging off because there were lectures or speeches that still had to be written. He was off to Washington next week for a reading at the National Gallery, then a talk before the city's Episcopal Fellowship. Concord Academy's commencement was set for the afternoon of June 3, followed by Harvard's two days later.

It was the time of year of endings and beginnings, weddings and graduation ceremonies. Gardeners were pruning bushes and mowing campus lawns, and the beautiful spired chapels of New England were booked solid with weddings. In New York, Rusty Lane was getting married to one of his former students in between his performances on Broadway.

The war was over, and people were moving on with their lives. Why couldn't we write a new chapter, too?

* * *

I awoke to a rattle of rain on my windows. It was not a good omen. By tradition, the academy's graduation exercises were held outside, underneath the shady elms and amid the bushes at the peak of their flowering beauty. Now the lingering downpour would drive the ceremonies inside, to the gym that I knew would grow hot and stuffy as the speakers droned on. Miss Tucker had cut back on the number of meaningless awards, but Governor Bradford was speaking, and then Tom would get his turn.

He had told me it would be easier if we did not try to meet up until the ceremony was over. There was logic to that plan, but still I was disappointed. I longed to spend time with him, to take his emotional temperature. And I wanted to show him around the school, to introduce him to my colleagues, my students, their parents. I *was* the famous poet's good friend.

But instead, I found a seat near the front, in the section reserved for faculty members. Tom walked out on the platform with Miss Tucker, the governor, the president of the trustees. He looked tired, I thought. Gaunt and stooped, like this was the last place in the world he wanted to be. He pulled out his glasses, then stared at his notes, as if editing his speech one final time before he delivered it.

The procession started. Twenty girls in white dresses and white shoes, each carrying a bouquet of roses. They were all lovely, I thought, but it would have been so much lovelier to be outside, amid the early summer greenery.

The choir rose to sing a Bach chorale. It was the familiar "Now Thank We All Our God," a reminder that I should try to catalog all the things for which I should be grateful. The war was over. I had a good job. Tom was free to marry me now. But outside the rain still came down, and with it, the nagging sense that the world was not right.

Now the president was introducing Tom. "We have with us a revolutionary, but a revolutionary within form, not a revolutionary for revolution's sake....It is a great pleasure, but more than that, a genuine privilege...."

Tom looked up startled, as if he had lost track of the program. But he regained his composure, smiled, and rose to take his place at the lectern as the audience responded with applause.

He began with a joke, observing that most commencement speeches turned out to be forgettable. The audience laughed and seemed to relax.

He went on. "This audience, unless it is very different from other commencement audiences, probably contains two different types of listener: those who write, or want to write, poetry themselves, and those who object to being asked to read poetry. Of course, there are some who don't want to write poetry and at the same time don't object seriously to reading it, but these are probably a minority. So I shall try to say something for those who would like to be poets, and to those who see no use at all in poetry, hoping that those who neither want to write nor object to reading will find something worth listening to as well."

I wondered if the graduates would remember this speech in their later years. He talked some about success, and writing to please oneself, and the need for humility. He could have talked more about his own life choices, his unconventional education, his decision to pursue a path his parents had opposed. But no, he was a poet, and so he was going to lecture them about poetry.

Chairs creaked, programs shuffled. The girls could return to thinking about their futures, their parents to the memories of their daughters' school years. There would be no test at the end of the talk.

When he finished, he folded up his speech, took off his glasses, and sat back down. Again, the audience applauded, but if he appreciated their response, it did not register on his face.

"I wrote 'The Waste Land' to relieve my emotions." That line of the speech stayed with me. He might have written that poem to relieve his emotions, but now he seemed to have lost them altogether.

Of course, I reminded myself, he was still dealing with the shock of Henry's death. Tom was now the patriarch of the Eliot clan, responsible for managing all of the women's financial affairs, while he marched his way through a soul-killing schedule of speeches and readings, fighting off students seeking autographs and academics slinging critiques.

It was time for the diplomas to be presented. Each girl crossed the stage as her name was read, a final moment in the spotlight in the warm cocoon of the Academy. Tom joined in the applause for each of them. He had found his way back to the moment.

* * *

There was no chance to talk at the reception afterwards. Tom was the celebrity guest, and as a faculty member, I was expected to help play hostess to all the family members. There were final hugs to be given, photographs to be snapped. And by the time the punch bowl was emptied, Tom was ready to retreat.

"I promised Theresa I'd set aside some time today to go over Henry's finances."

I was disappointed, but in the wake of Henry's death, Tom's family had to come first.

"Were you able to get an extra ticket from Harvard?"

"I'm glad you reminded me." He reached into his jacket. "I'm afraid it's not a very good seat." For a change, he sounded apologetic. "I should have thought to ask as soon as they invited me."

"It doesn't matter," I lied. "I don't care where I sit, as long as I can be there."

"They've filled up the day with receptions and such. We can connect again when it is all over."

When it is all over. Would I ever be a part of his present?

* * *

Unlike Concord Academy, Harvard was blessed with a beautiful day for its Commencement. And this time Tom did not have to perform. That role fell to Secretary of State Marshall. Actually, there would be two speeches. Harvard had recruited Omar Bradley before Marshall finally accepted his invitation. Even Harvard University, Tom joked, could not order former generals to step down.

Harvard Yard was crowded when I arrived. Last year's graduation was a pared-down affair, a recognition of how the war had disrupted the lives of so many students. But now the campus had settled back into the old, familiar traditions.

Twelve men were set to receive honorary degrees, and as they took their places for the procession to Memorial Church, I craned my neck to catch sight of Tom. Finally I spotted him, his ears jutting out from underneath his mortarboard. I was struck by the mix of academic gowns and business suits. Bradley wore his uniform; Marshall was dressed as a civilian. J. Robert Oppenheimer was also easy to pick out. I did not recognize any of the others in caps and gowns, but the program identified them as the president of the University of Chicago, a former dean of Harvard, the principal of Deerfield Academy, and Ivor Richards, an old friend of Tom's who was now teaching at Harvard.

Tom had submitted his dissertation years ago, and at last he would get a Harvard doctorate. I closed my eyes. *This was how it should have been*. He would have finished up his year at Oxford, found his way back home, completed his dissertation, studied for his orals, earned his degree. We would have gotten married. He would have found a job teaching philosophy or figured out a way to pursue his poetry.

Or would he?

"I wrote 'The Waste Land' to relieve my emotions...."

He had achieved literary greatness, worldwide celebrity, but was it worth the cost? He was a sad little man now, shrunken, depressed. I remembered the Harvard student, his arms and chest built up by rowing on the Charles. Now, compared with the men striding beside him, he looked stunted, diminished.

And what about me? Was it worth the price I'd had to pay?

Alone in the crowd at Harvard, I remembered that time. I was always by his side but never acknowledged to his friends. It was the same today. He could have requested a ticket in the priority seats, treated me like a special friend or family member. Vivienne was dead now. There would be no scandal. But he was still playing the monk, wearing a hairshirt and flagellating himself for his sins, real or imagined.

President Conant was describing him now. "Once again, the English-speaking people hail a religious and learned poet, whose words the world will not willingly let die."

I did not want to think about the years that had been lost, the years that could never be reclaimed. I could take care of Tom now. I could restore him. He might never produce another line of great poetry, but I could make him happy again.

Why was that so hard for him to accept?

* * *

The date on the calendar taunted me, the rapidly approaching day when Tom would return to England. He filled his days with activity, and when we were finally together, it was as if we were just going through the motions. I could feel the despair welling up inside me like a tumor lodged between my heart and my ribs. And I felt the unspoken questions of others: Edith and John, Margaret and Willard, Paul and Lorraine. Former students waiting for the next chapter of my ongoing saga. Would that page never be turned?

And then one day he turned up on my doorstep.

"Come in," I said, as if in a dream. He caught me in the middle of baking a cake. I wiped my fingers on my gingham apron, then nervously checked the tight bun at the nape of my neck. I wrestled with the knotted apron strings, then turned off the gas to the oven.

"You didn't call," I said.

"I'm sorry," he mumbled. "I discovered I had a few hours free and decided I had better make use of them."

Why does it have to be so hard?

"I was about to fix myself a cup of tea," I lied. "Would you like one?"

He nodded.

I busied myself with filling the teapot, relighting the stove, getting out cups. "I remember a time when we both drank coffee," I said brightly. "But it seems we have both moved on to tea."

Tom lit a cigarette, took a long draw, and then coughed.

"I'm sure this trip has been very hard on you," I said.

"I did not want to come," he acknowledged, "but I didn't have any choice."

He didn't want to come. "I'm sure Theresa has appreciated all your help."

"She told me I had to talk to you before I went home."

The teacups rattled in my hands.

"Why?"

"Because I can't give you what you want."

"And what do I want?"

He did not presume to answer.

"You are free now, Tom. That's the important thing. We can be whatever we want to be."

"No, Emily," he said softly. "It's something I have come to realize since Vivienne died. You are a very special person, and I am grateful that you have loved me. But I've realized it's too late for me now. I should have realized it sooner. It wasn't fair to you."

"It wasn't fair to me?" I repeated. "It wasn't fair to me? And how fair is this?"

"What future did you think we would have?" he asked.

"What future?" I must sound like an idiot. "What future? I never lived in the future, Tom. I lived only in the present, a day snatched here or there, weekends in England, a week or two in California. I thought we shared a world of our own. I thought we had found a place where we could be happy.

"But I wanted something more...and I thought that you did, too. When you wrote me that Vivienne had died, I thought you were free. Free to follow your heart. Free to spend the rest of your life with me."

He spoke slowly. "If I have ever been in love—and I think I was before—I have never loved anyone but you. But after Vivienne died, I realized I have no love left in me. I have become an old man and I'm growing older every day. This is the worst moment of my life, to feel as if I have lost the desire for all that was most desirable."

Now panic was welling up inside of me. "Please," I begged him. "Let me help you. You are tired, you're not well. Your only brother has just died. You have exhausted yourself with your appearances. Please take some time....We've waited all these years. I know I can wait longer. Nothing has to change."

"No," he said. "I can see now that my life was predestined long ago. I dreamed I could be happy, but I know now that it is not possible for a man like me."

I shook my head. "I don't understand you. I have studied your face all these years, I knew each contour like it was the back of my own hand. But now I feel I don't really know you. I listened to your voice, whether you were speaking just to me or reading a poem to a roomful of admirers or onto a record. And it always thrilled me, it echoed through my dreams.

"But now I no longer recognize it. It is dry and empty and devoid of life. It reminds me of the *scritch, scritch, scritch* of crickets, the ones we used to hear on those nights in New Hampshire.

"I see now that I dreamed of another person, I thought you were someone that it turns out you could never be. I should have known better. I should have known it from the start. It's so...it's so...it's so..." I buried my face in my hands. "It's so humiliating."

"There is no reason you should feel humiliated...."

"Don't think *you* can humiliate me. It's something I've done to myself. I thought we shared something wonderful. But now I realize I was simply your diversion. So, of course, I feel humiliated."

The tea kettle was shrieking. I looked around the room, wanting to be somewhere else. But this was my home, my haven. Tom was the invader.

"I think you'd better leave."

He rose from his chair, gathered up his hat, and headed for the door.

"I hope you have a safe trip back to England," I said. "And whatever is left of your life, I hope it is happy."

* * *

Days and nights went by before I could sleep again. It felt like death, I realized—a vast, lonely emptiness. But unlike Theresa Eliot, I had no lawyers, coroners, or financial advisers to fill up my hours. Josephine Tucker had nothing but praise for lining up their commencement speaker. But I wanted no part of it now. Over the summer, I submitted my resignation. I needed a change of scene. I had received a small inheritance from Mother's estate. I was going to go back to Vermont. Perhaps there would be more roles if I put my mind to it. Who could object now?

Had Tom's love just been a figment of my imagination? Even now, I could not believe that was true. But who could I trust? Not the Eliots, for sure. They would certainly take Tom's side of the argument. Even Edith would assume I had made some fatal miscalculation.

Then I thought of Lorraine Havens. Lorraine would remember that magical time Tom and I had shared in California. I could write Lorraine, explain what I was going through. Lorraine would tell me if I was crazy.

> ...I am going to tell you, dear friend, that what I confided to you long ago of a mutual affection he and I have had for each other has come to a strange impasse whether permanent or not, I do not know. Tom's wife died last winter very suddenly. I supposed he would then feel free to marry me as I believed he always intended to do. But such proves not to be the case. We met privately two or three times to try to sift the situation thoroughly as possible—he loves me—I believe that wholly—but apparently not in the way usual to men less gifted i.e. with complete love thro' a married relationship. I have not completely given up hope that he may yet recover from this—to me—abnormal reaction, but on the other hand I cannot allow myself to hold on to anything so delicately uncertain....

* * *

Eventually, I found the courage to phone Theresa. Was there anything I could do to help? Would she like to meet for lunch or take in a play?

"I'm sorry, Emily."

"What do you mean?"

"How this has all turned out. I don't understand Tom. After all these years...I had always thought he would marry you."

Alone in my rooms, I gripped the handset and closed my eyes, trying to stanch the tears.

"I pushed him to make time for you when he was here last spring." Theresa hesitated. "And he was never so angry with me in his life."

The End of Exploring

IT WAS NEVER THE SAME after that.

Oh, Tom pretended that nothing had changed. He still wrote almost every week, the same kind of long, breezy letters we had shared for more than 15 years, the minutiae of his life, and his most unvarnished thoughts.

But I read the letters differently now. I was not a scientist, but I tried to emulate their dispassionate methods. I dissected the letters anew, asking myself, over and over, what clue had I missed? When did Tom change his mind? Or had I misread his words from the start? Had I so embroidered a fantasy of our life together that I had been too quick to seize on any phrase, any sentence that would confirm it was his fantasy, too?

I didn't know the answer, and it didn't matter now. He still wanted friendship, so we might as well be friends. There was still a cachet, after all, to being on a first-name basis with T. S. Eliot—even if I no longer flaunted it. And Tom had, in fact, been very ill. He had finally scheduled his surgeries and taken several months to recover. In the fall, he wrote me, he'd had all his teeth extracted. I wondered whether he would be able to keep up with his speaking engagements or his broadcasts for the BBC.

But over time the pace of the letters slowed. They arrived every other week now, sometimes only once a month. He was working on a new play; he seemed to enjoy his renewed celebrity. For more than a year, the Institute for Advanced Study at Princeton had been trying to recruit him as a fellow, and at last he decided to accept. Two months in the fall of 1948.

He said he would look forward to seeing Willard and Margaret again. But he did not suggest that I should come and visit them, too.

* * *

For a change, I enjoyed being lazy. No classes to teach, no plays to organize. I remembered Judith's line from *Hay Fever:* "I've reached an age now when I just want to sit back and let things go on around me—and they do."

I located a small, unfurnished apartment on Lexington Road, and for the first time in a long time, I enjoyed unpacking and sorting the things I usually kept in storage. I reread all the letters, reopened all the books, paged through the fragile pamphlets.

I had been thrilled whenever Tom had sent me a book or an essay, but now I read the inscriptions with fresh eyes. There were, I had to acknowledge, no words of affection or shared memories. Just my name, his name, and a date. But he had been married almost all of those years. The books might be opened or borrowed. There was a public face that had to be maintained.

It was the new year, a time for resolutions. A good time to send some of the books to Scripps. But I wanted it done right. Perhaps I could make a visit, present them in person. I wanted Ruth George to be recognized. There was still that matter of designing a special nameplate.

As I wrote back to President Hard, I grew more excited. Perhaps they would like me to come give a talk? I had often done readings of Mr. Eliot's work, but I could lecture on other topics as well. I knew quite a bit about the theater.

My schedule was open now that I was no longer teaching. Perhaps spring would be nice, or better yet, commencement. It would help if the college could pay a small honorarium, something to help cover my travel expenses.

In the dead of the Boston winter, in the loneliness of my rooms, my spirits lifted. I remembered the sunshine of Southern California, my old friends, the easy informality of those years at the new college in the West, the theater in Claremont. I needed all of that again.

* * *

If Tom had felt his best days were over, no one else seemed to agree. As part of the New Year Honors, King George VI awarded him the Order of Merit.

I knew about peerages, of course. The thought of Tom arising as Sir Thomas S. Eliot with the touch of a sword blade had always amused me. But this honor put him into even more select company. Only 24 recipients at a time. And when you died, the king took back the medal to award to someone else.

Tom, I knew, would feel conflicted about it. Secretly, he loved the recognition, but not all the public fuss. Still, it underscored the fact that he was now regarded as a true and proper Englishman.

* * *

President Hard was sorry, he wrote, but there was no room on the college's calendar for me to give a talk. Marjorie Nicholson had been invited for commencement, and the Columbia professor's visit would drain the available budget. But if I ever found myself in the area...well, then, the college would be happy to welcome me.

I was disappointed. Still, I had admired Marjorie since her days as dean of Smith. And if Scripps was now able to attract speakers of her caliber, I knew I couldn't compete.

My books, however, were another matter. If they were going to be consigned to storage space, I might as well pass them on to Harvard. Emily Hale might be a nobody, but T. S. Eliot certainly deserved better.

I was ruminating about the books when Marguerite Hearsey phoned. We had been friends as children back in East Orange and reconnected when Marguerite attended Radcliffe. Now she was headmistress of Abbot Academy in Andover. The school's longtime drama teacher had died suddenly; all of the semester's plays were in jeopardy. Could I come rescue them?

It was good, I realized, to feel needed again. It was not as if my telephone was ringing off the hook with acting offers. I was 56, and even if a director was able to track me down, the roles for a woman my age were few and far between.

But I could always teach speech and diction. I could always pull out a script and put on another play. I knew how to turn a student into an actress, if only for a semester.

* * *

Outside the brick wall, in front of the iron gates, I paused to read the inscription: "Enter into the understanding that you may go forth into nobler living."

I had always tried to live a noble life. But, oh Lord, I could use some more understanding! And what had that "noble life" earned me? I gasped as my gaze shifted inside the doors of the gate. Three red brick buildings, situated on three sides of a semicircle. The scale was different, the buildings spread farther apart. But it was Milwaukee-Downer all over again. This was what it had come to.

I thought of the lines from "Little Gidding:"

...and the end of all our exploring
Will be to arrive where we started
And know the place for the first time.

Was this the end of my exploring? What had happened to the dreams of that young woman who'd left another red-bricked campus to cast her fate with a married man?

What kind of "understanding" did Abbot Academy hope to impart to its young women? Would my students have the courage to step onto a stage, not knowing whether they would be greeted by applause or catcalls? Or would they be groomed to become the perfect wife to the perfect man, the kind of boy now getting educated on "the Hill" in another set of red-brick buildings that were bigger and better than the ones where the girls lived and studied?

On the other side of the circle, in her office in Draper Hall, Marguerite Hearsey was waiting to talk to me. I knew I would have plenty of time to answer those questions.

* * *

I thought of the teachers who had gone before me. Bertha Morgan Gray was 65 when she died. Emily Brown had soldiered on to 75. I supposed that if I had to, I could go on teaching drama until the day I died. Abbot was a bigger school, older and more prestigious than even Concord Academy. I could do a lot worse than to work there.

And so I said yes, but only half-time at first. I worked two long days in Andover, then retreated to Concord for the rest of the week. And it seemed to work out well. I kept the Abbot Dramatic Society afloat. Mrs. Gray had cast the roles for *Outward Bound* before she died. With time running short, the grieving girls had decided to do just a reading of the play. I focused instead on organizing the commencement production.

At the end of the semester, Marguerite asked if I would stay on full-time. I said I would accept, but only if the school provided me with housing. Much to my surprise, she said that wouldn't be a problem. The trustees had just purchased another large house across School Street, and I could have a few rooms there. They would even spruce up the place with my choice of paint or wallpaper.

It was not the beautiful lakefront home that Smith had renovated for Hallie Flanagan. But it was a nice offer all the same. It was an offer, I acknowledged as I reviewed my dwindling bank accounts, that I was in no position to refuse.

* * *

Tom arrived at Princeton in October, having survived all the celebrations the British people rolled out for his 60th birthday the month before.

I could tell from his letters that he was happy to be back in America, freed, for a time, from the self-inflicted pressures of his daily routines and the incessant deadlines of the publishing business. Spoiled now by Margaret and Willard and other friends he had made over the years. Surrounded by brilliant colleagues and even more adoring students. Oppenheimer had just arrived to direct the institute, and Tom was looking forward to continuing the conversations they had started at Harvard about the perilous state of the planet.

He was working on a new play, and he relished his new stretch of uninterrupted time. Each of the institute's offices came with a blackboard, an empty canvas on which the scientists and mathematicians could puzzle out their theories with their colleagues. So he had decided to give it a try. He explained to me how he had assigned a Greek letter to each character and begun diagramming his plot lines.

The play was a comedy, based on Euripedes's *Alcestis.* Tom's comedies, I mused as I read his description, would never rival *Hay Fever* for laughs. The play had started off as *One-Eyed Riley,* but he now called it *The Cocktail Party,* a better choice, I thought. He was sending drafts to his old director, and Martin Browne was enthusiastic.

But as the weeks went by, he had not shared a draft with me. Had he found my suggestions for *The Family Reunion* useless? Had my critique annoyed him? Or was it another way for Tom to draw a line and move on with his life?

On the list of ways in which Tom Eliot had managed to wound me over the course of our lifetimes, this slight was hardly worth cataloging. He was a world-famous poet and playwright. His works were sought for Canterbury Cathedral, the best theaters of London and New York. I was a drama teacher at a girls' school in Massachusetts. What possible help could I provide?

So I focused on my own plays. I had picked out a new one this year. *Letters to Lucerne* had opened on Broadway right after Pearl Harbor and had the advantage of being set in a private school, with mostly female roles. It would give the girls a chance to wrestle with the still-fresh tensions of wartime Europe. And I could begin to forge my own era at the Academy.

Tom would come to Boston eventually. He would want to see his sisters, his in-laws, his cousins. But it was best if I had no expectations of my own. We were still friends, after all. I was lucky I had that.

* * *

The announcement came in November. The Swedish Academy of Literature had awarded Tom the Nobel Prize. He was now formally in the company of Kipling, Shaw, Yeats, and Bergson. And, I thought with amusement, that missionary's daughter, Pearl Buck.

Still, I was thrilled for him. I could imagine Margaret and Willard in Princeton, breaking out a bottle of champagne to help him celebrate. But I knew that while he would love the recognition, he would still hate being thrust into the spotlight.

I supposed that when the Swedish Academy described him as "a pioneer" of modern poetry, they had been referring to "Prufrock" and "The Waste Land." Credit Vivienne for most of that. She had made him miserably unhappy, and out of those dismal years, great literature—now, apparently, for the ages—had been produced.

The ceremony in Stockholm, he explained, would force him to cut short his sabbatical. He would come to Boston before he left and would try to make time to see me.

Would he be willing to do a poetry reading at Abbot?

As soon as I sent off the letter, I regretted it. I still wore our friendship like a badge of honor, solidifying my status at each new school where I taught. Emily Hale could get a Nobel Prize winner to make time on his schedule for a poetry reading at our school.

And Tom was willing to do it, as long as there was no publicity; he would get in trouble with his agent for making his own arrangements and forgoing a fee. By now he was used to speaking and reading. It did not seem to matter if he was tired or bored, or whether he read one poem or two—the audience was never disappointed. But I knew he would rather be writing than reciting, that he preferred the company of one to an audience of one hundred.

And I would have preferred to have Tom all to myself, too. But it was awkward now. It felt as if we were falling back on memories and old conversations, never fully confronting our loneliness, two aging lovers now paralyzed by our pasts.

So his poetry reading filled the time, provided a structure to his visit. It was easier for me to play the hostess, to introduce the famous poet to the starstruck older students, to escort him around campus, impressing everyone from Marguerite on down. And at the end of the day, he would head back to Boston, then catch a flight back to London and ready himself for another evening of adulation, this time on one of the world's most prominent stages.

* * *

We had talked briefly about his schedule in Stockholm. He was still not satisfied with his speech; I expected he would keep fussing with it right up to the last minute. When the stories and photographs were transmitted back to the States, I devoured them. Tom shared the stage with three scientists, including Paul Mueller, the Swiss chemist who had put DDT on the map. Despite his age, Tom still looked dapper, this time in white tie and tails, the Order of Merit medal dangling from a ribbon around his neck. He could pass for a member of the Swedish royal family, I thought, the men sporting their own sets of medals, the women their tiaras.

"When I began to think of what I should say to you this evening," Tom said in his acceptance speech, "I wished only to express very simply my appreciation of the high honor which the Swedish Academy has thought fit to confer upon me. But to do this adequately proved no simple task: my business is with words, yet the words were beyond my command...."

I should have been there. I belonged by his side.

I was shocked at the rush of anger I felt, the burst of jealous rage. Tom had never promised me marriage. I had no claim to his fame. But there, I named it. There was still a well of anger, of grief, buried inside me.

I took a long breath, steeling my emotions. *Focus on the speech.* The words were so much like Tom. "Painting, sculpture, architecture, music, can be enjoyed by all who see or hear. But language, especially the language of poetry, is a different matter. Poetry, it might seem, separates peoples instead of uniting them."

His written words always seemed to calm me. It was better, I thought, that he had been honest with me last year. Better to be rejected by a man who had decided he could no longer love me than to be rejected because I was no longer good enough for him. I had never felt that with Tom; I did not want to feel that way now.

My business is with words, yet the words were beyond my command....

Yes, I thought. Tom had never been able to find the right words for me.

* * *

A typewritten draft of *The Cocktail Party* arrived in the new year. He was under pressure to finish it—it was already scheduled for the Edinburgh Festival next summer. But he did not ask for suggestions, and as I leafed through the script, I realized there was no way I could have provided them.

A cocktail party was underway at the Chamberlaynes' home, but Lavinia Chamberlayne had failed to appear. The guests included a young woman named Celia Coplestone, and as the drama unfolded, it was revealed that she and Lavinia's husband Edward had been having an affair.

I always looked for myself in Tom's poems, but except for "Burnt Norton," I had rarely found anything. This was different. Celia was younger and more attractive and pursued by another male. But as the second scene began, I read words that I knew I had spoken to Tom, if only in my imagination.

You know I accepted the situation

Because a divorce would ruin your career;
And we thought that Lavinia would never want to leave you.

An older woman—a woman not unlike Aunt Edith—arrived and departed, and then Edward and Celia were left alone again. He told her that it was over, that it was too late for him, that he felt old and middle-aged, that she deserved better. And I remembered those words. They were in verse now and sharpened with Eliot imagery. But it was that painful afternoon in Concord when Tom had told me he couldn't marry me. It was impossible to forget, and now I never would. The whole world could experience my humiliation—that's what Celia called it—in the latest play by T. S. Eliot.

Edward makes a declaration of love of sorts:

If I have ever been in love—and I think that I have—
I have never been in love with anyone but you....

I supposed I should try and hang onto that. But then Celia calls out Edward. And I remembered my anger and how empty I had felt after I asked Tom to leave.

I put the manuscript aside at the end of Act One, needing my own intermission. I began casting the roles. Tom and Martin hoped to get Alec Guinness to play The Unidentified Guest, the psychiatrist at the center of the drama. Which young Hollywood starlet would make the perfect Celia?

Fortified with a glass of sherry, I returned to the script. Lavinia had returned, and the psychiatrist was working to patch up the Chamberlaynes' marriage. And then Celia returned for a scene of her own.

I mean that what has happened has made me aware
That I've always been alone. That one always is alone.

Tom does understand me. Even if he is incapable of acting on that understanding.

The God-like doctor dispatches Celia to his sanitorium and leads her friends in a prayer over another round of drinks. Sanitoriums, I mused, are always a convenient way for men to get rid of difficult women.

There was one more scene, back at the Chamberlaynes' flat, an echo of the play's opening. Celia was gone now. She had become a missionary, nursing to the people of the fictional land of Kinkanja. An insurrection had broken out, but she had stayed on with the natives, who were dying of a pestilence. And then she was captured, and her body had been found.

And Tom might have stopped there, but he didn't. Celia had died a terrible death, crucified, her body left near an anthill, and smeared with a juice that would attract the ants.

I threw the script to the floor. I rubbed my arms, willing away the sudden tingling of my skin. *Where does he get these ideas?* It was *Sweeney* all over again, but this time *I* was the woman dying the horrible death.

I calmed myself with another glass of sherry. Perhaps Martin Browne will tell him it's too much. The play is supposed to be a comedy! The audience would never forgive him for killing off Celia, particularly in such a graphically gory way.

What was going on in his imagination? Had I ever been as saintly as Celia? Did some part of him want to kill me off, too?

I flipped back through the pages, looking for answers. I found the scene where Celia says goodbye to Lavinia:

I should like you to remember me
As someone who wants you and Edward to be happy.

I *had* been patient and undemanding. What if I had been as difficult as Vivienne? Could I have forced Tom's hand? Would he have loved me more if I had?

And could I still love a man who was so impossible to understand?

* * *

I went back to England in the summer of 1950. John and Edith were both too old to travel now; John was too frail and Edith was nearly blind. So I invited Marguerite to join me and share expenses. Tom rearranged his schedule to meet our train. There was always that frisson of excitement when my train pulled up to the platform. Would this summer be different? Was this the year my life would finally change?

But no, we were simply friends now. He was an aging editor, meeting an old friend on a railroad platform, offering to squire two teachers to the theater or the museum. Doing what polite people did, what polite society expected.

Yet it was quickly apparent that Mary Trevelyan was now running his life. He tried to keep our outings separate, to give each of us some time and attention. Still, it was clear, more than ever before, that he relied on Mary to make his decisions, schedule his doctors' appointments, steer him to the speeches and readings.

I should be jealous, I told myself. But it was easier to be objective now. Tom treated Mary no better, and in some ways even worse, than he treated me. Mary had to live with Tom's moods, his hypochondria, his eccentricities. She got all the fussiness that Tom's admiring public never saw.

She was the one who had to live with all of that, day in and day out— and through all the privations of postwar London and English winters. I, on the other hand, could leave that all behind at the end of the summer, knowing that Tom Eliot's beautifully written letters would still find their way to my mailbox.

* * *

Christmas was a special time at Abbot, rich with its own set of rituals. At the end of the term, I had no energy left for an Emily Brown-style extravaganza. But perhaps, I told Marguerite, I could do a reading one night in the chapel, help to center the girls before they headed home for the holidays.

I organized a short program and slipped in some lines from "O Light Invisible."

In our rhythm of earthly life we tire of light. We are glad when the day ends, when the play ends; and ecstasy is too much pain....

It was as if Uncle John had been listening. A week later, two days before Christmas, he died at home in his bed.

Edith, as usual, swung into action. It was as if she had learned a thing or two from all the royal secretaries. Over the holiday, the staff of King's Chapel worked overtime to be able to honor their pastor emeritus on the day after Christmas.

John had been like a second father, I acknowledged. Still, he had lived a long, full life—to the ripe old age of 88. I worried instead about Edith, but if she ever gave herself permission to break down and cry, it would happen farther down the road of grief and loneliness, and certainly not in front of the lions of the Unitarian church.

The newspaper obituary described her as "once a nationally known lecturer on gardening," and I suspected she had supplied the words. But I had to admit that the flowers in the church were magnificent. The Christmas wreaths and garlands had been kept in place, providing a backdrop of dark green and the scent of woodlands. There were masses of red roses, white chrysanthemums, and lilies, and smaller arrangements of spring flowers, placed along the window ledges and at the base of the sanctuary's pillars. It was as if Edith was taking us to yet another English garden. It would comfort her to make arrangements for all the flowers; as for me, they only brought back memories of springtime in the Public Garden or the roses of Burnt Norton.

As the procession began, six men balanced the casket on their shoulders, being careful to keep the flowers in place. There were three wreaths: two of tiny yellow roses, and another of Oregon cedar. I wondered how Edith had managed to locate a touch of the Pacific Northwest on such short notice. And from the casket trailed more sprays of evergreen. *Choisya ternata*, Edith had made a point of telling me. Otherwise known as Mexican orange blossom.

There was nothing unexpected; the hymns, the prayers, and the readings were all in excellent taste. A choir of eight men closed with "God be in my head and in my heart," and after the benediction, the organist began the slow cadence of Handel's "Largo." I steadied Edith on my arm as we headed back down the aisle, following the casket. Her eyesight was fading, but she still nodded to the pews on both sides of the aisle, knowing there were people there who should be acknowledged. It was as if she were the queen herself.

Outside it had begun snowing, so I helped her settle quickly into the shelter of the hired limousine. There was to be another short service, this time a private one, in the chapel at Mount Auburn Cemetery.

"I thought it was a nice service," Edith observed as the car headed to Cambridge.

"Everything was perfect," I assured her. "All of your flowers were so beautiful."

Neither of us spoke on the ride across the river. Uncle John's service had been as lengthy as Mother's had been short. Edith had wanted to savor every minute of the pomp and ceremony she could order up for the last honors of John Carroll Perkins. As for Emily Jose Milliken Hale, she had been buried as quietly and quickly as possible.

The snow was falling harder now. I thought of another scene, one I had only heard about but that continued to trouble my dreams. Another snowy day. Another crazy woman. Tom and Maurice and the Fabers burying Vivienne Haigh-Wood Eliot. A desolate day in January, four long years ago.

* * *

How long, I wondered, would Uncle John be remembered as a leader of the Unitarian church? How long, for that matter, would Tom's poetry be studied and recited?

I looked longingly at the *TIME* magazine cover from last year. Tom certainly qualified as "a great man." Nobel Prize winner. Order of Merit. Despite all its flaws, *The Cocktail Party* was still running on Broadway. When Tom invited me to join him for a performance at the Henry Miller's Theatre, I plastered a smile on my face and agreed to go along.

I said nothing about the parallels to our own lives. Celia still died a gruesome death, but Tom had toned down some of the grisly details. And who was I to critique the ending? The play had won the Tony Award for the season's best play. The Broadway cast had made a recording. Alone in my room, I listened to Alec Guinness and Irene Worth. I told myself I was honing my craft. Still, I kept returning to Act One, Scene Two, re-playing the dialogue between Edward and Celia, wishing I could rewrite their words.

I was sorry now that I had sent my favorite photograph of Tom to Scripps. I had hung onto a photo of an older Tom, one who looked stern and distant. I kept it now by my bedside, the last thing I saw before I fell asleep, the first thing I saw in the morning when I awoke.

And what about me? In the end, I was irrelevant. But I knew Tom's letters weren't. Someone would want them someday. It was important to protect them.

I did not want to embarrass him. I did not mind if they were locked up until both of us were long gone. But I yearned for one small thing: I wanted him to save my letters, too. I was, after all, a small part of his story.

I should spend more time thinking about this—after all, we weren't getting any younger. Willard and Margaret would help me. More than anyone I knew, they were friends of mine and friends of Tom, and people who would know what scholars needed.

I could count on them to help me get it right.

* * *

It was time to take Abbot Academy's drama program to a new level. It was easy to fall back on *Dear Brutus* and *Hay Fever,* and to cast half the girls as men. But there were boys' schools situated all around us. Why not join forces, do something more challenging?

I knew better than to propose working with Phillips Andover. Everyone at Abbot was nervous about what might happen if it became too easy for the boys on the other side of Main Street to fraternize with the girls. The Brooks School was a better choice: coed, less threatening. I had met Chychele Waterston, the head of the English Department and the drama program, and I liked him. He was a quiet Scot, a well-educated man who spoke several languages. He had worked in British intelligence during the war and then become a U.S. citizen.

He reminded me of Tom, without all the complications.

We put our heads together and decided to tackle *Antigone,* Jean Anouilh's adaption from Socrates, updated during the Nazi occupation of Paris. There were eight parts for boys and four parts for girls. From the start, I knew who I would cast as Antigone. Carol Hardin was a boarder from Darien, Connecticut, a smart girl and a natural leader. She could act, but more important, she had a presence.

Chychele filled out the male side of the cast list, but he was sensitive about one choice. He wanted to cast one of his children as the page. But if I thought he was playing favorites, I should let him know.

However, Sam turned out to be a gifted little actor and perfect for the role. He was smart and attentive; he learned his lines quickly and never missed a mark.

None of my students had gone on to great dramatic careers, but I loved following the careers of my friends who had. Rusty Lane had broken out on Broadway in *Mister Roberts*. Tony Perkins, Oggie's son, had just landed his first movie role in *The Actress*. It was clear Sam Waterston loved acting just as much as I did when I was his age; if he decided to pursue a career in theater, I was confident he would go far.

I had never minded playing a male role or teaching girls how to lower their voices. Still, a mixed cast was always more satisfying. There was a distinctive interplay between men and women, a tension that persisted even among boys and girls. It made the product more real and ultimately more successful. And Chychele and I complemented each other, bringing out the best in our cast. It was the best production I had done in years.

Afterwards, he sent me a sweet note, still insisting on calling me "Miss Hale":

> *It is almost certainly obvious to you and to the Abbot Academy cast of Antigone that all the Brooks boys (in which category I include myself) found it extremely pleasant to work with the Abbot girls. The standard which the girls set and which you set for them was extraordinarily helpful to some of the boys.*

He referenced the boy who had played the First Guard. He was "a rather erratic soul," but under the influence of the Abbot Academy women "has shown all sorts of improvement in all sorts of ways other than dramatic." His colleagues, he said, had taken notice.

> *This is only one example of the understanding cooperation which I constantly felt and appreciated all through the play and I wish there were some way of conveying to the girls, without mentioning personalities, how very valuable it is when ladies know how to use their powers as a civilizing influence. So stated the idea sounds pretty trite and point blank. Can you express it for me more tactfully?*

I smiled as I read his last request. Wasn't that what society always taught us, that the future of civilization ultimately rested on the shoulders of women?

"Antigone's" parents sent me some flowers, and her mother followed up with a note. They were truly overwhelmed, she wrote, at their daughter's understanding and interpretation of her part. "I constantly relive it all, for it was a very high point for us all—and I hardly need say was an extraordinarily deep and climactic experience for Carol—a truly spiritual one."

Yes, I thought with a smile. Tom Eliot might find his spiritual sustenance in churches and cathedrals. But like a girl from Darien, I would find it on the stage.

* * *

Another university. Another milestone. Another honorary degree for T. S. Eliot. Washington University in St. Louis was marking its 100th anniversary in 1953, and the grandson of its founder had agreed to return home to deliver the commencement address.

"It has been 20 years since I passed through St. Louis," he wrote. "When the invitation came, I discovered I was eager to return, to visit my parents' graves, and meet with my Missouri cousins."

To see me?

It was hard to believe 20 years had passed since Tom had made his trip out West. Twenty years since those magical days at Claremont and Balboa Island. I wondered if he ever thought back to that time the way I did. The train arriving at dawn. The smells of eucalypts, oranges, and frangipani. The bright California sunlight. The squeak of white sand between our toes as we walked on the beach.

It was a different time, and I was a different woman. And he was a different man now, too.

* * *

Eventually, Tom asked if I would like to make the trip with him. The university president planned to host a reception in his honor. No Marshall or Bradley or Oppenheimer among the honorees this time. But I was intrigued by the prospect of meeting Fannie Hurst and Lillian Gilbreth, the engineer who had managed to pursue a distinguished career while raising 12 children. In Hurst, Tom observed, the university had apparently decided to recognize an alumna for her ability to make very good money by churning out very bad novels. Perhaps, he added, they were hoping for a bequest. I made a note to bring along my copy of *Imitation of Life* to get Hurst's autograph.

Eliot cousins were also coming, from as far away as California and Oregon. Marian, he wrote, would travel with him from Cambridge; perhaps I would like to invite Dorothy Elsmith to join the entourage?

There was a time, I mused, when Tom had traveled light. Now, it seemed, he needed companions, people to buffer him from too-eager admirers and attend to his growing list of needs. But I enjoyed Dorothy's company, and if we shared a hotel room, it would help reduce my expenses.

We were all old friends now. Once together on the train, we settled into easy conversation, sharing news, recalling summers in New Hampshire or at Dorothy's place in Woods Hole. Remembering times with Henry and Ada, and how much we missed them. But we were feeling the years more and more. Marian needed a steadying hand when she stepped down onto the platform. We retired earlier to our berths and felt twinges of stiffness when we crawled out in the morning. Eyeglasses came out to study the menu in the dining car. And if the waiter disappeared for too long, it was easy for Marian to forget what she had decided to order.

If she ever wondered why her precious younger brother had never remarried, she never asked about it—and certainly not in front of me. All of the sisters took their cues from Tom, treating me like a close cousin and nothing more. Their brother was a genius, a man who deserved to be protected and coddled. They were not about to shower him with advice on how to manage his love life.

As St. Louis approached, Tom seemed to come alive again, stretching to peer out the train window and be the first to catch sight of the Mississippi River. I remembered the day I had ventured into London's financial district and walked along the Thames. Hoping for what? The sight of Tom? Had my risk been rewarded?

Twenty-five years of waiting? A spot in the entourage of the celebrity poet? It was hard not to feel bitter. But the Hales of Chestnut Hill were never permitted to be bitter. There was always another Sunday. We had to be the face of piety, gratitude, charity. Our congregants expected it. Our livelihood depended on it.

I returned to watching Tom as he pointed out different ships to Dorothy and speculated about their cargoes. The happy Midwestern boy might have always been drawn to poetry, but if he had stayed in St. Louis, he never would have won the Nobel Prize.

The river disappeared behind us, and just as quickly, Tom's boyish excitement did, too. The conductor walked through the carriage, announcing our imminent arrival. As we gathered up our things, Tom donned his invisible mask, hiding his youthful joy behind tired eyes and pursed lips. It was time to be the dutiful celebrity again. To sit for an interview with the local newspaper and expound on the state of contemporary literature. To don a gown and mortarboard, make a speech, accept a degree, acknowledge the applause. To shake hands in the receiving line at the president's house and pose with distant cousins he barely remembered.

He had had a choice, and this was the life he had chosen.

* * *

When I returned from St. Louis, it was time to pack my bags for Britain. Tom's family might think I was chasing him across the Atlantic. But each summer, the British Drama League held a school for actors and directors, and this year I had been accepted.

The school was set at Alnwick Castle, the ancestral home of the Duke of Northumberland. The castle turned out to be a maze of bone-chilling passageways, but I was delighted to discover my room was at the end of a long spiral stairway in one of the castle's turrets. As I looked out over the River Aln and the English countryside, I thought of princesses in other castles, of Snow White and Cinderella, of Cocteau's Belle and her Beast. Would I ever find my "happily ever after" the way they had?

I recalled the words I had written for the Abbot alumnae magazine. Every actor or actress "loves to escape from his or her personal world into the happy land of 'make believe': loves to be someone else, to enjoy the illusion of becoming another personality than the one familiar to himself; enjoys 'dressing up' and 'pretending' as do boys and girls in childhood."

I was too old to play ingenues and almost too old to play their mothers. I needed a good role here, an escape from Boston and girls' schools—and the dreaded state of spinsterhood.

For years I had come to England each summer and played the most challenging role of my life. I had put on a smile and tried to provide whatever Tom Eliot needed. A walk in the country, conversation over lunch. A teasing laugh, a sympathetic ear. All the time locking away the years of disappointments, pretending they could be forgotten.

But what choice did I have? Edith was all I had left now and someday Edith would be gone, too. I would be on my own, and unlike Cinderella and Belle, there would be no escape from my own tower of solitude.

* * *

The wet chill of my tiny room was dispelled by the friendliness of my fellow students. As the only American, I stood out among the rest, but the barriers broke down quickly as we explored the labyrinthine hallways and got lost on our way to the Great Hall. At the end of the day, I huffed and puffed my way up the 60 steps to my bed, knowing it was good exercise for my lungs and my aging knees.

I signed up for the classes in production, acting, and choral speaking, and was pleased to be cast in one of the one-act plays that would be performed at the end of the week. I asked for just a small part because I knew I would miss a rehearsal; I had gotten permission to spend a day away at the Edinburgh Festival, attending the premiere of Tom's new play, *The Confidential Clerk*.

The night turned out to very awkward. Tom's niece, Theodora, was visiting, and she occupied the prized seat next to him in the box at the Lyceum. The two of them had been close since her mother had died nearly 30 years before. Now, at 50, she guarded her aging uncle like he was fragile, precious cargo.

Mary Trevelyan had also been invited, and we exchanged friendly greetings when we passed in the lobby. Fortunately, the play had three acts, giving each of us an intermission to visit Tom in his box.

Unlike his earlier plays, I had seen no drafts of this one. Considering that Tom had written it, I found it surprisingly funny. Denholm Elliott was particularly good in the role of Colby, the clerk.

My seat was in the Grand Circle, and when the first act ended, I took the stairs down to the boxes. I was pleased to find Tom in a good mood.

"The play's very funny, Tom," I declared. "From up where I'm sitting, I think the audience is really enjoying it."

Theodora's eyes flashed. *She thinks I'm complaining about my seat.*

I quipped quickly: "If James Barrie were here, I think he'd say you finally mastered the drawing room."

Tom smiled. "That good?"

I nodded. "I'm sorry I won't be able to see you after the final curtain. I'll have to rush to catch the train back to Alnwick."

"Write and tell me what you think. Your opinion is always important to me."

Mary's turn came at the end of the second act. I could have stayed in my seat, the perfect spot to spy on their interaction. But I wanted no part of that. I retreated to the ladies' room instead.

When the curtain went down and the actors returned for their bows, the crowd rose to their feet, applauding enthusiastically. The actors turned to acknowledge Tom in his box, and he saluted them in return.

I left the warm glow of the theater and scurried to the station to catch my train. It was two hours back to the castle, leaving far too much time to ruminate as I stared out the train window into the growing darkness.

I imagined the scene: arriving back at the castle and tracking down my classmates after dinner. "I've just been to see my good friend, T. S. Eliot," I could announce with pride. But I knew that I wouldn't. Here it was my secret. To speak otherwise would be pretentious, self-serving. And besides, what relationship could I claim anymore?

On the last day of our classes, Martin Browne came to lecture. He had directed the premieres of nearly all of Tom's plays, including this one. The rest of the class had gone to see the play the night before.

After he had finished and taken some questions, he lingered a while longer to talk with the students. I held back until I could talk to him alone.

"Hello," I said shyly. "I enjoyed your talk. I wanted to introduce myself." I extended my hand. "My name is Emily Hale."

"Tom Eliot's friend?" Martin's face widened in a smile.

"Why, yes," I replied, surprised.

"I think we both gave him some suggestions when he was writing *Family Reunion*. And, if I remember correctly, we were telling him the same thing."

I smiled. "Well, he didn't take all of my advice."

"Nor mine," Martin replied.

"I saw the premiere of your new play. I think the two of you have another hit on your hands."

"Perhaps," Martin replied. "But somehow it wasn't as exciting for me as all the other ones."

He turned to gather up his lecture notes, then paused and studied my face. "I have an impertinent question to ask."

"Go ahead."

"Are you the model for Celia?"

I froze, not knowing how to answer. It was presumptuous to say yes, but Martin might already know the truth.

"Never mind," he said. "You don't have to answer." Then he smiled. "But I'm sure you agree that Tom never should have killed her off the way he did."

The Confidential Clerk

ABBOT ACADEMY WAS CHANGING, AND not necessarily for the better.

Marguerite had decided to retire, and the trustees had chosen Mary Crane to replace her. Like Marguerite, she was a student of English literature. But she also was a widow who arrived on campus with four girls of her own. Unlike her predecessor, she did not have time to play "mother" to all the other girls at Abbot.

And more and more of the faculty members wanted to escape the dorms. After years of living in them, I loved having quiet rooms of my own. But I missed the bonds of family that were forged along the old corridors. The girls no longer sought my romantic advice or trusted me with their secrets.

Still, I tried to mold each of my casts into a family, if only for the weeks of rehearsals and the run of the play. The Class of '56 was a fun group of bright girls. The Senior Mids were doing Barrie again, this time *The Admirable Crichton*. As actresses, I explained, it was just as important how they "listened" on stage as how they spoke. I still worked on their accents, finding the few key words where the "r's" and "a's" of Massachusetts and the Midwest could be softened into something that sounded more British. I taught each girl a mannerism to help transform her into a believable butler or a lord or a lady. There was, I demonstrated, a certain way to hold a teacup. And after long afternoons of work, I whipped up impromptu dinners for them in my rooms.

After the last show was over and we were rewarded with full houses and standing ovations, the cast presented me with something I valued more than a bouquet: a folder full of letters, telling me what they had learned.

There were nearly 20 notes, some more literate, some more heartfelt. But I treasured each one, reminding me of the girl-about-to-be-a-woman who had taken the time to write it.

You have impressed upon me, even more fully, that acting is not merely a recitation of lines but the ability to understand and portray, mostly through pantomime, another person's character.

Above this, you have made me realize the great need for cooperation and patience in any organization. Miss Hale, you have shown this to me through your own patience, your sense of humor, and your ability to bear the disappointments and hardships that we have caused you.

But even above this, you have shown me a higher sense of values. You have proven to me that to give up temporary pleasures for an ultimately greater reward, is a goal that I must work to achieve in order that I may do it with pleasure.

I stored the folder away carefully in my drawer. Someday the letters from England might stop. These letters would help fill the gap if they did.

* * *

But for now, Tom—and his letters—kept coming.

He arrived before the end of the school year, eager to visit his family. Margaret was now 85 and Marian 79. All the Eliot siblings knew their time together was running out.

Tom was lucky to have been able to make the trip at all. He had spent five weeks in the hospital in February fighting off bronchitis and, this time, wracking bouts of coughing and choking. All the years of smoking had taken their toll, and, to my eyes, he was frailer than ever before.

But there was no time for him to rest. He set off quickly to the University of Minnesota to deliver another lecture. It had been booked for the main auditorium, but when 16,000 people wanted tickets, they moved it to the basketball field house. How could I ever expect him to do another talk at Abbot?

Still, once again, he agreed—as long as there was no publicity. Mary Crane was thrilled that I could land a Nobel Prize winner, even if we couldn't send out a press release—or taunt the Phillips faculty with our literary coup.

We kept the group small: just the two oldest classes, gathered in School Room, upstairs in Abbot Hall. Once again, Tom read "The Waste Land." I often listened to the Decca recording on nights when I had trouble falling asleep. Now I closed my eyes again, listening to the familiar lines, mulling the mysteries of Tom's inner being.

The girls applauded politely when Tom finished; the bravest deigned to ask a question or two. Then I stepped in. "Thank you, Tom, for making some time to join us today." I meant it on behalf of myself as much as I did for the students.

The girls filed out. Mary Crane shook his hand and thanked him again. At last we were left alone.

"Would you have time to get something to eat?"

He checked his watch. "I think so."

"Come then," I said. "We can walk over to the Andover Inn."

I led him back down the marble staircase, then around the oval to School Street. The campus was breaking out into the best of springtime. I remembered other walks—the Public Garden, the Cotswold hills, the serenity of campuses, Harvard and Scripps, the beach at Corona del Mar.

My students, I suspected, looked at us and saw two doddering old friends stuck in "the good old days." But I still remembered the thrill, the stirring throughout my body, no matter the kind of love Tom was capable of sharing with me now. In that stretch of street beyond the campus, before we reached the corner of Main Street, I threaded my arm through his, protectively, possessively. I wanted to remember what it felt like.

We crossed over to the Phillips campus. The inn was so different from other places where we had snatched a quick cup of tea. The boys' academy had built it on a prominent spot to house parents and other visitors. There was really no other place to go.

The front porch, graced by Georgian pillars, beckoned this time. It was a place to see and be seen. But old habits died hard. I still did not want to be seen.

He paused before opening the door as if he had read my mind. "You're sure this won't ruin your reputation?"

I smiled. "Oh, dearie, you know we're too old for that sort of thing!"

We were led to a table by a window and began, as usual, by sharing a pot of tea. Across the room I spotted one of my Senior Mids huddled with her parents, the ticket for her admission to the inn. Tom lit a cigarette but coughed after taking the first puff.

I turned back to him. "I've been worried about you."

"My doctor says I should give up smoking. But I find that very hard to do."

I regarded him more clinically now, the way my students might have. I did not like what I saw. When had he aged so much? Britain, I knew, had finally moved beyond the deprivations of the war years, but it could do nothing about the damp chill of its winters or the poisons lurking in the greasy London fog.

Tom lived a simple life now, with Mary to nag him, his roommate to keep him company, and the young secretaries at Faber to draft his letters and manage his calendar. How much longer would he have? What if this were the last time I would ever see him?

The thought startled me, causing me to tremble.

"What is it?" he asked.

"Nothing," I replied. Death was one thing we never discussed.

I wondered what my student across the dining room would think if she spotted us. I was the matronly teacher who directed her plays. Could any of them imagine that I had ever been in love?

And what would I tell them if they still sought my advice? About choices in life, about colleges and careers, boyfriends and marriage? A few months ago I had needed a girl to step into the lead in the play we were doing with the Brooks School. My best candidate had declined, saying she would be away the weekend of the performances. Only later did I learn she was going to a dance at Exeter. Why hadn't she told me the truth? *Did she think I would disapprove if she chose a dance over drama?*

"You look lost in your thoughts," Tom remarked.

I smiled. "That's supposed to be my line." I took a small bite, then set down my knife and fork. "I was thinking about what my students must see when they look at us…and I was thinking that no matter how many years have gone by, I still look at you and see the student at Harvard.

And you are not the world-famous poet, and I am not the director of the drama department. No, we are two young people, still trying to figure out who we are, and still having trouble expressing how we feel."

"I wish I could turn back the clock, Emily...."

"Well," I replied, matter of factly, "as you said yourself, back when Henry died, it's too late for that. Prufrock, it seems, is still wearing his trousers rolled."

"I wish it could have been different."

"No matter," I said. I summoned up all of my acting experience and forced myself to smile. "I've always treasured our friendship, Tom, and I know I always will. I always felt we understood each other in a rare and beautiful way. Even when we were apart, I knew you were still with me."

"And you were always a part of me."

I felt the tears start to well in my eyes. This was no time to cry here, in the dining room of the Andover Inn, surrounded by parents and students, faculty members and tourists, some of whom might recognize Tom.

I dropped that topic. There was still something else I had to discuss.

"When I heard about your lecture in Minneapolis and how you filled the arena there, it reminded me that, like it or not, you have become a famous person. And so I've been thinking about your letters. I want to make sure that someone takes care of them."

"Why do you have to do anything?"

"I won't live forever," I said. I willed my voice to stay even. "I've talked to Willard and Margaret. They agree that your letters should be preserved, and by a library that will know what to do with them. You and I used to talk about saving our correspondence, but guarding it for a while after our deaths. Willard has put me in touch with the top librarians at Princeton. I think they could be trusted to follow our instructions."

"I hate the idea of every two-bit academic poking around in my past," Tom said. "They all love to speculate about what I was trying to say—and they are usually wrong."

"You can't fight it, Tom. They're going to do it anyway, whether you like it or not. As the years go by, there will be more people trying to make their reputations by cutting you down to size. They don't know you the way I do. They don't know the man who wrote me all those letters."

I paused. "Your letters are my dearest possession, but I don't have any heirs. I have to make sure that someone will take care of them after I'm no longer here."

He looked stricken, and I could not fathom why. I reached across the table and patted his hand gently. "Your words will be immortal, Tom, but we won't be. Down the road, scholars may have a fine time gossiping about us, but we'll never know about it. Who would be hurt? We'll both be long gone. Vivienne is dead. We have no children...."

There was one final point I wanted to make. Would this be my last chance? But still I hesitated. I had refrained from saying the words all these years, keeping them buried, locked in my heart.

"I'm a nobody, Tom. The only reason anyone would care about me is because of you. And that was always enough for me. I didn't mind if your Harvard professors didn't know me. I didn't care when your famous literary friends wouldn't make time for me. I stayed in the shadows. I minded my tongue. Your secrets were safe from Vivienne. And after she died, I never tried to claim you. I was satisfied with whatever part of you that you were willing to share.

"But I'm getting old, too, Tom. And someday I'd like someone to know that there was more to me and more to us than anyone ever knew."

I waited for my words to sink in. "If I decide to donate your letters, do you care which library I choose?"

"No," he replied. "They're all the same to me."

I cleared my throat, then reached down to find my purse underneath the table. "You probably need to be getting back to your sister's."

"Yes," he said. He snuffed out the cigarette and pulled out his wallet to take care of the check.

He walked me back to my house as the early evening shadows lengthened. We had said all there was to say. The years and months went by, and nothing ever changed. And, I supposed, it never would.

"Give your sisters my regards," I said. "And thank you again for coming. It's something these girls will always remember...and it's something very special for me."

"It was good to see you again, Emily."

He took me into his arms, and I closed my eyes to help me remember the embrace. The arms were frailer now, the muscles no longer hardened by hours spent on the water. But I still clung to him, not wanting the moment to end.

He kissed me quickly on the forehead, then turned to head down the street where he had parked his sister's car.

I watched as he walked away, feeling a pang in my heart. What if I never saw him again?

"Have a safe trip home," I called after him. "And take care of yourself!"

Too late, I realized how loud my voice was. Would my neighbors notice? What about my older colleague upstairs, boiling kettles of cabbage as if she hoped the smell would ward off a male visitor who might be tempted to spend the night?

I smiled, realizing that I no longer cared. I remembered that summer night in Boston more than 40 years ago. And I knew that if I had only found my voice then, if I hadn't worried about what a woman was expected to do or what the neighbors might think, if I had found the courage to chase after Tom and tell him that I loved him, it might have all turned out so differently.

* * *

I was right to be worried. Two days after the *Queen Mary* sailed from New York, Tom's heart began racing again. Tachycardia, the doctors called it. I no longer had to rely on Eleanor or Theresa for the news. United Press International was stationed on the docks in Southampton when Tom was wheeled off the ship and taken by ambulance to the French Hospital in London. His six weeks in the States had "exhausted" him, the reporters said, but he was slowly recovering.

I considered changing my summer plans and heading back to England. But Tom needed his rest, and I knew Mary would take care of him. I'd had enough of his carefully crafted schedule, juggling visits to try to keep his women happy, but always apart. It wasn't fair to Mary, and it certainly wasn't fair to me.

So I wrote him long letters, urging him to listen to his doctors and follow their advice. And I, in turn, boarded a train for a trip out West, traveling north through the Canadian Rockies and then down to Seattle. I still loved the West. The scenery was so different, the views so vast. It made me feel young and free again. It made me feel that for a short time at least, I could shed all the baggage of my past.

I headed down the Pacific Coast but went no farther than Berkeley. It was tempting to travel to Claremont, but the memories were too bittersweet. All of my closest friends had moved on or retired. I had heard that Marie McSpadden had gotten married, but I had lost touch with all of my students from Scripps. President Hard would never find time for an appointment. And I feared that I would arrive at the Denison Library and discover that my treasured books were still in their boxes, waiting to be unpacked.

It was better to leave the memories behind and head back East to Andover, to the girls of Abbot Academy and another year of trying my best to mold them into actresses.

But the journey had given me time to think, and I decided I no longer wanted to wait. I wrote Willard and told him that because of our close friendship, I had decided to give the letters to Princeton. Tom knew about my plans but said he didn't care which library I chose.

Willard responded quickly.

I do wish you had been here to see my face when I opened your letter and read of your decision to give to Princeton this fall all your letters from T.S.E. Sam was in the next room, so Margaret and I had to have a discreet session of rejoicing out in the garage. This is one of the nicest things that has happened to the Thorps and we bless you for it. Margaret can't lick her whiskers, but I lick mine—as you said I might well do. I hope it will be a long time before scholars have access to this correspondence but when they do they will surely find a treasure-horde.

I was amused that I could help Willard win an academic competition. Princeton would get the letters, not Harvard, Yale, or even the Bodleian Library. But I still wanted his advice. How long should the letters remain sealed? Twenty-five years should be long enough, but perhaps it should be 50. That's what Tom and I had always discussed.

Princeton had a new head librarian, and Mr. Dix could not have been nicer. He helped me make the arrangements for securing the boxes and shipping them to New Jersey. I felt a sharp pang as the truck drove away, but it was better this way. I would miss my letters, but I knew they would be protected and preserved.

In November, Mr. Dix advised me that the letters had been arranged in chronological order and repacked into 12 boxes. They would be formally appraised for tax purposes, then sealed with steel bands and placed in the library's fireproof vaults. I could donate them in installments if that suited my financial planning. I didn't care about those considerations; I paid so little in taxes anyway. But it was good to know that someone else thought the correspondence was valuable enough to care.

There was nothing left to do but to write Tom that I had followed through with my part of our agreement. It took me a long time to write the letter; I was not sure how he would respond. I covered all the logistics—except the appraisal. I stressed how they would be locked away for long after we both were gone. Then I tried to express what they had meant to me:

> *The letters are my life's greatest treasure. They fill up twleve boxes now—more than a thousand of them the last time I counted. I have carefully packed them along with me, over all these years and to all the places where I have lived.*

> *But the time has come to let them go.*

> *It was important to me to find a place that would cherish the letters as much as I do. I am confident we can count on the Princeton Library staff to protect our privacy, while giving future scholars another window into the nature of your literary genius.*

As I brought the letter to a close, I stopped short of asking the question that still nagged me: What have you done with mine?

* * *

Christmas was coming. Over the years, my Christmas reading had become an Abbot Academy tradition, marking the end of the first term and the start of the holidays. I briefly considered reading Tom's old poem about his memories of Christmas trees, but I opted for a safer choice instead.

Kate Douglas Wiggin had graduated from Abbot more than 80 years before, but *The Birds' Christmas Carol* was still a children's classic. Carol

Bird was the sickly child who managed to inspire everyone around her—rather like a female Tiny Tim Cratchit. This Christmas, I preferred to share the story of a saintly little girl instead of the musings of an aging English poet.

> *It was very early Christmas morning, and in the stillness of the dawn, with the soft snow falling on the house-tops, a little child was born in the Bird household....*

It was a challenge to capture the girls' attention in the hubbub of the holidays. But Christmas was, at its core, a celebration of the simple things. Of a family that would never find a room at the Andover Inn. Of an optimistic child with a crutch in Dickens's holiday story. Or Kate Wiggins's Christmastime Pollyanna. But as I read the story, I hoped I could open my students' eyes, help them see their privileged world through a new and different lens. And perhaps, later in life, they would find themselves returning to the same classic stories when they had children, or even grandchildren, of their own.

* * *

Tom's letter arrived two weeks before Christmas. I held it for a moment, afraid to tear it open. His letters now were different, cool and distant, almost obligatory. They were unlike all the letters I had sent off to Princeton.

I opened the letter and read Tom's words. I read them a second time, not believing the angry words that I held in my hands. He was astonished that I had let an archivist at Princeton read his letters. He had assumed they would have been sealed up immediately. And then to underscore his point, he conjured up another terrible image. It brought back memories of the ants crawling over Celia. But this time Tom was the one who was being devoured.

I crumpled the letter as I burst into tears. This letter would definitely not be sent to Princeton.

* * *

Ten days into the New Year, a Nor'easter rolled in, plunging temperatures below zero and dumping a foot of snow on most of New England. I had come to appreciate the reliability of my paper boy, and this morning was no different. *The Globe* arrived with a *thwumph* against my door, and I listened to the crunch of the teenager's boots as he moved down the street through the snow.

In the old days in the dorms, the noisy babble of girls racing for the bathroom was my backup alarm if my own clock had failed. Now it was the boy who delivered my paper, trying always, it seemed, to hit an imaginary target on my door.

I opened my eyes and saw, as I did every morning, my photograph of the middle-aged Tom gazing down at me, looking dapper and distinguished. No matter what, I would always own the inscription he had written.

I liked my early morning quiet now, dawdling with a cup of tea and the paper before dressing and heading across School Street to my classroom. I knew it would take more than freezing temperatures and a few inches of snow to force Abbot Academy to cancel classes. So I put on my robe and slippers, filled the teapot with water, and turned on the stove. Then I padded out to fetch the paper before it turned into a soggy roll of wet newsprint.

I fixed a quick bowl of cereal, then scanned the headlines quickly. I began to read about the weather. Boston, it seemed, had been spared the worst of the storm, but more snow had fallen in the suburbs. Transportation was disrupted to the north and to the west.

I turned inside to read the rest of the story. My hand froze when I saw the headline at the top of the page.

"T. S. Eliot Weds 'Confidential Clerk'"

For a quick moment, the cleverness of *The Globe*'s headline writer confused me.

And then I focused on the words in a tinier typeface on top: "He's 68, She Is 30."

I read the words over and over, as if that might make them change.

LONDON—Jan. 11 (Reuters)—Literary London was surprised to hear today of the marriage of 68-year-old American-born poet Thomas Stearns (T. S.) Eliot to his "confidential clerk," Valerie Fletcher, 30.

The wedding took place yesterday in an unpretentious church in West Kensington, a genteel, boarding-house section of London. Only the poet's lawyer and the bride's parents were present.

This was Missouri-born Eliot's second marriage. His first wife, a ballet dancer when he married her in 1915, died 10 years ago.

Miss Fletcher has worked as private secretary to Eliot for seven years. As a teenager, she read his work and idolized him.

The story went on with a few more inches of background, reminding all of Boston why they should care about T. S. Eliot's second marriage: Harvard graduate. Poems that were modern classics. Plays performed all over the world. Essays that were a major contribution to 20th-century literature. Nobel Prize. Order of Merit, French Legion of Honor. Heart attack on shipboard on the way home from his last trip to Boston, seven months before.

And then it concluded:

Today the pessimistic poet who described an aging man pondering over a life frittered away ("I have measured out my life with coffee spoons") was abroad somewhere on his second honeymoon.

Each time a different phrase jumped out at me. 68 and 30. Unpretentious. Another wedding at dawn with two witnesses. A ballet dancer? A second honeymoon.

I closed my eyes and tried to picture Valerie Fletcher. Miss Fletcher, another in the long line of Faber secretaries who had greeted me with a sweet smile before Tom and I headed out to lunch. A picture of efficiency, always quick to return to her work, that never-ending stream of correspondence to T. S. Eliot that someone had to manage. Always there to remind Tom of his next appointment, always there to keep him on track. Always there to nag him to take his umbrella because the forecast called for rain.

Of course, the paper *would* highlight the difference in their ages. *Nearly 40 years!* I recalled a young woman who was pleasant looking, a bit on the plumpish side. Lips and fingernails painted a bright crimson.

Certainly no blonde bombshell. My mind flashed to the recent news photos of Arthur Miller and Marilyn Monroe. If Tom had married Marilyn Monroe, that might be easier to accept.

Twice in my lifetime. How could a man be so cruel? A man who professed to be a practicing Christian, a man adored and admired by so many people? From the King of England to the Swedish Academy, from Harvard, Yale, and Princeton to a jam-packed arena at the University of Minnesota?

How could I have been such a fool?

I felt that my world was crumbling around me. For 40 years, I had lived a fantasy. A thousand letters, they were all just lies. I thought of the day that Eleanor had told me about his marriage. I thought of his sisters, and Henry and Theresa, treating me like a family member. I thought of the students with whom I had shared his letters. I thought of the actresses who had played Celia, my humiliation staged night after night on the stages of London and Broadway.

How much was I expected to bear in a lifetime?

The kettle was whistling now, and like a robot under someone else's command, I found my way to the stove and turned off the burner. Out of old habits, I went next to my bedroom to get dressed. Across the room, the photograph taunted me. The anger rose up in me, telling me to grab it and fling it against the wall. But no, it was far too valuable. Instead, I simply reached for the frame and placed it face-down on my dresser.

Then I did something I had never done in all my years of teaching. I dialed the phone number of Mary Crane's secretary and told her I was sorry, but I had taken ill. So ill that I would not be able to manage my classes today.

Then I turned off the lights and climbed into bed, pulling up the blankets around me. I buried my head into my pillow, which was rapidly becoming damp. And I hoped against hope that when the newspaper arrived tomorrow, this would all turn out to be just a very horrible nightmare.

Much Future Happiness

SOMEHOW I MANAGED TO HOLD myself together.

The Hales always "carried on," and carry on, I did. A week after the news was splashed all over the world, I led my students into Boston to see *Macbeth*. Rehearsals continued with the Brooks School for *Playboy of the Western World*. And the Senior Mids got started on *You Can't Take It With You*.

My predecessor had died in February, and I remembered how it had thrown all of the school's plays into turmoil. I could not quit now, not when so many people depended on me. And the work, I knew, diverted me.

If I showed any emotion, if I shed any public tears, it would only telegraph how deeply Tom Eliot had wounded me. Yes, I said to anyone who asked, I had met Miss Fletcher but did not know her well. And yes, I acknowledged, I was surprised by the news, like all of Tom's friends were. But that was Tom Eliot. He had a penchant for secrecy. He had, after all, done the same thing once before.

Each night I wracked my brain, searching for any clue I might have missed that Tom had fallen in love with his secretary. But I couldn't find one. Valerie Fletcher was there when I arrived at Tom's office and there when we left. She spoke softly and always seemed to be preoccupied with her work. I could not imagine what the two of them had in common, except, perhaps, ensuring the immortality of T. S. Eliot himself.

And as I lay awake in my single bed, another thought occurred to me. It was ten years to the month since Vivienne had died. Ten years before that, she had been committed to the asylum. Tom had done his penance when she was alive and another long penance after she had died. But ten years, it appeared, was long enough.

In late January, Mr. Dix sent me a copy of the letter he had written Tom. He had dutifully explained the details of my gift and emphasized that the letters would remain sealed until 50 years after the latter of our deaths.

In the darkness, I did the math in my head. Tom's health was so precarious, I had always assumed I would outlive him. If I died at 75, the letters would be opened in the year 2016. It seemed like such a long time from now. And yet if Valerie lived to 90, she would still be alive. Who could have dreamed that a second wife might be there when the boxes were opened?

Tom's letters had always been my joy, my comfort, the one thing I could cling to in the lonely moments of my life. And now, I was quite confident I would never receive another one.

* * *

Dorothy Elsmith had gotten divorced a decade ago, and among the couples I knew, there were a handful who had dissolved their marriages. While everyone usually promised that we would always remain friends, I knew it never worked out that way. People had to choose sides, and so it would be with Tom and me. The Atlantic Ocean provided an easy dividing line, but not in every case. I could accept that I would fall out of touch with his family members, and I knew I would miss Theresa's friendship most of all. Edith remained loyal, but still I knew she was very, very disappointed. Eleanor managed to keep a foot in both of our camps; I was grateful that our ties from childhood proved very strong indeed.

I had no illusions about which friendship was ultimately more valuable to most of our mutual acquaintances. And thus I was particularly heartened that from their perch near the top of the Princeton English Department, Willard and Margaret stuck by me.

At spring break, they invited me to come for a visit and stay in their beautiful home, set back from the traffic of Nassau Street. With no children of their own, they loved managing the lives of others. Students, junior faculty members, visiting celebrities, girlhood friends. They hosted parties, staged weddings, huddled late into the night, talking over drinks in a cozy world walled with books.

The night I arrived, we enjoyed dinner, then Willard poured all of us tumblers of brandy. Then, uncharacteristically, he left Margaret and me alone to talk. He went to his piano and began to play. It was Chopin, a perfect choice. Romantic, filled with passion, just a little bit sad. I wondered if the two of them had planned the plot in advance. But if they had, I didn't want to quiz them about it. I was afraid I might start to cry.

"It's so exciting about your honorary degree," I said brightly, shaking off my sad memories. Over dinner, Willard had shared that Smith was giving Margaret one this year. "It's about time *you* got recognized."

I had always admired her hard work and discipline. She had published five books, including a surprising one about the movies and a biography of President Neilsen. Still, it was always "Willard and Margaret," not the other way around.

"I've been thinking about you, too," she replied. "I think it's time for you to tell your side of the story."

"But Tom's is the only one they will care about."

"Of course, that's what most of the scholars will focus on," she conceded. "Tom was very good at churning out words. Princeton now has more than a thousand letters to prove it. But he is a very complicated man, and the world needs to understand that, too." Then she added softly, "I find that I am very, very angry with him right now."

Calm, congenial Margaret. I had never seen *this* Margaret before. It helped that someone else could acknowledge my pain.

"Only you—and Tom—know what all those letters say," she continued. "And when people read them in the future, they may be able to figure out what was really happening between the two of you. But you can't control what Tom does or says now. And I think the world should understand what you were doing and thinking."

"But it's all too painful and personal," I protested. "It wouldn't be fair to Tom."

"When was Tom ever fair to you, Emily? Look," she persisted, her voice turning more maternal. "I know this is hard for you. It is like a death. We are all grieving in a way. Still, I think it would help to get it off your chest. It might make it easier for you to move on with your life."

I took a sip of brandy. "I'll think about it," I said at last.

Margaret smiled. "We believe in you, Emily. And if you decide to tell your story, you know you can count on us to give you whatever help you need."

* * *

I took Margaret's words to heart. I asked for a pen and some paper and stayed up late that night, pouring out my thoughts as an introduction to the letters. It might have been easier if I could still refer to them. But perhaps this was better. I could keep it short, base it on my memories, avoid getting bogged down in a research project.

In the morning, I reread what I had written. It was a mess of scribbles, deletions, and inserts. Willard and Margaret often teased me about my bad penmanship, and these pages were worse than usual. But that was all right. I would read the words over breakfast. If they liked what I had written, I would take it home and type it up and send it on to Mr. Dix.

Margaret was right. I felt better already. It was an exorcism of sorts. The sun had come up. Downstairs, bacon was cooking on the stove. It was a new day.

One step at a time.

* * *

When June came, I submitted my resignation. Mary Crane said nice words and expressed her disappointment that I had decided to leave. But, she made clear, I would have to be out of my rooms by the time they found my successor. I hated the prospect of becoming a vagabond again. But it would be easier to move this time; I no longer had to manage the boxes and boxes of letters.

Still, I needed a place to move to. It was summer now, and my thoughts turned to Chipping Campden. It was beautiful there this time of year; it was a place where I had always been happy. When friends asked where I was going, it sounded better to say, "I'm traveling to the Cotswolds" than to say "Concord" or "Boston," or worse yet, "I don't know where I'm going."

So I set off bravely across the Atlantic, then caught the train from Southampton. I tried not to mind that I was alone, that there was no one to meet my train this time. When I finally arrived back on High Street, I took a small room above a pub.

But as soon as I arrived, I knew I had made a mistake. Too many years had gone by. I missed having someone to talk to. I missed Edith and John, stodgy as they were. But most of all, I missed Tom. Strangers were living in Stamford House and in my cottage. All the old, familiar faces—the postmistress, the banker, the green grocer, the vicar—had died or moved away. I wandered the streets aimlessly, hoping to turn up a familiar sound or smell. But the place seemed rushed and noisy, and each summer day, the streets echoed with the accents of loud, brash Americans, seeking to cram all of England into a week. Burnt Norton had been transformed into a school during the war years. I could not bear the thought of going there now.

When I rode the train into London, I considered phoning Mary Trevelyan and suggesting we meet for lunch. I wondered if Mary had known about Valerie or if she, too, had been shocked by Tom's early-morning wedding. But I could not bring myself to make the call. We had always been cordial but never, ever friends. Tom had kept both of us dangling. That he had managed to keep two women in his life—before he had chosen a third—only made me feel more foolish.

I knew Tom still wrote to Eleanor and Dorothy. Had they told him I was there? Could he feel my presence, walking the streets of London or biding my time in the Cotswolds? Did he worry I would show up unannounced on his doorstep? Another mad woman on the loose in Kensington?

And as I mulled my own craziness, I wondered about Vivienne's. Did Tom contribute to her madness? Did I still trust the stories he had told? Or did we all want to believe Tom's version of his marriage? He was the great English poet, after all. Our friendships were at stake.

Summer turned into fall, and like so many times before, I prepared to sail home from England. It was a place that had once brought me such joy and happiness. I still had friends from the acting program and playbills from its theaters. But now I had seen all that I wanted to see. And I knew I would never come back again.

* * *

I was touched to learn that some of my former Abbot students had raised the money to create a drama award in my honor. The fall edition of the alumnae magazine included a gracious farewell:

Sorry to Say Goodbye

Miss Emily Hale has this year retired from Abbot, and will live for a time in Chipping Campden, Gloucestershire, England. During her nine years at the school she has contributed greatly to the development of the Speech and Drama Department. Extremely interesting plays have been produced under her guidance, and many Abbot girls speak with more confidence and grace because of her teaching.

Her skill in casting the school plays was widely recognized and resulted in outstanding performances. She worked as carefully with the girls having minor roles or backstage duties as she did with the "stars."

She has a particular concern for the place of speech and drama within the whole framework of secondary school education, and has worked hard for a wider recognition of the importance of this form of training.

Miss Hale has introduced many girls at Abbot to a variety of cultural interests, of a kind to broaden, deepen, and enrich their experiences. Her sympathetic concern for the students as individuals has won her a great group of affectionate friends, who will wish her much future happiness.

"Much future happiness." Was that reasonable to yearn for? I appreciated the kind words, the sanitized version of the truth. But I expected no less from the school. I was not the first teacher to resign or retire, and I would not be the last. And, I knew, broken hearts were as common in the halls of Abbot Academy as poodle skirts and bobby socks.

* * *

The first cold winds of winter had arrived by the time I arrived home. I felt drained by the ocean crossing. Each day began with a headache that never dissipated. When I went to visit Dorothy, she ordered me to see a doctor. And within a matter of days, I found myself flat on my back in a bed at Massachusetts General.

The doctors prescribed a long list of tests, each one more draining than the last. Edith managed to come visit me, but she provided little in the way of comfort. She missed Tom's letters and attentions and pestered me with questions. Had I seen his marriage coming? Had he given me any clue? How could he do this to me?

Outside the door of my hospital room, I overheard hushed voices musing about the possibility of a brain tumor. I closed my eyes wearily. Perhaps that would be easier, just to curl up and die quickly. But the X-rays came back negative and the talk turned to "breakdown." Yes, that was it, I decided. Tom Eliot had broken my heart, and the rest of my body had "broken down." The doctors concluded that there was nothing they could point to, not much they could do. Perhaps I would benefit from bed rest, a stay at McLean.

I could not bear the thought of that. I was not Emily Jose Milliken. I was not Vivienne Eliot. I was a teacher, I was an actress. I had a life.

Dorothy took me in again to help me recuperate. I wrote some letters, circulated my résumé. In March, I found a job with the Oak Grove School in Maine. But my heart wasn't in it anymore. The weather in Vassalboro was worse than Boston's, and the girls more interested in heading for the ski slopes than tackling Shakespearean plays. I had no energy left for teaching. And when the semester ended, I decided that at the age of 67, it was time to retire for good.

* * *

I was still up in Maine when the story made the front page of *The Globe*, but Eleanor had put it aside for me. "Part of me tells me I should save you from all of this," she apologized when we got together. "But the other part of me knows you would never forgive me if I did."

And I told her she was right. I was hungry for every clue that might unravel the mystery of Tom's inexplicable behavior, even as each new clue only deepened my pain.

"Introducing Valerie to U.S.": T.S. Eliot and Bride Visiting Cambridge

Nobel prize–winning poet-dramatist T.S. Eliot, American born and London bred, has arrived in Cambridge on the last leg of a trip to "introduce my wife, Valerie, to the United States."

Clutching the hand of his attractive 31-year-old bride of a year, Eliot, 69, spoke avidly last night of his newest play, "The Elder Statesman," scheduled to open at the Edinburgh (Scotland) Festival in August. . .

I turned to page five, where the story continued, and swallowed hard when I saw the photo of the happy couple. Tom was smiling broadly, his cheeks were full, his suit fitting well again. Valerie was close to him, wearing multiple strands of pearls and a chicly tailored dress. Her skin appeared soft and milky white, her rosebud mouth painted with dark lipstick. The "clutching" hands were out of sight; I was spared that by the way the photo had been cropped.

I continued reading:

Here primarily for the purpose of introducing Mrs. Eliot to relatives and friends in and about Cambridge and Boston, the world-renowned poet, playwright and publisher will take time out on May 14 to deliver the David Steinman Lecture at Boston College.

He had given readings at Columbia and the University of Texas and in Dallas, the article explained.

But in Cambridge, "we feel really at home," Mrs. Eliot interjected.

I set the article down. "I assume you met her."

Eleanor nodded.

"What did you think?"

"Are you sure you want to know?"

"Yes."

She shrugged. "What you'd expect. She was very young, very British. A little bit pudgy, but she makes the most of what she has. She was eager to win us over, a bit too eager if you ask me. She is obviously very devoted to Tom, and I must say he does seem very happy. And he's looking better than he has in years."

"I'm happy for that," I murmured.

"You're too nice," Eleanor said. "I kept hoping that I could get a private moment with him. To give him a shake and ask him how he could do this to you. But Valerie stuck to him like glue. It was impossible to spend a moment alone with him. And he seemed to like it that way.

"At one point, she insisted that he had to lie down and take a nap. So I had a chance to talk with her alone. She is definitely very smart. Still, her story is rather odd. She told me that she had been in love with Tom since she was a teenager. Since she had first heard Gielgud's recording of 'Journey of the Magi,' if you can believe that. She started attending Tom's poetry readings. On her second glass of sherry, she admitted that she had even gone to services at St. Stephen's once, hoping to catch sight of him. And at some point, she made up her mind that she was going to find a way to get hired as his secretary.

"Eventually, Faber had an opening, and she had a family connection that helped her get an interview. And eight years later, she got herself a husband."

"I remember her from those days," I said softly. "She was always hard at work, her head bent over her typewriter. If Tom and I were going out to lunch, she would always ask when he expected to return and what she should tell his callers. She would remind him what was on his calendar that night.

"But I've wracked my brain over the past 18 months, and I can't remember ever seeing any sign of affection or flirting between them." I shook my head, looking down again at the clipping. "I will never understand him."

"Nor will I," Eleanor acknowledged.

"I'm happy he's happy," I said at last. "And I'm happy his health is better. But I would have taken care of him, Eleanor. I may be an old woman, but I'm sure I could have made him happy."

"I know that." Eleanor took back the clipping and folded it away. "But unfortunately, we *are* old women. And this, apparently, is our destiny."

Curtain Call

I CONSIDERED THE ALTERNATIVES AND decided to settle in Northampton. It was easier for an older woman to navigate than Boston, and a better place for a fresh start than Andover or Concord. It had all the things I needed for a "full life": a Unitarian Church, a woman's club, a chapter of the League of Women Voters, a good amateur theater. Most of my old colleagues at Smith had moved on; Hallie Flanagan had been diagnosed with Parkinson's disease and retired back to Poughkeepsie. But I still stayed in touch with a few of the Abbot girls who had gone on to Smith.

Tom Eliot seemed to have found his own fountain of youth, but all around me, friends were aging and in some cases dying. In September, it was Edith's time. She had made her wishes known: a private service and burial next to John, along the Bellwort Path at Mount Auburn Cemetery.

At least it was fall, and the trees there were approaching their full autumn glory. I had worked with her over the years to compile all of her achievements for her eventual obituary. She was, of course, notable as John's widow, but she *was* a gardening authority, too. A medal from the Garden Clubs of America for her work on cultivating bulbs. A member of the Royal Horticultural Society, which had received all the slides from her trips to the major gardens of England. The ones from Glamis Castle, where the Queen Mother had lived as a girl, were her particular pride and joy—along with the fact that T. S. Eliot had been the one to present them to the society a decade ago.

I did not include that detail in the text I sent *The Globe*.

Now I was really alone. I had already lost the Eliots. But now I had no mother, no father, no aunt, no uncle, no brother or sister, not even a first cousin. When Edith's attorney invited me to his office, I had no idea what kind of estate Edith had left, or what, if anything, I might receive. The Millikens, the Hales, the Perkinses didn't talk about money. Edith and John always had enough to travel—and to take me with them. And up until recently, she had lived at a fashionable address in the Back Bay. But John had been a minister, not a banker or a lawyer. They probably had left most of their estate to the Unitarian church.

So I was surprised when the lawyer told me the figure. I did some quick calculations. I had learned to live simply, but this would let me do more. I would be able to stay in my little house. I would still be able to travel abroad. And since I had no heirs, I might be able to pass some of it on to some good cause.

I reached into my purse for a hanky. I had hated the way Edith had always tried to run my life. Still, for all her faults, she *was* the mother I never had. She had dried my tears, nursed me when I was sick, given me a push when I needed one. Without her, I never would have had all of those summers in England with Tom.

And now, she, too, was gone.

My long bottled-up emotions finally caught up with me. And as Edith's lawyer looked on, embarrassed and perplexed, I drove up his fee by staying seated on the other side of his massive wooden desk and indulging myself with a good, long cry.

* * *

It helped me to keep busy. I liked volunteering at the library at Smith. The book-lined rooms were cozy in the winter, and I enjoyed being around students again and eavesdropping on their conversations. All I needed to make it perfect was a hot cup of tea. But I knew the rules: no food or drink on the tables when we were sorting the incoming materials and putting them in files.

I had gotten to know Margaret Grierson, the library's director, and knew that she was quietly plotting to build up the library's collections. What better way to assert Smith College's preeminence, she argued, than to create an archive of women's history? Or as we described it in our solicitations to celebrated women, the school's "rapidly growing special collection of women's contributions to the creative life of the world."

Margaret had already located some papers of Clara Barton and Carrie Chapman Catt that the Library of Congress had somehow missed. There wasn't much I could do to help, but I did offer to write Marianne Moore because the poet "was a friend of a friend." I remembered how Tom and I had talked about her work those summer nights in Chipping Campden. He had admired her poems and then began publishing them. Over the years they had corresponded regularly, and Tom had visited her in Brooklyn when he could.

I no longer dropped Tom's name the way I had around Scripps or Milwaukee-Downer. But for Margaret's sake, I was willing to make an exception.

"For many years," I wrote Miss Moore, "I have heard you spoken of by Mr. T. S. Eliot whom I have known since his graduate days at Harvard." I knew it was a bit of a stretch; I didn't really "know" Tom anymore.

Still, she sent a gracious reply. She explained that she was sorry, but she had already promised her papers to Bryn Mawr, her alma mater. But there was something more: She wrote that she felt she knew me—after all that she had heard from Tom and Theresa and Henry. She knew that I had helped Tom with his plays, that I was a collaborator of sorts. She knew how much I had helped all of my students. She wished that she had known more.

I smiled when I read the letter. Somebody knew, and somebody still remembered. I decided to take the letter home and keep it, another remnant of my past.

The staff crossed Marianne Moore off its list and strategized how to pursue the next famous woman. I returned to my usual work, opening boxes and envelopes as they arrived in the mail, eager to see what was inside. It brought back happy memories of Christmases and birthdays, the long-ago days when both of my parents were there to help me celebrate them.

* * *

I liked working beside Barbara, a fresh-faced junior from somewhere in the Midwest. She had taken a part-time job in the library to help cover her tuition. I knew she hoped to stay on full-time after she graduated.

One day she looked up from her work and pronounced, "You know, I've decided you can tell a lot about a woman's life by what she decides to keep until the end of it."

"How so?" I asked.

"Well, some women obviously felt they were responsible for preserving their family's history. They're the ones who keep the photos and birth certificates, maybe even a family Bible. And piles and piles of letters from their parents and their siblings. Then there are those who focus on their own memories. They hang on to their scrapbooks and keep all the snapshots of their friends. And then there are those who treasure their diplomas and every award they ever won, no matter how significant.

"But the best boxes," she said, waggling her eyebrows, "are the ones with the diaries and love letters. That's where the biographers will find their gold."

I didn't disagree with her conclusions. "But there's one problem," I said. "The boxes usually tell only one side of the story." I paused, not wanting to spill my own secrets. "Unless you're important, of course. And unless the person who received *your* letters was as compulsive about keeping them as you were about keeping theirs."

She smiled. "And lovers don't usually make carbon copies."

I did not tell her about the letters I used to have. But as I lay awake that night, I replayed our conversation. Margaret was nagging me to turn over the silly things that would qualify as "my papers," but what stories would they tell about me?

Barbara would probably conclude I was one of those "good girls" who preserved her family's memories. She would find all of Edith's letters to the Royal Horticultural Society about her garden slides. Correspondence about Great-Aunt Sarah's days in Australia. The programs from my plays, the snapshots from dress rehearsals, photos of me in my wigs and costumes. The sweet letters from the cast and crew of *The Admirable Crichton*. Some articles I had written, some lectures I had given. A graduate thesis marked with an "A."

But no journal, no diary, no love letters.

Still, I had a carbon copy of that letter I had typed at the library, and now, fresh from the mail, the response from Marianne Moore. On the surface, it was innocuous, but it was a clue nonetheless. A clue that there might be something more beyond my own inconsequential box—if you were able to wait 50 years.

* * *

Could I have made it as an actress?

Now that Edith was gone, I could not stop ruminating about the "might-have-beens."

Those summer plays in Vermont seemed faraway now, and I realized how much I missed acting. But what kind of role could I tackle? I knew how it worked with amateur theater companies. The plays were chosen to suit their long-time members, the club officers, the ones who sold tickets and badgered local merchants. Even if they picked a play that called for an older actress, would they be willing to give me the part?

My heart sank when I learned what the Circle Players had selected for the next season: *Solid Gold Cadillac.* It was a wonderful comedy, but the film had just come out, with Judy Holliday in the lead. Thirty-five-year-old Judy Holliday, fresh off her Oscar win. No one would think of casting a gray-haired woman in the role of Laura Partridge.

But then I remembered Josephine Hull. Hull had played the role on Broadway in her seventies, just a few years before she had died. Other than the little detail of the character getting married at the end of the play, there was no reason Laura Partridge had to be an ingenue.

The key was in the comic timing. Hadn't the critics always said I had a knack for it? And so I screwed up every ounce of courage I had and went to the audition. And much to my delight, they gave me the part.

The laughter and applause were wonderful to hear again. Even better, a small gaggle of my old students came over from Smith to see me perform. They greeted my stage entrance with a burst of applause. And after the curtain came down, they came backstage to say hello and present their own bouquet of carnations.

It *was* still possible to know love.

* * *

I was a regular now, and the next play was chosen for me. Ethel Savage was *The Curious Savage,* an elderly woman whose stepchildren had committed her to a sanitorium because she was keeping them from enjoying their father's inheritance. Lillian Gish had played the role on Broadway when she was a few years older than I was. Ethel Savage had her share of the funny lines, but she was also positioned as the drama's stable center, surrounded by a host of mentally ill residents and three selfish relatives.

I loved the fact that among Mrs. Savage's reputed eccentricities was that she had taken up acting in her old age. She had backed a one-night run of *Macbeth* on Broadway, featuring herself in the role of one of the witches. "As a girl," I could say with conviction, "I was sure I could have been a great actress. So, with no responsibilities and time running out—I decided to be one."

And when it came time to explain my love for my late husband, I reached down deep into my memories. "I married Jonathan when I was 16. I loved him from the moment I met him until the moment he died.... It meant that my only aim in life was to make him happy—to want what he wanted—to anticipate what would please him. And that meant that all the other things I ever wanted had to be forgotten."

But as rehearsals went on, I grew more troubled. It was too easy to laugh at the residents of The Cloisters, their delusions, their phobias, their shattered histories. The Florence character was the most difficult one. The actress carried around a doll that she introduced as her five-year-old son, John Thomas. I remembered the sad trips out to McLean. *Had Mother ever clutched a doll to take the place of Billy?*

Had Tom's friends laughed at Vivienne behind her back?

I took it up with the rest of the cast. I knew something of the pain of these people. Were we making it too easy to laugh at them?

John LaBarge, the director who was also playing Jeffrey, reminded me that the playwright had had the same concern. "Read John Patrick's foreword. If you're still bothered, we can put something in the program. We can use what he wrote, or you can adapt it."

I liked the idea. And, once again, putting words on paper seemed to help. I started with the playwright's words, then added some of my own.

A play comes to life only when the actor is in sympathy with the playwright's intentions. The wrong interpretation of a play distorts its meaning.

We have intended, with the "Curious Savage," to present the inmates of "The Cloisters" with warmth and dignity, and not to place over

emphasis where none was intended. These good people are not "luna-
tics" and we have endeavored not to exaggerate the roles to rob them of
their charm and humor. To depart from this point of view for the sake
of easy laughs would distort the play of its meaning.

We hope you'll enjoy "The Curious Savage" and will agree with Lord
Byron that: "If you laugh at any mortal thing—'tis that you may
not weep."

As the cast gathered at the front of the stage for its final curtain call, I felt a sense of relief. It *had* been a good production and a good role to perform. I had always loved the challenge of playing a dramatic role like Lula Bett. But I still preferred doing comedy.

Lord Byron was right. Laughter had always helped me fend off the tears.

* * *

I could not remember when I had first heard the story of Emmanuel and Tiny McDuffie, how Booker T. Washington had recruited them at the turn of the century to start a school for Negroes and how they had hiked from Alabama to North Carolina to do it. It was probably at some Unitarian meeting, back in my days in Boston. And now I heard about the school again. With an impressive name such as "the Laurinburg Normal and Industrial Institute," it was hard to forget. And everybody around me had Celtics fever, and Sam Jones, the team's top scorer, was crediting his alma mater with putting him on the road to success.

I was still itching to do something significant with my inheritance. I had loved that aspect of Ethel Savage's character, giving away money to causes that others found preposterous. But it was hard to pick one school or college from all the places I had taught, particularly when most of them already had substantial endowments.

I stopped by the bank to recheck the totals in my accounts. I would start with one check to the institute and see how it was received. I had learned that lesson with the books and letters I had sent to Scripps. The gift needed to be appreciated. And if the institute put the money to good use, if I felt it could make a difference, I would be happy to keep sending checks as long as I could.

* * *

When I heard about the little house on Church Green in Concord, I decided I couldn't pass it up. I had always dreamed of owning my own home. It would mean moving away from my "families." There were the members of the Unitarian church and the casts of the plays, the women who worked at the Smith library, my friends at the historical society. I had served as president of the Woman's Club in Northampton, but one term was long enough. I loved all of my families, but as I turned 70, it was getting hard to keep up with all of them. Concord was quieter, smaller. I knew it was what I needed now.

I had one more "family," an odd one that was spread out all over the country: Willard and Margaret, Eleanor and Dorothy, Paul and Lorraine. They were the friends who knew about Tom, the friends who guarded my secrets, the friends who shared my disappointments.

It was impossible to escape Tom. Boston College invited him for a poetry reading and 4,500 people filled the arena. *The Cocktail Party* had opened downtown and every church group seemed to be scheduling *Murder in the Cathedral.* The Boston Cat Club was kicking off its championship show with a dramatization of "Gus: The Theatre Cat." Tom's Harvard colleagues and classmates, his translators, his competitors, his relatives were all dying—and their deaths generated headlines simply because they had known him.

Eleanor would have kept me posted if I had asked, but she didn't have to. In the "Travel" section of the paper, I could read about the Barbados hotel where Tom and Valerie had vacationed; amid the foreign headlines, I could read updates on his hospital stays.

His silence, my silencing still nagged me. How many years were left to tell our story? I reread the introduction I had sent to Princeton. I had dashed it off so quickly, there was so much more that could be said. But did I have the energy to put it all down?

I went over to my hi-fi and pulled out my recording of Tom reading the "Four Quartets." It took close to an hour to listen to the whole thing, but the idea came quickly, within the first stanzas of "Burnt Norton." *I* could make a recording; it would be so much easier that way. I could tell what he had meant to me and what I had meant to him. And when I was finished doing that, I might find the courage to write him one more time.

* * *

Willard was my best director, coach, friend. If I gave him an opening, he would push me across the finish line and take care of the details. And so it was with my tape recordings. I found it surprisingly easy to unburden myself and send the tapes off to Princeton. I figured no one would be interested. But Bill Dix assigned his secretary to transcribe them, and my memories were ready for the Thorps to read when they returned from vacation.

My heart leapt when I read their reaction.

To Margaret and me this is a precious and moving document, and it will be a revelation (to put it mildly) if it is published hereafter. I think you "come through" wonderfully. Your training and experience make this possible. Remember how amazed I was when I read the transcript of the first recorded remarks of my own. I sounded like General Eisenhower in a press conference! You, emphatically, sound like yourself.

As the wise editor he was, Willard suggested I should now take the time to clean up the manuscript, double-check the titles, names, places and dates. He urged me not to be perturbed that Bill Dix's secretary had turned the "Bodleian" into "Bowdoin" and "Scripps College" into "Squibbs." I faulted myself for those errors—I didn't articulate the words clearly enough when I recorded them. Willard acknowledged that he and Margaret could not resist making some edits themselves. "But we decided to stop," he explained, "because this is yours and must be as you want it to be."

Margaret had come up with another idea: I should write a brief autobiography that could stay with the transcript and be published at a later date. "You have moved about a great deal, from one teaching position to another, from America to Europe. A possible future reader will want to know how your movements here and abroad correspond with Tom Eliot's. (His will be ferreted out, we may be sure.)"

Was I really that important, I wondered? Tom and Valerie were public people; I decidedly was not. Was it all too personal and painful?

I returned to Willard's letter. Margaret had come up with another suggestion, one that Willard acknowledged might be more difficult to accept. "Could you, would you, care to say in which poems of Tom's, or parts of poems, you figure? In 20 years, 50 years, this will be *the* question to which critics and scholars will very much want to have an answer."

He was right—that was a tougher question. Did I see myself in Tom's poetry? It would be presumptuous to suggest I was the inspiration behind every female image he had ever used—and I didn't think I was. There were the memories of Burnt Norton, of course, but other than a reference to "we," I didn't really appear in that poem. I recognized an image here or there, a flash of our shared memories. But they were all Tom's experiences, and Tom had been with many women. Who was I to say that I was the one?

No, if I were to go back and puzzle over every poem, it would only slow me down. I would leave that for Willard's students—and Willard's students' students—to figure out. I was much too close to it.

"Later," I finally wrote them back, "I shall try to write out what M. suggested—tho' there is *mighty little* of me in any poetry!"

* * *

The long train trips always helped me clear my head. It was particularly true of those long hours when there was nothing outside of the window but miles and miles of flat prairie. Tom and I had talked about it once. He described the chants of the monks in the retreat houses he had visited; I recalled the monotonous clatter of metal train wheels, hour after hour rolling on the tracks.

It had been good to get away again to Seattle, but now I faced a decision. I pulled out Willard's letter again. "Whatever may come of this enterprise," he had written, "I want you to know how much I admire your understanding of the need for the recording and your courage in making it. I have some idea of the courage you summoned to the task."

Courage. I felt I had so little of it now. Oh, I rarely had stage fright, but going on stage was completely different. In real life, I had always held back. I had been taught to bite my tongue. It was the recurring theme of my relationship with Tom.

But who knew how much longer we had? He had been married for seven years now. I no longer posed a threat to the couple's obvious happiness. Surely Tom would remember our friendship, appreciate my point of view?

I could try to recapture my side of our story. But I was an old woman now, and I knew my memory was failing. There were so many trips to England, so many little episodes. I could not remember all the dates and the places. But my letters had them all. If only he would let me have them—or share them with the rest of the world.

And so I made up my mind to write him. This time, I was even more careful than the last time. I knew another woman would be reading my words.

September 12, 1963

Dear Tom,

It is difficult to break the silence which has existed between us for the last several years, but you would be the first to admit I think that the changing circumstances of our lives and increasing years necessitate that we both face certain facts and problems with courage and objectiveness.

I told him that Willard and Bill Dix had asked if he would agree to shorten the embargo on his letters. And, by the way, whatever happened to mine?

The question has also been asked in Princeton if these two collections should not be under the same roof....It would seem to me if you are still preserving my letters, that your consent in placing them in this country would be the only correct practical solution, don't you think?

And then I turned to the personal.

I think you will be aware that for me to consider my life as important because of its relationship to you—a noted world figure—is very difficult. I must as now act impersonally for the sake of the future in raising these questions, equally difficult for both of us but wholly professionally and historically correct. I do hope you will accept what is thrust upon us—shall we say—because you are you.

I took longer to decide how best to close the letter. It would be so easy to be angry, to lash out at him with all the hot words that I held in my heart. But that would get me nowhere. The truth was, I still yearned to be friends, even as I knew that was probably impossible.

Further, I hope your health is better than I know it has been lately. I learn of you from time to time from the Cambridge relatives.

In the thought of past friendship,
Emily Hale

I walked to the post office to make sure I purchased enough postage. Then, after checking that no one in the lobby was watching, I kissed the seal on the letter, pushed it through the mail slot, and then went home to wait.

* * *

One month passed, and then another. I decided, on the spur of the moment, to travel to Seattle to visit old friends and recall my youthful triumphs. I was there when the news broke, just before lunchtime, that the president had been assassinated. I remembered when I heard the news of President Roosevelt's death. It was late in the afternoon, after classes had let out. I could not imagine what I would have told my students this time.

The young president's sudden death cast an even deeper pall over everything. By the time I got home to Concord, there was a letter waiting from Willard. Now that the term had ended, he said he had time for other important things. "And none more important than this strange impasse with your letters to T.S.E. His silence, after your careful (and gentle) letter of last September is incredible, unless, as you suggest, he may not be well."

He acknowledged that Tom was free to dispose of my letters but that I controlled the right to publish them. "One would think, therefore, that he would like to know what your wishes are in the matter." He said he would consult with Bill Dix on what to do next.

In the meantime, they had finished editing my transcripts and would get them retyped. "It will be a sober year ahead," he concluded, "but we must have some joy from it."

* * *

The lines seemed to pop out of nowhere these days. From the recesses of my brain, mostly from the plays I had done more than once. Roles I had loved, moments I had relished. I often thought back to *Hay Fever*. It could still make me laugh, but Judith's lines now had a double edge. The world was moving on without me. My time on the stage was past.

I tried hard not to think about Tom. It was easier now, now that the newspapers no longer carried stories of his speeches or trips to Cambridge or the Bahamas. When we met for lunch, Eleanor shared that he was slowing down. Every time he caught a cold, it turned into a medical crisis. The family members all thought Valerie was a saint, but there was only so much even she could do for an elderly man who had lived for his cigarettes.

Dorothy invited me to Woods Hole to welcome in the start of 1965. It was bitterly cold and windy on the coast, but my friend's rambling home and the warmth of a crackling fire brought back good memories, of vacations with Tom and his now-dead sisters, of our last train trip all together to St. Louis.

I was there when the word finally came. And despite all I knew of Tom's failing health, the news still stunned me. T. S. Eliot dead at age 76. Another story in *The Globe*. Another January morning, eight years after the last shocking story.

The obituary quoted the closing lines from "The Hollow Men": "This is the way the world ends, not with a bang but a whimper."

I began crying softly as the obituary recalled the chapters of his early life. Born in St. Louis. Entered Harvard College in 1906. Contributed poetry to the *Harvard Advocate*. Between 1910 and 1915, studied at the University of Paris, at Harvard and at Oxford University. Put down roots in England in 1915 when he married Miss Vivienne Haigh of London.

It was better to be staying with Dorothy than to be on my own in Concord. Still, I wanted to be alone. I bundled up in my winter coat, found my boots and scarf and hat and gloves, and headed out into the bitter day. It was a short walk to the coast, and as I headed into the wicked wind, my eyes began tearing up. Was it the weather or was it the hole that had opened in my heart? I looked out at the ocean, stretching out beyond Cape Ann, past the Dry Salvages to a faraway land called England. And as the whitecaps transformed into memories, breaking in, one after another, on the shores of my life, the tears turned into sobs, shaking every inch of my body. The wind muffled their sound, allowing me, for one final time in my life, to let go of all that I had kept locked up inside of me for the past 50 years.

"When you go to sleep—today ends." I remembered the lines from *The Curious Savage*. "And when today ends—tomorrow begins. Today we're safe. Tomorrow may be filled with disaster."

Today *was* filled with disaster. Tomorrow still might be.

I turned to head back to Dorothy's house, to the warmth of a fireplace and shelter from the wind. It was done now. There would be no more goodbyes. There would be no more chapters. There would be no more pain.

And there would be no more poetry.

* * *

Father had always said that funerals were for the benefit of the living, not for the dead. Westminster Abbey, I later learned from Eleanor, had volunteered to organize a funeral for Tom, but he had left very specific instructions. There was to be a brief service at St. Stephen's in Kensington, and then he wanted his body to be cremated and the ashes taken to East Coker.

Harvard, however, could not resist honoring its celebrity son. On a snowy day two weeks later, I stepped carefully along the slippery walks of Harvard Yard, back to Memorial Church. I remembered that sunny Commencement Day, when my heart burst with pride over Tom's great achievements, even from my seat on the sidelines. It was like that again today. I found a spot, in a pew near the rear, as the leading lights of the English Department and the literary establishment rose, one after another, to extol Tom's contributions to the world of poetry and prose.

Two professors read some of the poems: "Ash Wednesday," "Journey of the Magi," "Bride of Salvation," and, inevitably, "Four Quartets."

Time present and time past
Are both perhaps present in time future.

As I listened to "Burnt Norton" one more time, I started to cry softly. There would be no more time future.

About half of the congregation were students. Tom, it seemed, still had quite a following. Nevertheless, I kept waiting for the real man to be revealed in all of the proceedings. It was all too cold and antiseptic. Where was the Tom I had known? The Tom of Harvard was clever and funny. Where was the laughter, the spirit now?

I read all the obituaries, all the news articles, all the remembrances, looking for him now. But all I felt was pain. I gave it up after reading Conrad Aiken's article in *LIFE*. He recalled the time Tom had cabled him to arrange flowers for a girl. Instructions so precise he could remember them to this day. But Conrad actually *didn't* remember it correctly. Tom, he wrote, had arranged for a dozen American Beauty roses. To a "girl cousin of his, to whom he was devoted."

* * *

Margaret and Willard reached out to me, sharing in my sorrow, asking how I was doing. In truth, I wasn't sure. We were all joined now in managing my intimate secrets, but I could not figure out how I felt. "Some of it has come back so vividly," I wrote Margaret. "It has not been easy; and having the public know *nothing* is at once a blessing and a burden."

I remembered how Ethel Savage had explained what love was all about: "People say it when they say, 'Take an umbrella, it's raining'—or 'Hurry back'—or even 'Watch out, you'll break your neck.' There're hundreds of ways of wording it—you just have to listen for it, my dear."

As the days passed, my thoughts were shifting. I was grateful that Tom had known a few happy years, that Valerie had been there to take such good care of him. I tried to articulate it to Willard. "I have no feeling of anything else towards her, nor any feeling about T except to *accept* it all without any bitterness or unkind thoughts."

There was a way, I realized, that I could still demonstrate that I had never stopped loving him.

All of our private secrets were at Princeton, waiting for my memoir to be opened. If I died tomorrow, Valerie might still be alive when that story was told. By then she would be an elderly woman, forced back into the headlines, with gossip and speculation swirling around her.

I wanted my transcript back. I needed to tear it up.

...I feel that the letters alone give enough evidence of so abnormal (or is it normal) a story—and for the sake of my caring for him, as friend and a loved one—I should not underline the miscarriage, so to speak of what seemed to be so perfect a solution to the long years of waiting for happiness.

It might not have been happy, or right, had the relationship been consummated, and I must always remember I was unaware of the complexities of both the situation and his nature—or ready to believe in a side I knew so well of his nature. Be what it may, I hope you and M can realize I shrink from the intimacy of personal disclosure.

They all urged me to reconsider. Bill Dix suggested I could re-edit the text, remove the most personal details. But this was my life. All the eulogies at Harvard had come from men, dissecting the life of a fellow academic. Willard was my friend, but he also was a competitive scholar. And this time he pushed too hard.

I tried to help the Thorps understand. "There are other elements in life which I think equally as important as the objective literary professional point of view you both have."

And in the end, I decided to honor Tom's wishes. It was too late to retrieve his letters, and I had come to believe that my own had been destroyed. Had Tom been the one to do it? Had he killed me off along with Celia? Had he thrown out the letters before he purchased Valerie's engagement ring? Had he turned them over to a colleague, like a pile of unsolicited manuscripts? Or had he used them to keep a fire going back in the days when coal was scarce in England? Had the letters helped to keep him warm as he fed them, one by one, into the embers on a drizzly London night?

It no longer mattered. For whatever reasons, he had decided to bury our secrets. And I could still choose to believe that I was the one he wanted to protect.

* * *

When I celebrated my 75th birthday, I remembered my long-ago calculation. Every day that I lived lengthened the odds that Valerie would still be alive when Tom's letters to me were opened. By all accounts, from

Eleanor and Willard and the librarians I knew at Harvard, Valerie was a challenge to deal with. She guarded her husband's papers and reputation with a ferocity they had rarely seen. I was sympathetic, but I also hoped that she would never be able to stretch her reach to my own boxes at Princeton.

My world was growing smaller and definitely quieter. I didn't mind it that much. It was getting harder to drive, particularly in winter or at night. Most of all, I feared a fall or a stroke, the kind of thing that would land me in a nursing home. But I still had circles of friends who could help me get where I wanted or needed to go.

I delighted in following the old friends who had made it as actors. Oggie Perkins would be proud of his son, with Oscar and Tony nominations already to his credit. Almost every week, I could find Rusty Lane on TV, popping up on everything from *Gunsmoke* to *McHale's Navy*. Even Sam Waterston, that page from *Antigone,* had gotten a bit part in a movie. I made a point of going to see *Fitzwilly;* it was a silly comedy, but I loved seeing him just the same.

That's how you build an acting career: Get your foot in the door, accept any role, stay in touch with your friends.

But I still desperately missed the stage. The Concord Players had given me a bit part in *The Visit* three years before, but the late-night rehearsals were draining and I feared I would stumble on my lines. Last year, they'd drafted me as a speech coach for *Much Ado About Nothing.* It was good to make new friends and feel I could be useful. But it would never substitute for that moment when the curtain rose and the audience hushed, the bright lights blinded you and you entered another world for a few wonderful hours.

As the holidays approached, I began working on my annual Christmas poem. I used to joke to the Thorps that if Faber could distribute one of Tom's poems every holiday, I could send out one of mine, even if it was nothing more than doggerel.

I was working on the 1967 version when the phone rang. It was Don Harper from the theater troupe, wanting to stop by to talk. It had been a while since I had entertained anyone, much less a "gentleman caller." But I straightened up my place as best I could, filled up my teapot, and rounded up a few Oreos that had not yet gone stale.

When Don arrived, he got right to the point. "The Players are doing *My Fair Lady* this spring. My wife and I are directing, and several people have said you would be the perfect person to play Henry Higgins's mother."

It took a moment for the words to sink in.

"Who recommended me?"

"Don James. Bill Travers. And Chris Davies." He smiled. "All the people you coached for *Much Ado*."

I still wasn't sure how to respond. It was such a wonderful play. And I had seen the movie several times. Cathleen Nesbitt would be another hard act to follow.

"Chris Davies is going to play Higgins. You won't have many lines to learn. Still, your part is critical to building the tension between Henry and Eliza."

I liked the way Don Harper thought.

"You make a compelling argument, Don, and I'm truly flattered that you asked." I hesitated. "But I think I should take a day or two to think it over." I cocked an eyebrow. "You don't happen to have a script handy, do you?"

"As a matter of fact, I do." He pulled it out of his briefcase. I knew the story, of course. I loved singing the songs in the shower. But there were more practical concerns. How many lines would I have to learn? How long would I be on my feet? Did I have enough energy?

"I promise to get back to you by the end of the week."

"It's going to be a lot of work," Don acknowledged, "but we're going to have a very good team."

He polished off the final cookie, then said he had to leave. I refilled my teacup and settled into my favorite chair.

I always loved opening a script for the first time and reading the playwright's vision for his set.

Outside the Royal Opera House, Covent Garden.

TIME: After theater, a cold March night.

AT RISE: The opera is just over. Richly gowned, beautifully tailored Londoners are pouring from the Opera House and making their way across Covent Garden in search of taxis....

I closed my eyes, remembering my own nights at Covent Garden, the thrill of a great performance, the surge of humanity into the streets afterwards. These were the Edwardian years, those last years before The Great War, when Tom and I were still in Boston. The Boston Symphony. *Madame Butterfly.*

I opened my eyes. *Get practical. How many scenes?* I flipped quickly through the script to confirm what I remembered of the part. Four scenes. Two at the Ascot races. The promenade outside the ballroom. And the critical scene near the end, in the conservatory of Mrs. Higgins's home. It *was* an ambitious play for a community theater company to mount. But the Concord Players had high standards—and a cozy little venue with a couple hundred seats. I would get to wear big hats and beautiful dresses and show off my best British accent.

I read the script more critically now. Henry Higgins, I realized, was not unlike Tom Eliot: both learned men, consumed by their own self-importance, determined to preserve their worlds and their rules.

Why can't a woman be more like a man?

Why not, indeed?

I reread my final scene, the confrontation between Henry and Eliza.

Higgins: Don't you dare try that game on me! I taught it to you! Get up and come home and don't be a fool! You've caused me enough trouble for one morning!

Mrs. Higgins: Very nicely put, indeed, Henry. No woman could resist such an invitation.

In the end, of course, Henry would find a girl who was willing to fetch his slippers. Just as Tom Eliot had.

I remembered my long-ago acting classes. I was not the mother of a priggish English son, or even a mother for that matter. But it would be oh, so satisfying to put Henry Higgins in his place. To tell Tom Eliot that he had treated me shabbily, never appreciating the Edwardian girl he should have married until it was too late.

I waited until morning. (Edith had always stressed the consequences of a woman appearing to be too eager.) And then I called Don Harper and told him I would love to play the part.

* * *

The reviews were great, and the run had sold out. Every aspect of the production had been done with class and care. Twenty seamstresses fashioned more than a hundred period costumes. Ten sets constructed. Clever choreography, backed up by a well-trained ensemble.

It was, I realized, the first time I had ever performed in a musical. My voice had faded over the years, but I still could carry a tune. My role did not require singing, but I considered asking Don if I could join the chorus for the "Ascot Gavotte." I would be in the wings then, and it would be mostly for fun.

But then the director in me reconsidered. I was not a diva. The success of the song, the inherent humor, lay in clipping consonants precisely the way upper-class Brits would do. To do it right, the chorus had to be able to see the conductor, and I would not be on stage. So I mouthed the lyrics from my spot in the wings, waiting to make my first entrance.

My part was small, but the play still thrilled me. I remembered the call for "places" when the curtain was about to go up. I recalled the importance of timing and how hard that was to practice in advance. Could the audience hear us? Did they have a good sense of humor? How long did it take for a line to travel to the back of the auditorium and the laughter to roll its way back?

It was a subtle thing. At the girls' schools, I was always grateful if my students could get into character, if they mastered the physical and vocal tics I suggested, if they actually memorized their lines. But a two-week run—seven performances!—that was a true luxury. If you loved the play and you loved the part, you could always come back the next night and try to do it better. You always had the chance to fix your mistakes.

If only life were like that.

* * *

It started with the newspaper reviews. It was just a bit part, hardly worthy of a mention. But one critic praised my "professional style." The other one wrote: "Aspiring actresses would do well to study the performance of

Miss Emily Hale. As Higgins's mother, she dominated every scene that she was in."

Joan Wood, who played Mrs. Pearce, had stepped out to watch my final performance from the back of the hall. That same night, Joan sent along a single rose with a note: "No one in the cast has received as much adulation from press, friends, neighbors, co-actors, etc. etc!! xxoo."

I could not believe the number of friends and neighbors who tied up my phone line or sent flowers and handwritten notes. There was one I particularly relished: "Gee Wizz Mrs. Higgins! You sho put that good-for-nothin' stuck-up-prig-of-a-son right where he ought to be in the gutter. And you were the best thing in it! (the show)."

But the sweetest note came from Don and Sabrah Harper. It was so easy, I remembered, to be depressed after the final curtain came down. I had always tried to thank my students for all of their hard work.

"Productions of the all-over high caliber of LADY do not just happen," the Harpers wrote to all of us. "It takes dedication and devotion on the part of ALL concerned whether chorus member, lead, stage crew, seamstress, prop girl or what-have-you to make all the parts fit together."

And then Don had scrawled a postscript:

"Emily—

Our bow to you for such a grand job. A perfect Mrs. Higgins."

A poem was written on paper and could last for the ages. But a performance was a moment, and a play, a few days in a lifetime. You would always have the script, of course. You might have the memory. But you could never recapture that moment in front of the footlights, the tears, the laughter, the flubs, all of it. The best you could do was to be grateful that you had been there, that you had been part of that moment, that shared special time on the stage.

Epilogue

BARBARA OPENED THE MANILA ENVELOPE and tried to decode the handwriting on the note Miss Hale had attached.

I am sending you some further publicity about myself—rather against my natural feeling—to be placed with an envelope in the Sophia Smith Collection which surprisingly bears my name. One of my most long-time dear friends read these notes, clippings, etc., and thought they should be kept for such future reader or relative, as I have no younger generation to be interested, or even children or grandchildren of close friends. I....

She stopped there, unable to figure out the word, and resumed reading the next paragraph.

I did have a VERY happy, rather remarkable "come back" in this last role of Mrs. Higgins and it gave me a warmth of friendliness each night from all on the scene—stage hands and actors.

Barbara felt a pang of bittersweet regret. She was glad Miss Hale had apparently died happy, but she felt guilty she had never managed to drive over to Concord and visit her before she died. She recalled the fun they'd had at the library, playing a guessing game about what they would find when they opened a box or a fat envelope like this one.

The staff had continued to nag Miss Hale about adding her papers to their collection. She *had* taught at Smith, after all. But she was touchingly modest. "You've got Katharine Cornell and Eva Le Gallienne and Agnes de Mille," she told them. "Who would be interested in me?"

Yes, her father had worked with Edward Everett Hale, but their families weren't related. Or if they were, it was centuries ago in Massachusetts history.

But Margaret Grierson had persisted. Every woman had a story, and Emily had one, too. And she was part of the larger story of women. Someday a researcher might want to learn about community theater groups in the early 20th century. Or what the average woman thought about earning the right to vote. Or what women's colleges were like in their heyday.

Emily Hale was part of that tapestry. And now she was gone.

The funeral was announced with a short notice buried deep in the *Boston Herald-Traveler.* Services at 11 a.m. Thursday at First Parish Church in Concord. The announcement revealed that Miss Hale was 78 when she died. In lieu of flowers, contributions in her memory could be made to McLean Hospital in Belmont. It seemed, Barbara thought, like an odd choice.

She asked for a few hours off so she could attend the funeral. After all, Miss Hale had been one of their most loyal volunteers.

It was a beautiful fall morning, and on a day like today, she didn't mind escaping the library. The church was filled with flowers, an explosion of colors, arranged more informally than they usually were for a funeral. On the altar, a glass vase held a profusion of long-stemmed pink roses. She wondered if they held a story, too.

At the start, Reverend Jellis explained that Miss Hale had left behind very specific instructions, including a list of her favorite hymns. The service was simple, based on the standard order of worship. The pastor noted that Miss Hale's father had been a Unitarian minister; he said very little about her mother. Barbara knew Miss Hale had no close relatives, and from the turnout in the pews, it looked like she had a dwindling number of friends.

She stayed long enough to sign the guestbook before returning to Northampton. Back at the library she clipped and dated the obituary and pasted it onto a sheet of paper so it wouldn't get lost. Then she placed it in Emily Hale's "Biographical Material" folder. It seemed like a too-short coda for nearly 80 years of life.

But a few weeks later something else arrived in the mail. A four-page remembrance, printed on green-trimmed vellum. Reading it, Barbara discerned that the friends who had stayed on for Miss Hale's memorial reception had decided she deserved something more.

They had designated two memorials where donations could be made in her name. One was a school in North Carolina. Miss Hale's own gifts to the institute had been large enough that a building had been named in her honor. Who would have known?

The other designation was the Concord Players' endowment to build a new theater. Who, they asked, could forget Miss Hale's performance in *My Fair Lady* last year?

... The love of her life was, after all, the stage, the world of the theatre. Her productions were outstanding in the originality of her stage sets, her taste in costuming, her sense of effect, her insistence on the clear spoken word, her way of bringing out latent abilities.

Her skill in production was matched by her own dramatic ability, one that, had circumstances permitted, might well have justified a professional career.

Her performance as Mrs. Higgins, they concluded, "was her crowning achievement, her pinnacle of happiness."

There was more about her career and her travels. Her "flair for friendship," as they described it, "was one of her special gifts," after you got past the "New England reticence."

The whole thing was framed by a few lines of poetry. The poet was not identified, but Barbara recognized the verses. She had studied the "Four Quartets" in her sophomore English Literature class. Now she pondered the well-known stanzas again. Did they hold some special meaning?

In the beginning is my end;
We must be still and still moving
Into another intensity...

But no, she decided. They were the kind of lines that were being chiseled onto many tombstones these days. Emily Hale had never talked about T. S. Eliot. Her papers, Barbara had to admit, were ultimately rather disappointing. No diary, no memoir, no love letters.

Someday she should look through Miss Hale's box more carefully. But there was no time today. She filed the folder back into the box and placed it on the cart to be put back into storage. If Emily Hale had secrets, the sweet old lady apparently had decided to take them to her grave.

Fact and Fiction

A NOTE ON SOURCES

I HAVE PREVIOUSLY WRITTEN BOTH fiction and biography. When asked which was harder, I usually replied, "Biography, because you can't make it up." Still, the life of T. S. Eliot has been—and continues to be—so well-researched that there are few details of his life that can be left to the imagination. One exception, however, is his relationship with Emily Hale.

This novel was completed before the release of nearly 30 years' worth of letters that Eliot sent to Hale. But we will never fully know her side of their story, because Eliot reportedly arranged for her letters to be destroyed.

I have tried to keep the story within the parameters of the facts we do know, but this remains a work of fiction. I wrote about their known encounters but created some new ones—based on what I believed was possible and plausible.

The Eliot-Hale relationship first became known to the wider public in 1973 with the publication of T. S. Matthews's unauthorized biography of Eliot, *Great Tom: Notes Towards the Definition of T. S. Eliot.* At that time, Eliot's second wife, Valerie, would not let Matthews quote from Eliot's works or access his unpublished letters, and Matthews provides no footnotes. But among the persons who provided "help" were Hale's friends Willard Thorp and Dorothy Elsmith and Mrs. Robert Gibney (a.k.a. Nancy Flagg Gibney of the Smith College Class of 1942), whom he credited for the "time and energy she spent in tracking down the surviving friends" of Hale. He incorrectly wrote that both of Hale's parents died when she was young, and some of his chronology of Hale's life was also inaccurate. But he did place Hale with Eliot at Burnt Norton.

I am greatly indebted to literary biographer Lyndall Gordon for fleshing out much of Emily Hale's story in her biographies of Eliot and for encouragement she gave me as I completed this novel. Gordon's books began with *Eliot's Early Years* in 1977, followed by *Eliot's New Life* in 1988 and then *T. S. Eliot: An Imperfect Life* in 1998. As her research progressed, some of Hale's friends and students shared memories and/ or letters, including Hale's August 7, 1947, letter to Lorraine Havens, which Gordon published. Gordon provided a more nuanced view of Hale than many Eliot biographers did, and one that some of Hale's closest friends could affirm before their deaths. Gordon's next book on Eliot will be *Eliot Among the Women,* focusing on his relationships with the key women in his life, including Hale.

Among the hundreds of other books written about Eliot, I turned most frequently to *T. S. Eliot: A Life* by Peter Ackroyd, published in 1984, *T. S. Eliot: A Friendship* by Frederick Tomlin (1988), and *Young Eliot* by Robert Crawford (2015). For more on Eliot's relationship with his first wife, I drew from *Painted Shadow,* Carole Seymour-Jones's biography of Vivienne Eliot (2002). James F. Loucks's 1996 article "The Exile's Return: Fragment of a T. S. Eliot Chronology," in *ANQ: A Quarterly Journal of Short Articles, Notes and Reviews,* tracked the year Eliot returned to Harvard. E. Martin Browne's *The Making of T. S. Eliot's Plays* (1969) provided useful details about Eliot's playwriting career, though it ignored Hale's role in it.

When the first volume of *The Letters of T. S. Eliot,* covering the years 1898-1922, was published in 1988, Valerie Eliot described her husband's anger over Hale's decision to donate his letters to Princeton and recounted his version of their 1914 parting. By then, Hale had been dead for nearly 20 years. My own version reflects Mrs. Eliot's comments while trying to understand Hale's side of the story.

To date, eight volumes of Eliot's letters (through 1938) have been published, variously under the editorship of Valerie Eliot, Hugh Haughton, and John Haffenden. Other key resources were the two-volume *The Poems of T. S. Eliot,* edited by Christopher Ricks and Jim McCue; *Critical Companion to T. S. Eliot: A Literary Reference to His Life and Work,* by Russell Elliott Murphy; *The Complete Prose of T. S. Eliot: The Critical Edition,* published online by Project MUSE; and *T. S. Eliot: A Chronology of His Life and Works,* by Caroline Behr. Details on Eliot's inscriptions to

Hale came from the 1985 essay "T. S. Eliot and Emily Hale: Some Fresh Evidence," by William Baker, in *English Studies*.

As a literary device, this author created letters. Unless listed here, the letters in my novel are fictitious but based on known details. Real letters, used with permission from sources and archives acknowledged elsewhere are: Henry Ware Eliot to his son (April 11, 1914); two letters (October 14, 1914 and September 5, 1916) from Eliot to Eleanor Hinkley; Henry Lefavour to Hale (May 6, 1918); Lucia Briggs to Ellen Sabin (June 2, 1921), Hale to "Friends," undated (circa spring 1935); Julian P. Boyd to Hale (July 7, 1942); Hale to Frederick Hard (September 20, 1945); Hale to Lorraine Havens (August 7, 1947); Leslia Pelton to Hale (June 1955); Hale to Marianne Moore (September 24, 1959); letters between Hale, the Princeton University Library staff, and the Thorps concerning the disposition of the Eliot letters; and Hale to Eliot (September 12, 1963), seeking the whereabouts of her letters. I was disappointed that the Eliot Estate would not permit me to quote from Eliot's November, 27, 1956, letter to Hale about her decision to donate his letters to Princeton. The letter has not been formally published, but some of the text was cited in a footnote in the compilation of Eliot poems edited by Ricks and McCue.

The letters from Eliot to Hale in the Princeton University Library collection begin in 1930; no earlier letters have been published. The text of the letter Hale wrote Eliot from Florence in May 1927 is fictitious, as is Eliot's response. But the letter itself was sent. This exchange is based on William Force Stead's oft-cited story in his unpublished memoir *Reminiscences* in the Osborn Collection of the Beinecke Library.

Hale and others contributed correspondence, dramatic programs, photographs, and the remembrance prepared after her death to the Smith College Archives. I drew as much as I could from Hale's own descriptive reports, including those about her uncle's funeral and her visits to Cambridge, England, Alnwick Castle, and other parts of Europe. None of these reports mentioned Eliot. The 2001 film, *Creating Women's History*, produced by Joyce Follet and Terry Kay Rockefeller, provided more information on the Sophia Smith Library and its staff.

Details about Hale's acting career and the lives of her contemporaries were drawn from *The Boston Globe*, *The New York Times*, the *Milwaukee Journal*, the *Milwaukee Sentinel*, the *Capital Times* (Madison, Wisconsin), the *Boston Post*, the *Cambridge Chronicle*, and the *Cambridge Tribune*.

Additional reviews came from clippings from unidentified newspapers in Hale's papers. Articles and reviews about Eliot are cited from *The Boston Globe*, the *New York Tribune*, and *TIME* and *LIFE* magazines.

Thanks to these archivists for the specific help they provided in answering questions and retrieving resources: Smith College archivist Nanci Young; Simmons College archivist Jason Wood; Erin Dix, former archivist of Lawrence University; Paige Roberts, director of Archives and Special Collections at Phillips Academy (Andover); Sabina Beauchard with the Massachusetts Historical Society; Susan Halpert, Leslie Morris, and Christine Jacobson with Harvard's Houghton Library, and Dorran Boyle at the Ella Strong Denison Library at Scripps College.

Additional sources on more specific topics included:

Boston courtship and Hale's early acting career: Lyrics for songs performed at the "Stunt Show" are from the sheet music collections of the Library of Congress ("Ecstasy" and "A May Morning"), the Lilly Library at the University of Indiana ("Mavourneen"), and the Music Collection of the Daniel A. Reed Library at the State University of New York at Fredonia ("Julia's Garden"); "Recollections of the Cambridge Social Dramatic Club," by Richard W. Hall, from Volume 38 (1959-60) of *The Proceedings of the Cambridge Historical Society,* and other records about the de Gozzaldi family in the society's records; Programs of Boston Symphony Orchestra concerts, including Philip Hale's program notes, from the symphony's online archives; Richard S. Kennedy's *Dreams in the Mirror: A Biography of E .E. Cummings;* records of the Berkeley Street School Association from the Schlesinger Library at Radcliffe College; *The Legacy of Tracy J. Putnam and H. Houston Merritt* by Lewis P. Rowland, MD; *Through an Uncommon Lens: The Life and Photography of F. Holland Day,* by Patricia J. Fanning; *Anthony Perkins: A Haunted Life,* by Ronald Bergan. Bertrand Russell described the Fullers' garden party in a May 11, 1914, letter to his friend, Lucy Donnelly.

Hale's father, his church and other Unitarian clergy: *A History of the Chestnut Hill Chapel* by Mary Lee; *History of the First Church in Chestnut Hill, Newton, Massachusetts, 1861-1986,* by Elmer Osgood Cappers; *Heralds of a Liberal Faith: Volume 4,* edited by Samuel Atkins Eliot; and the minutes of the March 1918 meeting of the Colonial Society of Massachusetts. In June 2018, I interviewed the Rev. Joseph Bassett, pastor of the First Church in Chestnut Hill from 1969-2007. Information on the founding of University Unitarian Church in Seattle was retrieved from the church's website, http://www.uuchurch.org/our-church/, on April 17, 2019. My friend the Rev. Jane Ranney Rzepka reviewed files on Hale's father and uncle in the ministerial records of the Unitarian Universalist Association in the Andover-Harvard Theological Library at the Harvard Divinity School.

McLean Hospital: *Gracefully Insane: Life and Death Inside America's Premier Mental Hospital* by Alex Beam (2003).

Simmons College and the 1918 influenza epidemic: All volumes of the college's yearbook, *The Microcosm,* are available online through the college's archives; "Influenza Epidemic" (circa December 1918) from the Records of the Office of President; and the Boston chapter of "The American Influenza Epidemic of 1918" (www.influenzaarchive.org/cit-ies/city-boston.html#).

Hale's Milwaukee-Downer College years: "T. S. Eliot's Secret Love," by Phil Hanrahan, which first appeared in the Summer 1990 issue of *Lawrence Today*; "The Milwaukee-Downer Woman," by Lynne H. Kleinman (Lawrence University Press, 1997); "Faithfully Yours, Ellen C. Sabin: Correspondence Between Ellen C. Sabin and Lucia R. Briggs From January, 1921, to August, 1921," edited by Virginia A. Palmer in the *Wisconsin Magazine of History* (The State Historical Society of Wisconsin, Vol. 67, No. 1, Autumn, 1983); volumes of the college's yearbook, *Cumtux,* and issues of the student magazine *The Kodak,* from the Lawrence University archives in Appleton and the Wisconsin Historical Society in Milwaukee. Margaret Farrand Thorp's letters in the Willard Thorp Papers (C0292) in the Department of Rare Books and Special Collections of Princeton University Library provide details about her trip with Hale to England. Information about Professor Emily Brown and her Christmas plays came from several sources, including an article by Marguerite Schumann, Milwaukee-Downer Class of 1944, for the *Appleton Post-Crescent.* Of many sources, "Laura Sherry and the Wisconsin Players: Little Theater in the Badger State," posted on May 12, 2011 by historian Joshua Wachuta on his blog, Acceity (www.acceity.org), was particularly useful. Finally, I interviewed *Milwaukee Journal-Sentinel* reporter Mary Spicuzza about her late aunt, Mary Spicuzza Schmal, and reviewed Schmal's scrapbook and those of other Hale students at the Lawrence archives.

Scripps College and Eliot's visit to Southern California: "The George-Eliot Collection at the Ella Strong Denison Library," a compilation of letters and sources prepared by student Sam Cross in 2005; "Search for Eliot's Claremont Connection," by Kay Koeninger, in the November 18, 1982, *Los Angeles Times*; and *La Semeuse,* the college's yearbook.

The Thorps and Princeton Library: The *Princeton University Library Chronicle* (winter-spring 1993); the Willard Thorp Papers; and "Sealed Treasure: T. S. Eliot Letters to Emily Hale," a May 16, 2017 blog post by Don Skemer, published in the university's *RBSC [Rare Books and Special Collections] Manuscripts Division News.*

Hale's years at Abbot Academy: The school's yearbook, *Circle,* and the *Abbot Academy Bulletin,* available through the Phillips Academy Archives and *A Singular School: Abbot Academy, 1828-1973,* by Susan McIntosh Lloyd. I am indebted to Jane Christie, a member of the Abbot Class of 1958, who shared many vivid memories of Hale in interviews and email exchanges. Thanks to Jane, I interviewed other Hale students at her class's 60th reunion in June 2018. I conducted phone interviews with Nancy (Donnelly) Bliss of the Class of 1954 and Anne (Woolverton) Oswald of the Class of 1956. The exchange between Eliot and Hale on the steps of the Andover Inn, a possibly apocryphal story shared among Phillips Andover students and teachers, was described in the "Class Notes" section of the Winter 2015 issue of *Andover* magazine, for which Philip R. Hirsh Jr. and Oswald served as correspondents for the Class of 1956.

Other Eliot appearances: "Harvard Hears of the Marshall Plan," by Robert Smith in the May 4, 1962 issue of *The Harvard Crimson Review*; Eliot's Nobel Prize acceptance speech was retrieved (April 23, 2019) from the website of the Nobel Prizes at https://www.nobelprize.org/prizes/literature/1948/eliot/speech/; "T. S. Eliot in Concord," by Richard Chase, *The American Scholar,* Autumn 1947.

Smith College: *Hallie Flanagan: A Life in the American Theatre,* by Joanne Bentley (1988), and Margaret Farrand Thorp's *Neilson of Smith* (1956).

OF COURSE, ELIOT SCHOLARSHIP CONTINUES, but even with the help of T. S. Eliot societies on both sides of the Atlantic, it is challenging to keep up with all of it. The future publication of Eliot's letters to Hale, which will be compiled and edited by John Haffenden, will certainly provide an opportunity for fresh analysis. In the meantime, the author humbly offers this take on Emily Hale's story.

Portrait of Emily Hale, 1914
Courtesy of Smith College Archive

Acknowledgments

MY APPRECIATION BEGINS WITH DONNA Cartwright for suggesting that our women's group discuss the poem "Burnt Norton," which she remembered fondly from her college days. That was how I first discovered Emily Hale and then yearned to find a way to tell her story.

Several friends—my sister Sue Woodard, Jean Parvin Bordewich, Lauren Marcott, Richard Lovell, and Alice Schmidt—provided feedback on an early draft, as did Karen Coe, who also shared memories of her great-uncle, Smith College chaplain Burns Chalmers. Richard is part of a circle of friends who studied "The Love Song of J. Alfred Prufrock" with my favorite high-school English teacher, Marilyn Bright, a few years after Eliot died. Sally VanderWeele, another member of that circle, shared a memory from our high school days that provided unexpected encouragement exactly when I needed it. Judy Yoder and Tommye Morton Campbell, members of a now-disbanded critique group, also provided the kind of support and friendship that helps to sustain authors. Jane Ranney Rzepka and Arthur Howlett provided hospitality and guidance about 20th century Unitarianism, and Jane and her English professor husband Chuck led me on a tour of Gloucester, Massachusetts, making sure I could actually see the Dry Salvages.

I appreciated the thoughtful suggestions of novelist Susan Coll and other participants in Susan's "Novel Year" workshop at The Writer's Center in Bethesda, Maryland. Although my classmates—Paul Feine, Joanne Hyppolite, Mary Ann McLaurin, Rita Mullin, Andrea Neusner, and Aaron Tallent—were working on very different kinds of novels, they took time from their own projects to help me with mine. Thanks, too, to

Sue Alterman and Meryl Gordon for sharing their contacts, and Michael Palgon for more useful advice.

I appreciate the support of the staff of the Thought & Expression Company, and in particular Chris Lavergne, Noelle Beams, and Kristina Johnson Parish for shepherding my book into the world. Thanks also to Cathy Johnson for sharing her marketing expertise and to my former business partner, Orin Heend, for more than 20 years of helping each other refine crazy ideas.

Finally, I want to thank my late husband, Walt Wurfel, a writer and journalist who was always with me in spirit while I toiled on my own projects, and never once complained that I was spending too much time at my computer.

"..... All the world's a stage, And all the men and women merely players," by Emily Hale, *Abbot Academy Bulletin*, May 1951, Phillips Academy Archives and Special Collections.

"Sorry to Say Goodbye," Abbot Academy Bulletin, October 1958, Phillips Academy Archives and Special Collections.

"Dramatic Art" by Emily Hale, *Milwaukee-Downer College Bulletin*, November 1928, the Milwaukee-Downer College collections at the Lawrence University Archives.

The Simmons College Review, "Faculty and Administration Notes: Course in Voice Culture," Volume 3, Number 5, March 1921, Simmons University Archives.

The author also acknowledges using excerpts from these novels, poems, plays, and songs, which are now in the public domain in the United States:

"The Love Song of J. Alfred Prufrock, "The Waste Land," "Journey of the Magi," "Ash-Wednesday," and "Marina" by T. S. Eliot.

Romeo and Juliet, by William Shakespeare, 1597.

"The Owl and the Pussycat," from *Nonsense Songs, Stories, Botany and Alphabets*, by Edward Lear, 1871.

"How Do I Love Thee? (Sonnet Number 43)," from *The Sonnets From the Portuguese*, by Elizabeth Barrett Browning, 1859.

The Birds' Christmas Carol, by Kate Douglas Wiggin, 1888.

Miss Lulu Bett, by Zona Gale, 1920.

*The Mollusc: A New and Original Comedy in Three Act*s, by Hubert Henry Davies, 1907.

Alice Sit-by-the-Fire, by J. M. Barrie, 1905.

Fanny and the Servant Problem, by Jerome K. Jerome, 1909.

"An Irish Love Song (Mavourneen)," anonymous lyricist, music by Margaret Ruthven Lang, 1895.

"A May Morning," by Luigi Denza, 1894.

"Ecstasy," by Amy Marcy Cheney (Mrs. H. H. A.) Beach, 1892.

"Julia's Garden," lyrics by Charles Edward Thomas, music by James Hotchkiss Rogers.

"You Made Me Love You (I Didn't Want to Do It)," lyrics by Joseph McCarthy, music by James V. Monaco, 1913.

"If You Were the Only Girl in the World," lyrics by Clifford Grey, music by Nat D. Ayer, 1916.

"Glory Be to God on High," words by Theodore C. Williams, set to the hymn tune *Gwalchmai* by Joseph D. Jones, 1889.

"It Came Upon a Midnight Clear," by Edmund Sears, 1849.

About The Author

SARA FITZGERALD was an award-winning journalist and new-media developer for *The Washington Post*, *National Journal* magazine, *The St. Petersburg Times*, *The Miami Herald*, and the *Akron Beacon Journal*. A major in honors history and journalism at the University of Michigan, she writes both fiction and nonfiction, sharing the stories of little-known women who might otherwise be lost to history. Her biography, *Elly Peterson: "Mother" of the Moderates*, was recognized by the Historical Society of Michigan and by the Library of Michigan as a Notable Book of the Year.

WWW.SARAFITZGERALD.COM

```
THOUGHT
CATALOG
Books
```

THOUGHT CATALOG BOOKS is a publishing imprint of Thought Catalog, a digital magazine for thoughtful storytelling. Thought Catalog is owned by The Thought & Expression Company, an independent media group based in Brooklyn, NY, which also owns and operates Shop Catalog, a curated shopping experience featuring our best-selling books and one-of-a-kind products, and Collective World, a global creative community network. Founded in 2010, we are committed to helping people become better communicators and listeners to engender a more exciting, attentive, and imaginative world. As a publisher and media platform, we help creatives all over the world realize their artistic vision and share it in print and digital form with audiences across the globe.

ThoughtCatalog.com | Thoughtful Storytelling

ShopCatalog.com | Boutique Books + Curated Products

Collective.world | Creative Community Network